when
we were
innocent

BOOKS BY KATE HEWITT

when we were innocent

KATE HEWITT

bookouture

Published by Bookouture in 2022

An imprint of Storyfire Ltd.
Carmelite House
50 Victoria Embankment
London EC4Y 0DZ

www.bookouture.com

ISBN: 978-1-80314-386-6
eBook ISBN: 978-1-80314-385-9

To Cliff, for his limitless patience in listening to me talk about my stories, his wonderful help with research, and just for being a fantastic husband! Love you!

CHAPTER 1

LIBBY

It looks like someone has been shot.

I hold the shirt up—a white silk blouse by Tory Burch, probably once worth at least five hundred dollars, its entire front covered in what looks like bloodstains but is probably red wine. "Do you think somehow they didn't notice?" I ask my friend Grace, an edge to my voice.

She shrugs philosophically. "Hard to see how they couldn't."

"Incredible. I suppose they think they're doing someone a favor." I toss the blouse into the "attempt to fix" pile, which is bigger by at least fifty percent than the "good to go" one. Grace and I are sorting through this week's donations to the charity she volunteers for and I manage—Fresh Start, to support disadvantaged women, including refugees and economic migrants, entering the workforce. It was started by a senator about ten years ago, first aimed at women in the DC metro area, but has now expanded to twenty-four branches across the country. I manage one of them, in Charlottesville, Virginia. "How is someone supposed to wear a blouse with a huge stain on the front?" I ask Grace as I pick up a Ralph Lauren tweed blazer with a deep rip in the lining. I know I should just let it go, but I'm annoyed by the blouse and its stain, by the nameless woman who thought it was okay to donate it. "And to a job interview, no less?"

"With a sweater?" Grace suggests, smiling, practical as ever. She's used to my mini-diatribes about our questionable donations.

"If the stain doesn't come out, I'll toss it." I'm not willing to show a ruined piece of clothing to one of the vulnerable women who has finally worked up the courage to ask for help. Fresh Start receives a lot of donations from very rich women, so the clothes are often designer but not always in good shape—the careless castoffs of the privileged. Too many people think that because women are poor, they should be grateful for whatever they receive. A little kindness, thoughtless as it sometimes is, is supposedly better than nothing, but I don't agree.

I reach for the next item of clothing in the pile, an over-the-top evening gown in gold silk, not exactly the kind of thing one of our clients can wear to a job interview. At least it's not stained, but again I'm irritated by the thoughtlessness. *Some people*, I think, as I toss the dress into the "good to go" pile.

"Coffee?" Grace asks after we've sorted a few more items into either "the attempt to fix" or "good to go" piles. The first one is still bigger by far, as it almost always is, and a lot of it will unfortunately have to be discarded.

"Yes, please."

As Grace moves into the kitchen, I gaze around the shop floor and feel the usual warm glow of contented pride at all we've achieved here. Fresh Start sells basic work pieces for women who need outfits for interviews and the like; we charge bargain-basement prices rather than give them away for free, as one of the founding principles of Fresh Start is that people value that which costs them something, even if it's only very little. It also gives them dignity, to know they're not accepting handouts. There's a difference between outright charity and a helping hand.

We also offer courses in basic computer skills and admin-type abilities; we assist women with finding jobs and we coach them for interviews. Since this branch opened five years ago, we've helped over four hundred women get into work. Whenever I think about that, it feels good.

"Libby?"

I turn around, expecting Grace to be handing me a coffee, but instead she's got my phone, which I must have left in the kitchenette.

"It's Em."

Em, my eleven-year-old daughter, who is being sort-of babysat by her older brother Lucas. She has a habit of calling me several times during the few hours I'm at work, to check on just about anything—yesterday it was whether the mango in the fridge had gone off. When I assured her it hadn't, she called me back five minutes later to ask if she would get sick if she ate the whole container. I suggested she eat only half, and then ten minutes after that she called again to say she was worried she was getting a stomach ache.

My husband Tim and I have been trying gently to wean her off asking so many questions; she struggles with anxiety and OCD and they manifest themselves in a hundred different ways every day. It can be hard to know what is being supportive and what is negatively enabling the behavior, and I often feel like I walk a tightrope between the two, wanting to help her but also knowing how much she needs reassurance.

"Hey, Em." I keep my tone upbeat as I angle myself slightly away from Grace, who heads back into the kitchen.

"Mom?" Her voice is already high-pitched with strain and briefly I close my eyes, determined to summon all my patience and gentleness. What is it this time, I wonder—whether the bread is too stale for a sandwich, or maybe about the small red mark on the base of her thumb that she's worried might be cancer, because she's googled something on WebMD?

I know where Em gets her anxiety from: me. As a child, I couldn't go to sleep unless I'd lined all my shoes up exactly straight, to the millimeter; I used to stay awake imagining the disasters that might befall me when I was sleeping, and figuring out ways to safeguard against each one. A poisonous spider bite? I'd sleep with the covers over my head. A flood from the faucet I'd worry I'd left on? I'd go and twist it several times, just to make sure they were properly off. All these little things to help me to feel in control, to be able to keep those looming disasters at bay.

My father was endlessly patient with me, waiting by the door to say goodnight as I checked my shoes or the faucet one last time. I try to be as patient with Em as he was with me, taking comfort in the thought that I grew out of it—sort of—and so, surely, will she.

"Yes, honey," I ask, "what's up?"

"The police are here."

Shock jolts through me, as if I've stuck my finger in an electric socket, and my eyes snap open as thoughts of browning mango or stale bread vanish in an instant. It's one of my childhood disaster scenarios come to life, and after all this time I can't quite believe it. "*What?*"

"They're asking for you." Her voice trembles with anxiety, and I can picture her in our kitchen, one leg twisting around the other like a stork, a finger twirling through her long, strawberry-blond hair. "They say they want to talk to you about... about Grandad."

"Grandad?" I repeat incredulously. The vague images swirling through my mind of Tim in a car accident, or worse, evaporate in an instant. What could the police possibly want with my father? He's ninety-six years old and he has lived us with us for the last ten years; for the last three, he's hardly ever left his in-law suite, which is where he is right now, watching TV or most likely dozing. I'm glad Em called me rather than brought them straight into my dad; I wouldn't want him upset. And yet why would they be there at all?

My mind races to construct some plausible scenario that has the police knocking at my door about my dad, but there simply isn't one, and so I take a steadying breath as logic takes hold, along with a trickle of relief. If the police want to ask me about my dad, it must be about something innocuous—a fundraising drive for the community day center he doesn't like to attend, or maybe some kind of census thing for over sixty-fives? Do the police do that? But why else would they be there?

I feel a ripple of unease about it all, but nothing more, and when I answer Em, my voice is relaxed. I've learned, over time, to conquer my anxieties, or really, bury them deep down where they can't bother me so much, or be seen by anyone else, which would be worse. "Okay," I say to Em. "It's probably no big deal. Can you just tell them to come back another time, sweetheart? Whatever it is, it can't be that important. I'm working from home tomorrow. Tell them to come then."

"Okay..."

"Or ask Lucas to tell them," I suggest, because I know Em gets nervous about talking to strangers. I picture two burly, blue-uniformed policemen, holsters on their hips, looming in our doorway and I'm not surprised she sounds so strained. Having the police knock on the door would unnerve anyone, and I am, unreasonably perhaps, annoyed at them for doing such a thing.

"Lucas went for a bike ride," she tells me.

"He's not supposed to leave you alone," I reply before I can think better of it. That's a conversation to have with Lucas, not Em. "Okay, well, if you don't mind telling them, Em—"

"Okay." Her voice wobbles, but then thankfully firms. "Just a sec..."

I wait on the line while the phone clatters onto the counter, and I hear Em move into the front hall.

"Um, excuse me...?" she calls nervously, and the rest fades to silence.

I feel another ripple of irritation; surely if the police are collecting money or something like that, they'd go as soon as they realized I wasn't at home? Although if they realized I wasn't at home, and Em was virtually alone, would they be concerned? Consider it negligence, even? Chasing that ripple of worry is a deeper, darker one of anxiety as I have a sudden, ridiculous vision of some *Home Alone* scenario where criminals pretending to be the police force their way into the house. Did Em even ask to see their ID?

"Em," I call, even though I know she won't be able to hear me. "*Em.*" My heart starts to race.

"Mrs. Trent?" The male voice that comes onto the line is smooth and assured, with a trace of an accent—Brooklyn, maybe? For a second, my mind spins and then stalls out as my half-joking scenarios suddenly morph into awful reality.

"Who is this?" I bark.

"My name is Simon Baum and I'm with the Department of Justice's Human Rights and Special Prosecutions Section. I'd like to talk to you about your father."

The Department of Justice? I've never even heard of the Special Prosecutions whatever. What on earth can he be talking about? My mind continues to spin like wheels stuck in mud, going nowhere.

"What about my father?" I finally ask, helplessly, because I don't have a frame of reference for this conversation, or even this man. What is he doing on my phone, in my house?

"It's a little complicated to explain, and I think it would be better to do it in person. Would you mind coming home?"

"Now?" I hear the disbelief in my voice. My mind is still spinning.

"Yes." There is a steely note in Simon Baum's voice, and my confused incredulity crystallizes into something more like fear. Terror, even, because I have no idea what this man might want to say to me about my father, but in this moment, I'm pretty sure I don't want to hear it.

I am grappling to come up with a reason, even a worst-case one like the envisioned disaster scenarios of my childhood, but I can't think of anything, and that makes this feel even worse, because there's nothing I can do to mitigate the utterly unknown. What is it that I'm missing—that I've already missed?

"I..." I feel a stubborn, instinctive need to resist immediately acquiescing; I'm at work, and he came to my home—*into* my home—without any warning. He upset my daughter. "Is this really that urgent?" I ask, a bit stridently.

"Yes," he replies, and again I hear that steel, that certain calm. "It is."

Grace comes in from the kitchenette, holding two mugs of coffee, a frown on her face. "Is everything okay?" she mouths, and I give a jerky shrug in reply; I don't know the answer to that question.

"Okay," I finally say to this Simon Baum, because whatever this is, clearly it needs sorting out. "I'm at work, so it will take me about ten minutes."

"I'll be waiting."

In my house? With my daughter? Fury suddenly bubbles up inside me. Surely that isn't even *legal*?

"Could you put my daughter back on the line, please?" I ask him shortly.

A few seconds later, Em's breathy voice comes on the line. "Mom? What's going on?"

"I don't know, sweetheart, it's something about Grandad." My voice automatically goes into soothing mode, although my heart and mind are both racing, racing. "I'm coming home, and

I'm sure it will be sorted out super quick. In the meantime, why don't you go back and sit with Grandad?"

It's eleven o'clock in the morning, and my father will be watching *Parking Wars* or some other ridiculous reality TV show. He keeps it on like background muzak while he naps.

"And the police?" Em asks uncertainly. She sounds so young and so scared, and I blame Simon Baum for that. This is the last thing my daughter needs, something else to worry about, something that will surely end up being nothing, because I still can't figure out what it would be.

"Put the policeman back on the line, sweetie, please."

"Okay."

A few seconds later, I hear Simon Baum's voice again. "Mrs. Trent?" he asks, all politeness.

"I'd appreciate it if you'd wait outside my house until I come home," I tell him coldly. "You have frightened my daughter, and I don't believe you're allowed inside my house without a warrant." I speak with far more authority than I feel.

"As it happens," he replies, as unflappable as he's been the whole time, "I do have a warrant." *What?* My mouth opens, but no sound comes out. "An arrest warrant," he clarifies. "For your father."

I cannot even begin to compute that. "Stay outside," I manage to gasp out. "Please." And then I end the call, because I don't trust what might come out of my mouth and I need to get home. Immediately.

"Lib?" Grace's voice is full of concern as she puts my mug down on the counter. I am clutching my phone to my chest like it's a life preserver—or a stick of dynamite. Abruptly, I thrust it away from me, so it clatters on the counter, as if I can distance myself from whatever this is—and the trouble is, I don't *know* what it is.

My heart is thudding, my palms clammy, and I am desperately trying to think of a reason why the police would be arresting my father—but I still can't think of anything. My father is the kindest, gentlest man I know. Plenty of people say that kind of thing about the people they love, I know they do, but with him it's actually true. He raised me on his own since I was four, when my mother left us both, never being in touch again. She had mental health issues, I try not to blame her, but sometimes it has felt like a vacuum at the center of my life. Still, my dad was parent enough. More than enough. He never lost his temper—well, *rarely*—and he has always been caring, affectionate, loving, *good*.

"What's wrong?" Grace asks.

"I don't know," I tell her. I scrub my hands over my face, fighting a sudden urge to burst into tears, which I really do not want to do. "I don't know," I say again.

"Who was on the phone?"

I shake my head; I can't explain it all to her now. I don't even know how I would. "I've got to go home for a bit. Can you finish sorting through all this on your own?"

Her frown deepens, her eyes soft with sympathy and concern. She's been a good friend since we met at a toddler gymnastics class nine years ago. Her daughter Violet wrestled Em to the ground and sat on top of her, triumphant. They're good friends now, even though they're polar opposites in just about every way. "Of course," she tells me. "No problem."

Fortunately, we don't have any client appointments or classes today; it's the middle of a muggy July and there's not much going on besides the usual maintenance and admin—sorting donations, making arrangements for our classes that will start in September.

I take a deep breath to try to calm myself, but it just feels like I'm hyperventilating, and for a second, as stars dance across my vision, I think I might actually pass out. All my attempts to control my anxiety, my panic, are deserting me now.

Think, Libby, think.

But I don't know what to think.

"Can I do anything?" Grace asks, and again I shake my head.

"Just... this." I gesture to the pile of clothes in the middle of the shop floor.

"Okay..." She nods slowly, her forehead furrowed. I can tell she wants to ask me a million questions, but I don't even know how to begin to answer them.

"Thanks," I say, and then I scoop up my phone and my bag. With one last tense smile for my friend, I hurry out the door.

The humidity hits me like a brick wall as I step outside the air-conditioned store and start to wilt in the one-hundred-and-two-degree heat. Fresh Start is located in a small, rundown strip mall—cheaper rent—a mile outside Charlottesville, just a couple of faded storefronts with a row of parking spaces. By the time I make it to my car, I am already sweating.

A warrant for my father's arrest? The words judder through my mind, like a broken record, the needle stuck in a relentless groove. *Warrant for his arrest. Warrant for his arrest.*

For *what?*

As I start the car and turn the AC onto high, I finally manage to scrape together a semblance of calm. Either this is about something ridiculous, like parking tickets from twenty years ago, or there has been a mistake somewhere along the line. I don't know what this Simon Baum wants with my dad, but I am starting to believe that he must have gotten his wires seriously crossed. That's the only acceptable answer, the only one I can possibly envision. There's no way my dad has ever done something worthy of arrest.

My dad is pushing one hundred, after all. For the last decade, he's done little more than watch TV, occasionally potter in the garden, once in a blue moon go out to the doctor's or the grocery store, or, if he has to, the senior day center.

A warrant for his arrest? Impossible.

Improbably, I find myself smiling, and a little huff of laughter escapes me as the ludicrousness of the whole situation hits me. I imagine the headline in Charlottesville's newspaper, *The Daily Progress*: *Senior Citizen Mistakenly Arrested*. I can picture it already—this man, Simon Baum's embarrassment, the apologetic grimace, the shake of his head. *"So sorry... I didn't realize..."*

No, I think, *you certainly didn't.*

I breathe in and out, force myself to relax. It's typical of me to jump to the worst conclusions, that habit from childhood I have yet to break. When my kids were small, it was choking on Cheerios or mysterious rashes that could be the symptom of some deadly disease. As they got older, it became more nebulous anxieties about their emotions, their friends, their schools, a swirl of vague what-ifs going round in my head, but in this case, I can't even think of any, not in relation to my dad.

It's going to be fine. Resolve floods through me, hardens my will. It's going to be *fine*. This has to be some sort of mistake, and I am going to sort it out. Quickly.

By the time I pull up onto my street in Charlottesville's Village Place neighborhood, fifteen minutes have passed since I disconnected that call. The street is an oasis of peace and privilege, rows of Arts and Crafts-style houses with deep front porches and American flags wilting in the sultry air, just minutes from Charlottesville's historic downtown and the UVA campus, where my husband works as a research chemist.

For no more than a second, I think about calling Tim, letting him know what has happened, but then I decide not to. I don't want to worry him, and I'm pretty sure I can handle this by myself. By the time I tell him, it will be an amusing anecdote, nothing more. *Can you believe that guy...?*

I pull into the drive, noting first the battered sedan parked on the road outside my house, and then the man sitting on my front porch, in one of the Adirondack chairs, one leg crossed over the other. He doesn't look like a police officer, and he seems to be alone. I am definitely going to ask to see some ID.

I take a deep breath and then open my car door, closing it with not quite a slam as I squint up at him, lifting one hand to shade my eyes from the sun's hazy glare.

"You must be Simon Baum."

He rises from the chair. "And you must be Elizabeth Trent."

I don't reply as I head up the steps to the porch. The shade is welcome, but the heat is still oppressive, the humidity like a heavy, wet blanket wrapped around me. My shirt is already sticking to my back, my shorts to my thighs. As much as I am tempted to, I know I can't conduct this conversation outside.

"Why don't you come inside," I say, keeping my tone firm, "and we can sort out this misunderstanding."

My words are pretty pointed, but they seem to roll right over Simon Baum. He smiles and springs forward to open the screen door for me, something that annoys me. It's not his house, and he has no right to be here.

A warrant for your father's arrest. No.

I fumble with the front door, which Em must have locked, and then, with something close to a gasp of relief, I step inside the house's dim, air-conditioned coolness. As I head to the kitchen at the back of the house, I glance at the door to my dad's suite, and I am glad it's firmly closed, with the strains of some TV show audible through the door. The last thing I want is for him to be upset by all this nonsense.

In the kitchen, I place my bag on the granite island and turn to Simon Baum, who is standing in the doorway, his hands in the pockets of his khakis, seeming relaxed. He looks to be in his mid-fifties, maybe seven or eight years older than me, with a pleasantly crinkled face, faded blue eyes and curly gray hair. His button-down shirt and khakis are good quality but baggy and creased, like he's the sort of man who doesn't care about what he wears.

"Do you have any ID?" I ask a bit abruptly.

With an easy smile, he pulls out his wallet and then shows me a laminated card. *Deputy Chief, Human Rights and Special Prosecutions Section, Department of Justice,* it reads. Like something out of a superhero movie, the kind Tim takes Lucas to see, because I can't stand all those violent action sequences. Silently, I hand it back.

Simon Baum doesn't speak, merely waits for me to, and for a few seconds I struggle not to fidget. All around us, the kitchen stretches silently; there are cereal-encrusted bowls piled up by the sink, and I forgot to switch off the coffee machine, its red light glowing like a rebuke. From the TV in my father's room, I hear a distant, tinny burst of applause.

"So what exactly do you think this is about?" I finally ask, my tone both brisk and just a little bit forbidding. *Because whatever it is, you're wrong,* is what I'm not saying, but I'm pretty sure, from the twitch of his mouth, that Simon Baum heard it all the same.

"I'm here with a warrant for your father's arrest—"

"Yes, so you said," I interject, unable to keep a sharp edge from serrating my voice. "But for what, exactly?"

His blue gaze meets mine with the same kind of steeliness I heard before in his voice. "For Nazi war crimes, perpetrated in Poland during the Second World War," he states flatly.

CHAPTER 2

LIBBY

For a second, it's all I can do to stare at him. Simon Baum stares back coolly, but with a light in his eyes—the light of a zealot, I think. A man on a mission. Does he actually think he's captured a war criminal here? My *father*?

"Are you serious?" I finally ask, hearing the scorn in my voice, a defense mechanism, perhaps, but really this beggars belief. My father, a *Nazi*? It's utterly laughable. All right, yes, he's *German*, but not every German was a Nazi. My father was only nineteen when the Second World War started, practically a boy. He married a woman who was Jewish, or at least half-Jewish. He has donated to a dozen charities, including ones for Holocaust survivors, and when the Holocaust Museum in DC was being built when I was a teenager, he drove me into the city so we could watch the cornerstone being laid. He had tears in his eyes as President Reagan helped to put it down. There is absolutely no way he is—was—a *Nazi*. It's impossible.

Simon doesn't break his gaze as he answers, "I can't think of anything I'm more serious about."

"All right—yes." I nod my head, an exaggerated up and down. I feel like I've turned into a parody of myself, maybe because this feels so absurd. I think of my gentle father, giving me his whimsical smile over a bowl of Campbell's chicken soup with saltine crackers, the classic dinner of my childhood. Waltzing with me to the radio over the cracked linoleum of our kitchen. Playing chess with my son. Falling asleep in his chair. "Yes, of course it's a serious matter," I say as I finally stop nodding. "Absolutely. Nazi war crimes are very serious. The most serious." A statement that hardly needs saying, and I feel faintly ridiculous for stating it out loud. "But you've got the wrong man." I speak firmly, and with a sudden new sympathy, because I am that sure. There is simply no way my father could have been a Nazi. *War crimes?* Simon Baum has wasted his time. He's going to be disappointed he's got the wrong guy, but I can't help that.

"What did your father do during the war?" he asks, his voice as calm as ever. He sounds as sure as I feel.

"During the war?" This comes out surprised, as if this isn't relevant, and it *isn't*, because this simply has to be a case of mistaken identity. A different Daniel Weiss, maybe. "He was an accountant."

"Where?"

For a second, appallingly, my mind blanks. I try to think of the name of the city, but I can't. I know it, of course, but my dad has never really talked about his childhood in Germany, the suffering he endured both before and during the war. "It was a terrible time," he's said more than once, his tone final. "No one wants to hear about it." He came to America in 1947, and as far as he is concerned, his life started then. "Um..." My mind continues to spin.

"Stuttgart?" Simon Baum fills in helpfully, and I stare, struggling not to feel annoyed, or worse, actually afraid.

"Yes," I reply after a second's pause. "That's right. Stuttgart."

He nods, and I suddenly feel like I need to sit down. Simon

Baum clearly knows a lot about my father, or at least he thinks he does. But I'm still sure he's wrong. I can tell, though, as I look at his calm but firm expression, the way he stands in my kitchen like he will not be moved, that I need to think coolly and logically about this. I need to get my head around whatever it is this man think he knows, what he *wants* to know, because looking at him, I'm pretty sure he wants this to be true. He wants to catch a criminal today. My father.

"Look," I tell him, resting one hand on the kitchen island to anchor myself, the granite smooth and cool beneath my palm, "clearly you've done some research and you think you know who my father is, but I'm pretty sure this is a misunderstanding of some kind. But—" I offer a conciliatory smile, a mere stretching of my lips, "I'd still like to hear what you have to say. The sooner we can get this cleared up, the better for both of us, right? Then you can find the real perpetrator, wherever he is, because he obviously needs to be prosecuted." My smile widens, like an elastic band about to snap. "Would you like something to drink? Coffee, tea, something cold?"

"A coffee would be nice, thanks," Simon says. "No milk, two sugars."

I spend the next few minutes thankfully employed by that task, emptying the pot of its burned-smelling dregs and refilling it, my back to Simon. He doesn't speak, but I feel his presence, the intensity of him, hidden by that oh-so casual stance. He must have some pretty compelling evidence, I realize with a sudden, plunging sense of dread, for him to come this far. Obtain that warrant. This obviously isn't some *whim*.

Whatever evidence he has, it's wrong, I know this absolutely, but I recognize that it might be difficult to convince him that my father isn't who he thinks he is. In the hazy reaches of my mind, I recall some documentary I watched one night, while flicking through the channels, about Nazi hunters. A case of mistaken identity, some Polish farmer whom several people identified as the guard who tormented them in a concentration camp. They'd come all the way from Israel for the trial, but as it turned out, there was no way he could have been that guard; he'd been innocent, a forced labor conscript sent to Germany to dig ditches. Eventually, after years of struggle and heartache, the case had been thrown out.

I switch the coffee machine on to brew and then turn around, fold my arms. "So what exactly do you think my father did during the war?" I ask, trying to keep my voice friendly. Because, of course, technically, *absolutely*, I'm on Simon Baum's side, the side of justice. Nazis need to be condemned. Arrested, tried, sent to prison, no matter how old they are, because of the heinous crimes they committed during the war. Of course I believe that, and my father does, as well. I'm sure of it.

Simon regards me quietly for a moment, as if he can see right beneath my pseudo-friendly stance. "He was a bookkeeper at the extermination camp Sobibor in eastern Poland from September 1942 to October 1943," he states without a ripple of doubt.

The precision of those dates, their complete matter-of-factness, unsettles me, but I do my best not to show my unease. "Sobibor," I repeat, nodding. I've never heard of it, but the word *extermination* echoes ominously through my mind.

"Did your father ever mention the place?"

No, because he wasn't there. "He rarely talked about his war years, or anything from his time in Germany." And in case this sounds incriminating, I add quickly, "That's fairly common, I think, for German refugees, as they had such a terrible time, both before the war and during it. And after, as well. He lost his parents during the war... you know, that's how he came to this country? As a refugee?"

"As a displaced person, yes, in 1947."

The coffee machine beeps, and I turn around to pour two cups. I wonder how Em is doing, if she's trying to overhear our conversation from my dad's room, or if she just wants to keep out of it. Lucas might come back from his bike ride soon, sweaty and disheveled, wanting to down a quart of milk straight from the carton. I have a desperate, deep-seated urge to keep my children from hearing this conversation, from having to worry about their beloved grandfather. From wondering if he is a Nazi.

No, of course he isn't a Nazi. That nanosecond's flicker of doubt infuriates me as well as fills me with shame. Simon Baum might sound sure, but he has to be wrong. I know my father. I know what he's capable of, what kind of man he is. He was my whole world when I was a child; he's lived with me for much of my adult life. I love him. Of course he can't be a Nazi, because I would know. I would sense it; there would have been clues, flickers of doubt. He would have revealed himself some way, something would have slipped out... and nothing ever did. *Nothing*. The realization both reassures and strengthens me.

"So," I say as I turn around and hand him his cup of coffee, "there must have been a Daniel Weiss at this camp, Sob—" I stumble on the name, and Simon fills in tonelessly,

"Sobibor."

"Yes. Sobibor." It's not my fault I've never heard of it, but I feel a twist of guilt about it all the same, like I should have. "And you've confused him with my father."

"There was a Daniel Weiss at Sobibor," Simon tells me before he takes a sip of his coffee. His blue gaze, over the rim of the cup, never leaves mine. "But he wasn't a bookkeeper." A pause, weighted, deliberate, while I do my best to remain still, to keep my expression neutral but also alert, interested. "He was a prisoner, one of the few hundred Jews the Nazis kept alive to do the manual work of running the camp for them."

"How could my father be both a prisoner and a Nazi?" I ask after a second, feeling both confused and a bit exasperated. If he's doing this slow reveal for dramatic effect, it's starting to get annoying. Why not tell me straight out what he thinks happened, so I can refute it? And then he does.

"He wasn't," he states in that same calm voice. "Because your father isn't Daniel Weiss. His real name is Hans Brenner, and he's been going under the alias of Daniel Weiss since the end of the war."

Another silence, this one stretching on. I am gaping, but I can't help it. I don't know what to say, what to think, what question to ask first. "Hans Brenner," I finally say, and it sounds like a stranger. It *is* a stranger. My father is Daniel Weiss; I was Libby Weiss for the first thirty years of my life, until I changed to my married name. Who is Hans Brenner? Not my father. "Why... What evidence do you have that my father actually is this Hans Brenner?"

"There was a Hans Brenner who was an accountant from Stuttgart. He worked at his family's accountancy firm until he was called up to serve as bookkeeper at Sobibor in September 1942. After the war, Hans Brenner disappeared as if he'd never existed, and a Daniel Weiss—allegedly an accountant from Stuttgart—applied for emigration to the United States. Your father."

"That's it?" I blurt, and as Simon Baum's mouth tightens, I see a flare of anger in his eyes. "I mean," I amend, "there could be any number of explanations." I am trying to think of one, but the facts feel slippery, elusive. *Stuttgart. Sobibor. Daniel Weiss. Hans Brenner.* I can't keep hold of any of it. My father, making up a name? The name of a prisoner? *Why?* "What I mean is, there's no real link between the two men, is there?" I press, as reasonably as I can. "Besides the fact that both Hans Brenner and Daniel Weiss were accountants from Stuttgart?" How big a city was Stuttgart back then? How many accountants might there have been? Surely quite a few.

"And they were both at Sobibor," Simon adds. There is a

sardonic edge to his voice that I don't like, as if he thinks I'm being deliberately obtuse, and I'm not. I can't be.

"My father wasn't at Sobibor," I return quickly. "Daniel Weiss, the prisoner, must be another person with the same name. It must have been a fairly common name, back then, in Germany." I meant to make it a statement, but it comes out like a question.

"And there was no Daniel Weiss from Stuttgart who was an accountant," Simon continues evenly. "Not in any record that exists today. The Daniel Weiss who was at Sobibor was a Polish German-speaking Jew from Poznan. He, his wife, and their son and daughter were taken to Sobibor in November 1942. His wife and daughter were gassed upon arrival." I flinch and Simon Baum notices. "Daniel and his son remained at the camp until the prisoner revolt of October 14, 1943. At that point, Daniel's son witnessed Hans Brenner shooting and killing his father in cold blood, right at the gates of the camp."

For a second, I can see it—an SS guard, a raised arm, a pistol. The crack of a gunshot, the fallen body. I might as well be picturing a scene from *Schindler's List*. It feels like that—a dramatic scene, the climax of some war film, not anything actually to do with me—or my father. "And you think my father is this man?" I restate, unable to keep the disbelief from seeping into my voice. "Who shot someone? Killed him?" No way. *No way*.

My father doesn't like killing *spiders*. He used to catch them and let them outside, while I cowered in the corner. Kill a man in cold blood? That is truly, utterly impossible, and the knowledge fills me with a sudden, almost buoyant relief. I had a tiny twitch of doubt, yes, but now I know absolutely. Simon Baum really is wrong.

He seems unfazed by my skepticism, but he is holding his mouth tightly now, and there is another flash of ire in his eyes. It gives me hope, because it makes me wonder if he actually has the watertight case he wants me to think he does. What if he came here trying to trick me, or even my father, into saying something incriminating so he'd have some more evidence? Except, of course, there isn't any.

I throw back my shoulders, meet his level gaze head-on, a hint of challenge in my eyes. "My father did not kill a man," I state.

"Leo Weiss, Daniel Weiss's son," he states, "has identified your father by photograph."

Again, I think of the Polish farmer, accused of being a Nazi guard, based only on testimony, and I shake my head, the movement firm, sure. "That's not possible."

"It is."

"What photograph?" I am already starting to bluster, as if my outrage is hiding something and it *isn't*.

"This one." Simon takes out his phone, swipes a few times, and then, to my shock, he shows me an image I recognize. It's a screenshot of a photo I took myself, three years ago, a fundraiser for Fresh Start that I put up on social media. My father came to the charity gala; he's with me and Tim, Em and Lucas and a few other people, all gathered around a table. There are half-empty wine glasses and silver balloons, a tablecloth splotched with red wine and a wilting orchid as a centerpiece. My father looks so tiny and frail; his best suit hangs off his shoulders, and his face is as wrinkled as an old prune.

"He recognized him from this?" I can't help but sound disbelieving. "How, if he hadn't seen him since the war, when he himself must have been no more than a child? My father would have been in his twenties then, and he's ninety-three here. How could he possibly say he was the same man? I'm not sure I would recognize a photo of my father as a young man." There aren't any, nothing from before he emigrated to America, anyway.

"Leo Weiss saw him shoot his own father. I think he might remember the face of the man who did that, don't you?"

"You don't know that for sure," I reply quickly. He's treating these assumptions as facts, and it is beginning to make me angry. I take a deep, steadying breath. "There might be some similarities in their appearances," I allow, as if I am being generous in conceding that much, "but that's all." I nod toward his phone, clenched in his hand. "Is that all the proof you have?"

He doesn't answer for a long moment, and I feel another rush of relief flooding through me, making my knees weaken, so I put one hand out to the counter to steady myself. That's all he has, a single photo of my father as an old man. This really is a case of mistaken identity. I knew it was, and yet I am still grateful to be even more sure.

"Tell me," Simon says, his tone turning conversational, "if your father *was* a Nazi, if he did once work as an accountant at the Sobibor death camp, and you could be absolutely certain of those facts, would you want to see him prosecuted for his crimes?"

"But—"

He holds up a hand. "I know. You think he isn't. But if you knew he was. If you *knew*." He pauses. "Would you?"

As I stare at him, I feel myself start to flush. How am I supposed to answer that? Of course there is only one way I can. "Yes, I would," I finally say, my voice stiff. "If there was incontrovertible proof, yes, absolutely, I would." I do believe that; I believe Nazis should be tried for their crimes, of *course*. What kind of monster doesn't? "But there isn't proof." I state it as a fact because that is how I feel. What I believe.

"There could be," he replies.

"Such as?"

He shrugs. "A photograph. A memento. You'd be surprised

what these old Nazis like to keep around, even though it incriminates them."

These old Nazis. The words reverberate through me and I feel a confusing welter of emotions—irritation at his contemptuous tone, and then guilt for feeling it. He's talking about *Nazis.* But my father isn't one.

"You don't have any photographs of Hans Brenner from the war?" I surmise slowly.

"Not any in which he could be easily identified."

My heart leaps, although whether with fear or hope, I don't know. "But you have some?"

Simon nods slowly. "A cache of personal photographs from Sobibor recently came to light. They were handed over by the grandson of an SS deputy commandant at the camp. I believe Hans Brenner is in some of the group shots."

"May I see them?" I ask, even though I'm not entirely sure that I want to. Of course I'm not going to recognize this Hans Brenner, but I still don't want to see him.

"I have copies at my office."

Am I meant to go to DC, or wherever his office is? Is it on me to prove who my father is, and who he isn't, when really it should be on Simon Baum, and whoever he represents? I feel as if we've been going around in circles, getting nowhere.

"All right," I ask after a moment, "so what happens now? Are you going to talk to my father?" I don't want him to, but it occurs to me how strange it is, that he's talking to me, and not my dad.

Simon Baum hesitates, and then he blows out a long breath. "Look, I'm going to level with you," he says. "I don't have as much document evidence as I'd like in order to proceed with this case."

I stare at him, blinking, shocked that I have already been so easily vindicated. *Of course you don't,* I almost want to say, but I manage to keep myself from the pointless snark. "What do you mean, exactly?" I ask instead, my tone polite but cool.

"The District Court of Western Virginia is reviewing the case for extradition—"

"You said you already had a warrant for his arrest," I interject, my tone sharpening.

"I have applied for it—"

"So you lied." I can hardly believe it. He's supposed to be the good guy, and yet he lied to worm his way into my house? My family? I think of how scared Em was, and I feel a flash of fury.

Simon Baum's eyes flash again, with his own restrained ire. "I will have the warrant," he replies evenly.

But it wasn't in his pocket, the way he'd made me believe. "You misrepresented yourself," I state coolly. "Why should I believe anything you say?"

"Because I'm on the side of justice." For the first time, his voice rises, and I sense his passion, what drives him to do what he does. "I want to prosecute a Nazi war criminal. Surely you can't argue with that."

"But my father—"

"I said I needed more evidence," he cuts me off, "not that I didn't have any. Trust me, I have a significant amount."

I raise my chin. "A single photograph."

"There are other considerations, factors."

I'm not sure I believe him. I'm not going to ask what they are, besides what he has already mentioned. "So why do you need even more evidence?" I ask. "If it's as cut and dried as you implied?"

"I didn't say it was cut and dried—"

"You basically did." My tone is rising; I am starting to feel properly angry. He tried to trick me. Is that how these guys work?

"Libby." His tone gentles, the use of my nickname

surprising me. How does he even know it? "We're on the same side here."

"Are we?"

"You said if you had incontrovertible proof that your father had worked at Sobibor, you'd want to see him prosecuted." He sounds so reasonable, and yet something in me resists. I press my lips together, wait for more. "I need you to find that evidence," Simon Baum says.

"Find the evidence? So you can put my father in jail?"

"I'm not going to put your father in jail. That's not my job, and in any case he's not considered a flight risk. I just want him to stand trial for extradition, to determine if he can be extradited to face criminal charges in Germany."

"Extradited." I stare at him blankly. I really don't know enough about any of this. "He'd have to go to Germany?" It's obvious from what he said, but I can't make myself believe it. "He hasn't been back there since he left, right after the war."

Simon's expression remains implacable. "There are people in Germany who want to see him tried."

People? What people? They feel like shadowy figures, ominous, alarming. "And what if my father really isn't Hans Brenner?" I ask.

He shrugs. "Then you won't find any evidence. You can have a clear conscience about that."

What, I wonder, does my conscience have to do with anything? But then, of course, I know the answer. If there is any chance, any chance at all, that my father is Hans Brenner, that he was a Nazi... I can't hide that fact, can I? I can't participate in some sordid cover-up, I can't refuse to cooperate. I shouldn't even want to. Simon Baum is right, and in this moment I hate him for it.

I wish Tim were here, with his logical scientist's brain. I've always been too emotional, even if I do my best to disguise it, to present a smiling face of calm to the world, but I don't know how to handle this. My bravado, my certainty of who my father is, it doesn't feel like enough in this moment. I put one hand to the side of my head as if I've suffered a blow. I feel as if I have, as if my head is ringing, the room blurring before my eyes.

"What is it exactly," I ask slowly, "that you want me to do?"

"Find some evidence, to prove he was at Sobibor."

I gape; I can't help it. Actively work against him? Turn my father in? How can he possibly ask me even to consider such a thing? And yet I *know* my dad isn't Hans Brenner. He's asking me to find evidence that doesn't exist. Before I can say any of this, Simon speaks.

"Look," he says, "I'm not some wild cowboy going solo, chasing some vendetta here, okay? There have been a lot of people involved in your father's case, from officials in the German government to the U.S. Department of State to the Human Rights and Special Prosecutions team that I'm part of. There have been human rights lawyers, Holocaust survivors, historical researchers, all weighing in with their expertise and evidence. We've been building up a file on your father for a couple of years now, ever since Leo Weiss saw that photo."

"There's a whole file?" I ask dazedly. There are who knows how many people, all working against my father?

"We have evidence, but nothing absolute. Which is where you come in."

I blink slowly as dizziness sweeps over me, pulling me under. This is all sounding a lot bigger than I thought it was. A lot more frightening, a lot more real. When I speak, I fumble for the words, form them slowly. "But if this has been such a huge enterprise... why didn't you approach my father or me until now?"

Simon's mouth tightens. "We like to have an airtight case before we go public. Do you know how many of these guys claim a case of mistaken identity? Especially with so many of the Nazis' records destroyed during or after the war?" He shakes his head. "Pretty much all of them."

"But what if it is a case of mistaken identity?" I press, because it has to be. *It has to be.*

"Then prove it. Find the evidence that shows he was at Sobibor—or that he wasn't. I confess, I'm pretty sure, but right now so are you." The looks he gives me is one of challenge, like he's daring me to do it. "So prove it to me," he states coolly. "Prove to me that your father wasn't there."

"Why should I?" I flash back. "Shouldn't the burden of proof be on you?"

"As it happens," he replies evenly, "it is, which is why I don't have the warrant yet. But I'll be honest with you, it's likely that I'll get it, and I'm not saying that as wishful thinking, but reality. That's how these cases go. And if you decide you're going to try to tie things up with some case of mistaken identity, it might slow things down a bit, it's true, but do you really want your father's last years of life to be consumed by a trial? I should warn you, the publicity these cases generate isn't pretty."

"I don't want his last years to be spent in prison," I retort, and Simon gives me a level look.

"You do if he really is a Nazi."

I look away. I don't know how to respond. He's got the moral high ground, I know that, but it feels more complicated. More personal. I also know that I can't think about this anymore; my brain is on overload, full of static like a snow screen on a TV. I can barely formulate thoughts, never mind words, and Em is probably going out of her mind with worry. My father will be getting concerned.

My father. I could just storm into his room, ask him to tell me the truth, solve this in a heartbeat, because I know he would be honest with me.

Wouldn't he?

That second's doubt silences me utterly.

"What kind of evidence do you mean?" I ask weakly. I hate that I'm asking the question. I hate that I'm even thinking about doing what he asks, even if it's to exonerate my father, because he isn't Hans Brenner.

"Anything that links him to Sobibor. A photograph, a memento, some little trophy—"

I rear back, shaking my head, revolted at the thought. "A *trophy*? You don't know my father at all." I shake my head, angry again. "You think you do, but you don't."

Simon presses his lips together. "You'd be surprised."

I think of what he said before—*what these old Nazis keep.* But that's not my father. I know that, absolutely.

I shake my head, the gesture as firm as my tone when I speak. "My father has never shown me anything like that."

"He wouldn't have, but he might have it in his possession all the same."

My stomach cramps at the thought. "And you want me to give it to you?"

"Libby." He says my name like he knows me, like we're friends. "I've learned a little bit about you, from the research I've been doing on your father. Your family." Which is alarming in itself, but I stay silent. "I know you work for a charity that helps disadvantaged women," he continues, "including refugees —women like the ones who would have gone through Sobibor, clutching their few belongings, desperate for a chance to live." I swallow hard. "I've heard your speech at that fundraiser online, and I've read some articles where you've been interviewed. I know you have a concern for the disenfranchised, a heart for the weak and the poor. I believe you are someone who desperately wants to do the right thing, and who does it, no matter what the cost." The flattery, baseless as it might be, makes me flush with an uneasy sort of pleasure. He pauses. "And I think you know what the right thing to do is, in this situation. Even if it's hard. Even if it hurts, almost unbearably."

A tear pools and then threatens to spill down my cheek and I brush it away, pretending I have an itch to hide the movement, but I'm pretty Simon knows I'm trying not to cry. I'm also pretty sure he knows how to play me, with those compliments. He can't possibly know all that about me, can he? And yet he's right. I *do* want to do the right thing—just as my father always taught me. So how can potentially turning him in be the right thing in this situation? And yet if he was a Nazi...

But he *isn't*.

"Do you know how many Jews died at Sobibor?" Simon asks quietly, and he doesn't wait for my response. "As many as two hundred and fifty thousand. In just under eighteen months. It wasn't a concentration camp, not like Auschwitz or Dachau or any of those places. Those were horrendous, God knows, but Sobibor was something else. Something even worse." He pauses, and I simply wait, because what can I say to any of that? How could Sobibor be worse than Auschwitz or Dachau? "Sobibor was a death camp," Simon states flatly. "And only a death camp. An extermination camp, that existed only for the systematic mass murder of Jews—and only Jews. There were three extermination camps in total, all in eastern Poland—Sobibor, Treblinka, and Belzec. Operation Reinhard, they called it, in Heydrich's memory. Do you know how many survived those three death camps?"

I shake my head. I feel like a child being scolded, that this is something I should have known, although how could I possibly have known it?

"Eighty-seven. Eighty-seven out of a million and a half."

Again I cannot speak. There is, really, nothing at all that can be said to that.

"People don't always realize," Simon continues, "that these camps were different than the others. That they existed solely to kill Jews. They kept a few hundred prisoners on to work for them, to do all the things they didn't want to do—hauling bodies, cleaning out the train cars—but they swapped them out after a while, killed them and took others. Same with the *Kapos* —you know who those are?"

"Jewish guards?" I offer hesitantly, half-remembering from the historical novels I'd read.

"Yes, guards. They put some prisoners in charge of removing the bodies from the gas chambers, taking them to the crematorium—but I'm getting ahead of myself. First, they came to Sobibor in trains—cattle cars usually—and they were met at the platform by SS Oberscharfürher Hermann Michel. He wore a white coat to make it look like he was a physician. He told them they were going to be put to work, but they needed to be clean first, so there wouldn't be any outbreaks of typhus in the camp."

"Don't..." I protest weakly. I know where this has to be going, and I can't bear to hear any of this, not in relation to my father. Not in relation to anyone.

But Simon hasn't finished. "They were forced to undress— the men, the women, the little children. They were promised they would get their clothes back later, and they were even given towels. *Towels.* Then they were led down the Himmel-strasse—the 'Road to Heaven,' as the SS liked to call it. It was also known as the Tube—*Schlauch*, in German. And then they were put into sealed rooms that were supposed to be showers, and they were killed by carbon monoxide. In some camps, you can still see the marks made by their fingernails on the walls, the doors of the gas chambers. The camp at Sobibor, however, was completely destroyed—by the Nazis. They wanted to hide the evidence of what they'd done from the advancing Soviets. From everyone."

I shake my head, unable to speak.

Simon stares at me, a fierce light burning in his blue eyes. "Do you know the average amount of time a Jew spent in Sobi-bor, before they were killed?"

This time he is waiting for my reply, and so I take a deep breath as I dab at my eyes as discreetly as I can. "No, of course I don't."

"Twenty minutes," he tells me, and I can't keep from letting out a small, choked sound of distress. The horror is unimaginable, impossible to fully comprehend. I don't even want to, and yet my father...

My father.

"As the camp's bookkeeper, Hans Brenner would have been on that platform for every arrival. He would have watched thousands and thousands of people go to their deaths. Parents. Children. Babies." I make another sound, one hand fluttering uselessly in front of me, but Simon plows on, remorseless now. "And then he would have supervised the sorting through of all their belongings—their money and their jewels, their precious photos and keepsakes. Their gold teeth, pried from their mouths after they'd been killed. He would have made a record of all that stolen treasure, before sending it on to Berlin for processing. They put all the money into an SS account nicknamed 'The Saint.' Charming, eh?" He presses his lips together. "And your father did that for an entire year."

I just shake my head yet again, because I have nothing to say. I wipe my eyes once more.

"I'm not pretending this is easy," Simon says, his tone less strident now. "Far from it. But it is right, and I think you know that. If your father really is Hans Brenner, then he should be prosecuted for his crimes. You believe that, don't you?"

"Yes..." I part with the word reluctantly, knowing I have to believe it, yet also not wanting to. My father *cannot* be Hans Brenner. He cannot.

"Then find that evidence, whatever it is. A photograph. A memento. Something. Make it easier on him, in the long run. See justice is done, for your sake, for his, for the sake of the two hundred and fifty thousand people who died under his watch."

I take a deep breath, desperate to clear my head. "You're assuming that if he is Hans Brenner, he will deny it," I say slowly, the realization occurring to me for the first time. "How can you be sure of that? If I ask him directly, if you do..." Although I don't really want Simon Baum confronting my frail father. "He's an honest man," I persist, but Simon looks unimpressed.

"They all deny it," he replies grimly. "Every single time." He takes out his wallet and hands me a business card. "Contact me at that number and email address, any time, day or night."

"And what about your warrant?" I ask shakily. "Should I— we—expect something?" Police with handcuffs? Officious paperwork in the mail?

"I'll let you know if and when anything changes," he tells me. "In the meantime... see what you can find."

Is he really asking me to do this? I fight not to close my eyes, to wish this all away. Simon Baum is already turning toward the door. It takes me a stunned second to realize he's actually going. I feel as if a tornado has blown through my house; as if I am standing amidst ruins. I have a million questions to ask, but I don't know what any of them are. I don't know if I can bear to hear the answers. All I know is I have to find a way to prove my dad *isn't* Hans Brenner. I'll find the evidence, but it won't be the kind Simon Baum is expecting.

As Simon turns to go, Lucas, sweaty from his bike ride, comes through the front door. He looks young and innocent and completely unperturbed. I think of how I was cross he left Em, and how ridiculous that seems now.

Lucas glances at Simon with an indifferent sort of teenaged curiosity, and I watch, sagging against the counter, as he walks out of my house, closing the door behind him with a surprising gentleness. Lucas opens the fridge and peers inside.

"Who was that?" he asks.

CHAPTER 3

SEPTEMBER 1942

Stuttgart, Germany

"Anni, have you been listening at all?"

Hans Brenner shook his head as he gazed at his younger sister with affectionate exasperation. She was lying on the sofa, her head thrown back, her dark hair spread out over the faded cushions as she surveyed the ceiling as if it were utterly absorbing rather than a stretch of peeling white plaster.

"Listening?" she repeated vaguely. "Yes..."

No, she hadn't been. She hardly ever was. Ever since she was a small child, Anni had happily lived in her own world, and one she'd matter-of-factly stated was far more interesting than the living and breathing one all around her, people included. *Him* included, her only sibling.

Hans sank into the chair by his desk, shaking his head slowly. "What has been capturing your imagination this time?" he asked, his tone a mixture of weary resignation and amused affection. He'd actually been saying something important, and now he'd have to say it all over again.

"I've been thinking about aleph null," she replied in a

dreamy voice, her gaze still on the ceiling. She twirled a strand of chestnut hair around one finger.

"Aleph null?" He'd never heard the term before, but that was hardly surprising.

"Yes, you must know it, Hans." Finally, Anni deigned to lower her gaze from the ceiling, glancing at him with mingled surprise, exasperation, and hope. "Of course you do."

"I don't," he replied on a sigh. Of course he didn't.

"Aleph null? The smallest of infinite numbers?" She swung her legs down to hit the floor, her elbows braced on her knees as she stared at him expectantly, her hair in a dark cloud around her face.

"The smallest?" He raised his eyebrows. "How can something infinite be small, never mind the smallest?"

"Oh!" She made a sound of impatient dismissal, as if his question was too ridiculous for words, which for her it probably was. Long ago, Hans had learned that while he, as an accountant, saw numbers as useful, manageable tools he handled to some effect, Anni viewed them as dear friends. She preferred their company to anyone else's, even his own, her only living relative left.

Their father, when he'd been alive, hadn't understood her fascination with mathematics at all, exasperated by Anni's seeming otherworldliness. He hadn't seen any point in Anni having any more opportunities of education than any other girl in Hitler's Reich, trained to take up the duties of wife and mother, and fortunately Anni hadn't, either. She found school dull and her *Bund Deutscher Mädel* meetings even worse.

"Why," she would ask Hans, "do I need to learn how to walk a tightrope?" The BDM required all sorts of athletic training and gymnastics in addition to its domestic education. Anni was, predictably, completely dismissive of such activities, along with the Nazi dogma that blared from the radio, the newsreels, her schoolteachers, everywhere. Fortunately, now that she was almost eighteen, she would be finished with the BDM, and the *BDM-Werk Glaube und Schönheit*, the Faith and Beauty Society for young women up to aged twenty-one, was voluntary. She would, he knew, not be joining.

"All right," he said as he leaned back in his chair, one elbow braced on the armrest. Outside, the leaves of the black walnut trees lining their street in Stuttgart-Mitte were just starting to turn yellow, the sky a pale blue, edged with white, a harbinger of winter. "Tell me about aleph null."

"Well," she said, "you do know that you can discover the cardinality of every set?"

"The cardinality," he repeated. "Yes." That much he knew from his training as an accountant; numbers could be neatly counted and organized into sets.

"Well, it's the same for infinite sets, of course."

"Of course," he replied with a smile. "Although I thought the whole idea of infinite numbers was that the numbers in them could not be counted?"

"That is such a simplistic idea, Hans." She sounded as severe as a teacher. "Look." Quickly, her movements light and graceful, she went over to his desk and rummaged among his books and files for a scrap of paper and a stub of pencil, while Hans looked on, bemused. "Here." She wrote the numbers one, two, three in brackets. "A set of cardinal numbers."

He shook his head with a small smile. "I'm not in kindergarten, Anni."

She slid him a quick, laughing look, her brown eyes lightening to gold before she turned back to the paper. "Infinite sets work on the same principle. You just have to keep counting."

"Forever."

"Well, yes, of course forever. That's the point." She shook her head impatiently. Another ridiculous question, then. "Such sets are the countably infinite, and they're shown by this." She made a mark on the paper like a cursive N, followed by a small zero. "Aleph null, the smallest infinite."

Hans threw his hands up in the air. "I'm sorry, you've already lost me."

She pushed the paper away and lay back down on the sofa, one arm stretched above her head as she surveyed the ceiling once more. "Do you know some mathematicians argued against the idea of the infinite? Wittgenstein, for one. He decried mathematical proofs for God."

"*Is* there a mathematical proof for God?" Hans asked skeptically. How had they gone from talking about aleph null to God?

She gave him a sideways look. "If there is an absolute infinite, then it must be God," she stated, as if it were obvious.

Hans shook his head. They'd had enough debating of such abstract, esoteric topics. He had real information to impart, information that would make a difference to both of them. "Anni," he said, and the gravity of his tone had her sitting up again, her expression turning serious, a little alarmed. Ever since their father had died six months ago—hit by a bus during a blackout, an ignominious end to a quietly and soberly lived life —Anni had suffered from anxiety; she struggled to sleep, she bit her nails, she found it hard to eat. Or perhaps, Hans considered, it had started before then; beneath her laughing demeanor, there had always been an edgy fractiousness, a sense of worry about the world. A teacher had once called her high-strung.

In any case, Anni dismissed all her physical symptoms as absurd, signs of weakness she refused to entertain, even as her nails looked red and raw, and her lovely eyes had deep violet shadows beneath them. She refused to allow her mind to succumb to her anxiety, even as her body did, again and again.

"What is it?" she asked, and now her voice sounded tense.

"Do you remember when I went out yesterday morning?"

"Of course I do. It was only yesterday morning, after all."

He took a deep breath and then let it out slowly. "I wasn't merely running errands, as I'd told you. I had a summons—from the regional SS office."

"The SS!" Her eyes widened. Their father had joined the *Allgemeine* SS ten years ago as a functionary to look after some of the SS's many business interests, and much of his work had been the bookkeeping for their different companies and enterprises in the area. A quiet man who had been grieving the loss of his wife from pneumonia four years earlier, Walter Brenner had found a camaraderie among the other local SS officers, all of them volunteers—dentists, doctors, accountants, and the like—who, as far as Hans could tell, did little more than proudly put on their uniforms to march in parades and hand out pamphlets. He had not yet joined the SS himself; at twenty-three, he suspected he was considered too young, although all that had changed yesterday. "Why were you summoned?" Anni asked, and now she really sounded anxious.

"I have been called upon to take up a position out east," Hans told her. Refusing, he had known from the start, would not have been an option. "As an accountant at some sort of camp." He could not quite keep a note of something almost like pride from creeping into his voice. It was not every twenty-three-year-old newly qualified accountant who would be recommended for such a role.

"A work camp?"

He shrugged his assent, because he didn't know and the *Gruppenführer* hadn't told him.

"You mean with Jews?"

He shrugged again and they were both silent; there were hardly any Jews left in all of Stuttgart. After the old synagogue and Jewish cemetery had been destroyed at *Kristallnacht*, they had begun rounding up all the Jewish males and sent them to Dachau. Then they'd turned the old Trade Fair grounds in Killesbergpark into a ghetto. Since last December, they'd both seen the trains that had gone through the city with ominous regularity, a succession of rattling cattle cars, their rough wooden slats hiding their pitiable loads.

Their parents had had no great love of Jews—"those murderous thieves," as their father would rant after a stein or two of beer—but Hans had always supposed he felt a bit more ambivalent about the matter himself. He suspected many of them were indeed greedy, grasping, materialistic and ambitious, although perhaps not quite as much as the newspapers and film reels so vehemently declared. His father had liked to say, half-joking, half-serious, that Hans should double-check any column of figures totted up by a Jew. But even so, did they deserve to be rounded up into that wretched ghetto? You could smell the place from a block away. Or put onto trains to God knew where... except, of course, he *would* know where, because he and Anni were leaving for a place called Sobibor in just three days. It was hardly enough time to make arrangements, but the *Gruppenführer* hadn't cared.

"You are needed by the Reich," he'd told Hans, who had stood in front of his desk, his hat in his hands, his heels clicked together like a soldier, and tried not to betray his nervousness. "Your father's loyal service has been noted, Herr Brenner. And yours, as well. You joined the *Hitlerjugend* when you were ten?"

"Yes, *Gruppenführer*."

The group leader had grunted his approval; Hans had joined the HJ years before it had been a legal requirement, back in 1929, when the Nazi Party had been seen as little more than a bunch of upstart rabble-rousers. He'd started at the same time as his father had joined the Party, simply to be like him, and admittedly he'd enjoyed the hikes and campfires and marching songs. As a quiet, brainy sort of boy, he'd never been particularly popular at school, but in the HJ he'd felt accepted, and later, as a young man of eighteen and a leader himself of a group of younger boys, he'd relished a small sense of authority and importance.

"You are a loyal servant of the Reich who now commands your service in a delicate matter that requires the utmost discretion," the *Gruppenführer* had declared rather grandly, and Hans had bowed his head in humble acceptance of this compliment even as he could not keep his chest from swelling a little in pride. *He* had been chosen. Admittedly, he did not know what for, but it had to be something at least a little important.

Back when the war had started, at only nineteen years old, he'd been excused from army service thanks to the nature of his work, as well as a weak chest. He'd chafed at that, even as he'd been secretly relieved not to have to fight. Like his father had, he wanted a quiet life, and yet at the same time, he longed for a chance to prove himself. Perhaps, finally, this was his opportunity.

Since their father's death, and even before, he and Anni had lived quietly in their parents' apartment; she managed their household affairs in a rather lackluster way, and he ran the accountancy office underneath. He was a Party member, just as his father had been, and he attended the rallies and meetings as necessary, gave to the *Winterhilfswerk* whenever one of the BDM girls came around rattling their tin pots for charity, but otherwise he'd kept his head down with work, his evenings and weekends spent with his sister, or on rare occasions out with a few school friends for a stein of beer, but not much else. He hadn't thought he *wanted* much else, until he saw the *Gruppenfuhrer's* encouraging smile and felt himself preen a little.

I could be important, he had thought, and was both attracted to and ashamed by the thought.

"Where are we going, exactly?" Anni asked. She still sounded alarmed.

"A place called Sobibor. It's in the east of Poland, near

Brest, on the Bug River." He sounded as if he were reading from a holiday brochure, but Anni wasn't fooled.

"Brest was given to the Soviets in the Frontier Treaty," she stated sharply.

"And taken back by us last year," Hans reminded her. "A glorious victory." Or so the newspapers had insisted.

"Will we be near the fighting?"

"We'll be perfectly safe, I assure you." He tried to sound relaxed, although the truth was, he knew he could be sure of no such thing. Although the *Gruppenführer's* compliments had appealed to his vanity, Hans did not particularly relish the idea of going so far east, almost all the way to Ukraine. He knew nothing about the camps, and he realized, when the *Gruppen-führer* had mentioned them, that he'd rather preferred it that way.

"And I am allowed to go with you, to such a place?" Now his sister sounded suspicious.

"I explained the situation to the *Gruppenführer*," Hans assured her. "How you were only seventeen—"

"Eighteen in a few months," she reminded him and he continued with a smile,

"And under my care. He understood the matter completely. He said you could accompany me and occupy yourself with our domestic arrangements. Apparently, it is quite a pleasant place —near a forest. There are cottages for all of the staff."

Hans had been initially surprised by the man's seemingly magnanimous manner; it was not an attitude he associated with those of rank, and yet the *Gruppenführer* had been all smiles and expansive shrugs.

"Well, yes," he'd said, "it is unusual—most women do not accompany their husbands or brothers while on duty. But if you say she has no one else... I daresay an exception can be made. And I see she has been a good, loyal maiden of the BDM? Yes, yes, I have her file here, as well." He'd patted the yellow folder on his desk, and Hans had wondered then if it was a warning. Perhaps not so magnanimous, after all. "I have heard it is a pleasant place, and the accommodation should be comfortable enough. You may consider this a promotion, Brenner. You will be inducted into the SS, with the rank of *Unterscharführer*."

Hans had stared at him, speechless with surprise. It was to be as easy as that, to join the SS, without an interview, references and racial profile checked, statement made, the blood type tattooed on his arm? What was it that he would be doing, at this camp?

"When do we go?" Anni asked, and with a smile for his sister, Hans tried for an optimistically bracing look.

"In three days."

"Three days!" She stared at him in dismay. "Why so soon?"

"You know how these things are. I am needed, and that is the end of the matter. We can take the train—there is a station right at the camp, apparently, but I believe we will be met by an officer at Chelm." He fell silent, thinking of those cattle cars, while Anni frowned, pleating her fingers together.

"And what about our apartment here? And your work?"

"We'll ask Frau Werling to look after things for us, and as for the business, what can I do?" He shrugged. Their neighbor, a widow, would be happy enough to mind the apartment, and the business would simply have to wait. He had to obey orders; they both knew that.

Anni got up and moved to the window, bracing one hand against its frame as she looked down at their sleepy street. Stuttgart had not suffered too much from the Allied bombing yet, although there had been air raids enough. It was a gracious city, built over a series of hills, filled with park and vineyards. Hans and Anni knew nowhere else. They certainly, he reflected, did not know Poland, or a camp.

"How long will we be there, do you think?" she asked quietly.

"I don't know."

"They didn't tell you much, did they?" she remarked a bit waspishly, throwing him an ill-tempered look over her shoulder.

Hans shrugged and spread his hands. He knew she was anxious about the whole thing and was attempting to hide it with bad humor. In truth, along with a sense of pride, he felt a little anxious, too, although he hoped he hid it better. In any case, they would be leaving for Sobibor in three days whatever they felt about it.

"It will be all right, Anni," he told her. "We'll be together, at least." He was glad of that, certainly. He'd always felt a fierce protectiveness toward his little sister; their mother had died when Anni was only four, Hans just nine. Their father had been too grief-stricken to bother himself much with either of them; he'd almost taken up an aunt's offer to "take the little one off your hands," but Hans had intervened, promising their father that he could take care of Anni perfectly well himself.

And he had—dressing and feeding her, teaching her to tie her shoes and even plaiting her hair for school. He'd been teased by his classmates for being womanish, but he hadn't cared. He would, he thought, do just about anything for his sister. Even if she'd started to love numbers more than him years ago. He couldn't begrudge her her brilliance, abstracted as it was. He loved everything about her, and he always would.

He crossed the room to put a comforting hand on her shoulder. "We'll be together," he said again, and she turned back with a tired smile, a silent apology for her snappishness, as she placed her hand over his.

Outside, a few yellow leaves fluttered down, and the shadows lengthened on the street as the clouds drew across the sky.

CHAPTER 4

LIBBY

"So who was that?" Lucas asks again, with only a modicum of interest, his head still stuck in the fridge.

I am standing in the middle of the kitchen, my fists clenched, my mind reeling. I feel as if my entire world has shifted, *shattered*, in the matter of a moment, and I do not know what to make of this new reality... if it really is a new reality. Surely it really is a mistake, and I'll look back on this day with a faint smile, a clench of remembered panic, nothing more. Maybe the warrant will never come through, the case dismissed by a judge with more sense than Simon Baum. *Maybe this will all go away*. That's what I want, desperately. That's what has to happen.

"Um, just..." I can't think how to answer. I don't want to lie, but neither can I bear to tell my son the truth. And what *is* the truth, anyway? There are still so many unanswered questions. "I need to check on Em and Grandad," I say instead, and I hurry from the kitchen before Lucas can reply.

Outside my dad's door, I take a deep breath, try to keep my shoulders from hunching toward my ears. My whole body feels as if it is vibrating with tension. My emotions are churning, far too near the surface; I feel as if I could burst into tears, or rant with rage, I'm not sure which, and I don't want to do either. Most of all, though, I feel afraid. For all my imagining of worst-case scenarios, absurd disasters, as a child tucked up in my bed, I never, ever envisioned something like this. I simply can't let it be true.

I take another steadying breath, and then I rap lightly on the door before opening it and poking my head through.

My dad is dozing in his plaid armchair, a colorful afghan I crocheted for his ninetieth birthday across his knees, despite the July heat. Em is perched on the sofa next to him, and she swivels from the drone of the TV to gaze at me with wide, questioning eyes.

"Everything okay in here?" I ask brightly.

My dad stirs, blinking sleepily. "Oh yes, yes," he says, and for a second, his German accent, now faint from the passing years and as familiar to me as my own voice, jolts through me. "We were just watching..." He glances at the television, his forehead crinkled, before turning to Em. "What were we watching, darling?"

"*Ice Road Truckers,*" Em replies, smiling at him. She and my dad have been TV buddies for quite a while. Em loves nothing more than sitting back with him and binge-watching a bunch of silly reality TV shows on cable. Their camaraderie has always warmed my heart, but now it makes something in me clutch with fear. What if everything changes? What if Em loses her grandfather? Even if my father is innocent—and I *know* he is— this trial might still go ahead—unless I can find evidence to prove he couldn't be Hans Brenner. At least, I think that's how it works, but I'm not even sure of that.

Now that he's left, Simon Baum's lack of explanation about so many things is starting to both frustrate and frighten me. I was in too much shock even to figure out what questions to ask

—I barely know now—but what I *do* know is that I don't know enough.

"Grilled cheese and tomato soup, okay?" I ask, although I know it is. It's what my dad has every single day for lunch.

"Perfect," my father replies, and his beaming smile, so tender and warm, floods me with both fear and guilt. Fear of the future and what it might hold, and guilt because no matter what I keep telling myself, there still is a tiny, relentless what-if flickering at the edges of my consciousness that I am desperate to suppress.

What if... But, no. *No.* Of course my father wasn't a Nazi, working in some camp, watching thousands of innocent people be marched to their deaths, cataloguing their stolen belongings. Of course he didn't shoot a man in cold blood. That, more than anything, really is utterly beyond the realm of possibility.

And yet Simon Baum's words still slosh around in my mind. *Stuttgart. Sobibor. Daniel Weiss. Hans Brenner.* For a second, standing there with my mind racing, I am tempted to ask my father point-blank right now if he's ever heard of Hans Brenner, just to see if his expression changes, a flash of recognition or, God help us both, even guilt in his eyes. Will he have to hide his shock, or will he be completely confused by the unfamiliar name, the question out of nowhere?

But I don't ask, because Em is sitting right here, and my head is spinning, and I'm not ready to bring this out into the open just yet, not until I know more, feel more prepared. Not, I acknowledge, until I have to. I do need, though, to call Tim and tell him what is going on. I need his calm scientific brain to keep me from descending into total panic. He'll talk me down from this terrifying ledge; he'll point out how little evidence Simon Baum has, how we can prove who my father is—and who he isn't.

"Grilled cheese and tomato soup it is," I practically chirp, and as I head back to the kitchen, Em trails after me. Lucas has already disappeared to his room, and I am reminded that I need to talk to him about not leaving Em alone. It hardly feels important now, with all this looming over me, but I know it still is. Just as I know how the conversation will go—Lucas will say he didn't leave her alone, because Grandad was here, and I'll tell him that it's not the same. Em loves her grandfather, but she is anxious about being left alone with him, "in case something happens."

What if he chokes? I don't think I could give him the Heimlich. What if he falls from his chair? I'm not strong enough to lift him. And on and on.

Then Lucas will tell me Em isn't a baby, and when *he* was eleven, he was babysitting her by himself, which is more or less true. But, four years ago, my dad was quite a bit spryer, and Lucas has never suffered from his sister's anxiety issues.

A small sigh escapes me; I am wearied by having that conversation in my head, never mind in actuality with my son, and I certainly don't have the emotional space for it now.

"So what did the policeman want?" Em asks as I open the cupboard and root around for a couple of cans of soup.

"He wasn't actually from the police," I say as I emerge from the cupboard, banging my head on the door. I wince, take a deep breath, and put the cans down on the counter. My hands, I realize, are shaking.

"Who was he then?"

"A kind of lawyer." At least, I assume that's what Simon Baum is, what a deputy chief of the Department of Justice needs to be. I focus on opening the cans of soup, so I don't have to meet my daughter's worried gaze. I don't know what to say to her, how much to reveal or explain. As little as possible is my instinct, but I know Em will keep pressing and pressing. She always does. She can't help herself; it's a self-soothing mechanism, but in this case, it's not going to work.

"Why did he come here?"

"He had some questions about Grandad. His... history." I

try to keep my voice both light and matter-of-fact, but by the way her eyes widen, my daughter isn't fooled. Either that or she's just careering toward the worst-case scenario, because, just like me, that is what she does. Except this time, I can't let myself.

"His history? What does that mean?"

"It's nothing to worry about, Em," I tell her, and now I make my voice firm. I can't have this conversation, not yet, not until I have talked to Tim, processed it myself. Maybe, I think, even talk to a lawyer. Or Simon Baum again. Something.

I reach for the opened can of soup, and then knock it over by accident. I can't keep from swearing under my breath as viscous orange liquid starts to spread over the countertop. Em lets out a little gasp and starts to chew her nails.

"Mom... are you sure everything is okay?"

"Yes," I tell her, and finally, thankfully, my voice and hands are both steady. I wipe up the mess and then pour the remaining soup into the pot and give it a stir, my back to Em. "I can't tell you more now because I don't know anymore, but it's nothing to worry about, I promise." As the words leave my lips, they feel like a lie, but what else can I say? Already this whole situation feels impossible, and I'm afraid it's barely begun.

"But what history?" she presses, just as I knew she would. "What does that even *mean*?"

I take a deep breath and reach for the loaf of bread. "Just some stuff about his work a long time ago, what he was doing, where, that sort of thing. Please, Em." I turn to smile at her, blinking back the sudden threat of tears that crowd under my lids. I cannot let my daughter see me cry. "I'll tell you more when I know more, okay?"

And I know from the way she looks at me—her eyes wide, her face pale, her lips bloodless—that I've managed to make her more worried, not less.

. . .

Somehow, I get through the rest of lunch without too many more questions. I take my dad his lunch on a tray; he's fallen asleep again, his head lolling forward, chin to chest. I stand in the doorway for a moment, my heart contracting with love. He looks so *old*. Of course, he's looked old for most of my life; he's ninety-six, after all. But he looks *frail*—diminished somehow, as if he is shrinking by the minute, as if I can see it happening, like time-lapse photography, second by precious second.

His hair is thin and wispy and white, the cuffs of his shirt hanging off skinny wrists, bagging around his narrow shoulders. My father wears a shirt and tie every single day, even if all he's going to be doing is sitting in his favorite armchair. Today he's wearing a pale blue short-sleeved shirt, a wide, darker blue tie, both at least forty years old.

As I come forward, he stirs and opens his eyes. "Ah... *liebe*, Libby." The German endearment is one he's always used for me, as my name is so close to the German word for love, but again, stupidly perhaps, it jolts me.

"Sorry to wake you—"

"Ach, no, I was just resting my eyes." The smile he gives me is both wry and knowing, so typical of my dad. "They close so much more easily these days, I find." He leans his head back in his chair, watching me as I put his tray down. "Thank you," he murmurs, and I mumble something back. I am just stepping back when he asks quietly, "Who was at the door earlier?"

Am I imagining that hint of understanding in his voice, almost as if he knows? I glance at him a bit sharply, but his smile is the same, his shaggy white eyebrows slightly raised in expectation. "I didn't think you heard the doorbell," I say a bit stupidly, and his eyes crinkle in concern. My father is a smart man; he can tell when something is off.

"Emily was watching TV with me and she went to answer it. She said they were asking for you."

"It wasn't anyone important." I am struck again that Simon

Baum asked for *me*, and not my father. I am the linchpin that holds this all together, because I am the one who can find the evidence he needs. I am the one who can turn my father in. The prospect makes everything in me shrivel with horror.

"No?" My father cocks his head as his gaze, faded yet still shrewd, sweeps slowly over me. "Are you sure? Because Emily seemed a bit anxious."

Yet even Em didn't tell my dad that a policeman was asking about him. We both want to protect him, I realize, and that feels right, but Simon Baum is asking me to do the exact opposite.

Somehow I summon a small smile. "You know how she is."

I busy myself by tidying up the room a little, plumping pillows on the sofa across from his armchair, refolding the blanket at the foot of his bed. My father watches me silently, until I can't find anything else to keep me busy.

"You'd tell me," he says quietly, "if something was wrong?"

And I know from his tone he's not worried for himself, but for me, for Tim, for the children. He's always thought of us before himself; he was reluctant to move in here, ten years ago, because he thought he'd be a burden to us.

"Of course I would, Dad," I say, and I hear how false my voice sounds—too hearty, yet with the choked threat of tears behind it. Does he hear that, too?

My dad smiles and reaches for my hand. "Thank you, *liebe*," he says, and I pat his hand, feel the raised, knobbly veins, his fingers now bent and twisted with arthritis. My heart swells with love and my mind buzzes with fear.

"Let me know if you need anything," I tell him, and then I hurry from the room.

Even though I know I probably should, I decide not to call Tim to let him know what has happened, not only because Em has the hearing of a bat and eavesdrops, as she says, without even meaning to, but also because he'll be in the lab and I'm not meant to disturb him, except for an emergency. Is this an emergency? It feels like one, and yet the warrant hasn't even been issued; there might not even be a trial.

What I can do, I decide, is get some information, so I feel less as if I am swimming in ignorance. I tell Em she can go on the iPad for half an hour, which makes her eye me suspiciously, because I'm usually fierce about screen time. Then I take my laptop up to my bedroom, close the door, and breathe a deep sigh, not of relief but of utter weariness.

I settle myself in the armchair by the window overlooking the backyard, the branches of a dogwood tree brushing the windowpane.

I sit with my laptop on my knees, my fingers hovering over the keyboard. I've nursed both my children in this armchair; I've read them bedtime stories here, and combed their damp hair, smelling of strawberry shampoo. I've curled up here with a book or just a daydream, my gaze on the yard outside—bursting in blossom with spring, verdant in summer, a riot of yellows and reds in fall, heaped soft and white with snow in winter. It's been a place of peace, an oasis of calm in a busy life, and yet right now I feel as if I am poised to shatter it all with a tap or two of my fingers.

What to google?

After a few seconds of hesitation, I type *prosecution of Nazi war criminals* into the search box. My stomach clenches as I click return. I scroll past the first few hits, which are all about the Nuremberg trials, and then land on an article about why there has been a renewed effort to prosecute the last remaining Nazis.

Apparently, the law changed only a few years ago; before 2011, only Nazis who were accused of killing someone directly could be prosecuted, but now anyone who assisted in the functioning of the camps, acting as an accessory to murder, could be tried for war crimes. I read, with a jolt, about the landmark case of John Demjanjuk, who was a guard at Sobibor and was convicted of aiding in the murder of over eighty thousand Jews.

That's the second time I've heard of Sobibor in one day, which feels ominous, like some sort of omen. Is there a connection? Was Simon Baum involved in Demjanjuk's case, and that led him to Hans Brenner? To my father?

I keep reading, but after nearly an hour, my brain starts to blur, and the lines of text dance before my eyes. I've read about a dozen different cases tried in the last few years, mainly of camp guards, but in one case, it was an accountant at a camp, like my father. Or, I quickly correct myself, like Simon Baum believes my father to have been.

Oskar Gröning was known as "the Accountant of Auschwitz" and was tried and convicted in Germany for "knowingly assisting mass murder" just last year. He is currently appealing the verdict.

I close my laptop and lean back, my unseeing gaze on the bright green leaves of the dogwood outside. What *did* my father do during the war? As far as I can recall him telling me, he stayed in Stuttgart, managing the family accountancy business. His father died during the start of the war, his mother when he was fairly young. But he rarely, if ever, talked about anything from that time, and I learned not to ask about it. I have a memory of peppering him with questions when I was twelve or so and in the grip of a fascination with all things to do with the Second World War, and especially the Holocaust. It was one of the only times I remember him getting angry with me.

"It was a long time ago, a very painful period of history," he'd snapped at me. "There is a reason why people don't talk about such things, Elizabeth. A reason why I came to this country—to forget!"

And then he'd stormed out of our kitchen, leaving me feeling more bemused than chastened, because the outburst was so unlike him. I never asked him anything again.

I hadn't been able to ask my mother about it, either, since she'd left us when I was just four. I never saw her again and she died when I was sixteen, from breast cancer; a nurse at the hospice where she spent her last months had the kindness to write to us and let us know, something that always made me wonder. Had my mother given her our address? Had she ever thought of writing us—me—herself? I'll never know, and it's a part of my history I tell myself I've moved past, or at least I try not to dwell on, and I don't usually tell anyone about it, either, mostly because no one ever knows what to say. Maybe I'm like my father that way, I think now, on a sigh. *There's a reason why people don't talk about such things...*

What's your reason, Dad?

The question both frustrates and frightens me. Why am I actually doubting him, just that tiny, treacherous little bit? It feels so wrong, and yet I can't keep myself from it, from wondering about that awful what-if. *Could* my father have served in that camp? Could he have shot a man—shot Daniel Weiss, in fact? *But he is Daniel Weiss.*

Again I consider asking him directly. It's the easiest thing to do, and yet so very hard. Impossible, even. Once I ask, I can never un-ask. It might change things between us, forever. It almost certainly would, whether he is guilty or not. Am I prepared for that? Do I have any choice?

I take a deep breath and then I walk downstairs. My heart is thudding, but I am fired with purpose as I skirt the family room, avoiding Em, and knock very softly on my father's door. He'd tell me the truth, I tell myself, but I am remembering how he was all those years ago, when I pressed him about his war years. What if he gets angry? What if he's hurt?

And what if he's not?

No. I square my shoulders and then open the door. I don't need to be afraid, because he *will* tell me the truth, and the truth will be that he's Daniel Weiss. All these nameless fears circling in my brain are just my old anxieties coming back to bite me—the worst-case scenarios of my childhood, just with a different, more dangerous slant. I don't need to be afraid of them. I can keep them from controlling me.

And so I slip into his room, smiling at him in expectation, except he's asleep, his chin tucked to his chest, his jaw slack. I can hear him snoring, a slight wheeze. I stand there, knowing I can't wake him up to ask him. He'll be sleepy, disorientated, agitated. This isn't the right time—and, shamingly, I am relieved.

As I head back out, Em slouches out of the kitchen. "Mom?" She looks worried, her gaze darting toward my dad's door. "It's been over an hour."

"Sorry, love." I smile and she nibbles her lip, regarding me uncertainly.

"Why didn't you come tell me to get off the iPad?"

"Sorry, I was just trying to finish up some work, and then I went to check on Grandad." More lies, and they trip just as easily off my tongue. "Hey, why don't we head out to Critzer's? We can pick some strawberries and peaches. I'll make a cobbler."

Em always likes a trip to Critzer's Family Farm, half an hour west of Charlottesville. There's ice cream in the summer and apple cider in the fall, tractor rides and pick-your-own of whatever is in season.

"Can we?" she says, brightening, and I nod, more enthusiastic than I normally would be about such an outing, because I am so desperate to escape my own buzzing thoughts, to spend time with my daughter that is simple and easy.

"Sure. Maybe even Lucas will come along."

"What about Grandad?"

I hesitate, because bringing my dad with his now limited mobility will be a major effort, but I don't like leaving him alone, either, although he insists he is perfectly capable of managing.

A care assistant comes in three times a week to help him with the personal stuff, but he's not coming in today. And, I acknowledge, part of me wants to escape from my dad, from both the reality and the possibility, just for a little while.

"He's asleep, but I'll check on him again in a bit and see if he wants to come," I tell Em, and she beams.

As I pass by her in the doorway of the kitchen, I pull her into a quick hug, which she returns eagerly, always up for affection.

"I love you," I tell her, and she looks up at me, smiling but a little confused, because I probably don't say those three words enough. Everything is usually so busy, and if I'm honest, Em's endless anxiety can sometimes be a little wearying, just like my own. But right now, I bury my nose in her strawberry-scented hair—the same shampoo I used with her when she was a toddler—amazed that she already reaches past my chin. She wraps her arms around me and we stand there for a few seconds, as if we both, without needing to say a word, understand the fragility of life, the preciousness of this moment.

CHAPTER 5

LIBBY

By the time we get back from Critzer's, Tim is home. In the end, it was just Em and I who went to the farm; Lucas was absorbed with the PlayStation and my dad, having woken up to thank me for the invitation, said he didn't want to miss *Storage Wars*—although, really, I knew, he was more worried about leaving the house, managing stairs, having to be on his feet for too long once we got to the farm. Mentally, he's mostly there still, although he does have his occasional senior lapses, but physically he's become quite frail. He was never a very big man—barely topping five eight and with a slight build—and the years have shrunk him further.

It made me wonder how on earth he could handle a trial or even two—one for the extradition, if it happens, and presumably a criminal one in Germany. But I didn't want to think about any of that that afternoon; even after just a few hours of considering the possibilities, the implications, my brain needed a break. And despite the typical muggy heat of Virginia in the summer, it was a beautiful day, with a hazy blue sky, sunshine streaming over the meadows and trees as we drove from Charlottesville up into the foothills of the Blue Ridge Mountains.

Em took control of the playlist, programming in a dozen different boppy tunes that she sang along to as I opened the sunroof and let the sultry breeze blow through our hair. She grinned at me, delighted; it was so easy to please her, sometimes, and I knew I too often forgot that, under the weight of her anxieties. I even sang along to the songs I knew, although there weren't many.

Once we were at the farm, we sweated in the heat as we picked punnets of peaches and strawberries, and then sat in the shade with our cones of hand-churned ice cream. I picked up a hanging basket bursting with pink begonias for our front porch, and a passel of fresh green beans for dinner. Em asked if we could buy a tub of vanilla ice cream to accompany the peach cobbler I'd promised to make, and I agreed easily enough, because I think I would have agreed to anything just then. Anything to keep this day, so golden and sweet, going, so I wouldn't have to think about my father or his past or the grenade Simon Baum had lobbed into our lives, the one I was now holding in my hands. What would I do with it? Would I confront my father? Would I look for evidence? I couldn't bear to think about either possibility, and yet already I felt as if I had no choice.

"Daddy's home!" Em cries as I pull into the driveway a little after five. She scrambles out of the car while I move more slowly, collecting the peaches and raspberries, the beans and the begonias. The ice cream, I notice, has already started to melt.

I hang the basket on the hook by the front door, reveling in that small task, the simple pleasure of it—the sweet, citrusy fragrance of the flowers, the beauty of their blooms. The soul-sucking heat of midday has transformed to something bearable; there are pale pink and lavender clouds heaped on the horizon, like wisps of cotton candy, and the street is quiet and peaceful.

I walk into the house. Tim is in the kitchen, listening to Em tell him about our afternoon while he loosens his collar and then cracks open a beer. As I come in, he smiles at me, eyebrows raised—an afternoon trip to Critzer's isn't the usual—and I smile back, or try to, although now that I'm home, everything has come back in a rush, overwhelming me. Even though I've enjoyed the last few hours, I still feel as if I'm teetering on the edge of a precipice, as if I could fall in at any moment, and never clamber out again.

"Good afternoon?" he asks me, and I nod, not trusting myself to reply normally.

"I'm just going to check on my dad," I mumble, and Tim calls after me,

"I checked on him already. He was dozing."

I act as if I haven't heard as I tap softly on my dad's door and then slip inside. He is asleep again, just as Tim said, his head lolling back, his legs stretched out in front of him. The TV is on mute, which means he was serious about napping. He sleeps so much these days, and while I know that has to be normal for ninety-six, it can still make me feel anxious. I can't bear to think about losing my dad, and yet now I have to think about it more than ever, if in an entirely different way. But, of course, I remind myself, it might never happen. The warrant, the trial, any of it. Right now, it's all just possibility... and yet it looms in a way that makes my stomach swirl with dread.

I glance around the room—the double bed, made up neatly, a photo of me on the bedside table, about eight years old, gap-toothed and grinning. There are no photographs of my mother; we have hardly ever spoken of her, since she left forty-four years ago. My dad never mentioned her, and I learned not to, for his sake more than mine. It was easier that way, for both of us.

When I first asked about her, as a child, my father told me not to blame her, that she, a German refugee like himself and also half-Jewish, had had a difficult war and it had left emotional scars that made it hard for her to let herself love people, including me, apparently. Something that I try not to think about, and yet at times feels as if it has defined me—the fact that my own mother was able to walk away and never return, never even send a postcard. It's both hurtful and humiliating, a wound that never quite heals over, but which I do my best to pretend is nothing more than a faded scar, because my dad has always been enough. He's made sure he was, and so have I.

Now, briefly, like it's something forbidden, I let myself think about her. In truth, I can barely remember her beyond a few hazy memories of a quiet woman with dark hair, the smell of lavender, the cool press of a soft palm on my cheek. I know most of her family, including her own parents, had died at the ghetto near Müngersdorf, or later at Theresienstadt. As a categorized *Mischlinge* of the first degree—half-Jewish—she wasn't deported to a camp, but survived the war staying with similarly categorized relatives and had emigrated to America as a young woman in the 1950s. She met my father at some event in New York City for German refugees in the sixties; they married a few years later, when she was thirty-eight and he was nearly fifty.

But if my father really was Hans Brenner, how could he have been a card-carrying Nazi and married a woman who was half-Jewish? Has Simon Baum considered that?

"*Liebe?*" My father stirs in his chair.

"Hey, Dad." I rest one hand briefly on his thin shoulder. "We just got back from Critzer's, and I was about to make dinner. How does lasagna sound?"

"Lovely." He smiles up at me, an understanding in his eyes that makes me think he hasn't forgotten about the visitor earlier. Could he possibly suspect? *But if he was innocent, why would he?* Should I ask him now?

I start to open my mouth, but then I hear Em in the kitchen, and my father pats my hand. This isn't the moment, I tell myself, but I don't know when it will be. It is never, I know, going to feel either right or easy.

"I'll come out in a minute," he promises. "Stretch my legs. Maybe Lucas will deign to play me in chess?"

"I'm sure he will." Even if I have to pry him off the Play-Station.

My father is the only person in the family who can actually beat Lucas at chess, and they usually have a game most nights. Such moments feel precious, now more than ever.

I smile and pat his shoulder, and as I move out of the room, I find my gaze scanning the familiar objects—his bureau, with the small, carved wooden box for his cufflinks on it, and his bedside table, whose drawers contain, I believe, only medications and tissues. If my father has some memento—and he doesn't, he *can't*—I have no idea where it would be, or how to find it.

He spent his adult life in New York, just outside the city, where he worked as an accountant and I grew up. He sold the little ranch house we lived in right after I married Tim nearly twenty years ago, and then bought an apartment in Charlottesville so he could be closer to us. We went through all his things together back then, bagging up old clothes for charity, and selecting what books and pictures he wanted to take with him. All in all, there really wasn't that much. As he had told me many times, he came to America with a single suitcase.

"Libby?" he asks, and I realize I am standing in the doorway, looking around the room as if I am searching for something. "Is everything all right?"

"Yes." I give him a quick, fleeting smile. "I was just thinking I should dust in here." And then, fearing he'll see the lie written on my face, I slip out of the room.

Back in the kitchen, Tim is sprawled at the table in the breakfast nook, sipping his beer and scrolling through his phone. Em is lying on her stomach on the sofa, the iPad in front of her.

"Em," I say warningly, "I don't think you need any more screen time today, do you?"

She gives me a look full of appeal. "I'm just drawing on it, Mom."

Em loves to draw; for her eleventh birthday, we gave her a special pen that works on screens so she can draw right on the device. I was resistant, preferring a real pencil and paper, but Tim, ever the scientist, told me the electronic pen was superior, and anyway, this was where the future was.

I leave it for now as I start to unpack the stuff from Critzer's; I forgot to put the ice cream in the freezer and it is now practically liquid.

"How was your day?" Tim asks. "Em said someone stopped by, asking about your dad?" His voice is casual, barely interested, assuming it was nothing.

"Yeah." I shove the ice cream in the freezer, trying to keep my tone just as casual, because even though she is absorbed with her drawing, I know Em has to be listening. "I'll tell you about it later."

"Nothing to worry about, though, right?"

"Not really." If I'm trying to sound nonchalant, I'm pretty sure I fail, and when I turn from the freezer, Tim gives me a surprised, narrowed look. I glance pointedly at Em, and he nods. We'll talk about this later.

For the rest of the evening, I manage to maintain a semblance of normality, for both Em and Lucas's sakes, as well as my father's. Lucas comes down to play chess with my dad, while Em draws and Tim helps me make dinner. It all feels so peaceful, as the light fades from the sky and the cicadas begin their incessant summer chorus. With Tim taking charge of the lasagna, I have time to make a peach cobbler and we all eat it outside on the patio with the ice cream.

Afterwards, I make coffee—decaf with two sugars for my dad, same as always—and bring it into his room. I settle him in his chair in front of a rerun of *Jeopardy!* while he glances up at me, smiling with a tenderness that makes my heart ache.

"Thank you, Libby."

"You gave Lucas a good run for his money with that chess game." I pat his hand, fluff his pillow, and then leave him to his trivia. I'm too tired to ask him now, I tell myself. It feels like a reprieve.

Back in the kitchen, Lucas has disappeared back to the PlayStation in the basement rec room and Em has gone upstairs to shower. Tim is stacking plates in the dishwasher, but as I come into the room, he straightens to give me a serious look.

"So who was this guy who came this afternoon? Because Em told me she thought he was from the police."

I open my mouth to start to explain—although I'm not sure even how to begin—and find I can't. I close my mouth and bite my lips to keep back the sob that escapes, strangled, as I put my hands up to my face.

I have always hated having anyone, even Tim, see my cry. It feels too much like a weakness, a vulnerability that leaves me raw, exposed. I've been this way as long as I can remember, even as a kid. My father used to tell me how I'd pull away from his hug when I hurt myself, wanting to be alone even as I craved comfort, needing to seem strong even when I felt weak. I suppose some habits are hard to break.

"Oh, Lib. Libby." Tim's voice is tender as he puts his arms around me, and I rest my head on his shoulder, trying to hold back my tears. He strokes my back like I'm a child. "It's okay, hon. Whatever it is, it's okay."

"It isn't." The words come out on another sob that I swallow down. "At least, it might not be. I don't actually know..." How likely is it that Simon Baum will get that warrant? Maybe not likely at all. Maybe only likely if it's up to me.

"Tell me what's going on."

I gulp and nod and step back, scrubbing at my face, trying to reassemble my composure. "I think I need a glass of wine first," I announce and he nods, frowning, as I take out the bottle of white in the fridge and pour myself a particularly large glass.

We move together to the family room off the kitchen; Tim puts the iPad on charge before sitting down as I curl up in a corner of the sofa. He's a wonderful man, Tim, so calm and competent, steady and unflappable. There was a time, early on in our marriage, when I almost wanted him to storm and rage, or at least *emote* a little more. I'd grown up with a father who, while loving and tender, was similarly calm, while I lurched from emotion to emotion, trying to hide all the complicated feelings I had jumbled up inside, afraid to let them out and reveal me. Now, as I order my confused thoughts, I am grateful for my husband's placidity. It steadies me; it's what I need.

"The man who came wasn't the police, he was a lawyer. A deputy chief of—" I take a breath—"the Human Rights and Special Prosecutions office of the Department of Justice." What a mouthful. I take a slug of wine.

"Human rights?" Tim frowns, and I can practically hear his brain ticking over. "Isn't that the office that investigates Nazi war crimes?"

I gape at him for a second, shocked at how quickly he jumped to that conclusion. It's the right one, but I'm still both irritated and frightened by how easily he made the leap. Why did he, when I couldn't, not in a million years?

"Yes, it is," I reply, trying to keep my tone even. "And this man—Simon Baum—believes my father..." I pause as my voice trembles. I can hear the TV from my dad's room, the shower from upstairs. Even so I lower my voice, steady it. "He believes my father is actually someone called Hans Brenner, who was an accountant at one of the camps in Poland. So-Sobibor."

Tim is silent for a long moment, absorbing all I've said, and part of me wishes he would *react*, jump up and say what outrageous nonsense that is, that of course my dad isn't Hans whoever. It seems I still do want him to storm and rage, at least a little. At least about this. I want him to be sure... as sure as I am —or better yet, even surer. That's what I need right now.

"Why did he come to you today?" he asks finally. "I assume it wasn't just to tell you what he thinks."

"No, he came to tell me he's applied for a warrant for my dad's arrest." I almost go into how Simon Baum misled me, if not downright lied, but then I decide not to bother. "If he's granted it," I tell Tim, "there will be a trial here in Virginia to extradite my dad to Germany, so he can stand trial for war crimes there." I speak flatly, as if I can somehow distance myself from that awful, incredible reality. As if I'm simply stating facts that have nothing to do with us... and maybe they don't. Simon Baum doesn't have that warrant yet. Maybe he'll never get it. The possibility of my father being forced back to Germany is unimaginable, unendurable—for him, for me, for my children.

"In Germany, not here?" Tim leans forward. "So the Germans are instigating the charges, not the DOJ?"

He speaks with such innate authority, as if he knows how the whole process works, and, unreasonably perhaps, this annoys me. He sounds as if he is talking about a news program on TV, not my *father*, the man who has lived with us for the last ten years. How can he already be arriving at conclusions I have yet to come to, and with a level-headed practicality that feels hurtful? Why is he not exclaiming how absurd this all is, refusing to entertain such impossible notions for so much as a nanosecond?

"I guess so," I say, wishing again that I knew more, and yet also glad I don't, because I can barely deal with what I do know. "There's a man who identified my dad from a photo... I suppose he is in Germany." Daniel Weiss's son. I can't remember his name now.

"What photo?"

"One I took from that fundraiser a couple of years ago. He saw it on social media." Which I suppose makes this whole thing, in some ways, my fault. If I hadn't posted that stupid photo...

Tim sits back in his seat, still frowning. "Is that the only evidence they have?"

"He said there was some other stuff, but..." I draw a shaky breath. "Maybe not enough for him to get the warrant. He..." I don't want to say it, but I know I have to. "He asked me to find some evidence to convict my father."

"What?" Tim looks uncharacteristically shocked. "Wow, that took some nerve."

"He said I'd want to do the right thing," I reply numbly.

"Turn in your father?"

It's basically what I said myself, but for some reason I find myself in the unlikely position of defending Simon Baum. "If he was actually an accountant at a death camp," I tell Tim with a tremble in my voice, "then it's not an entirely unreasonable ask. Obviously I want all Nazi criminals to be prosecuted..." I trail off feebly, because I want that in theory, but in reality? When it might be my own dad?

Tim's eyebrows inch higher. "Even your father?"

"My father is *not* a Nazi criminal," I retort staunchly. "Simon Baum has got it wrong." Tim is silent, and I turn more strident. "He thinks my father actually shot someone, a prisoner at the camp, in cold blood. Can you see my dad doing something like that? It's ridiculous. Impossible."

Still Tim doesn't speak.

I lean forward, urgent now, a little angry. "Tim. Come on. You know my dad."

"It was a different time then, Libby," he says quietly.

"You actually think my dad could have been a Nazi? Could have shot a man?" I sound scathing. I feel it, too.

"What does Simon Baum think happened, exactly, back then?"

"I'm not totally sure." I draw a calming breath as I try to sift through what he told me. "There was a Daniel Weiss who was a prisoner at this camp," I tell Tim. "And his son apparently saw Hans Brenner shoot his father. Shoot Daniel Weiss." My voice wobbles, because *my* father is Daniel Weiss, not this stranger's.

"Daniel Weiss... so Simon Baum believes your dad took the name of the man he shot and emigrated to America under it?"

"I guess? I haven't been able to think through it all yet. And Simon Baum left so quickly. He said he'd call if he had any new information about the warrant or trial."

"And he wants you to find some evidence to back him up." Tim shakes his head as if he can't believe the nerve of the guy, and maybe he can't.

"If there was evidence," I say slowly, feeling my way through the words, turning them over in my head to decide if I really mean them, "I'd have to hand it in. Wouldn't I?" I'm not sure who I am asking—Tim or myself. Wouldn't that be the right thing to do? The only thing? And yet it doesn't feel like it, at all.

Tim is silent for a long moment. "Libby," he finally says, "I can't be your conscience for you."

"What would you do? If it was your father?" A question which is laughable, because his parents are as uncomplicated and American as apple pie.

"I don't know," Tim admits heavily. "When I think of your dad... he's lived an exemplary life for seventy years, as far as I can see. Who knows what any of us would do under pressure? If we were forced?"

"But I don't know that he was forced." Were any of the officers who worked at a camp *forced*? "I don't know that he was there at all."

"But if he was..."

"He wasn't. He can't have been." I speak firmly, because while Tim might be looking for loopholes, I refuse to stoop to such a thing. My dad did not serve at the camp. He could not have worked at such a place, done and seen such things, and still be my father—the man who tucked me in every night of my childhood, who taught me the importance of being honest, marching me back to the corner shop when I'd swiped a piece of penny candy at six years old, who told me when the class bully had targeted a friend that courage wasn't being unafraid, it was being afraid and still doing the right thing. I stood up to that bully, because my dad taught me to. Because he was both wise and kind, and that man—my father—was *not* a Nazi, because if he was, then he must be a liar and a hypocrite and someone I could never respect, never mind love. And it's my father who taught me to think that way.

"Maybe you should just ask him," Tim says quietly.

"I will. I just haven't found the right time." I speak with bravado, because I haven't exactly been searching for the right time, either, but who would, when it comes to this? "I will," I tell Tim again, and he nods.

I look away as I take another slug of wine. My head is already feeling a little fuzzy, which is a welcome relief. I thought telling Tim would make me feel better, but I am realizing it just makes the whole situation feel more real, and that makes me feel much worse. His willingness to accept the possibility that my father is involved is like a fist to my gut, to my heart, and I'm trying not to show how much I'm reeling.

"All in all," Tim says slowly, "it doesn't sound like this guy from the DOJ has very much."

This gives me a wild lurch of hope, even as I force myself to continue, "There is more. Apparently, Hans Brenner was an accountant from Stuttgart, but he disappeared from any records after the war. And there is no record of a Daniel Weiss from Stuttgart who was an accountant, only the prisoner at Sobibor."

Somehow, when I say it like that, the whole thing feels more plausible. *But it can't be.* It simply can't.

I lapse into miserable silence, closing my eyes against the awful possibility of it.

No. No, no, no.

"If there's going to be a trial, Lib..." Tim rakes his hand through his hair as he releases a long, low breath. "You know those are a big deal, right? They make national news. There are so few Nazis left to prosecute. They've all got to be at least ninety. The media have a field day whenever one comes to light."

I imagine my father's picture—my picture, maybe—splashed across the newspapers with lurid, attention-grabbing headlines and I immediately reject the whole notion. "But there might not be a trial," I insist stubbornly. "If he can't get the warrant. If we can get this cleared up before it comes to that. If it's a case of mistaken identity, which is what it must be." Tim is silent, and I continue, my voice rising a little, "Tim, whatever you think about how things were, you know my dad, right? You know how gentle he is? He married a woman who was half-Jewish, for heaven's sake. He took me to the Holocaust Museum when it first opened..."

I trail off as Tim remains silent. I've finished my wine.

"Libby," he finally asks slowly, "do you actually know what your father did during the war?"

I stiffen, hardly able to believe he's asking me that question. My own faintly flickering doubts are bad enough, but for Tim to ask that in such a serious voice, like it actually *matters*? As if there really is reasonable doubt about any of this? We need to be on the same team here, fighting for the same goal. My father's innocence. That is the only option. The only option I can possibly bear.

"He was an accountant," I tell him flatly. "In Stuttgart. He was excused from military service because of the nature of his work, and he had a weak chest, I think. He told me so himself."

"But if there's no record of a Daniel Weiss who was an accountant from Stuttgart?" Tim's voice is distressingly gentle.

"You can't be sure," I protest, my voice rising again. "So many records were destroyed during or after the war. It's not as if Daniel Weiss is an unusual name. There could have been a dozen Daniel Weisses in Stuttgart, half of them accountants, and Simon Baum just doesn't know about them. Besides," I continue, cutting across whatever Tim had been going to say, "I can't help but feel he's biased. It's like he *wants* my dad to be a Nazi. He wants to find and prosecute one, get the accolade, maybe. I've read about it, you know, on the internet." I realize how childish I sound, like reading a Wikipedia entry turns me into some kind of expert. "There have been quite a few cases of mistaken identity, where some prisoner thought someone was a camp guard or something. There was this Polish guy—"

"Frank Walus, back in the seventies," Tim says quietly. "Yes, I know the case."

I stare at him in surprise. "You've heard of it?" I never would have, if I hadn't gone digging on Wikipedia, but then I know Tim has always been a bit of a Second World War history buff. More than once, he's stayed up late watching a war movie or documentary.

"It was a famous one," he explains, "right at the start of the renewed search for Nazi war criminals. And it is one of the only cases that has been dismissed, which is what makes it particularly notable." His words are gentle, but they fall heavily into the stillness.

I reach for my wine glass, even though it's empty.

One of the only ones. Which means most of them aren't dismissed. Most of them aren't cases of mistaken identity.

"Libby." There is an ache in my husband's voice that makes me feel like crying again.

I don't, though. I stare blindly at my empty glass to keep myself blinking, from a tear falling.

"I know this is hard, harder even than I can possibly comprehend, but... you know, I've always wondered about what your father did during the war, how he never talked about it."

"You did?" That is news to me.

"Only because most Germans were supporters of the Nazi party, in one way or another. That's simple fact. And considering what's now come to light..." He takes a quick breath and meets my gaze levelly. "I know you've always idolized your father a little, but—"

"Idolized him?" I sound stung, even though I know it is at least a little true.

"Understandably," Tim replies quickly. "He's been great, and he adores you—"

And I adore him. I bite my lip, not wanting to follow where Tim is leading me, but I am drawn there inexorably.

"All I'm saying is," he continues, his tone firming a little, "we've got to seriously consider the possibility that your father really is Hans Brenner."

CHAPTER 6

SEPTEMBER 1942

Sobibor, Poland

It took them the better part of three days to travel from Stuttgart to Sobibor, with an overnight stop in Dresden, and then another in Warsaw. Hans had never been so far east; he'd never been out of Germany, and even though Poland was of course now part of the Greater Reich, it didn't *feel* like Germany. There was an uneasy feeling of subversiveness in Warsaw, a wary furtiveness in the way the porter at the hotel took their bags, or the waiter bowed with obvious obsequiousness, his eyes darting this way and that.

In the city center, some buildings remained in ruins, from the Siege of Warsaw in 1939. Hans knew the city had the biggest Jewish ghetto in the Reich; over five hundred thousand Jews had been housed in just over three hundred hectares, a high, forbidding wall surrounding the whole thing. Now, however, the ghetto was half-empty; he heard from an SS officer seated at the table next to them for dinner that two hundred and fifty thousand Jews had been sent east just that summer. He spoke casually, as if it was of little consequence; had they, Hans wondered, been sent to work camps like Sobibor? He didn't ask, but merely nodded, as if he knew this already, as if he was well acquainted with the management of ghettoes and camps. Anni merely pursed her lips and looked away.

She'd been silent for almost the entire journey, spending hours staring out the window, sometimes with curiosity, at the deep, green valleys rising up from the Elbe, and sometimes with blank indifference or narrowed eyes, as they passed through shabby towns or nameless cities.

The farther east they went, the more unfamiliar the names sounded, an odd jumble of mismatched letters. From the train, they could glimpse little more than the station, a few narrow streets. Sometimes Hans got off to stretch his legs on the platform; the people he saw glanced once at his uniform and then looked away, quickening their step.

Anni had been deliberately unimpressed by his gray *Allgemeine* SS uniform, with the *siegrune* on the collar, the splash of red on the sleeve, the stiff cap, which he'd put on the morning of their departure.

"I suppose you think you look very smart," she'd said, waspishly, and Hans had tried to hide his hurt.

"I have no choice in any of this, Anni, as you well know."

"Yes, but you like it, I know you do. I saw you preening in the mirror."

He'd blushed and said nothing, because he knew it was at least partly true. He did feel smart in the severe-looking uniform, and more intoxicatingly, he felt powerful in a way he never really had before. Yes, he'd had a taste of it in the HJ, but not like this. He saw the way people looked at him as they traveled, sometimes with approval, sometimes with fear, but always with awe and respect. When had anyone ever looked at him like that? He'd never been a particularly impressive specimen of manhood, not by Nazi standards, anyway. Small and slight, too clumsy for sport and with a weak, wheezy chest, he'd done well in the HJ only because he'd had a good memory for useless facts and fervent song lyrics.

In the gray SS uniform and cap, he felt taller, stronger. Braver, even, and more assertive. He'd discovered, on their first night in the hotel in Dresden, that he'd adopted a bristling, almost pompous, manner that was quite unlike him. He'd demanded a fresh napkin when he saw the one he'd been given was stained; normally, he would have accepted such a thing without a murmur.

"I'm just doing my job," he'd told Anni that first morning, unable to keep from sounding affronted, and she hadn't bothered to reply.

Their relationship had not improved on the long train journey; Anni's silence, which had first felt like a punishment, eventually was simply born of weariness. She barely spoke during their evening meal in Dresden, or again in Warsaw, despite the decent food they were given, thanks, no doubt, Hans had thought rather acerbically, to the uniform he wore.

At Chelm, they left the train and were met by an officer who introduced himself as Bauer; he was, apparently, the unofficial driver of the camp. Hans helped Anni climb aboard the Jeep before hoisting himself up. It was another half-hour to Sobibor, and Bauer, with his eyes on the road and a bored, sullen manner, did not seem inclined to talk. Anni had not even said hello to him, keeping her face turned to the window as dense woodland streamed by in a blur of green and brown.

Hans found himself completely uncertain as to what to expect as they bumped down country roads, marshy pine forest rising up on either side of the rutted track, the trees tall and straight, cloaked in an autumn mist that was both ethereal and eerie.

He did not know anything about these camps, except that they existed and Jews were sent to them, presumably to work. But why would such places need an accountant? Would the accommodation be as comfortable as the *Gruppenführer* had promised? He was worried for Anni more than for himself; how would she manage, in a camp full of officers and Jews, presumably all of them men? Would she have any contact with the prisoners? He had no idea. He was doing his best to hide his ignorance, but he could not keep it from himself.

Finally, they came to the camp, indicated by Bauer's nod and grunt as they passed by the small train station and then through a high gate. Hans's spirits lightened as he looked around. Why, it all seemed remarkably pleasant, he thought with surprised relief. It did not appear so much as a work camp than as a village lifted straight out of Bavaria, admittedly one enclosed by barbed wire and manned by wooden towers and guards with machine guns, but those were no more than necessary precautions, surely.

The train station was a small white, wooden building with painted green trim, and a cluster of similarly styled cottages, with wooden front porches, were, according to Bauer, the officers' quarters. Hans saw that some of them had whimsical names—the Swallow's Nest, the Merry Flea. A high wall separated the SS officers' buildings from those of the camp's labor force, kept in similarly styled yet admittedly more utilitarian barracks, behind a forbidding fence of barbed wire, but, as with the gate and the guns, such security measures were only to be expected.

It really did, Hans thought as he helped Anni down from the Jeep, look remarkably civilized. There were hanging baskets of flowers on the train station's platform, and pretty, painted signs directing people to various locations—the garage, the stable, the tailor, the shoemaker, the showers. Really, if the Jews knew how they would be treated here, he reflected, perhaps they wouldn't be so reluctant to leave their filthy ghettoes and come east, where land and opportunity were clearly plentiful. It was like a bustling little city, although admittedly rather quiet right now; he could not see a single person around.

"What is that smell?" Anni asked, wrinkling her nose, and Hans took an experimental sniff, before he recoiled at the sweetish stench heavy on the air. It was both unfamiliar and unpleasant, clinging to his nostrils, making his stomach roil.

"You get used to it," Bauer said, and Hans glanced at him sharply.

"Does it always smell like this?" he demanded.

The other nodded.

"Why?"

Bauer gave him a skeptical, suspicious look, and then walked on without replying.

"Never mind," Hans told Anni. "There are worse smells, I'm sure. Perhaps it's something to do with one of the factories nearby. A tannery or some such." He tried to speak knowledgeably, even though he had no idea. The very fact of the smell, pervasive as it was, made him feel uncomfortable in a way he did not want to examine too closely.

Anni gave him a narrowed look and said nothing.

Despite the smell, he was feeling determinedly cheerful as Bauer directed them to the large two-story administration building in the middle of what was, he told them, Camp Two, where the deputy commandant would welcome them.

"You'll soon be settled," Hans reassured Anni, who was looking both pensive and exhausted, violet shadows under her eyes, her hair half falling down from its once-neat French roll.

She simply shrugged; she had had barely a word for him throughout the entire journey, but he saw how her gaze moved around the quiet camp, its neatly tended buildings, its many fences and walls, in thoughtful assessment. Perhaps she was as pleasantly surprised as he was, even if she did not want to admit as much to him.

The administration building faced a bare yard surrounded

by high walls. They walked through a gate, past what looked like several storage sheds, everything quiet, empty, and still.

"There hasn't been a transport for a while," Bauer explained in answer to their unasked question—where was everyone? "The machinery has been broken, so we've had to stop. But you've arrived just in time. There should be one coming later this afternoon."

Hans nodded, as if he understood exactly what the man was talking about. As they entered the building, he hoped the deputy commandant would be able to inform him what his role would be; he also hoped he would not appear too ignorant, not already knowing.

"Hauptscharführer Niemann will see you now," Bauer said, and sloped off, back to the officers' quarters.

A man emerged from an office, dressed smartly in the same gray uniform Hans wore, although with two silver pips and a silver stripe on the black collar that Hans' more junior uniform did not possess.

"I'll wait here," Anni said, sinking onto a hard wooden chair in the hallway of the building, while Hans performed the *Hitlergruss* and then followed Hauptscharführer Niemann into his office.

Although a senior officer, the man did not look much older than Hans' twenty-three years; he was thirty, at most, with dark rumpled hair and heavy-lidded eyes. His smile, as he surveyed Hans, was a slow stretching of his rather fleshy lips; Hans could not tell if it was genuine or not. He almost seemed bored.

"So you have been promoted to *Unterscharführer* and sent to Sobibor," he remarked languidly as he flipped through a file on his desk, turning the pages without any real interest. "Do you know what happens here, Corporal?"

Hans hesitated and then replied neutrally, "It is a work camp."

"A work camp, yes." Niemann's smile curved upwards even

more, reminding Hans of a wolf, or perhaps a cat toying with a mouse. There was a sardonic amusement in that slow curving of his lips, a weary enjoyment that made him feel distinctly uneasy. "Yes, the Jews do good work for us here," he agreed. "Very good work." He let out a short laugh and Hans gave a small, polite smile, unsure of the joke, or if there even was one.

Hauptscharführer Niemann sat down in the chair behind his desk, and with a flick of his fingers, he indicated that Hans sit as well. He did so, his back straight, his cap on his lap, his manner alert and ready, which, judging by the twist of those fleshy lips, seemed to amuse Niemann.

"You were excused from army service?"

Was there a slight sneer to those words? Hans wondered.

"Yes, due to my position as an accountant." He decided not to mention his weak chest. "I was needed in Stuttgart." He paused. "My father's accountancy firm has managed the book-keeping for quite a few of the SS's business interests." He realized, as Niemann continued to look unimpressed, how proudly he'd spoken, and he fought a flush.

"And we will need your counting skills here," Niemann said, as if he were a child who needed a placating pat on the head. "There is much to count, once the transports start again."

"The driver said they had been temporarily halted, due to the machinery being broken?" Hans tried to sound as if he understood what this meant.

"Yes, that is right," Niemann replied, leaning back in his chair. "We have not had a transport all summer. The men get restless, without anything to do. It is not good for morale, to be idle."

"Indeed," Hans agreed, and Niemann smiled faintly, as if he had said something amusing. "I have not been told any of the details of my position, *Hauptscharführer*...?" he prompted politely.

Niemann shrugged. "It is simple. The Jews come off the

train, you meet them on the ramp. Guards will take their suitcases, their bags, their paper-wrapped parcels, to be sorted by the work detail. You'd be amazed at the amount of stuff they bring here—all sorts. Jewelry, photographs, documents, tins of food, brandy, chocolate. One man brought his violin. Stradivarius or something. Quite expensive." He shook his head, seeming bemused by such folly. He continued, "The work detail will sort through all their belongings in the storage sheds across there—" he nodded toward the window—"and then you will make an account of any currency or gold before it is shipped to Lublin for further sorting, and then on to Berlin."

He stopped then, as if he'd said all there was to say, and Hans asked, "Do the Jews not keep any of their belongings then, while they're here?"

Niemann stared at him hard for a moment, and Hans had the awful, prickling sensation that he'd just said something remarkably stupid.

"They don't need any of it while they're here," he answered at last, and Hans nodded quickly, determined not to make another mistake.

"I see," he said, and Niemann let out a short, rather ugly laugh.

"Do you? Well, you certainly will soon enough." He glanced down at the file again—a file, Hans realized, that had to be all about him. "You brought your sister here, didn't you?"

"Yes, she is just seventeen, and I am her only relative. The *Gruppenführer* back in Stuttgart said it was all right—"

"Yes, I suppose so." Niemann waved a hand in dismissal. "Although, admittedly, we have few women here, besides the local Polish girls who do the cleaning and the kitchen work, and a few Russian whores to keep the men happy." He gave Hans a narrowed look. "This isn't really the sort of place for a gently bred woman, you know. The commandant is married, and his wife has visited once, but she stayed nearby, at Count Chelmicki's fish-hatchery. Women don't always take to camp life, do they?" He gave Hans a commiserating look that somehow felt mocking.

"No, I don't suppose they do, but my sister is quite resourceful. Quite hardy." Hans swallowed, already wondering if bringing Anni here had been a good idea. *Russian whores?*

"Is she? Good." Niemann's eyes narrowed. "And she can keep her mouth shut, I presume." This was said flatly, in a way that made Hans tense.

"Naturally, we know to be discreet," he replied after a moment, his voice stiff.

Niemann chuckled dryly. "Good, good. Your sister will be comfortable enough if she keeps to the officers' compound. Under no circumstances should she go into the second or third camps, not that she'd want to. She should stay away from the guards' quarters, as well. They're all Ukrainians from a nearby training camp and they can be rough sort of fellows. There are a few Jews in camp one and two, doing specialized work in a couple of workshops—we've got a shoemaker, a tailor, a carpenter, that sort of thing—but she should keep away from them, too. If she requires something to be made or mended, she can ask you. You don't mind having your shoes mended by a Jew, do you?" He raised his eyebrows expectantly, and Hans had no idea if it was a serious question or a joke.

"No, I suppose not," he replied after a moment.

"Good, good." Niemann sat forward in his chair, flipping Hans' file closed with the same air of disinterest with which he'd looked through it. "All in all, it can be comfortable enough here, I suppose, and you get plenty of time off—a few days every six weeks, at the least. There is a rest hut for officers about twenty kilometers away that you are welcome to use. Your sister can come with you, of course—there are some female SS auxiliaries at other camps, who work as telephone operators and the like." He smiled thinly. "She might make a friend."

Hans nodded. "Very good, *Hauptscharführer*."

Niemann cocked his head. "You should join us for drinks tonight, at the commandant's house. That's Hauptsturmführer Reichleitner. He keeps to himself, doesn't like to see the Jews on the ramp." Niemann's lips twisted in what Hans thought was contempt. "He's certainly good for a drink, though. Bring your sister—she shouldn't wander outside of the camp, by the way. There's a minefield all around the perimeter, fifty feet wide. There are signs posted, so as long as she can read, she should be all right."

Hans swallowed, nodding again, his mind reeling, although he tried his best to hide his discomfort, wanting to seem unfazed by this strange new world. "I see. Thank you, *Hauptscharführer*."

Niemann's speculative, amused gaze swept over Hans, making him blush. This time, he could not hide his embarrassment. "Where on earth did they find you?" he asked. "The HJ?"

Hans, having no idea how to reply, remained tight-lipped.

"Well, you'll figure it all soon enough," Niemann remarked with a shrug as he rose from behind his desk. "You can see your sister settled—one of the staff will show you your quarters—and then you can meet me on the ramp. There's a transport coming in at four o'clock. You'll see what this is all about, then."

Hans lurched up from his chair as he gulped and nodded again. "Yes, *Hauptscharführer*. Thank you—"

Niemann merely shook his head, as if Hans wearied him, and he offered the *Hitlergruss* once more before leaving the office, knowing he was dismissed.

Anni glanced up as he came back out into the hall, her eyebrows raised in silent query.

"We're to go to our quarters," Hans said, a bit more brusquely than he intended. He felt as if Niemann's weary contempt had scraped him raw, and he was chafing from the man's thinly veiled derision. "And then I'm to meet a train."

They walked back through the empty yard and gate toward the SS officers' compound, just across from the railroad tracks and separated from the rest of the camp by a high wall. Everything in the camp remained quiet, strangely so. Hans supposed the prisoners worked outside the camp—felling trees, perhaps, as the area was so wooded.

He saw a man in the black uniform of a guard walking toward a barracks and he asked him where he should find his accommodation. The man looked blank, but then, in broken German, pointed Hans to a rough-looking woman who was hauling a basket of dirty washing, and eventually they were directed to a small cottage in a row with a few others. It had a sloping tin roof and a narrow wooden front porch, and while certainly small, it seemed serviceable enough. It would be their home for the foreseeable future.

The door creaked as Hans stepped inside and looked around—just two rooms, with the minimum of furniture—a wooden table and a couple of chairs in the first room, around a little wood stove, and two beds, a bureau, and a washstand in the second. Their suitcases had already been delivered and stood in the middle of the front room. He supposed it was better than most; on the way here, Bauer had told him, in a surly sort of voice, that many of the officers had to share rooms, and some of them slept in the administration building.

"I'll sleep in the front room," he told Anni, "so you may have your privacy."

She didn't reply, and he wondered what on earth she would do all day here; taking care of a few rooms would hardly occupy her time, and he supposed they would take their meals in the dining hall, with the other officers. Were there any other women for Anni to socialize with, besides the few rough-looking servants? Would she even want to?

Just then, a whistle sounded, a long, low, strangely mournful sounded that echoed through the camp.

"That must be the train," he told Anni. "I'll be needed on the platform. You can stay here and settle in, all right?"

She nodded without looking at him and he stepped toward her to kiss her cheek.

"It will be all right, *liebe*, you'll see. I know it's all a bit strange at first, but it does seem remarkably well organized. Did you see the flowers on the platform?"

Her lips twisted as she nodded, and he glanced at her uneasily; there was something both blank and jaded about her expression, so unlike her usual lively thoughtfulness. He missed her playfulness, her smile.

"What is it, Anni?" he asked. "What are you thinking about?"

Her mouth curved in a mirthless smile that did not assuage his fears at all as she finally spoke. "I am thinking about aleph null."

"Aleph null?" He frowned. Was she really thinking about that silly number again? "You mean... the smallest infinite number?"

"Do you know aleph is the first letter of the Hebrew alphabet?" she remarked, walking to the window that overlooked a small yard, the wall, and then the train tracks beyond, under a hard blue sky.

"No, I didn't. Why would I?" He feared he sounded a bit belligerent, but why on earth was she talking about aleph null now? He wanted her to assure him that she'd be all right; he wanted her to be cheered by the pretty cottages, the flowers.

"The smallest number of infinity," she murmured, one hand resting on the sill. "It could be how many natural numbers there are, or how many even numbers, or how many rational numbers."

Hans blew out an impatient breath. "I don't understand you, Anni. Are you trying to tell me something?"

"It could be how many Jews there are," she stated softly, her gaze on the empty yard. In the distance, they could hear the steady, labored chug of the train approaching the station. "How many Jews are there, do you think, Hans?"

"In the whole world?" he demanded incredulously. Why were they talking about this?

Anni kept her gaze on the window. In the blue sky, a gray plume of smoke, from the approaching train, curled upwards toward the setting sun. "Perhaps," she answered. "How many come through this station, this camp, do you think?"

"I don't know. How should I know?" He knew he sounded cross, but he wished she wouldn't speak in riddles. What did it matter how many Jews there were, in this camp or the world, or anywhere at all? Or was she, as always, just curious about the mathematics of it?

Anni turned away from the window, seeming to dismiss both him and the view. "Go and meet your train," she said.

CHAPTER 7

LIBBY

"Hey, Dad. Matt is here to take you to the day center." I pitch my voice cheerful, even though I am feeling completely strung out, anxious and exhausted, running on fumes. I've barely slept since Simon Baum came to our house three days ago, and yet my thoughts are always racing, racing, going nowhere.

Tim and I have been tense around each other, too, which hasn't helped matters; after he suggested I needed to consider that my father really was Hans Brenner, I simply got up and walked away, back to the kitchen, busying myself with wiping the already clean counter while he just sat there. I wasn't angry, not exactly, but I felt something I didn't want Tim to see on my face.

"Libby," he finally said, gently, as he followed me into the kitchen. "You know you must at least consider it."

"I can't believe you're telling me that," I replied, my voice caught between a waver and a snap. "Consider my father is—" I broke off, not even wanting to say the words. "Tim, you've known my dad for twenty years. You've seen what he's like. Are you actually serious?"

"I know how much you love him," Tim replied quietly, and I'd whirled away to face the counter, afraid I would cry. Again.

Of course I loved my dad. It had been just the two of us against the whole world, for virtually my entire childhood. My mother was nothing more than a shadowy ghost I did my best not to think about; my father was a warm and real presence. He'd been my ally, my cheerleader, my comforter, my friend.

When Tim and I had started dating, I'd made it clear to him that my dad and I were a package deal; I'd always intended for him to live with me one day. It was why I hadn't had many serious boyfriends before Tim; not many guys wanted to take that sort of commitment on. Tim had been unfazed, even enthusiastic, and it was one of the reasons I fell in love with him.

And now, after just ten minutes of conversation, he was telling me my father must have been a Nazi? Without any real proof, or even seeming to mind?

Just then, Em came downstairs, damp and fresh-faced from her shower, her anxious gaze darting between the two of us.

"Hey, honey." I smiled at her and tucked a tendril of hair behind her ear, desperate both to reassure her and put a stop to this conversation. Thankfully, Tim was willing to drop it.

Since then, we haven't really talked about it any further; when Tim has tried, I've basically shut him down, telling him I am not going to entertain the notion of my dad being a Nazi. "Not until there's proof," I told Tim, as if that were the end of it.

"And are you going to find that proof?" he asked, seeming almost disappointed that I might.

"No, because there isn't any."

But I am going to find the proof for his innocence, which is why he needs to go to the day center today, as much as he hates the place, with its overly cheery staff who push activities on him and the elderly people, who are, according to my father, 'practically insentient.'

"If I wanted to learn to crochet," he has snapped more than once, "then I would."

No matter how I explain that the staff are just trying to engage his interest, he's never softened toward the prospect. But today I need him to go, because I am going to search his room.

In the three days since Simon Baum has come to the house, even though I haven't been willing to talk about it with Tim, I've been thinking about it constantly. I have spent hours on the internet, searching Nazi war criminal trials and the Sobibor death camp. I've dug deep into Military Wiki sites, found lists of the officers at the camp, including a Hans Brenner, although there is no photo of him and little information online besides the facts Simon Baum told me—that he served at Sobibor for a year, that he worked as an accountant.

I've even found a map of the camp, with its officers' compound, the "Road to Heaven" Simon told me about, the barracks and buildings and gas chambers. I've read about the uprising in October 1943, when all the Jews who had been kept on to work at the camp revolted, killing nine SS officers and storming the gates. Three hundred escaped, many of them rounded up the next day, but fifty made it to the end of the war. It was the largest escape from a camp during the entire Second World War, a fact that astonishes me, because I'd never heard about it, or even about Sobibor.

The more I read, the more I am convinced my father had nothing to do with any of this. There is simply no way he could have participated in this kind of absolutely inhumane savagery. He could not have kept such a secret from me, even if he'd wanted to. I would have sensed it, like something dark lurking deep in the water. I would have known he was a man with secrets, I would have at least *suspected*. I am so sure, and today I am going to find evidence of that, of the truth that will set my father free. Or, barring that, I will not find anything that links him to Sobibor, and I will go to Simon Baum with a clear conscience, and he will not get the warrant for my dad's arrest, and I'll never have to trouble my father about any of this, ever.

That is why I haven't confronted him about it yet, or so I tell myself. I don't want to upset him, especially if there's no reason. If my father believes that I could have even *wondered* if he was at a camp, he'll be unbearably hurt. Why distress him for no purpose?

This was the conclusion I came to when I went into his room the morning after Simon Baum's visit. I'd barely slept that night and I was feeling achy and old and out of sorts, hardly in the right frame of mind for an intense conversation. Still, I thought about simply getting it out in the open. Clearing the air.

My father was still in bed; on the mornings his carer doesn't come, I help him out of bed, to the bathroom. It is a loss of dignity I know he dislikes, although I try to be breezily matter-of-fact about it all. That morning, however, I was feeling too raw, too emotional, the knowledge of Simon Baum's visit burning a hole through my heart. My dad could tell something was up.

"Libby? *Liebe?* What is it?" he asked, blinking sleepily at me.

I opened my mouth, shut it. Tried again. "I've been wondering about something, Dad..." I began in a terribly croaky voice.

He raised his eyebrows as he started to clamber out of bed. "Oh? Something serious, it seems." I reached over to help him up, and as his feet hit the floor, he stumbled, falling into my arms with a frightened gasp.

As I held him, I realized how *small* he'd become, how very fragile. His heart beat against mine and I breathed in his old man smell—mouthwash and medicine, a hint of leather and something stale—as he struggled to regain his balance, his dignity.

"What a clumsy old oaf I am," he said with a huff of laughter, but I could tell he was both embarrassed and distressed, and I righted him gently.

"It's okay, Dad."

I could not ask him, not then. Maybe not ever. I walked him carefully to the bathroom, my heart aching, my eyes smarting.

I didn't find another time to ask him about it. I couldn't.

Now my dad rises creakily from his chair. "I don't see why I have to go," he harrumphs, while his carer, Matt, a friendly, burly guy in his twenties, comes in to take his arm.

"I'm having the carpets steam cleaned," I remind him, which has been my excuse to get him out of the house. It's true that they could use a clean, anyway. "It's easier if you're out of the house, you know it is. Besides, you'll have fun." I say this as if he always has fun at the day center and he just needs to be reminded of that fact, when nothing could be further from the truth. I only resort to him going there when I can't come up with any other alternatives.

My father sighs and shakes his head, and Matt guides him out of his bedroom. "Come on, Mr. W. It'll be fun."

"Fun," my father says scornfully, and Matt and I share a commiserating smile, although I feel so nervy and strung out, I can barely manage the upturn of my lips.

My mind has been going round in circles for days now, and it's utterly exhausting me. That first night, Grace called to check up on me, and I could tell from her voice that she wanted details.

"So, what happened?" she asked as I sank onto my bed, utterly exhausted. "Was it Em? Is everything okay?"

"Yeah, it was just her usual anxiety," I replied after a beat. I hated lying to my friend, but there was no way I could admit the truth. If *Tim* had jumped to the conclusion that my father at least *might* be Hans Brenner, how would Grace respond? How many people in this town, in the whole country, would judge my father on nothing more than some scant evidence? I've seen how the world works, how a whisper on social media turns into a shout, a howl of fury, and what was nothing more than a rumor becomes an incontrovertible fact. People don't even care what the truth is anymore; they just want to be right. Even more, they want to be outraged. It happens all the time now; careers are ruined by tweets, lives by a blurry photo or a single caption. I am not going to let that happen to my father, when I know he is innocent. I *know* it.

"Okay," Grace said, and I heard a slight coolness in her voice that masked her hurt. She could tell I wasn't telling her the truth, at least not all of it.

"I'm going to work from home for the next few days," I said, trying to sound casual and most likely failing. "For Em's sake. Is that okay?"

"Of course it is. Besides, I'm only a volunteer." She definitely sounded stung then. "I don't get to decide your working hours."

"I know, but..." We've more or less been running Fresh Start as a team for years, even if I'm the only one who has been paid for it. Grace has never gone back to work after having kids; she doesn't need the money and she loves volunteering. Even though she isn't on Fresh Start's payroll, she is as integral to the organization as I am, something I'd assumed she was okay with, but right then I wondered. I hated feeling like I was keeping something from her, but I couldn't tell her this. Not until I knew more. Not until I was sure. "Let's catch up on the weekend, okay?" I said instead, injecting a conciliatory, hopeful note into my voice.

Grace wasn't entirely appeased. "Sure," she replied. "The weekend."

I push the memory of that conversation out of my mind—along with the three I've had with Em when she's continued to ask me if everything is really okay with Grandad, and the ones I haven't had with Tim or my father—as I stand on the front porch and watch Matt help my dad into the car. He'll drive him there, stay to see him settled, and then pick him up at four o'clock to bring him home. His services cost an arm and a leg, but they're certainly worth it.

As Matt drives off, I turn to go back inside. The house is quiet and empty; Lucas is at the library researching a summer project for chemistry, and Em has gone over to a friend's. More of my machinations, but I can't be distracted, not now. Not when I'm not even sure what I'm looking for.

The carpet cleaners really are coming at eleven, so I have a whole hour to search my father's room. But for what?

You'd be surprised what these old Nazis like to keep around, even though it incriminates them. I can hear Simon Baum's voice as if he's in the room with me. I haven't called him yet, although I think I need another conversation, more information. My plan is to call him after I've searched my dad's room, and I have found nothing to incriminate him, or even better, something that could actually exonerate him. I'm not sure what that might be, but if it's in this house somewhere, I am determined to find it. There *has* to be something to prove he wasn't at Sobibor. Something to prove he really is Daniel Weiss—a birth certificate, perhaps, or a photo, a dated letter, *something*.

As I step into my dad's bedroom, I close the door quietly behind me. The room smells of his old-fashioned aftershave with the medicinal tang of old age, perhaps from the medication he takes for his blood pressure. Or maybe it's just that he never opens the window. I crack one open now, welcoming the muggy heat, the freshness of the air. I breathe in and out, and then I turn to his bedside table.

I want to be systematic and not overcome by emotion, but already, as soon as I start, that feels impossible. As I bend down to open the top drawer, I glance at the photo of me on the table —I have Band-Aids on both my knees, from falling off my bike. I remember falling hard on the sidewalk, and how my dad picked me up; I squirmed away as usual, but then he tickled me and studied my bloodied knees, pretending he was going to have to amputate both my legs, using his hand like a saw. By the time he took this photo as proof of my complete recovery, I was laughing.

A lump forms in my throat and I swallow it down resolutely as I turn away from the photo and open the drawer. Inside, there is nothing but a pack of tissues and an ancient-looking tub of lip balm. In the cabinet underneath that, there are a couple of old Louis L'Amour Westerns, dog-eared and yellow-paged. I release a shaky breath.

I turn to his dresser, five drawers of neatly folded under-shirts and boxers, shirts and sweaters. His ties, trousers, and suit jackets are on hangers in the closet. There is nothing in any of the drawers besides the clothes I've folded and put there myself. I open the little wooden box on top of the dresser where he keeps his cufflinks, the only jewelry he wears, besides his wedding ring, which he never stopped wearing and never takes off.

It is a small box, intricately carved and lacquered, that he's had ever since I can remember. As a kid, I used to love opening and closing the lid, the satisfying snap it gave as it shut. My father always warned me to be careful not to pinch my fingers, shaking his head and smiling as he'd glance at me sideways.

And just like that I am transported back in time—my father is standing in front of the mirror, smoothing back his hair, while I perch on my tiptoes and play with the box. I am—what? Four, five? Before I went to school, anyway. My mother has already gone. He is getting ready for work and I am waiting for the babysitter to come—one of a succession of elderly ladies who sat and knitted and watched TV while I did whatever I liked. It was both liberating and lonely, an emptiness of days.

In the box, there are nothing but three pairs of cufflinks, all ones I recognize. I close it slowly. I've only been in here ten minutes and already I don't know where else to look. I feel silly, like a child playing detective. What did I actually think I was going to find? Did I think it would be that easy, like a treasure hunt and I just had to piece together the clues, present them triumphantly to Simon Baum like some middle-aged Nancy Drew? I can picture his scorn at such an absurd move.

I go into the bathroom and look through my dad's medicine cabinet, the drawers of the vanity, then head into the walk-in closet, rooting among our boxes of Christmas decorations and winter clothes, for the single file box of all his old papers. I am feeling half-hearted now, knowing I won't find anything, and I don't. There are no surprises, no hidden photos or letters or anything that could either incriminate or exonerate my father, just a handful of old bills and Social Security payments. What did I really expect?

The carpet cleaning guys will be here in half an hour. I feel as if I've failed, and I can't believe I actually thought—at least part of me did—that I'd find something important, something that would help. What—a letter, helpfully dated, showing he was in Stuttgart, not Sobibor, in 1943? A photograph of him with friends, perhaps, on vacation somewhere, helpfully dated and proving absolutely he couldn't have been at that camp? Easy evidence, tailor-made for the situation. As if.

Even if there ever was something, I know it was most likely thrown out when my dad moved down to Charlottesville fifteen years ago, or maybe when he moved in with us from his apartment. Both times, there were trash bags full of stuff—papers, books, clothes—that went either to charity or the dump. At least I can tell Simon Baum I looked and found nothing, but that doesn't feel like enough. I wanted proof, just as he did. But I wanted proof that my father is not a Nazi.

I glance around the room one last time, as if something will jump out at me.

My gaze rests back on the little wooden box on top of the

dresser. It feels important, although I'm not sure why. Maybe because it's the only thing I know of that he brought from Germany; it belonged to his father, a wedding present for his parents, I think.

I walk toward it, open it again. I take out the cufflinks one by one and peer into its small, velvet-lined depths; there's nothing. I pick it up, and that's when I hear it—a rattle. I shake it gently, and I hear the rattle again, a desperate sound, like something trying to get out, or perhaps I'm just being fanciful, because for the first time, I have found something hidden.

My heart is starting to hammer as I put the box down, stare at it. Its interior is small—too small, I realize with a jolt. There must be a false bottom or side, a secret compartment of some kind. I feel ridiculous, truly like a wannabe Nancy Drew, as I press the sides of the box. Nothing happens.

I shake it again. Rattle.

A groan escapes me and I consider smashing the box with a hammer, but of course I won't do that, because my father would notice. Besides, this box is special. Even if it has secrets, I don't want to destroy it.

I turn the box over and that's when I see it—a tiny lever on the bottom. I can hardly believe it; it feels too good to be true, or maybe too bad, I'm not sure which. I push the lever and when I look in the box again, the back has folded down. I reach in with two trembling fingers and pull out a photograph.

It's a photo of my parents, one I've never seen before, both looking serious, unsmiling, in their wedding clothes. My father was forty-eight, my mother ten years younger. Neither of them had ever expected to marry, my father once told me, having had the prime of their youth during the war. Their courtship had been cautious, hesitant, shy. She'd left him—and me—just five years later.

I study the picture now; my mother is pale and slender, with the same flyaway strawberry-blond hair as Em. There is an almost haunted look in her eyes, as if she is distant from the photo, the celebration. I know her parents went into Theresienstadt in 1941, when she was eleven, the same age as my daughter now. What did she experience, with a Jewish mother, in Germany during the war? What scars were formed, that never healed?

My father has intimated it was all very difficult, but I've never really asked about it, because we never talk about my mother. And, I acknowledge, I never let myself think about her, even as she always seemed to be skirting the fringes of my mind, a dark shadow, an unacknowledged longing, a mystery.

I stare at the photograph for a few more seconds as if I can discover something in her smooth, blank face, and then I put it aside. I reach into the box again and my fingers brush something metal—the source of the rattling—and then snag on another photograph. I withdraw it slowly; this one feels—and I soon see, looks—older. It is black and white, on thick paper with serrated edges, the kind you would have pasted onto the thick pages of an old album.

It is of a woman I don't recognize, although strangely she looks familiar. Her hair is heavy and dark, pulled back in a loose bun, a few wisps framing a face that looks both lively and intelligent, thoughtful and knowing. She is young, no more than twenty, I should think. She is standing on a wooden porch, one slender hand wrapped around the railing. She wears a dark dress and she is looking slightly off to the side, as if she doesn't care about the picture being taken, or perhaps doesn't even want to be in it.

I turn the photograph over to see if there is any inscription or date, any clue to who or where this is, but there is nothing. Still, my stomach clenches hard and my heart feels like a heavy weight suspended in my chest. Why would my father have hidden this photograph? I don't know who this woman is, and my father has never mentioned anyone from his past. His parents died before the war or during it, and he had no siblings, no other family, at least none that he ever mentioned to me.

I have a plunging feeling that this photo might be the clue to something, perhaps even the answer, although I'm not sure what. I put it aside, and then I reach one last time inside the hidden compartment. My fingers skim the metal again and then I pull out a piece of jewelry—a ring.

I roll it between my fingers as I study it. It is a delicate piece, made of twisted, tarnished gold; it looks like a woman's wedding ring. Whose wedding ring? My mother's? Or someone else's?

I stand there in my father's bedroom, the ring resting in my palm, not wanting to think too deeply about what any of this means. I realize, in this moment, that I didn't actually expect to find anything, no matter what my feeble hopes of exonerating my father had been. I was, I know now with a leaden certainty, hoping to report back to Simon Baum that there was nothing, *nothing*, no evidence at all, and that would be enough to keep this from going any further. The warrant wouldn't be issued. The trial could be dismissed. No charges pressed, because there simply wasn't enough evidence.

And yet here I am, I fear, holding some in my hand. Why did I even look? Was I really that sure? And what on earth do I do now?

The doorbell rings, its loud chimes echoing through the house, and I jump, nearly dropping the ring. The carpet cleaners have arrived.

CHAPTER 8

LIBBY

The Robert F. Kennedy Department of Justice Building is part of the Federal Triangle of government buildings in the center of DC, a grand colonnaded edifice taking up an entire block on Constitution Avenue. I must have walked by it a dozen times, on various family tours or while chaperoning school field trips, barely paying it any attention as we'd crane our necks for a glimpse of something a bit more recognizable—the Washington Monument or the White House, both practically within spitting distance.

Now I stand in front of its front steps and swallow, the ring and photograph heavy in my pocket. In fifteen minutes, I am due to meet Simon Baum, and I haven't yet decided what I am going to tell him, although I know it has to be something.

I've barely been sleeping since I found that ring, that photograph. I showed both to Tim, miserably, in silence, the night I found them, feeling how damning they were—and yet not actually knowing at all. We'd reached a sort of truce, in terms of my dad; Tim hadn't mentioned the possibility of him being Hans Brenner again, and I hadn't snapped at him for suggesting it in the first place. But now, with the photograph, the ring, I was, to my own misery and shame, starting to wonder. To doubt. My *dad*.

"A wedding ring," Tim said slowly, holding it in his palm just as I had.

"Don't say it," I implored, and he looked up at me, bemused.

"Don't say what?"

I shook my head, not wanting to put it into words. I'd read, during one of my many internet deep dives, how the Nazi camp guards often stole bits and pieces for themselves, from all the loot they'd confiscated. I'd seen a photo of an American soldier, right after the war, holding up handfuls of stolen wedding rings at Auschwitz.

Tim put down the ring and took the photo, studying it silently for a moment. "You don't know who this is?"

"No."

"She looks like you."

"What?" I reached for the photo, and it was only then that I realized why the unknown woman looked familiar. She *did* look like me—the same dark hair, the heavy-lidded eyes, the pointed chin. It took Tim to point it out to me. There were differences, of course; she was both younger and thinner, for a start. I had a more rounded face, freckles across my nose. But something about the eyes, the chin... there definitely was a resemblance.

"She must be a relative of yours," he said.

I shook my head. "My father didn't have any family left."

Tim didn't reply, which was kind of him. We both already knew my dad must have been keeping some secrets.

"Why don't you just ask your dad directly, Lib?" he asked after a moment. "About the ring, the photo? Or even about him being Hans Brenner? At least then you'll know, and that might be a relief." He paused. "Or are you afraid of what he'll say if you do ask?"

I flinched at that. "No," I said, not quite telling the truth. "It's just... I don't want to hurt him." I had pictured it so many times already, the way my father's face would crumple in disbelief and disappointment, and far worse, a sense of betrayal, that I could have ever thought such a thing about him, even for a moment. Or—like Tim had just implied—that his face *wouldn't*, and that instead a look of guilt would flash across his features, settle into the deep, haggard creases of resignation.

But, no. No. That couldn't happen. Even with this photo, this ring, I wanted to believe in other explanations. But I wasn't willing to ask my father about them.

"I'll talk to Simon Baum first," I told Tim. "These might be nothing. They're certainly not conclusive. But at least I'll have shown him I did as much as he asked me to."

"Is that so important to you?" Tim asked skeptically, and I gave him a sharp look.

"I'm on the side of justice, no matter what, just as my father taught me to be."

He sighed. "Justice isn't always black and white, Lib, and the ethics of it are often changing. I see this in scientific research—"

"We're talking about the Holocaust," I cut across him. "I think that's pretty cut and dried."

He fell silent then, but I didn't feel vindicated. I still felt wretched, about both the photo and ring. I wish I hadn't found anything. I wished I hadn't looked.

"You still need to talk to your dad," he finally said. "Especially if Simon Baum ends up getting the warrant." Was I imagining the hint of censure in his voice? Did he really believe I shouldn't hand any potential evidence in? "Because, in that case, there really will be a trial. He'll need to talk to a lawyer, tell his side of the story, whatever that is. We can't keep him in the dark, Lib. He'll need to prepare himself."

"You're making a lot of assumptions there," I reminded him. "This might not even be evidence. He still might not get the warrant."

Tim shook his head. "That photograph and ring must mean something."

I didn't answer, because I suspected he was right and I didn't want him to be.

"Besides," Tim continued, his voice turning firmer, "if the trial does go ahead, this is all going to come out publicly—and the proverbial will hit the fan, media-wise. We all need to be prepared for that. It could be pretty ugly."

I flinched, hating the thought, hardly able to imagine it. Would this really be in the newspapers, on TV? Would people care that much, about something that happened so long ago? The answer was obvious—of course they would. We were talking about the *Holocaust*. And yet, according to certain polls, two-thirds of teenagers today didn't even know what the Holocaust was. Mind-boggling, but apparently true.

"And we'll need to tell Em and Lucas," Tim added. "They need to be prepared too, Libby, for whatever happens. If this goes ahead, it's going to be big, one way or another. It's going to be hard."

"I know." And yet it already felt hard. How much harder would it become? How much would we all have to bear? I thought of Em, distraught about her grandfather; of Lucas, shocked and hurt but not wanting to talk about it. Of Tim, being so stalwart and yet for how long? And my father... at the epicenter of this mess, and yet so frail. So beloved. "Let me talk to Simon Baum again first," I said, a bit feebly. "I need more information. Then, if he feels he can proceed..." I swallowed hard. "I'll talk to my dad. And the children." I tried to speak as if these were nothing but ticks on a to-do list, rather than towering mountains to climb. "Then we can make a plan for how to handle the trial, if it happens, I promise."

Tim's face softened and he reached for my hand. "Do you want me to go with you, to see Simon Baum?"

I shook my head; I wasn't even sure why. I knew I could have used Tim's steady presence when facing Simon Baum again, but I had a deep-seated need to see this through myself. This was my dad; my responsibility. And part of me didn't want to see Tim acting all reasonable with Simon Baum, taking what he said as absolute truth, or watching me fall apart when he did. I felt exposed enough already, desperate to scramble some defense together, to protect both myself and my father. "You take the kids out somewhere," I told him, to soften the blow of my seeming rejection. "Maybe you could go to Busch Gardens."

"Busch Gardens?" Tim looked disbelieving. It was the big amusement park in Virginia, near Williamsburg. "That's two hours away, and in this heat?"

"Somewhere fun, then. The pool, at least." Although, at fifteen, Lucas was less impressed with a trip to the community pool.

Tim sighed. "I'll think of something."

"Thank you."

He didn't reply for a moment, and then, his gaze lowered, he said quietly, "You don't have to do this alone, you know."

There was a faint note of recrimination in his voice, along with one of sadness. I stiffened, not wanting to get into all that now. As much as I depended on Tim to be my steady rock, I knew I didn't always act like it. I didn't ask for his help. I didn't show him my weakness. I didn't want to, and I knew it probably had to do with my mother abandoning me when I was four. My mother's leaving has been like a black hole at the center of myself, one I am continually swerving to avoid, even as it can feel as if takes over my life, a cloud constantly hovering over me. I pretend it doesn't exist, but Tim still sees it.

He's encouraged me to talk about it sometimes, but I never do. I tell him I'm okay, that I've dealt with it, that I've got him, so it's all good, and he lets it be. We both do. But I still keep certain parts to myself; I still act as if I'm strong, because I'm afraid what might happen if I don't.

"I'm not doing this alone," I told him. "You've been amazing, Tim, helping with the kids, and..." I trailed off, embarrassed by my own prevarication. "You know, everything."

Tim raised his head to give me a weary, accepting look. "You know what I mean, Lib."

The words hung between us, heavy without being accusing. Not quite, anyway.

I looked away, and the silence ticked on.

After a few seconds, maybe a minute, Tim sighed.

"I'll take them to the pool," he said, and I nearly sagged with relief—both that he'd agreed, and that he'd let the other thing go.

"Thank you," I said, and he just nodded.

When I called Simon Baum and asked him to meet me, he didn't hesitate, just named the time and place. And so now I am here, standing in front of the DOJ, my stomach swirling with dread. I've only parked a block away, but already I am sweating in the sultry city heat, my cotton blouse sticking to my back from my nape to my tailbone.

The sun beats down relentlessly as I mount the stairs and a few seconds later, I am in the building's huge foyer, going through security, in blessed air conditioning. A few minutes after that, I am sitting in a small, nondescript conference room, across from Simon Baum.

He seems more serious this time, the affable exterior dropped for an attitude that is unsettlingly focused. His clothes are just as rumpled, but the look in his blue eyes is intent as he puts a folder down on the table and then rests his hands palm down on either side of it.

"So," he says, and I have to lick my lips because my mouth is so dry, "was there a particular reason you asked to see me?"

I know what he's really asking—if I've found any evidence. I'm not ready to talk about that yet, though.

"I wanted some more information." My voice sounds rusty. "Everything was such a blur, when you came to my house... I could barely take it in. I've done some research now, and we've also talked to our lawyer." Not that I really want to tell him what Tim told me our lawyer Kate said—that these cases don't get this far without enough evidence. The warrant, she told us, was more a matter of time and red tape than anything else, something I refused to believe. Simon Baum wouldn't have come to me if that's all that was stopping him, surely. In any case, I reminded myself, extradition trials were not about whether the defendant was guilty or innocent; they were just about whether a person could be tried for a crime. Even if this does go to trial—and that is not a given—my father could still be innocent. That could still be proved. But, if it does indeed get that far, it might have to be in Germany.

"All right." Simon's voice is measured. "What is it that you want to know?"

What to ask first? Part of me doesn't want to ask anything at all.

"Is Daniel Weiss's son the prime mover behind this trial?" I finally ask.

Simon's gaze narrows. "That's confidential."

"Is it? You're the one who mentioned him seeing that photo."

"I am not about to reveal any personal details of anyone involved in this case."

Now he's really sounding like a lawyer. "I'm just wondering," I tell him, "because if it's only the son's word against my father's, then how can anyone prove anything?"

His mouth thins. "So your father has denied it?"

I bite my lip, feeling guilty as I admit, "I haven't actually told him about any of this yet."

Simon raises his eyebrows, his expression cool. "Why not?"

"I don't want to upset him."

He lets out a huff of disbelieving laughter. "You don't want to tell a hardened Nazi what he already knows he did? You don't want to hurt his *feelings*?"

He sounds so scornful, and I am caught between embarrassment and anger. "My father is not a hardened Nazi," I fire back. "You don't know for sure that it was him. Hans Brenner."

Simon leans over the table, his palms pressed down on its surface. "I am surer," he tells me in a quietly lethal voice, "of your father's identity than of any other Nazi I've pursued in the twenty years of my career."

I recoil at that, shocked at his intensity, his certainty. This is a different man than the one who came to my house—why? Has he scented victory? Is he homing in for the win? Or, I wonder as my stomach hollows out, is he really that sure? How can he be?

"How?" I ask. I meant it to come out as a challenge, but it sounds more like a plea.

"Are you sure you want to know?"

No, not at all, not even one little bit.

Still, for my father's sake, or maybe my own, I bluster, "What else is there to know, besides what you've told me? There's no record of a Daniel Weiss who was an accountant in Stuttgart. Hans Brenner from Stuttgart was in Sobibor, but then he disappeared." I fling the words at him like they don't matter, but I know they do. I feel the weight of the evidence heavy upon me, upon my father, and it terrifies me.

In answer, Simon flips open the file. The first piece of paper he takes out is a photocopy of some sort of register, in the tiny, Gothic script of Nazi Germany. He hands it to me silently and I scan the list of what looks like, in German, different amounts of currency. At the bottom is a signature—Hans Brenner.

Is it my father's handwriting? I can't tell. The script used for this official form is styled and intricate, unlike his own current, spidery scrawl. I can't possibly compare them.

Simon hands me another piece of paper. It's a photocopy of my father's visa application, signed Daniel Weiss. The script isn't the same Gothic style, but I imagine I can see something of a similarity in the shape of the letters, their slight leftward slant. My stomach starts to hollow out. My mind is full of static.

"A handwriting expert has analyzed both specimens," Simon states tonelessly. "And he believes they are a match."

I don't reply; I can't.

Simon hands me another piece of paper. This one is a photocopy of a photograph, of a group of half a dozen men, all in SS uniform, sitting or standing around a table outside. There are half-empty glasses of liquor on the table, packs of cigarettes, an overflowing ashtray. They are all looking relaxed, collars unbuttoned, leather booted-legs crossed, hair ruffled by the breeze. One squints in the glare of the sun.

"They were just a few hundred yards away from the camp's gas chambers," Simon tells me tonelessly. "Not to mention the crematorium. You would have been able to smell it, you know, the burning bodies—an awful, sweetish smell. It never left the place. It clung to their clothes, their hair." I press my lips together and keep staring at the photo. "The man on the left is Johann Niemann, deputy commander of the camp. His grandson discovered this photo, along with hundreds of others, all taken during Niemann's time at Sobibor. The photographs are currently in Berlin, but we are hoping they might be exhibited one day at the Holocaust Museum here." He pauses. "I think your father is second from the right, the one in the back, who isn't looking at the camera."

I stiffen, and then I peer more closely, trying to determine the lines and angles of my father's face and body in the blurry sight of this stranger, standing in the background of the shot, looking off to the side, almost as if he doesn't want to be there.

"It's a bit blurry, I admit," Simon says. "But the man is otherwise unidentified. He is wearing the uniform of an *Unterscharführer*, which was Brenner's rank, as the camp's book-keeper. I think he's about the same height, the same build, which was somewhat unusual for an SS officer—they were normally a bit taller."

"I can't even recognize him," I protest, but strangely, it almost sounds like an apology. The sandy hair—could it be my father's? I've only known his hair as gray, or more recently, white. The line of his jaw, the shape of his ear—are they familiar? I can't tell. Yes, he looks to be about as tall, and it's true he's slight, the way my father is—but so were plenty of men, surely, even SS officers.

"There's this one, as well," Simon says, and hands me another photocopied photo. "From the same afternoon, which was sometime in the summer of 1943, we think."

I take the paper between numb fingers, and then my whole body goes rigid, because this photo is of the same table, the same men, but the photographer must have taken a step back for a wider shot, and now I can see a young woman standing to the side, the wind blowing a few strands of dark hair across her face. She looks pensive, gazing off into the distance, one arm wrapped around her waist; she seems as if she couldn't care less about the officious men all standing around, as if she is trying to ignore them. But more than that, I recognize her. She is the woman in my father's photo.

"What is it?" Simon asks sharply. "You've seen something?"

Of course he's been watching my reactions, to check if I recognize anything. Why else would he show these to me?

My mouth is dry and I open it to say—what? Am I actually going to lie? Why would I do that?

The answer is obvious: to protect my father.

If all they have is the word of this stranger's son, who must have been a child at the time, and a single blurry photo, the opinion of one handwriting expert... it's not all that much, is it, no matter how sure Simon seems? Without the evidence I found, he might never get the warrant approved. The trial will never happen. I could make this all go away, simply by lying in this moment. By telling Simon Baum I don't recognize anything, and keeping the ring and photo in my pocket.

It would, I realize, be so easy, so very easy. I'd go back to the life I love, I would have kept my family, my father, safe. I'm not even sure anyone would blame me if they knew; Tim has sounded as if he wouldn't. And who would I really be hurting? Almost everyone connected to Sobibor is dead. Like Tim said, my father has lived an exemplary life for seventy years. Does he really need to pay for these decades-old crimes at his age, whatever they were? It really would be so easy simply to say nothing, and yet...

It was my father who taught me to tell the truth. To be brave, even when my knees were shaking. To stand up for the underdog, whether it was the girl bullied in third grade or the refugee who has the courage to walk through the doors of Fresh Start. My father has made me who I am, and he is the reason why I can't lie now.

And yet... if my father was really at Sobibor, if he really did do those things... then he's not the man I thought he was. The man I've loved. He *should* be prosecuted, just as Simon Baum said, just as I had agreed, and yet I cannot reconcile those two realities. This is my father. My *father*.

"Elizabeth." Simon's voice is urgent yet also surprisingly gentle. "Tell me what you see."

"The woman," I finally say, the words drawn from me inexorably, yet with deep reluctance, as if pulled from deep within by a string. I cannot lie, even though part of me still longs to, desperately. "I think... I think I recognize her."

"From where?"

I hesitate again, knowing that if I tell him the truth, it will change things, perhaps forever. Almost certainly forever, or for the rest of my father's life, at least, and the rest of mine, as well. *My children's.* I picture Em's distress, Lucas's shock, my father's absence in their lives a terrible, gaping hole. Nothing, I know, will ever be the same again.

"From a photograph," I say slowly, each word painful to form, to say, *hurting* me. "One I found in a box of my father's." In a hidden compartment, which is even more damning, but I don't say that.

I don't have to, because already I see a blaze of triumph flash in Simon's eyes and suddenly I feel sick. What have I done? I've condemned my father. I know I have. Why? Why would I do such a thing?

And then I realize that my father has condemned himself. If this woman was at Sobibor... he must have been, as well. He must have served there as an SS officer. As a Nazi. He *was* the accountant on the ramp, watching innocent people be herded toward their deaths. He was complicit, at the very least. Perhaps worse, hiding a cruelty or at least a cowardice that I had never, ever even guessed at. The reality slams into me, makes me see stars as the room spins around me.

I drop my head into my hands, afraid I might vomit, or pass out, or both. I double over, pressing my forehead to my knees. I hear Simon move, the door open and close, and I try to concentrate on taking deep, even breaths. I really don't want to throw up. I don't want to pass out, either. I don't want to have to think about any of this and yet already the realizations are pounding through me.

A few seconds later, or maybe a few minutes, Simon returns. He puts something on the table and then a hand on my shoulder.

"Have a drink of water."

I raise my head, spots dancing before my eyes, my tongue thick in my mouth. I taste bile and I force it down as I reach for the water with a shaky hand and bring it to my lips. One swallow, two, and then I have to put the glass back down. I don't think I'm going to faint or vomit anymore, thank goodness, but I still feel weak and trembling. My father... a Nazi. In the SS. At a death camp. Even now I want to exonerate him, somehow, *somehow*, yet I cannot find a way.

"I'm sorry," I manage, unable to look at Simon. I don't want to see his pity, or worse, the triumph that I've just given him his trump card. Even if it was the right thing to do, and I'm not entirely sure it was, I feel sick inside. Sick with guilt and fear. With horror and a deep, abiding sense of hopelessness. My father. My *dad*.

"It's understandable," Simon says, "to feel shocked."

I shake my head. "It's not just shock. It's... if you knew my father..." Tears sting my eyes as I stumble over my words in my desperation to make him understand. "He was always the gentlest man. My mother left us when I was four, and he did everything for me. Everything." The words spill out of me, memory after tender memory. "Made me dinner every night. Brushed the tangles out of my hair. Taught me how to dance for the seventh-grade homecoming dance. Read me bedtime stories. Taught me how to roller-skate and to ride my bike. Talked me through my first period even though he was scarlet with embarrassment." A tear spills down my cheek and I brush it away, too devastated to be embarrassed, to feel exposed. "He's my hero," I say simply. Brokenly. "My *hero*."

Simon is silent for a long moment. When I dare to look at him, his expression is more pensive than sympathetic. I feel as if he is, if not entirely unmoved, then something close to it, and I feel a flash of anger. Why can't he understand how painful this is?

"I'm sorry," he says, and the words sound formal, rote. "I do appreciate how difficult this is."

"Do you?" I choke out, and his mouth tightens.

"I admit, I don't view it nearly as difficult as what other people are facing—the Weiss family, for example. Daniel Weiss—the *real* Daniel Weiss—his wife and daughter were gassed as soon as they arrived at Sobibor. His daughter was four years old. His wife was twenty-seven. His son, Leo, survived only by the whim of the camp commandant. Leo was just eleven years old when he saw his father die, shot by Hans Brenner—the same age as your daughter right now, I believe?"

I sniff back the last of my tears; I feel like I don't deserve to shed them. "It doesn't have to be a competition."

Simon returns to his seat and folds his hands on top of the table. "No," he agrees, "it doesn't. But I suppose I only have so much sympathy to go around."

"Do you hate my father?" I blurt, and he considers the question.

"No, but I have no real pity for him. He made his choices, just as we make ours. Everyone must face the consequences of their actions. That is the nature of justice."

"And mercy?" I ask quietly.

"He had his fair share of mercy during the last seventy years," Simon replies coolly. "When he enjoyed freedom and prosperity, had his own family, lived a full life, despite his crimes. Daniel Weiss didn't have any of that. He was denied it by your father and men like him."

I can't disagree with anything he is saying, and yet I want to. I *yearn* to pick holes in his arguments, find loopholes he's never seen. I stay silent. My head is aching and I feel as if I could sleep for a hundred years.

"Who is the woman in the photo?" Simon asks.

"I don't know."

I hesitate, and then slowly I draw the photo out of my pocket. Simon takes it, studying it intently.

"Yes," he murmurs, "it is the same woman, and also the same place, most likely one of the staff cottages at Sobibor—many of them had these front porches. There's nothing left now —they destroyed it after the revolt in '43—but they'd built the camp to look something like a Bavarian village, a holiday destination, to fool the Jews who had been taken there."

"Fool them?" How could anyone be fooled, when they were brought there in a cattle car, and, according to my research, as many as half the people died on the journey, from thirst, starvation, weakness, or being trampled?

"Yes, so they wouldn't panic as they were led to the gas chambers." He gazes at me thoughtfully, acknowledging my skepticism that they could be tricked in such a way. "You'd be surprised what people are willing to believe. It's a last desperate act of hope. A courage, of its own kind, or maybe just a way to cope. To survive in that second, even if you know you aren't going to, not in the long run."

I look down at the table. The ring feels heavy in my pocket. I don't know why I don't want to show it to Simon; my father has already been incriminated enough, surely.

"Did you find anything else?" he asks, and I wonder what gave me away.

Defeated, I draw the ring out of my pocket and lay it on the table. "It was with the photo."

"Do you recognize it?" he asks as he picks up the ring and studies it.

I shake my head. "No, I've never seen before."

Simon continues to study the ring, unspeaking. Is he wondering if it belonged to one of the prisoners? Did my father steal it from a woman headed for the gas chambers? Did he pull it off her trembling hand? The prospect feels ludicrously impossible. My father would never, ever do such a thing. I *know* he wouldn't. And yet I also know, now, that he must have done many things I would have never believed him capable of, or at least watched them being done.

I feel myself sag beneath the weight of everything I have learned, everything I now must know. There is no avoiding or ignoring anymore, no denying or rationalizing or trying to make sense of all the disparate parts, because, appallingly, they fit.

My father was at Sobibor.

CHAPTER 9

SEPTEMBER 1942

Sobibor, Poland

The sun was just starting to sink to the horizon as Hans walked up to the station platform, known by the officers, he'd learned, as the ramp. He saw Hauptscharführer Niemann standing by the station sign, his face expressionless as he watched the train pull up with a loud sigh of exhaust. A few other SS officers were waiting on the ramp, smoking and chatting, as well as some of the Ukrainian guards, known as Blackies for the black uniforms they wore—the old uniforms of the *Allgemeine* SS, in fact—who stood impassively, hands resting on the rifles slung across their chests. No one paid Hans any attention.

He turned toward the train, bracing himself for the sight of the dirty cattle cars he'd seen back in Stuttgart, only to be shocked by what he saw instead. These were normal train cars, more than adequate; through their windows, he glimpsed plush chairs, tables and lamps, more comfortable conditions than even those he and Anni had had for their journey here. He could also see some of the train's passengers inside—men and women in fedoras and furs, wearing watches and jewelry of silver and gold, carrying suitcases and handbags of expensive leather, all of it far better than anything Hans had ever owned.

The train doors opened and people began to spill out in a cacophony of sound, a blur of movement. He didn't recognize the language they were speaking as they called to each other, jostling on the platform, mothers holding children's hands, fathers holding their chins up with determined bravado. Despite their obvious wealth, they were clearly uncertain, afraid, looking around wildly as people surged forward.

"*Guten tag, Jeder!*" A tall, elegant-looking man wearing a white doctor's coat over his uniform, stood on a small table, calling out to the crowd, as if he were a performer and they were his audience. "Silence, please! I am Oberscharführer Michel, and I am here to welcome you! There is no need to be afraid. Please leave your suitcases and bags on the platform. Your belongings will be returned to you in due course, I assure you. It is time for Jews to become productive for the Reich. You will be transferred to Ukraine to work and live, where there is space for all of you. Families will stay together. Have no fear."

Hans felt rather than heard the ripple of relief move through the crowd. He saw a woman glance at her husband with tears in her eyes; he reached for her hand and squeezed, and she smiled in return. A child clung to his father's legs; Hans watched as the man reached down and caressed the boy's cheek, a look of naked relief on his face, softening his features.

"For the safety of those at this camp," Oberscharführer Michel continued, "we must ask that you shower before traveling onward. A necessary precaution, to prevent any outbreaks of typhus or other diseases in the camp. Women will have their hair cut—again, a necessary precaution, to avoid the spread of lice." He gazed around at all the faces—Hans thought there must be as many as a thousand Jews up and down the platform, surrounded by SS and Blackies—and smiled. "I promise you, there is no need to fear. You will be well provided for in

Ukraine, with plenty of space, air, opportunities to work, to live. But first, the showers!" He threw an arm out. "Women and children to the right, men to the left. Quickly, now! Quickly! *Schnell!*"

With a flourish, the man jumped off the table, and incongruously, waltz music started up, piped through speakers lashed to posts. The music had the effect of turning the event into something of a celebration, as couples hugged and children laughed and the feeling of relief, even of joy, was palpable.

Hans felt himself smiling. What, he wondered, had anyone been afraid of, after all? He watched as the Jews began to deposit their suitcases in a heap; some tossed them aside with careless abandon, while others lined them up with assiduous precision. He glimpsed a birdcage of gold wire with a brightly feathered parrot inside; someone else had brought an accordion, and it made Hans think of Niemann's remark about the violin.

All of it was left on the platform while the guards herded them along, toward a tunnel-like passageway lined with what looked like woven tree branches, but, Hans realized, were there simply to disguise the barbed wire.

As they left, he glanced around, surprised to now see an invisible army creep forward; he hadn't noticed them before, but in addition to the officers and guards, prisoners—at least he assumed they were prisoners, judging by their ragged and shapeless clothing, their gaunt faces—had been skulking by the platform and were now darting forward, taking the suitcases and hauling them toward a storage shed.

Hans looked about, bemused, uncertain. What was he meant to do, especially if the Jews would be given back their possessions, when they were transported to Ukraine? Although Niemann had said they wouldn't need them, he recalled. Well, what of it? He wasn't as naïve as all that; he suspected the officers and guards went through the Jews' belongings and took for themselves what they liked. He'd seen it in Stuttgart, the men who moved into Jews' lavish apartments, took over their businesses, put their paintings on their walls. It was, he supposed, the nature of war. Right now, the officers were simply loitering about, looking bored, and the guards had gone with the Jews, taking them to the showers.

He spied Hauptscharführer Niemann a few meters down the platform, smoking, and approached him with what he hoped was a confident air.

"*Heil* Hitler, *Hauptscharführer*. What is it you would like me to do?"

Niemann regarded him with the same weary air as before, making Hans feel like a child who had to be entertained. It was not a sensation he enjoyed.

"Ah, yes. Our little bookkeeper." Niemann jerked a thumb toward the prisoners hauling the suitcases toward camp two. "Once they've gone through that lot, you can start counting the money. This looked a rich bunch—I'm sure there'll be plenty of guilders."

"Guilders... they were from Holland?" Hans guessed, and Niemann gave him a sardonic look.

"Yes, from Utrecht. Off on a holiday, or couldn't you tell?" He let out a rather sharp laugh.

"Where should I go?" Hans asked, hating that he had to ask the question, that he didn't know.

"There's a room for you in the administration building, two doors down from mine. It might be better if you stay there, for the time being." Niemann shook his head slowly. "I'm not sure you're cut out for this work, Brenner."

"I'm quite capable, I assure you," Hans replied stiffly. He realized that although he'd been wary about coming east, working at a camp, he did not now want to be sent away in some sort of disgrace. "I am capable of whatever is required of me," he stated with a slightly pompous air that he immediately regretted.

Niemann regarded him thoughtfully for a long moment. "Are you?" he finally answered. "Good. There's another trans-port coming tomorrow—and they're not from Holland. Polish Jews, from Warsaw. You'll find the experience quite different, I think. But that's not a bad thing, for a *putzi* like you."

Hans flushed angrily. He was not a baby, for heaven's sake! He could handle this job. He could handle whatever Hauptscharführer Niemann or anyone else threw at him.

"I'll be in the administration building," he stated coldly, and he turned smartly on his heel and marched away.

An hour later, a guard brought Hans several boxes full of bills. He stared at all the money—guilders, just as Niemann had said, along with American dollars, French francs, a few German Reichsmark. The guard who had dumped the box on the table in front of him, in the bare room he'd realized was his own, turned away indifferently. Hans chose not to ask the man any questions.

So the Jews weren't going to get their money back, he thought as he reached for the ledger he'd been given and opened it to a fresh page. Well, that wasn't really a surprise. Of course the Germans wanted to keep it. It had to be expensive, shipping all these Jews east, especially on trains like the one he'd seen, with its fancy tables and lamps. Why shouldn't they make a bit of a profit?

And yet his stomach churned as he pulled the box toward him and started counting the guilders.

Two hours later, when the sun had sunk toward the horizon and then disappeared behind the fringe of pine trees, Hans walked slowly from the administration building to the cottage where Anni waited. There was a chill in the air and the camp was quiet, strangely so, considering the thousand or more Dutch Jews who had come through not long before. Had they already been moved on, perhaps onto another train to Ukraine? Hans had been so absorbed in his counting that he hadn't heard anything, besides the occasional barked command of a guard, indecipherable in the distance.

He glanced at the station platform; it was empty, devoid of its crowds of humanity, its heaps of luggage. He looked away, squinting in the darkness as he turned into the officers' quarters and then mounted the steps to the front porch of his new home.

As he came into the cottage, his heart lightened; Anni had unpacked their few cases, and made the sparsely decorated place as homely as possible. There was a jug of autumn leaves on the rickety little table, and the blanket their mother had crocheted for him as a boy had been spread over the bed, which Anni had dragged from the bedroom and set up in the corner of the front room.

"Anni!" He was so pleased, he was grinning. "How lovely it all looks."

"It isn't much." Her voice was flat, and his smile dimmed, just a little.

"We are meant to go to the commandant's house for drinks."

"Yes, I know. One of the staff stopped by to tell me." She gestured to her dress of crumpled silk. "Why do you think I'm wearing this?"

Hans raked a hand through his hair. He wanted to wash and change, but he had no spare uniform and there wasn't time to heat any water.

Anni stood in the doorway, her arms folded, an obdurate look on her face. The evening, which a few moments before had at least held the possibility of being pleasant, now loomed in front of him darkly. Between Anni's stubborn reluctance and Niemann's contempt, he feared it would be an interminable evening indeed.

"Then you're ready?" he said, injecting a note of determined cheerfulness into his voice. "How lovely you look." He leaned over to kiss her cheek, but she flinched away.

"We don't want to be late," she said, her voice tight.

Hans stared at her helplessly. "Anni..." he began, but he didn't know how to finish. What was bothering her, and did he even want to know? He thought he probably didn't.

Anni didn't look at him as she reached for her coat and then walked to the door.

Camp Commandant Reichleitner's house, known as the Merry Flea, was in the middle of the officers' compound, a more impressive two-story house amidst all the smaller cottages. A Polish maid took their coats and ushered them into the sitting room, where several officers were already lounging about on sofas and chairs, having helped themselves to the drinks table with its array of liquor bottles and glasses. Another table held more food than Hans had seen in some time, thanks to rationing —a whole salami, that had already been sawed into, and several tins of meat, even caviar, as well as a large, gooey round of French cheese.

The officers glanced at Hans with a boredom that bordered on indifference, but he saw their gazes sharpen when they caught sight of Anni, and instinctively he stiffened. He put his hand under her elbow as he guided her to a seat in the corner of the room.

"I'll ask if there's lemonade," he told her, and she glared at him.

"I'm almost eighteen and I'm currently residing in a camp," she told him. "I think I can have some schnapps, or at least champagne."

"Oh, champagne, champagne, of course!" Hauptscharführer Niemann stood in the doorway, holding a bottle of Moët et Chandon champagne by the neck of the bottle, the collar of his uniform unbuttoned. He popped the cork with a rakish flourish, the fizz flowing over his hand before he grabbed an empty coupe from the drinks table and filled it to the brim. Hans suspected the man was already drunk.

Niemann handed it to Anni with a courtly bow that seemed mocking; she took the glass with a stony look and a barely polite *"Danke."* Hans watched on, powerless to do anything about it. Anni had had champagne before, but only sips, and he felt deeply uncomfortable having her drinking it here, among all these wolfish men, most of whom didn't seem to encounter decent women very often, at least not at a place like this. Already he was regretting his decision to bring Anni to this camp; he supposed she could have stayed in Stuttgart, with Frau Werling, but he hadn't wanted them to be separated. Now he wondered at his foolishness.

"Brenner, a drink?" Niemann asked him after he'd made his introductions to the other officers, and Hans had barely taken in the names. Reichleitner, the camp commandant, had not even bothered to make an appearance at his own party. Niemann gave him the same kind of sardonic glance he had before, and Hans tried not to visibly bristle or blush under it.

"Thank you." He took a coupe of champagne, feeling slightly silly, for all the other officers were drinking schnapps.

"Cigarette?" Niemann asked, proffering his pack, and stiffly Hans shook his head.

"I don't smoke."

"Don't smoke!" Niemann let out a bellow of laughter while a few officers smiled on; one snickered. "Don't smoke. Where did they get you from, the HJ?"

A joke he'd made before, but one he still seemed to find amusing.

"I'm twenty-three," Hans replied, and for some reason this

made Niemann laugh all the more, even though he couldn't be all that much older.

"What a baby," another man said in a mocking voice.

Hans turned to see a tall, blond man of about thirty lounging in a chair, grinning. He was handsome, a perfect Aryan specimen with his blue eyes, his chiseled nose and chin, yet there was something off-putting about the sharp cast of his features, a coldness in his expression that made Hans instinctively tense.

"A real virgin, eh? Well, you'll wise up soon enough."

A few other officers snickered again, and Hans bit his lips to keep from saying anything that would make him even more of a cause for mockery. He took a sip of his champagne, and the conversation thankfully flowed on; they were talking of the transports, and how dull it had been when they had been stalled for the summer, thanks to the broken machinery, whatever it was. All the while, they tossed back schnapps as if it were water, and Hans had the sense that these men drank long and hard every single night. More and more, he wished he hadn't brought Anni here, that he hadn't been allowed to. What had the *Gruppenführer* been thinking?

"We're being rude." The blond man with the cruel face leaned forward in his chair as he turned his bright blue gaze on Anni. "Ignoring the one lady in the room. What is your name, *Fraulein*?"

Anni turned to the man with a haughty look, while Hans looked on, apprehensive. "Anna," she said in a disdainful voice, not giving the nickname Hans and his parents had always called her. "And what is yours?"

"Gustav," the man replied, with a wolfish smile. "Oberscharführer Gustav Wagner." He adopted a mockingly old-fashioned gentlemanly tone as he gave a little bow. "So pleased to make your acquaintance."

Anni merely inclined her head, and while Hans was glad

she hadn't made some smart retort, he saw the way Wagner's eyes narrowed, his lips thinned. No doubt such a handsome man was used to impressing the ladies—and Anni was clearly far from impressed.

"I hope you enjoy your time here," Wagner continued, his expression relaxing, although Hans thought he still looked annoyed. "Although you won't find many decent women for company." He leaned back in his chair, a faint smile on his face. "Maybe I should find a little Jew girl to keep you company."

"Wagner is in charge of the work detail," Niemann explained to Hans, who realized he must have been looking confused. "He selects which prisoners stay on for labor."

"Would you like that?" Wagner asked Anni, and it sounded like a taunt. "Would you like a little Jewess to keep you company, Fraulein Brenner?"

"I daresay it could be interesting," Anni replied tonelessly, and for some reason this caused Wagner to let out a guffaw of laughter. He tossed back the rest of his schnapps, seeming to dismiss Anni in a moment, and while Hans was glad his sister was no longer the center of attention, he felt a deep unease running through him, settling into his bones. He had no doubt that Wagner was a dangerous man—not just to the prisoners, but to his sister. To him.

"We should go," he said, after another quarter of an hour had passed and he felt he could leave without seeming too rude. "It has been a long day of travel, and as you said, there is another transport tomorrow, I am sure I will be busy." He addressed this to Niemann, but it was Wagner who answered.

"Oh, you will, Brenner, you will," he said, and once more his words sounded like a jeer.

Hans rose, bowed briefly, and then, taking Anni by the elbow, left the room.

Outside, the night was cold and crisp, stars pricking the sky like needlepoint. The air still held that unpleasant, sweetish smell, but already Hans found himself getting used to it. He took a deep breath and let it out slowly; his whole body was thrumming with tension.

"Did you enjoy yourself?" he asked Anni once they were back in their own modest quarters.

"No." Her voice was flat, uncompromising.

Still, Hans tried for a conciliatory tone. "I admit, the men can be a bit coarse, but I suppose that is the way with camps. Perhaps it is better if you keep to yourself."

"I shall."

He stared at her helplessly, longing for the closeness they'd once shared, the easy laughter, the simple companionship. She would tease him, and he would smile, enjoying her playfulness. It had never been hard with Anni, but ever since he'd told her they had to go to Sobibor, she had been cold, almost indifferent to him. It hurt Hans almost unbearably.

"Are you sorry I brought you here, Anni?" he asked quietly.

She glanced at him from under her lashes, a long, searching look. "Are you sorry you came?" she asked finally.

"I..." He hesitated. "I don't know," he admitted finally. "It is a promotion, of sorts, and we are at war. If I can serve my country..." He trailed off at the look of scorn that flashed across her face. "Can't you understand that?"

"Can't you do the math?" she returned almost fiercely, and he let out an exasperated breath.

"The mathematics, Anni? Really—"

"Yes, really. It's quite simple math, as it happens. On the other side of that wall—" she jerked her head to the wall that separated the officers' quarters from those of the camp labor force—"there are barracks. Assuming they crowd them in, and I'm sure they must, two or even three times as many as is advisable or sanitary, there is room for only four, five hundred. Six hundred at most, I should think, in those buildings."

Hans stared at her, nonplussed. "And?" he asked finally.

"How many Jews arrived on the platform today?" At his surprised look, she informed him shortly, "Yes, I saw them. You can see the train arrive from our window. Dutch Jews, weren't they?"

"Yes—"

"How many?"

Hans shrugged. "I'd say about a thousand."

"More like two thousand," Anni replied. "I don't think you saw how far down the platform they went, and with about a hundred per car..." It was simple arithmetic, he supposed, for her. She paused significantly, as if waiting for him to say something, but what?

"What of it?" he finally asked.

"Two thousand Jews, Hans, and that is just today. The machinery has been broken, I know, and they haven't had a transport in several months, but another one is coming tomorrow, or so the deputy commandant said. And probably another one after that. But since we don't know, we won't include it in our equation." She sounded like a schoolteacher now, and he felt stupid. "Say another two thousand, or even just one thousand, to be on the safe side. What's one thousand plus two thousand, Hans?"

"*Anni.*"

"What is it?" She barked the question.

He felt himself growing angry, but he decided to play her game. "Three thousand."

Anni nodded. "Three thousand, in just two days. And barracks for only six hundred, at most."

Exasperated, Hans shook his head. "That's easily explainable, Anni. The Dutch Jews aren't staying here. They are being moved on, further east, to Ukraine. They were told so themselves, on the ramp. The barracks are just for the ones who stay, the ones Wagner chooses, for labor." Without meaning to, he'd adopted a kindly yet patronizing tone, as if he were the one who now had to explain simple sums to a child.

Anni gave him a look full of weary disdain. "Did you see the train leave the platform?"

"No, I was working—"

"Well, I did. It was empty. Not a soul on it. Not one Jew."

He shrugged. "There must have been another train—"

"There wasn't."

"All right, then, the Jews are being kept somewhere else, and they'll be moved on later." He shrugged, impatient now, wanting this conversation to be over. "This camp must be bigger than it looks, and you can't see all the barracks, surely. Who cares?"

Anni nodded as if he'd finally given the right answer. "That's right," she said quietly, almost to herself. "Who cares. Who *cares*." She shook her head slowly as she stared out the window, into the night. "Do the math, Hans," she said quietly. "Just do the math. That's where the answer always lies."

CHAPTER 10

LIBBY

The day after my meeting with Simon Baum, I finally face talking to my father. I have to, because there is no avoiding any of it anymore. There are no more possible explanations of mistaken identity I can cling to. My heart is so heavy, it feels like a weight I am dragging behind me, a ball and chain I don't have the strength to keep pulling along.

When I came back from DC yesterday afternoon, the house was quiet; Tim wasn't back from the pool with the kids and my dad was still at the day center, for the second day in a week, a fact that had made him grumpy. I wandered through the house, feeling like a stranger, a ghost, as if everything around me was unfamiliar rather than beloved. I ran my fingers along the back of the sofa, the tops of picture frames, as if reacquainting myself with life as I had once known it. I opened the fridge and stared inside as though looking into a foreign country. All I wanted to do was sleep, but I couldn't. Eventually I lay in bed, gritty-eyed, staring at the ceiling, my mind utterly, purposefully blank, an effort that took all my energy.

After fifteen minutes or maybe as long as an hour—time had lost all meaning—I heard the sounds of the front door opening and closing, the babbles of voices, of life that was normal and easy, simple and right. Tim was home with the kids, and he'd picked up my dad, as well. I heard all their voices—Em's animated, Lucas's grunt, my father's dry chuckle, Tim's low rumble of a reply. I heard the blare of the TV, the squeak of the fridge door opening and closing. Welcome sounds, of home, of family, of life and love. They all felt so very far away. I heard Tim say something to Lucas about dinner being soon. I closed my eyes.

After another while, I wasn't sure how long, Tim came into the bedroom. "Libby?" he asked quietly. "How was it?"

I didn't open my eyes. "He was at Sobibor."

I heard Tim release a long, low breath. "You're sure?"

"Yes."

I felt the mattress shift as he sat next to me on the bed. He lay a gentle hand on my calf and I had a bizarre urge to shrug it off, even as I craved some comfort, anything to make this just a little bit better. And yet at the same time, I couldn't bear sympathy, not even his. It was as if I was covered in thorns, in barbed wire, inside and out. Nothing was bearable. Everything hurt. This couldn't be happening, and yet it was.

"I'm sorry," he said quietly.

I managed a shrug, my throat too tight to reply.

"Are you going to talk to him? Or would you like me to?"

"I'll do it." The words sounded rusty, scraping my throat. Of course I would do it. I was his daughter. This was my responsibility, my burden, my grief. No one else's.

"Libby..." Tim sounded hesitant. "This doesn't change who he is. Who he has been, I mean, to you."

I opened my eyes and stared at my husband, the look of compassion on his face. Compassion I couldn't bring myself to feel, not yet anyway, because my father had lied to me. Again and again, in the worst possible way. He wasn't the man I thought he was. He never had been. Somehow I had to find a way to make peace with that, and yet I didn't even know how to begin.

"Of course it does," I told Tim flatly. "It changes everything."

I am thinking about that conversation now as I stand in front of the door of my father's bedroom. Does it really change everything, the way I said it did? Does it have to? Even now, knowing what I do, I am hoping that when I talk to my dad, he'll have some kind of reason, something I could never think of on my own, something that will make this just a tiny bit better.

They held a gun to my head, Libby, it was terrible. I had no choice, no choice at all. I tried to escape, I was as good as one of the prisoners...

Of course I know he almost certainly isn't going to say something like that, even if part of me can't help but hope. But what *is* he going to say? Will it be enough to make a difference? I'm afraid that it won't. That it can't, and yet I still hope.

Tim has taken another day off work—one he can't really afford—to take the children out again, a treat that has made them suspicious, because it's not the usual, to go out with their dad on a weekday twice in a row. I know they both realize something is wrong; Em has been shooting me panicky, troubled looks for the last few days, and yet she hasn't asked her usual barrage of questions. It's as if she knows she doesn't want to know, and I understand that feeling all too well.

Even now, when I long for my dad to explain it all to me in a way I can understand, I dread having this conversation. I dread knowing more than I already do—and having to learn to live with it somehow, when that seems utterly impossible. The conflicting emotions inside me jostle and jar; I can't make sense of myself, never mind my dad, and yet I know I have to try, and so I open the door.

"Dad?" I ask quietly, and he stirs in his chair, lifting his head as he blinks the sleep out of his eyes.

"I wasn't sleeping," he tells me with a smile. "Just resting my eyes."

I come into the room, closing the door behind me with an air of import, and instantly he's alert, sensing my somberness.

"Libby? *Liebe*? What is it?"

"I... I need to talk to you." Already my throat is thick, my chest burning with both sorrow and anger that I force myself to choke down, at least in this moment.

My father pales. "It's not one of the children, is it?" he asks in something close to a gasp. "They're all right? Nothing's happened?"

"No, no, it's not that. Everyone's fine, Dad." God forbid he has a heart attack from shock now. And then I think, with an awful, macabre sense of humor, *But wouldn't that make everything easier?*

"Libby?" Now he sounds concerned, but not anxious. Not afraid. There is a tenderness in his voice that I ache to hear, because I know it so well. I *know* this man. He held Lucas when he was just a few hours old, his face suffused with love and wonder. He kissed my cheek with tears in his eyes after walking me down the aisle, when I married Tim. He was in the front row at my graduation, beaming with pride, even though it was only an associate's degree from a community college, because I hadn't wanted to leave him to go away for university. I know him... and he knows me. How could he have kept this secret from me, when for so long all we had was each other?

"Libby." He tries for a tone that is both smiling and stern. "Ach, you look so serious! Should I be worried?"

He is joking, maybe even a little nervous, and I can't bear it. I am angry, yes, but worse than that, I am so deeply, terribly sad.

I sit on the sofa across from him, resting my elbows on my knees. I stare down at the floor, trying to summon the strength for this conversation, but everything in me feels so *heavy*. I barely have the energy to lift my head and look him in the eye, and yet I do, because I have to. And maybe my dad sees something in my expression because the smile drops from his face and he goes still, attentive.

"I've thought you've seemed a bit low this week," he tells me, his tone cautious, and I almost want to laugh—or sob. *Low?* I have been so much worse than low.

I take a deep breath. He remains still, alert. Maybe part of him suspects what's next. Maybe part of him knows, has been waiting for this for years. Decades.

"Dad," I begin, "the man who came to the door last week—do you remember?"

"Eh?" He sounds a bit annoyed now, which is how he always sounds when he can't remember something, a way to mask his confusion.

"A policeman came to the door," I say slowly, carefully, as if I am talking to a child, "when you and Em were in here watching TV. I was at work. Em called me, and I came back and spoke to him for a little while. Do you remember?"

He gives a dismissive shrug, as if it doesn't matter. He really can't remember, I realize, and again I have an urge to both laugh and cry at the absurdity of it all. How can a man who can't even remember a visit last week be prosecuted for things that happened seventy years ago? And yet he can. He should be, because he did those things, whatever they are, and because I turned in the evidence he will be prosecuted, whether he remembers or not.

"That man was actually a lawyer," I tell my father. "A deputy chief with the Department of Justice—the Human Rights and Special Prosecutions office."

My father still stares at me blankly, and somehow this gives me a flicker of hope. Surely by now he should start realizing what I'm about to say. The light should begin to dawn, the flash of guilt... but I see nothing but a vague confusion in his troubled gaze.

Is there any way, any way at all, I wonder desperately, that that photo could have been taken somewhere else, *of* someone else? Any way for my father to be innocent, so he keeps looking at me with that blank expression, a faint puzzlement in his faded eyes? I so want there to be... and yet already I know there is not.

"It's the branch of the government that assists in the prosecution of Nazi war criminals," I state, saying each word with precision, like a fragile burden I have to lay down with care, and that's when my father's expression freezes. For the space of a second, not even that, his whole body tenses, and then the bright gleam of understanding comes into his eyes, like a flash of lightning, and is gone.

His shoulders hunch and his expression closes like a curtain coming down on a play and he looks away, as if he is dismissing what I just said. Dismissing me.

"Dad?" I ask uncertainly, after a moment, when it seems he is not going to reply.

He doesn't answer, just picks up the TV remote and starts stabbing the buttons.

"Dad?" I press, trying to keep my voice gentle but firm, not wanting to reveal the throb of anger, the pulse of hurt, I feel deep inside me. "Dad? Don't you have anything to say about that?"

"I want to watch that show about the man who is stranded," he says in a truculent tone, the voice of a child. "The one with no money, no clothes, nothing. It comes on around now." His German accent, I think, sounds thicker than usual.

"*Stranded with Cash Peters*?" It's a ridiculous show about a man who is dumped in some strange town with no clothes or money and then has to depend on the kindness of locals to provide for him. It all must be rigged, and I can't quite believe my father is talking about it now, when I consider what I've just said.

"*Stranded with Cash Peters*. Yes." He stabs the remote again, his fingers shaking.

"*Dad*." I cover his hand with my own, but he pulls away, with surprising force for a man so old and frail. He turns back to the remote, determined to find the right button, the stupid show. Does he really think this is going to work? That I'll just drop the whole thing? Why isn't he trying to explain it to me? There is not a flicker of recrimination in his face, and that steels me to push it further. "Dad, come on, please," I say. "We need to talk about this."

"I don't want to talk about it." His voice is flat, his gaze on that stupid remote. I can't believe he's being so *childish*, as if his refusal will make any difference to what is going to happen.

"Well, you have to," I tell him, an edge entering my voice for the first time. "*We* have to, because there is going to be a trial." If I expect my words to shock him into sudden honesty, a broken repentance, they don't. He just keeps pushing the buttons. "Dad, the man who came here now has a warrant for your arrest." Or he will, very shortly, thanks to me. "You're going to be tried in the district court, in order to determine whether you should be extradited to Germany. *Germany*, Dad. And then they want to try you for war crimes, back in Germany." My voice is rising with each statement, and now I sound as if I'm more angry than afraid. Maybe I am. I didn't expect my father, my kind, gentle dad, to respond like this. Like a spoilt child. Like, perhaps, the man he really is, deep down. The man he has always been, and I just never saw it, and yet I still resist the notion. "Dad," I plead, my voice both rising and breaking, "do you realize what I'm saying?"

He presses his lips together and pushes another button. Suddenly *Stranded with Cash Peters* comes blaring onto the screen, with its ridiculous opening banjo music.

With a growl of frustration, I rise from the sofa, stalk over to the TV, and turn it off. The room is plunged into an awful silence, worse than the corny music, and my father glares at me mutinously.

"Dad, please." I take a deep breath, lower my voice, force myself to be calm. "We need to talk about this." Although what even is there to be said? What can be said, in this situation? Already I know there is no reason, no excuse, good enough, no matter what I've been futilely hoping. Nothing but the cold, hard truth I finally have no choice but to face. I take another breath, let it out slowly. Then I return to the sofa and sit down, my hands tucked between my knees. "I know you were at Sobibor," I tell him quietly. "You worked there as an accountant."

My father turns his head to look out the window, his lips still stubbornly pressed together. I've never seen him act like this, never. It's almost as if he's a different person, this obstinate, difficult child, not my gentle, loving father, the man I have known and loved. There is an intransigence to him that I sensed, back when I was twelve, but I never actually had to confront it so directly before, and it chills me now, because it makes me realize there really are depths to my father that I never knew, hidden and secret. As beloved as he has been to me, I have not truly known him. And if I have not truly known him, then how can I know what he was—is—capable of? *How can I love him?*

"Dad?" I prompt when he still has not spoken. "Don't you have anything to say about this?"

Nothing. He looks out the window, avoiding my gaze. I am caught between feeling exasperated, the way I would be with a toddler, and deeply, painfully sad—and yes, angry, too, although I am trying to suppress that emotion, unhelpful in this moment.

"Dad, please. I want to understand what happened back then. I know you," I continue, my voice starting to break before I manage to pull it back. "I know you're a good man. A lovely, loving man. You have always been so wonderful to me. And to my children. And Tim." I sniff back my tears. "And I don't understand how..." I trail off, shaking my head, because already I know there is nothing he can say that will explain it for me, at least not enough. Never enough. And yet I still try, I still hope, because it feels as if I have to. There has to be a way to make sense of this. "I just want to understand," I say quietly.

My father doesn't speak for a long moment, and I sense he is wrestling with himself. I wait, counting to ten in my head, and then twenty, thirty, one hundred. The seconds pass with agonizing slowness; I have to bite my lips to keep from snapping at him, or maybe screaming.

Finally, with his face still to the window, he says in a low voice, "You can never understand."

My breath escapes me in a rush; while I'm relieved he's finally spoken, it feels like he just blew away the last, faint dust of my ever so fragile hopes. Somehow, even now, despite everything, part of me wanted him to deny it. I still wanted the chance to believe it was a case of mistaken identity after all, even when I know, I *know*, it couldn't be. But it isn't. It isn't at all.

And that really does change everything.

"So you won't even tell me?" I ask, my voice caught between defeat and anger. "You won't even offer an explanation?"

"There is nothing to tell." He has turned stubborn again, mulish. "Nothing to explain."

"Dad—"

"I was given a job and I did it," he states flatly. "That's how it was back then. You didn't have a choice, you didn't question your superiors, you didn't mutter a word against anyone. Not one word! You just..." He gestures with his hand, a sharp, slashing movement. "You just did the work."

I swallow the acid tang in my mouth, my stomach churning. "What... what was it that you did, exactly?"

He thrusts out his lower lip. "I counted the money, that was all."

"In a death camp." The words come out hard, harder than I meant them to. But how? How could he have seen the things he must have, and borne them?

He shrugs, as if this is no more than a minor detail.

"But..." I sit back on the sofa, my mind starting to spin again, like a rat in a maze, trying to find escape routes. *If he just counted the money, if that really was all he did, stuck in some little cubbyhole somewhere...* I haven't actually thought past him being at Sobibor, past that one truth I couldn't bear to face, but now I find myself treacherously tempted to start rationalizing it all. It would be so easy to explain it all away, except, I know there is no way I can.

Still, my thoughts race toward that flicker of light at the end of this bleak, dark tunnel. My father wasn't like Demjanjuk, that guard who was prosecuted years ago. He wasn't a guard or a deputy, the kind who punished Jews, inflicting torture just for the fun of it, being cruel because they could. He was just a bean counter, off by himself, doing his job, keeping his head down. He probably didn't even interact with any of the prisoners...

Then I remember.

"What about the real Daniel Weiss?" I ask quietly. It feels so strange, to say that. My father is Hans Brenner. I was never Libby Weiss.

My father jerks his head round to look at me without expression, and then turns away again. The seconds tick by, slowly, painfully.

"The lawyer who came," I tell him, doing my best to keep my voice steady, "he said your real name is Hans Brenner, and that you took Daniel Weiss' name when you emigrated to America." I pause, waiting for him to reply, but he doesn't. "He says that you killed Daniel Weiss, during the camp revolt in October 1943."

My father is silent.

"Dad?" My voice has sharpened, because I am running out of patience, out of the ability even to want to understand. "Dad, did you kill him?" My voice is hard now, unforgiving. "Did you kill that man? The man whose name you took? *Stole?*"

"I don't want to talk about this," he says again, and then he reaches for the remote once more. A few seconds later *Stranded with Cash Peters* blares out of the TV once again.

I feel a surge of fury, and I am tempted to knock the remote out of his hand. To shout at him, to rail and scream and cry. *Talk to me.* Except right now, I realize, I don't want to talk to him. I don't even want to look at my own father. I swallow hard and then I stand up and walk out of the room.

CHAPTER 11

LIBBY

After I leave my dad's room, I move around the kitchen, tidying up, starting dinner, feeling almost as if I am existing outside myself. I am not thinking about my dad, or the trial that now looms, or Sobibor itself. I am just surviving each moment, second by painful second—focusing on each small task as if it takes up all my energy, all my concentration. Wipe this counter. Snap those beans. Stir that sauce. Behind that, my mind is blank, deliberately, utterly blank, and that is a relief.

The front door opens and Em tumbles inside, followed by Lucas and Tim. I forget where he took them today—minigolf or a trampoline park? But I turn to them with a huge, ready smile, like I've just been switched on. I've walked onstage to the play of my life; I feel like nothing more than a character, performing a role to an ignorant audience.

"Hey! How was it?" I ask, my tone way too enthusiastic, but thankfully Em is buzzing from being out and doesn't notice.

"It was great! I scored two hole-in-ones."

Minigolf, then. "Amazing, sweetheart." I give her another megawatt smile before turning to my son. "Lucas? Did you have a good time?"

He shrugs, already heading to the fridge for a snack. "It was okay."

"High praise, then," Tim says with a smile, and then gives me a silent look of inquiry that I pretend not to notice.

"Dinner is in about half an hour. Chicken pot pie."

"Yum!" Em says, and I am grateful for her easy joy in such simple pleasures. "Is Grandad awake?" She is already turning to go to his suite.

"I'm... I'm not sure," I say, after a second's pause that I know Tim registers. "But you can go see, I guess." I have no idea how my father will respond to Em. Surely he won't be as silent and stubborn with her as he was with me?

As Em goes off to see my dad and Lucas slouches down to the rec room with a bag of Doritos, Tim moves toward me. "How was it?" he asks in a low voice. "You talked to him?"

"Yes." I turn to stir the chicken, prodding the carrots to see if they're done.

"Are you going to tell me more than that?" Tim asks with just a hint of exasperation. I am, I realize, acting a bit like my father.

"He didn't say much, to be honest. He refused to talk about it."

"But—"

"He was there. That much was clear." The words come out in staccato, as if I've bitten them off and spat them out.

"I'm sorry, Lib." Tim puts a hand on my arm. I nod without speaking. "How do you feel about it?" he asks, and I wonder when my normally taciturn husband started *emoting* so much. He's still so calm himself, but he's probing my feelings in a way that feels like poking a raw nerve, an open wound. It *hurts*, and I don't like it. I certainly don't want to talk about it.

"I don't know how I feel," I answer woodenly. "Numb, I guess." Although underneath that numbness is a wild surge of emotions, of sorrow and grief and fury and fear. Simon Baum told me we'd receive the paperwork regarding the trial in a few days. Now that I've handed in evidence, everything has been set in motion, and it will all move quickly now, which makes me feel guilty, and then guilty for feeling guilty, and then angry at my father for everything, and then grief-stricken that I'm angry, that I have to be angry. I'm exhausted by my own emotions.

Tim is silent for a moment, his hand still on my arm. "We need to tell the kids," he says finally. "They'll need time to process it, be prepared for the trial, the publicity."

I nod, the movement mechanical. "Yes."

"And your dad will need to talk to Kate. Although if he admits he was at Sobibor, I'm not sure how much defense there is to make. All the judge will be determining is whether he should be extradited, not if he's actually guilty of anything."

"I know." I've read that much about extradition trials.

"But there might be some defense he can make," he continues. "You can't appeal an extradition, but you can file a request for a writ of *habeas corpus*, which would argue that his extradition violates his constitutional rights. There could still be a way around this, if we want to go that route. If your dad does."

The route of fighting Simon Baum, arguing against justice, finding the legal loopholes and wriggling through them, all the sort of things my father taught me not to do. My stomach cramps and I shake my head. "No."

"No?"

"I don't want to wriggle out of this. I don't want him to." Or really, I don't want him to want to, but it amounts to the same thing. "That wouldn't be right." I speak resolutely, even though it hurts.

"Libby, it's not *wriggling*. Your dad is ninety-six years old—"

"So?" Now I sound fierce, even if I don't feel it. Even if inside I am longing to agree with every word Tim says. *Yes, yes, let's find a way. Anything...*

"So," Tim replies, "he's an old man, he's lived a pretty exemplary life for seventy years. What, exactly, would be the point in him going to prison now?"

I've thought as much myself, but when Tim says it, it feels different. Wrong. "It was a *death camp*," I remind him quietly.

"I know."

"My mother's entire family died at Theresienstadt."

"I know that, too."

I shake my head wearily. "I get where you're coming from," I relent grudgingly, "but it doesn't change the facts. He served at an extermination camp."

Tim sighs. "I've always admired your certainty," he tells me, but he doesn't sound particularly admiring now, and the truth is, I'm a fake. I've never been less certain of anything in my life, and yet it feels like my principles—the ones my father instilled in me—are the only absolutes I have left.

We are silent for a moment, both of us lost in our own thoughts. Then Tim puts his hand over mine.

"Are you okay?" he asks quietly, and I give a jerky shrug. I am not remotely okay, but I don't want to say as much out loud. "I'm sorry for all of this, Libby. Truly." He folds me in his arms so I have to drop the spoon, and for a second I resist the hug—why? Because I am so raw and so prickly, and yet so numb? Because I feel that somehow my father's actions reflect on me? Or because I'm used to handling things on my own, and I'm scared if I lose control even for a few seconds, I'll never get it back, and Tim will see underneath the capable, can-do exterior I present to the world, to him, and maybe he won't like all the need and hurt he finds? I don't know. All of it, probably. I feel like a mess, and I can't hide it the way I want to. The way I usually do, because that is the only way I know how to be.

After a few seconds, though, I make myself relax, and I put my arms around him and rest my forehead against his shoulder. I breathe in the smell of him—soap, sunshine, a slight tang of summery sweat—and I close my eyes.

"I'm sorry," I murmur against his shoulder, the words drawn from me painfully. "I just feel really..." I try to think of the word, but I don't know of one that encompasses the maelstrom within me, both the churning emotions and the awful numbness. "Strange."

"That's understandable," he murmurs, and rubs my back.

Em comes back into the kitchen, and I step away from him, turn back to the chicken.

"Grandad was asleep," she tells us, sounding disappointed. "He usually wakes up if I turn the TV on, but he didn't."

Is my father just exhausted by our conversation, I wonder, or was he pretending to be asleep so he didn't have to face Em? Both prospects make me feel sad, but also angry. It's his fault we're in this situation. Is it wrong of me to feel that? I don't have any answers.

"Maybe just let him rest, Em," Tim says, and by the portentous tone of his voice, I already know what's coming next. "Mom and I need to talk to you and Lucas for a bit anyway."

Em's whole body twangs with alertness, as her alarmed gaze darts from Tim to me. "What—why?" Her voice rises to a high, shrill note of anxiety. "What's happened? What's wrong? Is it something with Grandad—"

"We'll talk you through it all," Tim says in a calming voice, but, of course, it doesn't calm her at all.

"Talk me *through* it? What does that even mean?" She knots her fingers together as she turns to me in appeal, sensing she won't get a straight answer from Tim. "Mom, what's going on? What's happened? Is everything going to be okay?"

I try to answer with my usual soothing platitudes, but this time they don't come. My lips tremble as I try to smile and then find I can't. *Is everything going to be okay?* I can't answer that question, because I really don't know the answer.

"*Mom*," she says again, her voice breaking; she is in full-blown panic mode now, her breath coming in pants, her gaze terrified, and all in a matter of seconds. My daughter can dial it up faster even than me.

"We'll talk about it later, Em," Tim replies, and I throw him a disbelieving look. Does he really think Em will be able to wait? She'll just wind herself up more and more, until by the time we all sit down to talk, she'll be near hysterical.

"Let's talk about it now," I say. "I'll just put the pie in the oven."

"Talk about *what*?" Em cries, and Tim hesitates, sighs.

Then, quietly, he says, "I'll go get Lucas."

He's making it worse, by being so somber about it all, but I don't suppose there's really any other way to be.

Em continues to pepper me with questions as I roll out the pastry and lay it on top of the chicken. "Mom, what's going on? Is something wrong with Grandad? Did something happen? Can't you tell me just a little—"

"Em, we're all going to sit down and talk about this in just a few minutes." I try to find my usual voice of steadying calm, but I sound almost as strained as she does. "Please, just wait."

As I am putting the pie in the oven, Tim comes back upstairs with Lucas, who is holding his half-eaten bag of chips, looking annoyed at being pried off the PlayStation.

"Let's all sit down in the family room, guys," Tim says, and now he sounds almost jovial.

Without speaking, we all move to the adjoining family room; Em curls up in the corner of the L-shaped sofa and Lucas flings himself on the other end, clearly wanting to get this over as quickly as possible. Tim sits between them, and I take the armchair.

We all sit in silence for a few seconds, and then Lucas throws me an incredulous, impatient look.

"Well? What's the big deal?"

I take a deep breath and glance at Tim; I realize he's waiting for me to speak. For some reason, I was half-expecting him to take on some "man of the house" role and be the one to explain, but clearly he thinks I should do it, or maybe assumes that I want to, the way I did with my father.

And really I should, and so I do.

"Do you remember the lawyer who came here the other day, about Grandad?"

"Yes, I thought he was a policeman." Em mumbles over her hand, which she's stuck in her mouth as she chews her already bitten nails. Lucas just shrugs.

"He was here because he identified Grandad as someone who worked in a... a camp during the Second World War."

"A camp?" Lucas perks up, interested in an academic sort of way, forgetting, perhaps, that we're talking about his grandfather. "You mean a concentration camp?"

Actually, worse. I think of Simon Baum's explanations of the extermination camps, the mere twenty minutes between arrival and death. "Yes, something like that."

"Grandad worked at one?" Lucas's eyes narrow, the academic turning personal as he absorbs what this means. "Was he a guard?"

"No, an accountant."

"An accountant? Why did they have an accountant at a camp?"

I glance at Em, who is silent and wide-eyed, still biting her nails.

"To count all the currency they took from the Jews," I say quietly.

"Grandad did that?" Lucas sounds surprised, but not actually disbelieving. There is a hint of censure in his tone that wounds me, even though I know it is more than deserved. I feel it myself.

"Yes, he did."

"He never said."

"No."

We are all silent for a moment, as Tim and I let them both absorb what I've just told them.

"So what does that guy want?" Lucas finally asks. "The one who came here?"

I glance at Tim, who takes over the narrative. "He came here because the German government wants to try Grandad in a court there for war crimes."

"What!" Lucas looks shocked, and Em's face has drained of color.

I feel lightheaded, woozy. Even though it's all I've been able to think about, it still comes as a shock every time; I keep expecting someone to interject how it's not going to happen that way, after all, but no one ever does, and I made sure of that.

"So he's going to have to go to Germany?" Lucas asks.

Tim explains about the extradition trial that will, according to Simon Baum, most likely take place in just a few weeks.

"And if they decide to do it?" Lucas asks while Em folds in on herself, her arms crossed, her expression shuttered. "He'll have to go to Germany? Will he go to *jail*?"

Tim glances at me and I have no idea what the expression on my face is. I feel numb again, and yet beneath that numbness is an incredulous kind of terror. My father in *jail*. In Germany. If that happens, he might as well have died. We'll never see him again. And yet he'll have deserved it.

"He might," Tim answers steadily. He's so calm about it all, it's as if it doesn't affect him. I find myself feeling resentful, and I know that isn't fair. I need him to be the steady one, and yet that steadiness still stings.

"But he just counted the money," Em protests, speaking for the first time. "He shouldn't go to jail if that's all he did. He didn't *hurt* anyone."

I'm not ready to talk about the real Daniel Weiss, and thankfully Tim doesn't mention him either.

"In Germany anyone who worked at a concentration

camp can be tried for Nazi crimes," he explains. "Because they are seen as having been an accessory to the murder of thousands, maybe even hundreds of thousands, of people."

"Grandad wasn't," she retorts fiercely, her face flushing, her eyes glittering with rage. "He *wasn't*."

"I'm not saying he was," Tim replies calmly, although as far as we know, he was. How can he deny that? How can I? "I'm saying," he continues in the same serene tone, "that's how the court sees it."

And surely that's how we should see it, too? Even if we don't want to? Even if everything in us resists.

Lucas has gone silent now, his arms folded, his expression completely closed. I wish I knew what he was thinking; I wish I knew how to respond. There are no parenting manuals for this type of situation. You won't find it in a chapter of *How to Parent Your Teen*. *How to Explain to Your Children That Their Grandfather is a War Criminal*. No, that won't be in the table of contents.

"Well, that's not fair." Em sounds stubborn now, as stubborn as my father. Her lower lip is thrust out, just as his was, and her arms are folded.

"Whether or not it's fair is for the court to decide, Em," Tim tells her gently. "The reason Mom and I are telling you this now is because there is going to be a trial, most likely in a few weeks. Not to determine whether he's guilty or innocent, but whether he should be taken to Germany for the criminal trial that will determine that."

Em's eyes go glassy and huge. "But I don't want him to go to Germany."

"None of us does, sweetheart," Tim says, and while that's definitely true, it's not *entirely* true. If he really is guilty... then surely I should want him to be tried. Or am I being unfair? Harsh? The way Tim seems to think I am.

"Can't we do something?" She turns to me accusingly. "You should be able to do something!"

"I'm not sure what we can do, Em." My voice sounds shaky and my breath hitches. If Em finds out I'm the one who turned in the evidence that gave Simon Baum the warrant to arrest my father, God help us all. "We're going to meet with our lawyer to go through our options."

"So he might be able to stay?" she asks eagerly, desperate for a way out of this.

Tim and I exchange glances. "We don't know," he replies quietly.

"But he *might*," Em insists and I want to tell her it's not going to work like that; I want to prepare her for what's ahead, but the words catch in my throat.

"It is likely to be in the news," Tim tells Em, glancing at Lucas as well. He is staring straight ahead, as if he's doing his best to ignore everyone and everything, as if he doesn't care about any of this. "Maybe even the national news, so I want you guys to be prepared for that. You don't have to talk to anyone about it, you can say you can't talk about it, because of the court case. But people will ask questions, and you might... you might see some upsetting things, on TV or YouTube or whatever. I'm sorry about that. I want you to know you can always talk to us, about whatever you see, whatever is bothering you. We both want to be here for you."

My stomach clenches. I picture things going viral on Twitter, the hate-filled messages that could spew out in an endless scroll, the hashtags that will trend, the essay-length posts on Facebook by people who don't actually know what they're talking about. Who aren't living it, minute by minute, hour by endless hour.

Neither of our children speaks. Lucas is still glowering, and Em has turned splotchy, her face mottled, a flush sweeping up her arms, which shows just how upset she is. Before either of us can say anything more, she scrambles off the sofa.

"Em—" I begin, but she's already running out of the room. "Em," I say again, uselessly, because her feet are thudding up the stairs and then I hear the slam of her door, hard enough to make the whole house shudder.

"Can I go now?" Lucas asks, unfolding his arms.

"Is there anything you want to ask us?" Tim manages to keep his voice calm despite everything. "Anything you want to know, that you're worried about?"

Lucas shakes his head as he rises from the sofa. "No," he replies, and then he goes back downstairs without another word. A few seconds later, I hear the sound of some video game on the PlayStation, and then Lucas talking to his friend through his gaming headphones. "Dude, you online now?" he says, before the rest is muffled.

A shuddering breath escapes me and Tim scratches his chin.

"I don't know if that went well or not," he says.

"They're processing it," I say shakily. "We all are." I feel as if I've barely begun.

"It is a lot to process," Tim acknowledges with a sympathetic smile.

Tell me about it.

I rise from the sofa to check on the chicken pie.

"Do you want me to talk to your dad about seeing Kate?" Tim asks as he follows me into the kitchen.

I open my mouth to say I'll do it, and then realize not only do I not want to, but I'm not sure I can. As much as I am trying to handle this on my own—out of instinct, out of need—right now I know I don't have the strength to talk to my father again, at least not in the calm, level way I know Tim will. I'm too angry. Too hurt.

"Yes, if you don't mind," I tell him wearily. "If he'll talk to you."

"I can try."

My dad and Tim have always had a good relationship. Tim is respectful in a way that my dad appreciates, but he can be lighthearted too, making my dad laugh. In return, my father both trusts and respects him, values his opinion, perhaps even more than mine. Tim is definitely the right person to talk to my dad about the legal stuff, but I still can't believe it's a conversation that needs to happen.

I take the pie out of the oven—it is perfectly golden and bubbling, sending up steam, smelling delicious. It looks like it could be on the cover of *Good Housekeeping*, or the centerpiece of a Norman Rockwell painting, yet for one heart-stopping second I have a sudden, wild urge to hurl it to the floor, to watch it all shatter and spill.

"I'll set the table," Tim says, as if this is a normal evening, as if our lives can simply go on and on as always—eating, drinking, sleeping, working, again and again. Look at us, a normal, happy family, living the American suburban dream.

I carry the pie to the table and place it in the center as Tim gets out the forks and knives.

CHAPTER 12

OCTOBER, 1942

Sobibor, Poland

Hans woke early the next morning, the first of the month, and fetched water from the bath block and breakfast from the kitchens, fresh bread from the bakery. He felt cheerful, enjoying these little tasks, as if he were visiting shops back in Stuttgart. There was a pleasing normality to it all that heartened him.

The morning was fresh and clear, the air crisp but still holding that strange, sweetish smell; Hans couldn't tell if it was from something burning or going rotten. Both, perhaps. Its pervasiveness made him feel uneasy, and even as he wondered whether to ask about it, he knew he wouldn't. He didn't want to betray his ignorance, but more than that, he didn't want to know its source.

With everything quiet and still, he took the opportunity to explore the camp a bit more, in the cool morning light. It felt as empty as ever, and the high walls and barbed wire fences, disguised by tree branches, made him feel as if he were in a maze. There was no clear view of anything, buildings and court-yards all marked off by high walls, and he got lost twice coming back from the dining hall. The trees in the pine forest surrounding the camp stood tall and straight, like silent sentinels, their beauty feeling somehow ominous, although he tried to brush such a fanciful feeling away.

Do the math. His argument with Anni still tugged at his conscience this morning, annoying him. Six hundred Jews to work in the camp, yes, he could see that. There was plenty to do, processing all the belongings. There must have been more than a thousand suitcases on the platform yesterday, as well as any number of cloth- or paper-wrapped parcels, picnic baskets, hatboxes, even toys. When he'd walked back from the administration building yesterday evening, he'd passed the storage sheds and glimpsed half a dozen prisoners sorting through huge heaps of clothing and blankets—and that was just one shed, one transport.

As for the thousand, or even two thousand, Dutch Jews that had come through? Well, they must have been loaded onto another train, and Anni simply hadn't seen it. She could be a bit of a know-it-all, his sister, and normally he regarded such an attitude with an amused affection, but right now it annoyed him, just a little. He was the one in charge here. He was the one wearing a uniform. Perhaps his sister needed reminding of it.

When he came back into their cottage, she was awake, although not yet dressed, a dressing gown thrown over her nightdress. She was huddled in one of the chairs, gazing out the window, and she didn't so much as turn her head as he came inside. The cottage was chilly, even for the first of October, and after putting down the breakfast tray, Hans went to the little wood stove and lit a fire.

"Ah, you're awake!" he remarked brightly. "Did you sleep well?"

Anni did not reply.

Hans focused on fanning the flames before he closed the door of the stove and then turned to his sister. "I've brought porridge and coffee, fresh bread as well. There's a bakery here, you know, and a few little shops." He remembered Niemann's warning about Anni keeping away from the Jews who worked in the shops, and added hastily, "If you need anything, just let me know and I will arrange it for you. New shoes, perhaps, or a coat?" He spoke cajolingly, wanting to please, never mind what he'd told himself about showing his sister who was in charge. He'd never been able to suffer Anni's frowns.

She threw him a scathingly disbelieving look, making Hans wonder if he'd misspoken. He supposed his sister was not much of a one for new clothes, but he was trying.

"Perhaps you could take a walk today," he suggested. "The sun is lovely and bright, and I think it will warm up by the afternoon. Would you like that, Anni? To get some air?"

Slowly she turned to look at him, and for a second Hans had the sense he was looking at a stranger—or she was. She acted as if she did not know him at all, as if she had never seen him before. "Go out?"

"Yes, perhaps in the wood?" He hesitated and then said, flushing a little, "There is a minefield all around the camp for fifty feet, but if you walk down the road a bit, you will be safe enough, I should think. The forest looks pleasant."

She stared at him for a long moment, slowly shaking her head. "Hans," she said at last, "what are we doing here?"

He tried to suppress the ripple of irritation he felt at such a pointless question. "You know what," he said and handed her a cup of coffee.

Anni took it, wrapping her fingers around the tin mug. "No, I don't," she told him. "I have thought and thought about it— why you? There must be dozens of accountants who are Party members. The SS owns so many business interests—granite works and meat packing plants, factories and quarries and mines. There will be accountants for all of them, or at least for most. Why did they pick you for this, when you weren't even in the SS?"

Hans shrugged uncomfortably, unable to meet her gaze. "I don't know."

"And you're young," she continued, making him prickle with annoyance again. He was five years older than she was. "Although perhaps they want someone young. Someone impressionable."

"I'm hardly impressionable," he protested. She was making him sound like a child, and a rather stupid one at that.

"And you want to please," she added, almost as if she were talking to herself. "I think that must be it. They saw your HJ record, how you'd turned up to every Nazi Party rally and parade—"

"If I hadn't, I'd have got into trouble!"

"But all the men here are SS officers," she continued musingly. "They've been picked for this job—I can tell. They have experience of this sort of thing. That Wagner..." Her lips tightened. "He looks completely savage. Do you know the prisoners call him 'the Beast'?"

Hans stared at her in open-mouthed surprise. "How could you possibly know such a thing?"

"I made friends with the Polish woman who cleans all the cottages," Anni told him with a dismissive shrug. "Jolanka. She hears everything."

"And what has she told you?" Hans asked, caught between curiosity and irritation that already Anni knew more than he did.

"She won't talk much, she doesn't want to say. She's afraid, and I understand why. She's Polish, after all."

Hans shrugged. "So?"

"Oh, Hans, why must you be so naïve?" Anni exclaimed. "So... so obtuse? Almost like you don't want to know. Perhaps you don't." She shook her head. "You saw the Polish workers back in Stuttgart—they worked on all the farms outside the city, and they stayed at that camp in Feuerbach. They were little more than slaves."

Hans shrugged again, uncomfortably this time, yet still annoyed. Yes, he'd seen the Polish workers—conscripted labor, with a P sewn on the front pocket of their shapeless uniforms. He hadn't thought too much about it; he supposed he'd assumed they were prisoners of war. But considering the thousands that had been sent to Stuttgart alone, he realized now they couldn't all be prisoners of war, and in any case, some had been women.

"Very well, what of it?" he asked. "What has this char-woman told you?"

"It's what she doesn't tell me that matters," Anni replied. "She won't speak of where the Jews all go. Only that some are kept here, in the barracks, to work."

Hans sighed. "They go to Ukraine, I *told* you—"

"Yes," Anni cut him off, shaking her head, and took a sip of her coffee. "So you did."

Irritated, Hans reached for his own cup and then moved to stand by the window that overlooked the small, weedy yard, the sky a square of hard, bright blue above it. "You ought to make the best of things here," he told Anni, his back to her. "Being difficult won't help you—or me, for that matter."

"What, are you hoping for, a promotion?" Her words sounded like a sneer.

"No, of course not." Hans felt his annoyance drain away, replaced only by weariness, as he turned around. "I just want to get through it, Anni, that's all. Get through it and get home, back to Stuttgart, back to the life we have there."

Anni's expression turned very still as she replied quietly, "We will never go back to that life, Hans. Never."

He blew out an impatient breath. "Don't say that! Of course we will. I can't imagine they will keep me here for more than a few months." He tried to speak confidently, but the truth was, he had no idea. No one had told him how long this position might be for.

"They will keep you here until they reach aleph null," she replied, and he hissed between his teeth.

"Not that again—"

"Although not truly aleph null," she amended softly. "For there is not an infinite number of Jews."

Hans shook his head and drained his coffee. He had no patience with her numbers, not today. "I must get ready," he told her. "I am meeting another train today." He hesitated and then said, a bit truculently, "Did you see them on the platform yesterday, Anni, from the window? Did you see their fine furs and jewelry?"

"Yes, and I saw how all of it was left," she replied flatly. "The suitcases, the clothes, the prized possessions. Why, you counted all their money yourself. It must have been quite a sum."

"I'm... I'm not saying it's right, to take everything they have," Hans told her, unable to keep a defensive note from creeping into his voice. "Of course I'm not saying it's right."

Anni merely stared at him, her eyebrows slightly raised. Hans realized he wasn't sure what point he'd been trying to make.

"I must get ready," he said again, and grabbing the pitcher of water he'd brought from the bath block, he stomped into the back room to wash and shave.

An hour later, with the freshness of the morning still lingering in the air, Hans made his way to the platform. He'd been told the next train was due around nine o'clock in the morning, and he wanted to be ready, alert and useful. He fully intended to show Niemann, and any of the others, that he knew exactly what he was doing.

Gustav Wagner was on the platform smoking when Hans approached, his step faltering slightly as he saw other man, the way his lips twisted into something close to a sneer.

"Ah, our little virgin. We're going to have fun today, Brenner, with this lot of Jews."

"Wagner." Hans nodded politely, choosing to ignore the man's jibe.

Wagner chuckled, as if Hans had said something funny. "I'm looking for a tailor today—the one who made my last jacket was shit. It ripped after only a week."

"Perhaps he can repair it," Hans suggested.

Wagner looked at him, his expression caught between disbelief and amusement. "He can't, because he's dead." He paused. "When my jacket ripped, I went back and shot him in the head."

Hans simply stared at him, having no idea how to reply. He'd sensed Wagner was dangerous, but he'd had not realized he was as much of a thug as that. Of course, he'd heard of such barbaric practices, back in Stuttgart. He wasn't as naïve as Anni seemed to think. He knew some Nazis, men in the Gestapo and the SS, liked to throw their weight around, show their power, shoot a man in the head, just because they could. Nazi policies appealed to savages as well as to rational men, just like any political party's, he supposed. As uneasy as that thought made him, he recognized it was one he had to accept. *See, Anni*, he thought, *I am not as naïve as you think.*

He didn't reply to Wagner, turning instead to stare down the empty expanse of railroad, a long, flat line of tracks leading to the blue horizon.

The other man laughed and threw the smoldering butt of his cigarette onto the track.

"Did Niemann give you a gun?" he asked, and Hans turned back to him reluctantly.

"I'm an accountant, not a guard."

"Or a whip?" Like so many of Wagner's words, it sounded like a taunt.

Hans pressed his lips together. "No."

Wagner snorted and turned aside, seeming to dismiss him. Hans supposed he wasn't very interesting to the man, without a gun or a whip. Wagner raised one hand to shield his eyes from the glare of the sun as he watched another officer, tall and loose-limbed, with a huge dog, some sort of mongrel St Bernard, trotting next to him.

"That bastard," Wagner muttered and spat onto the platform.

Hans glanced covertly at the officer strolling in such an easy way, almost as if he were on his way to a party. He had, Hans thought, the same cruel handsomeness about his face that Wagner did.

The men clearly did not like each other; as he approached, Wagner angled his body away from him.

"Bolender," he told Hans under his breath. "He set his damned dog on a Jew who had been making me a gold ring. Decent goldsmith, as it happened."

Hans glanced at the dog, black and white with floppy ears, tongue lolling out. He swallowed and said nothing.

Others were approaching the platform, as well; more SS officers, some of whom Hans recognized from last night, as well as a few Ukrainian guards in their black uniforms, rifles and whips at the ready, and then the prisoners, in their baggy, raggedy blue, creeping and skulking about at the edges, waiting to collect all the luggage.

Hans watched as an elegant-looking man approached, in dress uniform complete with gloves, a disinterested, arrogant look on his fleshy face as he stood slightly apart from the other men.

"That's Hauptsturmführer Reichleitner," Wagner told him. "The camp commandant. He doesn't often come to the ramp."

"Why not?" Hans asked, and a look of annoyance passed over Wagner's face.

"Niemann is right. You really don't know what you're doing here, do you?"

"I do," Hans protested, feeling indignant. He had not thought his question all that ignorant.

"Most of us were at Hartheim or Hadamar," Wagner remarked. "Reichleitner was, and Stangl before him. Bolender, too, and Niemann, Frenzel, Michel, Gomerski, Groth..." He paused, glancing at Hans up and down. "There are only one or two who didn't come from there." He paused, still eyeing him speculatively. "Have you ever heard of Hartheim? Hadamar? Sonnenstein? Do you know what we did there?"

Hans lifted his chin. "No."

Wagner shook his head, seeming about to speak, but then a whistle blew and they heard the sound of the train chugging steadily down the platform. Wagner grinned. "Here we go," he said, taking his Walther pistol from its holster and raising it up in the air, as if he was about to start a race.

Hans watched with a growing sense of unease and even alarm as the other officers and guards did the same, all of them poised with their guns above their heads and their whips at the ready. There was no white-coated doctor standing on his table this morning to assure everyone they would be taken to Ukraine; no waltz music being piped through the speakers.

Instead, there was a tension stealing through the place, a sense of expectation that felt, Hans thought with a sudden ripple of dread, evil. He could smell it, like something sharp and acrid. Even the huge dog was slavering and straining at its leash, as if it too knew something he did not.

He had a sudden, deep-seated urge to turn around and leave the platform, to go back to his office or the cottage and not see whatever was coming next. Instead, he remained rooted to the spot as the train came to a stop with a loud hiss of steam. It was not the elegant passenger train of the day before, but one made up of cattle cars and the smell emanating from them, even with the doors closed, was foul.

Hans watched as several guards stepped forward and yanked open the sliding doors of the first few cattle cars so sunlight poured into the dark, cramped space. Before Hans could even make out the people inside, the officers, Wagner included, had started firing their pistols into the air.

"*Raus, raus!*" they screamed as the air exploded with pistol shots. Get out. "*Schnell, schnell, raus!*"

Hans took a stumbling step back as Polish Jews began to emerge from the train, blinking like moles in the sunlight, wearing little more than sweat-stained rags, their gaunt, haggard faces frozen in stunned terror. He watched, his mouth agape, as the heavy whip of a guard whistled down on the back of an elderly man, forcing him to his knees on the platform. The man lurched upwards, stumbling forward, close enough that Hans could breathe in the smell of him, feces and sweat and something like decay. Their eyes met—the man's gaze full of panicked understanding, and then, quite suddenly, scorn. He stared at Hans for what seemed like a full minute but could have only been mere seconds, and then, to his shock, he spat at him full in the face.

Before Hans could even wipe the spittle from his cheek, Wagner had pointed his pistol at the old Jew and shot him in the head. He fell dead at Hans' feet while his still-warm saliva trickled down his cheek.

"Don't let them do that kind of thing," Wagner told him shortly, and then he turned to whip a young boy on. "*Raus!*" he screamed, his face turning ugly in his unholy rage, twisted and virulent and inhuman. "*Raus, raus!* Leave your belongings! Get to the yard!"

Hans stood completely frozen, longing to escape the dreadful scene that seemed straight out of hell, like one of

Bosch's terrible paintings come to life, all agony and fire, suffering and pain, and yet he was unable to. He wanted to put his hands over his ears, over his eyes, and block it all out— the couples clinging to each other, weeping; the mothers clutching their babies; the children who looked both terrified and lost, holding tightly to their parents' hands; the men trying to protect their families or look brave when they were utterly powerless, all of them being pushed down the platform, toward the camp and the yard outside the administration building, by screaming officers, their faces twisted with hatred and something worse, something almost, Hans thought, like ecstasy.

The guards were moving systematically down the train, opening more doors, shouting and firing their pistols, so more Jews stumbled onto the platform—weak, dazed, confused, terrified, everyone milling about, clinging to each other, weeping and shouting or shocked into silence, as the guards and officers, in an utter frenzy now, whipped and drove them onward, screaming all the while.

"*Raus, raus!* Leave your belongings on the platform! Don't take anything with you! *Schnell!*"

Unlike the Dutch Jews from yesterday, the Polish Jews had pitifully few belongings—cloth-wrapped bundles, the occasional battered suitcase. It all went into a heap to be sorted through later. There were no birdcages or accordions, no fedoras or furs, not today. Hans saw a photograph flutter to the ground; it was of a young couple, stiff-faced and dark-eyed, in their wedding finery, now trampled by the crowds streaming toward the *Schlauch*.

He watched, silent and horrified, as the Jews continued to be herded along, intermittently whipped, pushed, or shoved, off the ramp to the yard by the administration building, where he knew they would be forced to undress, before they had their showers. *Their showers*. He thought of the long, enclosed corridor, its barbed wire covered by branches, that led to—where? To what?

Do the math.

He caught sight of Wagner, peeling a baby away from its weeping mother, and he watched in stunned horror as, with an easy sort of carelessness, Wagner swung the infant hard against the side of the railroad car. It fell to the ground in a heap.

Hans made some sound; he didn't know what it was, but he knew then he could not bear to watch anymore. His stomach was roiling, bile rising in his throat. He stumbled away from the ramp with all of its hideousness—the wailing, the sobbing, the shouts and screams, the pistol shots, the terrible *thwack* of that poor tiny child hitting the railroad car—still echoing in his ears, and he walked blindly back toward the administration building, his heart thudding as he tried not to be sick.

As he came to the office, he glimpsed the enclosed yard with its high walls. Men and boys were undressing there, taking off their clothes with trembling hands. Hans watched a father help his son with some buttons; the boy's face was streaked with tears.

He watched for another moment as a guard screamed at them to go faster, *faster*, and another whipped a man for no reason at all. Then Hans turned and went into his office, carefully closing the door behind him.

He walked to the table where he had counted all the guilders yesterday, had made a neat note of the amount in his ledger, a day's work done. He pulled out his chair and sat down. He sat there for a few minutes, simply staring into space, and then he lay his head down on the table and closed his eyes.

CHAPTER 13

LIBBY

A week after we talked to the kids, I wake at 7 a.m. to someone knocking, quite determinedly, on our front door. It takes an explosion to wake Tim up, and even if the kids are awake, I know they're not going to answer the door, so it is up to me to stumble out of bed, throw on my bathrobe, and hurry downstairs. All the while, the knocking continues, a constant, insistent *tap tap tap*. What on earth?

It has been a difficult, endless week. The paperwork arrived a few days ago, with the date for the trial set in just three weeks. Seeing it there in stark black and white made it both more and less real at the same time. *How could this be happening?* And yet it was.

My father has maintained his tight-lipped silence, not that I've tried all that hard to break it, and he has refused to talk to our lawyer, Kate, despite Tim's patient exhortations. Em has been, at turns, tearful or angry; when I've tried to talk to her about it all, she's remained as tight-lipped as my father, although she has flung a few choice accusations at me. *"How can you let your own father go to jail?"* and *"Don't you care about him at all?*" As if I'm some unfeeling monster, as if I'm not hurting as much as she is. And as if I had a choice about any of this.

Of course, I *did* have a choice about whether to show Simon Baum that photograph, that ring. If I hadn't, perhaps my father wouldn't have been arrested. Perhaps none of this would be happening. When I think that way, I feel guilty for having done it, and then guilty for feeling guilty. My own father... and yet he was at that camp. Sobibor. What was I supposed to do? Cover for him? Lie, simply because he's old, he's lived a good life, and I love him? What about justice? About truth? I still believe my father would have wanted me to do the right thing, and yet his refusal to talk makes me question everything—him, me, the whole situation. What was the right thing to do, really?

I'm still not sure, and that has made me irritable, antsy, angry, emotional. I do my best to keep an even keel, to have our home and my work running as smoothly as possible, but I feel like a bad actor going through the motions, and all the while there is so much churning inside me, a maelstrom of feelings I am trying to suppress because I know I can't handle them, not yet. I certainly don't want to show them to anyone.

I've learned even more about Sobibor in the last week. I've made myself. Tim and I watched a documentary, after the children were in bed, about the escape attempt in October 1943, how the prisoners plotted together under the leadership of a Jewish Soviet soldier who had been captured at Smolensk. Sasha Pechersky was his name. Before the war, he was both an accountant and a musician. I wonder if my father knew him.

It is still so strange to think of my father knowing any of that world, never mind being an integral part of it. Even on the TV screen, captured in black and white stills or clumsy but well-meaning re-enactments, it all felt so grueling, so utterly harrowing—the bleakness of the place, the savage cruelty of the officers and guards, the cold-blooded, systematic murder of so many. I could hardly bear to watch for an hour, never mind live it for months, years, as my father did, and yet I still can't make it compute. At one point in the documentary, a survivor of Sobibor asked bleakly, "How did the guards see all that and choose to live?"

It's a question that has haunted me, because I cannot imagine the answer. How did my father—*my father*—see all that horror and still choose to live? And yet, I am glad, or at least grateful, that he did, because if he hadn't, I wouldn't be alive. Em and Lucas wouldn't be alive.

And yet... *how*? How did he do it? What does it mean that he did—for him, for me, for us, a father and daughter who were always a team?

The knocking continues, even louder now that I'm in the front hall.

"All right, I'm coming," I shout irritably, and then I open the front door, half-expecting to see someone looking for their lost cat, or maybe a determined Amazon delivery man, but instead I am greeted by the flash of cameras, the thrust of a microphone near my face. At least half a dozen people are crowded onto my doorstep.

"Elizabeth Trent? Are you the daughter of Nazi SS officer Hans Brenner?"

"Did you know your father worked in a concentration camp?"

"How do you feel about his trial?"

"Will you go with him to Germany?"

"Do you think he'll appeal?"

"Is he still living in your house?"

The questions assault my senses as the camera shutters snap and the faces blur in front of me. I stumble back and then I slam the door, breathing heavily. My mind is spinning. I was in no way prepared for that. The trial isn't for two and a half more weeks. I thought no one knew about it yet; I didn't think we'd have to deal with publicity until my father went to court.

Tim had warned me and the kids that there would be publicity, but I'd pictured it as something distant, a channel I could switch off, a newspaper I didn't have to read. I've already been doing my best to avoid any social media since Simon Baum came to my house. But this... people on my doorstep, invading my life, hurling questions and accusations at me. At my father.

I put my hands up to my face as I take a deep breath.

The knocking continues. Tim comes downstairs, rubbing the sleep out of his eyes.

"Who on earth is that?" he asks, heading for the door.

I fling out a hand. "Don't open it. It's... the press." I shake my head, everything in me still reeling. "They must have heard about the trial." Did Simon Baum leak the news? The thought sends a flare of fury through me. He warned me about the publicity, too. *It won't be pretty.* No kidding.

"The press?" Tim blinks a few more times. "They're not allowed on our property."

"Don't open the door—"

But he does, standing there calmly while the cameras snap and the reporters fire more questions.

"Were you aware Hans Brenner was a Nazi?"

"How do you feel about having a war criminal in your house?"

"I must ask you to respect our privacy as well as our property," Tim states politely, speaking over the questions that continue, a relentless, battering tide. "Please leave the premises, or I will have no choice but to call the police. My family will be issuing a statement in due course."

I stumble back toward the kitchen, unwilling to hear anymore. My stomach heaves and I pour myself a glass of water, bolt it down with my eyes closed. I hear Tim come into the kitchen. He rests a hand briefly on my shoulder before moving away.

"I'll make some coffee," he says, and I nod.

I listen to the comforting sounds of a regular morning—a spoon clattering against a counter, the gush of the faucet, the hiss of the coffee maker. Sunlight streams through the French windows and I imagine what this day could look like, if it were normal. A lazy breakfast in the sunshine before I kiss the top of Em's head, check on my dad, tell Lucas to keep an eye out, and go to work for a couple of hours. I come home to make a late lunch, maybe deadhead a few flowers in the garden or throw in a load of laundry, take a trip with Em to the farmers' market, think about dinner. Maybe Tim and I would have a glass of wine in the evening, out on the patio, watching the sun slowly sink to the horizon as the humidity thankfully seeped from the day. Perhaps my dad would join us, or sit in the family room and play a game of chess with Lucas. I'd hear his dry chuckle when Lucas made a good move and I'd sip my wine and think how lucky I was, slightly smug in the knowledge of my wonderful life.

It all seems so blissful now, and so impossibly out of reach. I wonder, distantly, if our lives will ever be the same again. If they ever can be. Even as I consider the question, I already know the answer. They won't. Things have already changed irrevocably; my father is not the man I thought he was. The man I loved.

"We need to make a statement," Tim says. "Kate said she'd help us draft one."

"Kate." I speak her name on a weary sigh. I've met her twice: once to do our wills and once to buy this house. "Does she have any experience with this sort of thing?"

Tim shrugs. "She knows us."

"Yes, but..." Does my dad need a proper defense lawyer, is what I am wondering. A criminal one? Honestly, all my legal knowledge has been gleaned from a couple of half-watched, late-night episodes of *Law & Order*. I'm completely out of my depth, in so many ways. We all are.

"Whatever statement we provide, it can be vague," Tim tells me, as if offering reassurance. I'm not sure it's much comfort. "The extradition trial doesn't go into criminal details. That's not what this is about, remember."

"I know." That will happen in Germany, if my father gets to Germany. I know enough already to realize he could potentially tie this case up in legal knots for months, if not years, the rest of his life. Most trials of Nazi war criminals last that long, often until their deaths. If my father chooses to fight, he might never have to go to Germany, and yet that means for the rest of his life he'll be living under a cloud, a stain, always heading to court, having to rake through the past again and again... and so will we.

"We should both meet with Kate, to talk about the statement," Tim continues. "I'll call her this morning."

"All right."

"We'll get through this, Lib."

I turn to him, trying to smile, but I can't summon the energy. "I know." But *how* will we get through, I wonder— bleeding, limping, scarred and never the same? Already Em seems like a different child; she's so *angry*. I shudder to think how she'll react if she finds out I turned in some evidence. And Lucas, so silent and surly. What if he's hiding something? Or am I just paranoid, because my father hid such a big secret from me for so long? For my whole life. I feel as if I can't trust anyone anymore, most of all myself. *How could I not have known?* Suspected, at least, or wondered. Will everyone else think that way too?

"But your dad really needs to talk to Kate," Tim adds as the coffee maker beeps comfortingly and he pours us both steaming mugs. "Do you think you can talk to him, ask him at least to speak to her once? She can't go into the trial blind."

She might have to. My dad has barely said two words to me since we had that conversation. He's acted with stiff, dignified affront, making me feel as if I'm the one who did something wrong, and maybe I did. Maybe I never should have looked for evidence. Maybe I never should have found it. And maybe I never should have given it to Simon Baum. And yet what was the alternative? To hide the truth? To live a lie?

My dad has, at least, been his same old self—mostly—with the children, watching TV with Em and playing chess with Lucas. Last night, he asked Lucas if he would look up something for him on the iPad, and they spent an hour closeted in his room. When I asked Lucas what it was about, he just shrugged and sloped off.

It feels like everyone is keeping secrets.

"I will talk to the lawyer."

Both Tim and I whirl around to see my father standing in the doorway to the kitchen. He's already dressed, even though it's not yet eight in the morning—shirt, tie, trousers—which must have taken some effort. His shoulders are thrown back, his expression somewhere between resigned and disdainful. When I look at him, I'm afraid I can see the ghost of the man he might have been, back then. The man who worked at Sobibor, who saw terrible things. Who did them.

"You will, Dad?" I speak carefully, unsure how to pitch my tone. Cheerful definitely doesn't feel right, and I don't even think I could manage it. Looking at him standing there, so small and dignified, remote and resolute, causes a surge of anger, a rush of love shot through with grief, both to go through me. "That would be great," I tell him. "Tim will call her today."

He gives a small, regal nod and then turns to walk slowly, painstakingly, back into his room, closing the door behind him with a firm click.

Tim and I exchange looks.

"That was easier than I thought," he says under his breath. "I wonder what made him change his mind?"

"Maybe he's finally realized this is inevitable." Something I am still coming to terms with, because heaven knows I'd hoped it would never get to this—a trial and all its ensuing publicity, a judge, a judgment. And yet it's my fault that it has.

"Maybe he wants to do the right thing," Tim counters gently.

"Maybe," I allow, but I can't help but think that it's about seventy years too late for that, although the truth is, I have no idea, no idea at all, what is going on in my father's mind—and I wonder if I ever did.

Kate agrees to come to our house that afternoon, at two o'clock. Most of the reporters have thankfully left, but a few remain camped out across the street, much to my neighbor's irritation. Barbara, a widow whose house they parked in front of, came out three times to ask them to move, and then knocked on my door to demand that I move them on, as if I could.

"I'm sorry for the hassle, Barbara," I said, wretchedly wishing I'd thought how I was going to tell people what was going on. Tim and I hadn't had that conversation yet; I'd thought there was still time. "I don't want them there, either, but as they're not on private property, there's nothing we can do."

She narrowed her eyes, clearly wondering what I was not saying. "Is someone in trouble?" she asked, her tone somewhere between concerned and suspicious.

"No, no, not in trouble, not..." I took a deep breath. "My father's citizenship is being questioned," I said, as if that were an explanation, even if it was true. When Kate spoke to Tim on the phone, she told him that part of the extradition trial would be the denaturalization of my father's citizenship, since he would have obtained it under false pretenses, a false name. I realized, with a jolt, that he would be addressed as Hans Brenner in the trial, in all the proceedings—the name of a stranger. *But he is a stranger, now.*

"And for that you have reporters and cameras?" Barbara huffed, and I gave her an apologetic smile.

"I'm sorry for the hassle," I said again, and gently closed the door.

When Kate comes to the house, the few reporters remaining spit out questions at her like bullets. Even though she's only a small-town lawyer, she has an officious, important manner as she walks briskly past them, head held high, without saying a word. She seems to be rising to the occasion; perhaps she's been waiting for a moment like this, to take the stage.

"So," she tells my father, Tim, and I as we all sit around the kitchen table, after introductions have been made; Lucas and Em are upstairs, by my decree, although I am sure at least Em is eavesdropping, and I don't want her to hear too much. "We have a few options that I can go through with you." She pauses. "I assume, first of all, that you do not wish to pursue mistaken identity as a potential defense, considering the evidence that has been submitted?" She glances at me and I bite my lip. I haven't actually told my father about the photograph and ring I found. I never got that far, but now it feels like I am keeping a secret, too.

My father, stony-faced, tilts his chin up a notch. "No, I do not."

"Right, then." Kate blows out a breath as she glances down at her notes. She is out of her element, I realize, as much as we are. "Speaking in general terms, extradition is permitted only if the requesting state has jurisdiction over the offense. Now, considering that these alleged crimes took place in Poland, we could offer the argument that the German government actually—"

"No." My father speaks quietly and firmly, and it takes Kate a second to realize he has at all.

She looks up from her notes, at a loss. "No?" she repeats. "To which part—?"

"All of it." My father's German accent sounds thicker than usual, and I think Kate notices it. She doesn't flinch or wince, but something close to it, a sort of spasm she suppresses. "I do not wish to contest any of the points," he states. "I waive my right to any extradition trial at all."

Silence greets this statement; Kate looks flummoxed, and I glance at Tim as if he can translate, but then I see that he looks flummoxed too, although I think I glimpse a gleam of something like respect in his eyes.

"So you won't have a trial," he says quietly.

My father shakes his head.

"Not have a trial?" I can barely process the words. Ever since Simon Baum came to my house, all I've been thinking about is this trial. And now it's not even going to happen? What does that mean for my father? "Dad," I ask, "what are you saying?"

"I will be extradited. I will not fight the proceedings. I will face a criminal trial in Germany." He glances at Kate with that same expression from this morning, half resigned, half disdainful. "There is no need for your services."

"I..." She blows out a breath, shrugs. "It's your decision, of course."

"Yes. My decision."

"But..." I realize then that, although I have been both deeply hurt and angry about my dad's involvement at Sobibor, although I have believed that every Nazi should face justice, including my own father, as agonizing as that was, I still assumed, on a subconscious level, that the extradition trial would last ages, that red tape would tie it up, that my father would submit the writ of *habeus corpus* or whatever else he had to. Whether that was the right thing to do or not is another matter entirely, but that's how all these trials have gone. They've lasted years, sometimes decades. I assumed we were in for a long haul, as hard as that was, but now it seems we aren't. I think of Simon Baum, telling me *they all deny it*.

Not my father, apparently.

And in the midst of my deep confusion, my wild grief, I feel a flicker of pride, because *this* is the man I know and love—and yet within that is the terrible realization that if he isn't going to fight it, then it really did happen. He is not making a defense, because he has none. No extenuating circumstances, no reason why, nothing to make me understand why it happened at all. He is guilty, and he knows it. He always did... which means I must have never really known him at all.

"There will still be a hearing," Kate says, gathering her wits together while Tim and I simply stare. "But it will be a simple matter, if you are going to waive your right to a trial. A formality." My father nods. "It will be in an immigration trial court, to denaturalize your citizenship. After that, immigration agents will arrange your transport to Germany. I imagine that, considering you are not contesting the extradition, you will not be seen as a flight risk. Once you are in Germany, you should be free to live your life as you please, within reason, of course, until the end of the trial."

My father nods again, as dignified as ever, but I feel a clutch of panic. *Live his life in Germany*? What life? This is happening way too fast. It feels as if he is already halfway out the door.

"When, though?" I ask Kate. "I mean, surely this all takes time...?" The bureaucracy, the red tape. It still exists, even without a trial—doesn't it?

"If he waives his right to a trial, that speeds things up considerably." She gives me an uncertain look of sympathy. "At a guess, the extradition could happen in a matter of weeks, maybe months, at most."

What? I swing around to stare at my father, but he isn't looking at me. He is staring straight ahead, his expression stony and stoic, and it feels almost as if he has already gone, as if he was never even here at all.

Part of me wonders if I should be relieved, but all I feel in this moment is grief.

CHAPTER 14

LIBBY

Simon Baum calls me that evening to let me know his team will be issuing a statement imminently. His voice is matter-of-fact, slightly cool, and I feel flat, almost uncaring about it all. I can't sustain this level of emotion, of hurt and anger and fear. *My father will be going to Germany. I may never see him again. Maybe I shouldn't even want to.* I haven't told Em or Lucas about what my dad decided, but I know I will have to, soon. And meanwhile, there is still a determined reporter camped across the street, waiting for some kind of scoop.

"What will your statement say?" I ask Simon dully.

"What they usually say in these instances. Mainly, that Virginia resident, Hans Brenner, who has been living under the alias Daniel Weiss, will be tried for extradition to Germany, based on his Nazi-sponsored acts of persecution while serving as an accountant at a Nazi death camp from 1942 to 1943. And that this demonstrates the Department of Justice's and its law enforcement partners' commitment to ensuring that the United States is not a safe haven for those who have participated in Nazi crimes against humanity and other human rights abuses." He speaks with a fluidity that denies the words' roteness.

"He won't be tried here," I tell Simon. I can't think of any reason to keep it from him. What does it matter now?

"What do you mean?" His voice is sharp; he must think we're trying to be slippery, find some get-out-of-jail-free card. *Like all the old Nazis do.*

"My father is waiving his right to an extradition trial."

Simon is silent for a long moment. "Is he?" he remarks, and he doesn't sound particularly impressed.

"Aren't you glad? Saves all the time and trouble of countless appeals, doesn't it?" I sound bitter; I can't help it. "He's not denying it, like you said he would. Like you said they all did." The implication is clear: my father is different, even if he is not different enough. It is a small mercy, indeed, considering.

"I'm glad he'll be extradited, certainly," Simon replies. "And yes, it will save time and money and hassle. But it also might mean your father doesn't want the details to come out in this country. He might just be saving himself—and maybe you—a lot of bad press."

Of course he sees it that way. I wonder if his job made him cynical—understandably—or if he was already. "Or maybe he just wants to do the right thing," I reply, stung, although I'm not even sure I believe it. My father is still refusing to discuss anything.

"Do the right thing?" Simon sounds skeptical. "Sorry, but no, I think he just doesn't want his family to hear about what he got up to at Sobibor."

"What do you think he 'got up to'?" I fling at him, unable to keep myself from it, although I'm pretty sure I don't want to know.

"I couldn't say." Simon's voice is measured. "But we do know he shot Daniel Weiss in cold blood. Who knows how many others?"

Others? I haven't even let myself consider such a possibility. I have not asked my father anything more about Daniel Weiss, and part of me hopes that at least in that there is some story, some reason. Even though my father's betrayal feels like a mortal wound, my instinct to defend him remains, and wars with one almost as strong to seek truth and justice, in all circumstances. One is deeply, painfully personal; the other feels morally right, and yet distant.

"I thought the extradition trial wasn't about the crimes he committed, anyway," I say finally. "Just about whether there is cause to try him."

"To find justifiable cause, they have to describe the crimes. It sounds like there's something your father doesn't want you to know."

"It sounds like you're making a lot of assumptions," I fire back, and Simon sighs.

"I appreciate this is hard for you, I really do, no matter what you think right now. But any assumptions I make are based on twenty years of experience of cases like these. I know what I'm talking about. Unfortunately." He sounds jaded now, rather than matter-of-fact, as weary as I am.

"How did you get into this line of work, anyway?" I ask, genuinely curious. "What made you decide to go after Nazis?" Most of whom would have been over seventy, if he started twenty years ago.

Simon doesn't reply for a long moment. "My father's family is from Czechoslovakia," he says finally. "He came to this country as a boy, in 1939, as part of a refugee program for under fourteens. His whole family—parents, grandparents, aunts, uncles, cousins—were all killed at Treblinka."

I am silent. What can I possibly say to that?

"I'm sorry," I tell him at last, my voice quiet.

"Your relatives died in Theresienstadt," he reminds me. "All your mother's family, if I recall correctly. Doesn't that make a difference to you and how you feel about this?"

Shock ripples through me. "I didn't realize you knew that."

"We investigate these cases very thoroughly."

"How do you think I feel about this?" I ask, wanting to know the answer. How can he know, when I'm not entirely sure myself?

"I think you feel conflicted, which is understandable. But I hope you realize you did the right thing—"

"In turning in the evidence that allowed my father to be arrested and tried?" I finish with an edge of bitterness. "Every time I think it was the right thing to do, I start to wonder."

"You don't need to wonder about that, Elizabeth." Simon sounds almost gentle.

I don't reply, because I don't want to admit that I know I always will. How can I not? I will never be free of the doubt that I am a good daughter, the fear that I made a mistake.

That evening, I knock on my father's door. I can hear *Wheel of Fortune* blaring on the TV, and when I step inside, Em is curled up on the sofa, my dad in his chair. She lifts her head as I open the door and then glares at me in angry accusation.

"What do you want?"

I blink, unnerved by her hostility, even though I've been facing it for a week. It feels so strange, coming from Em. So wrong. I wonder if she knows about the evidence I handed in, but I don't think she does. Surely she'd throw that at me if she did? It shames me, that I'm keeping it a secret, and yet I know I don't want to tell Em or my father. I don't want to imagine either of their reactions, face their condemnation, or worse, their hurt.

"I need to talk to Grandad, sweetheart," I tell her as pleasantly as I can.

"Why?"

"Leave it, *schatzi*," my father says, briefly touching Em's hand before muting the television. "There are things your mother needs to say, and they are not for your ears."

Em glowers at me, which hurts more than it should, perhaps, because I know she's confused and upset and frightened. She doesn't really blame me. At least, I hope she doesn't. She will if she finds out, I think, and then push that worry away for another day. It's hard enough to face her like this; Em has been my cuddly one, my go-to girl, always up for hanging out or a hug, and now she is looking at me as if she hates me.

"Fine," she huffs, and flounces out, slamming the door behind her.

I wince, and my father gives me a small, wry smile, the way he once would have, when we shared such things, and our relationship felt both easy and right. Then the smile drops and he turns his head away to stare at the wall.

"Em is finding this all pretty hard," I say, and he doesn't reply. I move to sit down on the sofa across from him while he remains with his head averted. Does he think I'll tiptoe away if he just keeps staring at the wall? It hurts that he won't even attempt to bridge the chasm that has opened up between us, that he doesn't seem to care enough to try. "Dad..." I try to speak as gently as I can, even though already I can feel the emotions rising—the anger, the hurt, the grief, the fear. "Will you please talk to me?"

"There is nothing to say."

"There is so much to say, I don't even know where to begin," I protest, my voice rising as a little of my anger and confusion slips out. "Please, Dad. I... I want to understand."

What follows is a long silence, while I wait with both hope and dread.

"Fine," he finally says. His voice is hard as he turns back to look at me. "What is it you want to understand, Elizabeth?"

When did he last call me by my full name? I feel like a kid

who has gotten in trouble. The look of stony challenge on his face is forbidding, and it doesn't make me want to ask any questions at all, but I know this might be my only chance to understand.

"Why did you go there?" I ask quietly. "To Sobibor?"

The corner of his mouth lifts in something almost like a sneer. "Because I was ordered to."

"Did you know it was a death camp?"

He stares at me for a moment, his face expressionless, before he replies. "During the second transport, I saw one of the officers shoot a man in the head. He fell down dead, right in front of me. The same officer took a baby and smacked it against the railroad car, the way you would with a... with a fish." His voice is hard, unyielding, without any regret or sorrow. "Of course I knew it was a death camp."

I blink, trying to absorb what he's telling me, the *way* he's telling me. This is the man who sang me to sleep every night, who brushed the tangles out of my hair so gently I barely felt it. Who took me to the Holocaust Museum both when the cornerstone was laid and when the museum was opened. Who told me, with tears in his eyes, that it was the most important museum in the world, because "those who do not remember the past are condemned to repeat it"—the words by George Santayana now inscribed over one of the huts at Auschwitz. My father had said them with reverence, with sorrow. How can this be that man? Which one is real?

"If you knew, why did you stay?" I ask after a moment, grappling to get hold of my thoughts, to make them make sense. I think of the survivor on that documentary—*how did they see what they did and choose to live?* How did my father? Day in and day out at the camp, and then for seventy years after?

My dad presses his lips together and shakes his head. It takes me a few seconds to realize he's not actually going to answer me.

"*Dad.*" I lean forward, one hand outstretched in supplication, which he ignores. "Dad, please. I'm trying to understand. I *want* to understand—"

"There's no understanding." The words are abrupt, almost dismissive.

I take a deep breath as I try to organize my thoughts once more, the jumble of questions. "Then if you won't answer that, at least tell me how you were able to marry—marry Mom, knowing she was Jewish?" I hardly ever refer to my mother as *Mom*. I can't remember calling her anything at all. I can barely remember her beyond a vague shape, a certain softness, the smell of lavender, the ghost of a memory.

"Half-Jewish," he corrects flatly, and I rear back, shocked he is choosing to make that distinction now, that he's using those words. What does it even mean now, to be half-Jewish?

"How?" I ask again, and this time my voice sounds raw.

He shakes his head once more. "I will not talk with you about your mother."

He sounds so firm, so final, so stern and unyielding. I realize he is not going to answer any of my questions, at least not so I am able to understand. He doesn't even *want* me to understand; he is not seeking my understanding, much less my forgiveness, and perhaps that is because neither are possible. Still, I want him to try. I want him to want to try, even if it doesn't get us anywhere.

"What about the real Daniel Weiss?" I ask, and now I am the one whose voice sounds hard. My fists clench instinctively.

My father's mouth tightens, but he still doesn't speak.

"Did you kill him, the way they say you did?"

My father is staring straight ahead, not looking at me, not even acknowledging my presence. The skin around his mouth is white, his eyes narrowed and flinty. I realize I am sitting upright in my chair, everything in me straining, because I *need* something from him—some explanation, some reason. Anything. *He was threatening me... it was a moment of anger... I've always regretted it...*

My father stays silent.

"Did you kill him?" I demand again, and now my voice is raw and hard and ugly.

Finally, my father looks at me. "I will not talk about Daniel Weiss."

The way he says his name jolts me, because it sounds as if my father has never really thought of himself as Daniel Weiss; it really was an alias, a mask. It also makes me think my father knew the real Daniel Weiss, knew him well. But did he kill him? Why won't he *say*? The answer seems obvious—because he did kill him. He must have. And yet, even after everything, I struggle to believe this.

The breath rushes out of me and I sag, the fight, the anger, gone, replaced by only bewilderment. I shake my head slowly; I feel too empty for tears. My father looks away again, as if he is dismissing me. I feel dismissed, as if I am merely pestering him with my questions when it is as if I am being wrung out, every last drop of me, so there's nothing left but an empty husk.

"Why won't you at least say?" I ask in little more than a whisper, and he simply shakes his head.

I decide to try a different tack; maybe it's time to tell him what I found. Right now, I don't even care if he's angry with me about it.

"I found a photo, in your cufflinks box," I say, searching for some reaction, a flicker in his eyes, a look of remembrance or loss or guilt. "And a wedding ring. I turned them into the Department of Justice."

Slowly, so slowly, my father turns to look at me again. I see a flash of pain in his eyes before his expression shutters. "You had no right to go through my things."

"They asked me to find evidence." I feel heady with the

recklessness of admitting it all now. "They needed it for the warrant for your arrest. I was so sure I wouldn't find any..." My voice chokes and I have to take a deep breath.

My father's mouth tightens, but he says nothing—no anger, no regret, just more silence.

I lean forward. "Who is the woman, Dad? In the photo I found? You're all at a table, in front of a cottage at the camp. At Sobibor. Tim said she looked like me."

He flinches a little at that, and then, after a long pause, he finally answers. "It is my sister, Anni."

"What...?" Once again, I am bewildered, lost, even though with the resemblance to me, I should have guessed. "But you never told me you had a sister." Which is a little ridiculous to point out right now, because there are so many things he never told me.

"She died."

"When?"

"An Allied bombing in February 1945 in Dresden." The words are toneless, without emotion.

"And she was with you at Sobibor? I didn't think women accompanied officers to the camps."

"They made an exception for her because she was only seventeen, and I was her guardian." A sound like a shudder escapes him. "But it was no place for a woman."

"Or for anyone," I say before I can keep myself from it, and my father gives me a weary look.

He looks as if he is going to say something, but then he just shakes his head.

"Did Mom know you worked at a death camp?" I ask. "Did she have any idea of what you'd done?"

"Why do you think she left me?" he retorts, before pressing his lips together and looking away. Again.

I stare, silent, appalled. *She left because she knew?* She

found out? This never occurred to me, not once since I found out my father was at Sobibor. Perhaps it should have; perhaps it should have been obvious. I wonder if Tim has suspected but didn't say anything to me. I know I haven't, not even a flicker, because I always thought, deep down, that *I* was the reason my mother left. I must have been. What mother, after all, leaves a four-year-old daughter behind, no matter what kind of tough time she's had? What kind of mother can do such a thing? And what does it say about her child?

"You told her?" I whisper to my father. He still isn't looking at me. "*That's* why she left? Because of you? Because she found out you worked in a camp, that you... you killed a man?" Maybe more than one. Maybe my father was like those savage guards, taking pleasure in pain, sadistic simply because they could be, with a gun, a whip. Why shouldn't it be true? I obviously didn't know him at all. I had no idea what he was capable of, and he is refusing to tell me anything. He won't deny anything, either. What am I supposed to think? What can I bear to believe?

My father nods tightly, his gaze still averted. "Yes, I told her. I wanted to be honest. I thought I could trust her."

"And she thought she could trust you!" The words burst out of me—savage, unforgiving. I cannot imagine the pain my mother must have felt, to realize the man she married had worked at a death camp, had been one of *those* people, when her entire extended family died either in the ghetto or at Theresienstadt. How could she have borne to look him in the eye? The answer comes all too quickly: she couldn't. She left. Left him, and therefore left me. I wasn't the reason; I was the casualty. The realization ricochets through me, scattering all my certainties.

"I don't want to talk about this," my father declares. He folds his arms, sounding stubborn, even petulant, and suddenly my fury rises up, unstoppable, endless. I have been trying to make excuses for this man ever since I learned what I believed was the unthinkable, the impossible, and have had to come to terms with it being neither, and *he's* acting like I'm the unreasonable one. He lied to me about *everything*—not just his time at Sobibor, but about my own mother. My own life. Mental health issues, he told me, when I was around ten and asking questions, before I learned not to. *She lost so many people, she had trouble forming attachments.* It made me fear I was unlovable; he let me live in that lie, that fear. He encouraged it. And all the while *he'd* been the reason.

"You don't want to talk about any of it," I hurl at him, the words tumbling from my lips in a torrent of rage. "You don't want to admit the truth. How have you lived with yourself, keeping such a secret from me for so long? I thought my mother left because... because of me! Did you know that? Did you realize—" I break off as I swallow back a sob. I'm too angry to let myself cry.

For a second, my father's stony mask drops and he looks wounded, anguished, one hand reaching toward me as I press back in my chair. "Libby, *liebe*, I never meant—"

"Don't call me *liebe*," I cut across him. "Don't call me that ever again."

He stills, and then he nods, and I have the sense that he has taken me at my word, and he won't, and it feels like a fresh grief. Grief upon grief, betrayal after betrayal. Tears sting my eyes and I shake my head until the world blurs. I am not going to cry. I want to stay angry.

"I thought I knew you," I choke out, and then, because I can't bear any more of his silence, his refusal to let me understand, his childish stubbornness, I rise and rush from the room.

Out in the hallway, I hear Tim call me from the kitchen, but I keep going. I call something back to him, I'm not sure what, and then I scoop the keys up from the table by the door and run out into the hot, humid night, the air damp on my face.

I start driving with tears blurring my eyes, not even knowing where I'm going. I manage to navigate three streets before I jerk the wheel to pull off the road, turn off the car, and then scream out loud, hard enough to hurt my throat, a howl of anguish torn from my lungs, echoing in my ears. Then I beat the steering wheel with my hands, over and over again, stinging my palms, as sobs shake my body, because I'm so, so angry, but I'm also so deeply, painfully sad, and I don't think I can bear the weight of either emotion.

There is no going back from this. My father—my *dad*—will never be the man I once thought he was, the man I loved and trusted and believed in, my hero and comforter and friend, and I simply cannot stand that thought. It's like an exposed nerve, an itching under my skin, a constant, agonizing pain I can't possibly learn to live with. And yet my father lived with worse for seventy years. How? *How?*

How can I ever make sense of this? How can I find a way forward for me, for my family?

Eventually, the sobs die down and I sag forward, folding over at the middle, my forehead resting on the top of the steering wheel. I am utterly spent. My eyes feel gritty and my body is limp with exhaustion. I don't ever want to have to move, to move on from this moment to whatever is next, and yet I know I have to.

When, after a few minutes, I glance wearily at my phone, I see there are four missed calls from Tim. I tip my head back against the seat and close my eyes.

Somehow I have to find the strength to go home and face it all. Face my father, but more importantly, help my children. See them through this. They are what matters now. My heart hardens, along with my resolve. My father made his choices, both seventy years ago and today. It's the future I have to think about. My family.

I open my eyes and stare straight ahead. The weariness has

left me, along with the grief. I've pushed it far down, with all those other jumbled emotions, where I can pretend I don't feel it. My lips pressed in a hard line, I start the car to drive back home.

CHAPTER 15

OCTOBER 1942

Sobibor, Poland

His third day at Sobibor, the day after the transport of Polish Jews, Hans went to see the camp commandant, Reichleitner. Yesterday, he had counted the money that had come in—the Polish zlotys and the precious gold pieces, the assortment of German Reichsmarks, French francs, even some Hungarian pengös. He had kept his head bent over the bills, his mind focused only on the task at hand, yet he could not escape the sounds of the shouts and cries he heard from outside the building, the whistling of the whip, the occasional, awful gunshot.

This was not like the first day, when the Dutch Jews had traipsed merrily down the camouflaged tunnel—the Road to Heaven, he recalled one of the guards calling it, and he'd stupidly assumed it was simply called that because it was the road to freedom, at least of a sort. He'd been so absurd, so deliberately obtuse, as naïve as Niemann thought or Anni accused, or really, worse. Far worse. No wonder his sister had looked at him with such scorn.

Do the math.

When he'd finally emerged from the administration building, he saw a couple of raggedy-looking prisoners on their hands and knees, scrubbing blood from the yard where the men had stripped. One looked up at him warily, his expression haunted before he ironed it out into smooth blankness and quickly looked back down again. The others didn't look up at all.

Hans had watched them for a moment, wanting to say something—but what? What could he possibly say to these people? He had thought of the man, spitting in his face. And then he had thought of Wagner, pulling out his pistol and shooting the man in the head with the same dispassionate indifference one might swat a fly. He had turned from the prisoners and walked on.

He didn't speak to Anni of what he'd seen on the ramp; he couldn't. In any case, he saw the truth of it in her face—the anguish in her eyes, followed by a flash of anger. She knew, and she knew he knew, as well, and yet neither of them spoke of it.

And so, the next morning, he walked heavily to Reichleitner's house, only to discover the man wouldn't see him.

"The commandant is busy," his housekeeper stated flatly, a dour-faced woman with lips pursed like a prune. "He says if you must speak to someone, to go find Hauptscharführer Niemann."

Hans did not want to talk to Niemann again. He did not want to see the contempt in the other man's eyes, the lazy mockery, and yet he had no choice if he wanted to get out of here. Still, he did not want to admit Niemann had been right. *I'm not sure you're cut out for this, Brenner.*

No, he was not, and he told himself he was glad of the fact. He did not want to become the sort of man who found killing commonplace, who could murder a baby, even a Jewish one, almost with a yawn. No, he was not cut out for this place at all.

Still, he did not relish the look on Niemann's face, when he came into his office. It was one of jaded knowledge, weary acceptance, bored mockery. Hans felt himself stiffening as he stood, shoulders thrown back, mouth drawn tight, his expression both sanctimonious and abject.

"What is it, Brenner?" Niemann asked in a lazy drawl.

"I... I wish to request a transfer."

Niemann raised his eyebrows. "A transfer?"

"I believe you were right." He spoke with difficult, bristling dignity. "I am not cut out for this sort of work."

Niemann sprawled back in his chair, arching one eyebrow with lackadaisical indifference. "No?"

"No." Hans stared down at his boots and waited for Nieman's response. It felt as if it was a long time coming.

"The thing is," Niemann said after an endless pause, "you can't really apply for a transfer, can you?"

Hans was forced to look up from the study of his boots. Niemann was smiling at him with a mixture of sympathy and scorn.

"I'll go anywhere," he said, trying for a regal dignity but knowing he sounded desperate. *Anywhere, anywhere at all but here.*

"Oh?" Niemann's smile turned into a sneer. "How about Stalingrad?"

Hans swallowed. "Stalingrad?" he repeated, as if he had never heard of the place, when, of course, it had been in the news since August, when fierce fighting had raged throughout the city, and the casualties on both sides had been devastating.

Niemann leaned forward. "Brenner," he said, "you don't think we can just let you go back to Dresden and work your desk job till the end of the war?"

"Stuttgart," Hans replied quietly. "I'm from Stuttgart."

Niemann waved a hand in dismissal. "It doesn't work that way, wherever you're from."

"Why not?" Hans could not keep himself from asking.

The other man sighed and turned to look out the window; it

was a quiet autumn morning, no transports scheduled till the day after tomorrow, the trees surrounding the camp cloaked in morning mist, their leaves turning crimson, scarlet, ochre. A beautiful day, save for the sweet, rotting smell that lingered in the camp and whose source Hans now feared he knew.

"Look," Niemann said finally, still staring out the window, "you're not the first man who has had some trouble of this kind."

You mean I'm not the first man to exhibit a shred of human decency? Hans thought, but did not dare say as much.

Niemann let out a long, weary sigh as he turned to face him once again. "Some find it... difficult... at first," he said and for a second, Hans felt as if he would choke.

Difficult? *Difficult?* Difficult was one of Anni's algebra equations, the kind that kept her staring at the ceiling for an hour at a time. Difficult was having to drink greasy, ersatz coffee that tasted like gasoline, or spend the night in a freezing air-raid shelter. This wasn't *difficult*. This was... this was... He could not even put into words what this was. He stood there silently, fuming and despairing. He knew there was nothing he could say.

"Look," Niemann continued, leaning forward with a creak of his chair. "It's easier if you just think of them as vermin. That's really what they are, you know. Vermin that need to be destroyed—like a rat or a roach. That's how you'd treat a pest, isn't it? Quickly, easily. They're not the same as you or me, Brenner." He smiled then, in appeal, while Hans' stomach churned.

The people he'd seen on that ramp had seemed very much like him—more so, he realized now, than he'd ever let himself acknowledge before. Some part of him had chosen to believe that Jews were... well, *Jews*. Different. If not actually *vermin*, then certainly inferior in some way, although he'd never quite said as much out loud, at least not to Anni, whom he had suspected would take a dim view of such reasoning. After all, the Jews hadn't seemed to mind so much when they were herded into ghettoes or onto trains; they hadn't protested very loudly. A proper German wouldn't have let himself be treated in such a fashion, would he? So, Hans realized, he'd let himself think.

He'd let himself believe Jews didn't have the finer feelings he did. In his mind, they were, somehow, a cross between a dumb animal and a sly thief; how he'd managed to make sense of two such notions, he didn't know, but he had. He'd drifted into thinking that way without even realizing he was doing so, complacent, unbothered, and the knowledge now of how he'd let himself be changed both startled and shamed him—and left him with what felt like an impossible choice. Sobibor or Stalingrad. Watching murder or committing it. Clinging to life here or courting death there.

He struggled to keep from closing his eyes, from trying futilely to wish it all away. What could he *do*?

"If it helps," Niemann said, "you don't have to be on the ramp for every transport. One of the guards can bring the money to you, in your office."

They'd been doing that anyway, Hans thought. There really was no need for him to witness the heinous, criminal tragedy that was the ramp, and yet—if he sat in his office, ignoring it all, did it change anything? Did it help anyone? It just made him a coward, and a complicit one at that.

"Brenner?" Niemann prompted, an edge of impatience to his voice. He'd clearly made as many concessions as he intended to.

"There's really no way for me to be transferred somewhere else?" Hans tried one last time, even though he knew it was useless. "I could do the accounts for *Granitwerke*, or one of the SS's factories..."

Niemann shook his head, a slow, firm back and forth, his tone, when he spoke, coldly final. "No, there is not."

"But why?" Hans burst out. "I wouldn't say anything..." Which also, he realized, made him complicit. No matter what he did—except die perhaps—he was damned. The thought was too awful to contemplate for very long. He forced it away and saw a look of something close to disgust flash in Niemann's eyes. It seemed almost humorous, in a horrible sort of way, that Niemann was disgusted by *him*, for protesting against all these brutal, systematic murders. And yet he clearly was.

"You don't get that choice," he stated flatly. "None of us do. And," he continued in a deliberately casual tone of voice, "just in case you weren't sure about this point, if you did speak about what happens here, to anyone, you'd be shot. You or your sister."

It didn't come as surprise, yet it still caused a ripple of dread to creep over his skin. He knew his sister, and he knew she wouldn't care what anyone said, not even a *Haupsturmführer* in the SS.

"I never should have brought her here," Hans exclaimed, unable to hide his bitterness. Why had the *Gruppenführer* in Stuttgart agreed to such a thing? Had he realized what this camp was like? What it was for? Perhaps he saw it as a way to control him—with his sister to protect, he might close his eyes to anything. Was that what he was now going to have to do? Anni should have stayed in their flat, Hans thought bitterly, safe and ignorant and far away, watched over by the beady eye of Frau Werling.

Niemann shrugged, unconcerned. "She's not the only woman who has come to the camp. Stangl was the commandant before Reichleitner and his wife stayed for over a month. Children, too. Offsite," he allowed, "but still. She knew what was going on, certainly. I'm quite sure of that."

Hans just shook his head.

Niemann glanced down at his file. "You applied to the SS before this," he remarked, and Hans flushed, a burn of shame. He hadn't told Anni about that, but yes, he had applied a few months ago, in the hope of being granted more lucrative contracts and also simply for the prestige, the honor. He'd wanted to be an officer in the *Allgemeine* SS, just like his father. How stupid he'd been! He'd never dreamed it would lead him here, to this.

"Really, this shouldn't come as a surprise to you," Niemann remarked. "Considering. You knew the Jews were being sent east?"

"Yes," Hans agreed, "but..." He found he couldn't finish.

Niemann released an exasperated breath. "What did you think we were doing, Brenner? Sending them on holiday?"

"Work camps..." Hans managed feebly. "Or to Ukraine, like..." He stopped at Niemann's blatant look of incredulity, that he'd believed Michel's lies on the ramp. "I suppose I didn't think about it too much," he finished lamely.

Niemann sighed, as if he'd had enough of him. "Well, no one likes getting their hands dirty, but here you are."

Hans swallowed and said nothing, and the other man's expression softened slightly.

"If you can separate it all in your head, you can have a pleasant enough time here. We play cards in the evening—you should join us."

It was a peace offering, and Hans knew he should take it with both hands, with gratitude.

"I don't play cards," he replied, and Niemann closed his folder.

"Go see to your sister, then," he said, a dismissal. He might as well have called him an old woman.

Hans offered the *Hitlergrüss* before walking slowly and stiffly from the room.

Back in their cottage, Anni was composing a letter to Frau Werling. She looked up when Hans entered. "Well?" she asked, and he had the sense she knew what he'd been doing even though he hadn't told her.

"I applied for a transfer," he replied dully. "They refused."

Anni put down her pen. "They refused absolutely? Just like that?"

He thought of the offer of the Eastern Front; no doubt Anni would tell him he should have taken it. He should choose death over living and working in a place like this. He hadn't realized just how fiercely she felt about the Jewish question, but he supposed he should have guessed. She had always seen things in mathematical terms, formulas for life in black and white. He was the one who had become mired in the shades of gray.

"Yes," he said as he looked out the window, the trees in the distance, silent and beautiful. "Just like that."

A few weeks passed and Hans stayed in his office. There were three transports during that time: two from Holland and one from Poland. He kept his head down and counted the money and pretended he couldn't hear the snarling dogs, the sudden gunshots, the anguished screams and grief-stricken wails. He didn't see the splashes of blood; he didn't watch the few prisoners who had been chosen for work grovel and sidle away, trying not to catch anyone's notice, their expressions caught between hardened acceptance and a deep, unspoken agony.

A few weeks was plenty of time for him to begin to understand how the camp worked, and what he learned only depressed him further. This bustling little city with its bakery and tailor, shoemaker and carpentry shop, had no real sense of order or law.

There was no army discipline, as far as he could see, no drills, no rules kept. Officers and guards sauntered about, doing whatever they liked. When they were bored, they made a sport of the prisoners, inventing ways to torture them and be entertained in the process. The whole thing made Hans feel utterly sick. He'd had to turn away from a particularly savage officer,

Gomerski, ordering a couple of Jews to do calisthenics until they collapsed, and then he'd ordered another wretched prisoner to whip their backs to a bloody pulp in punishment while he'd looked on, smirking.

It was all so barbaric, so needlessly cruel and utterly senseless, like little boys pulling the wings off flies, but on an incomprehensible scale. The sheer waste of it, along with the savagery, filled Hans with both disbelief and despair. He had always felt he'd had a respect for the law, a belief in both justice and the necessity of punishment. Before coming to Sobibor, he might have told Anni, in admittedly a rather pedantic and pompous sort of way, that she had to respect the government and that others knew better than they did how to rule, to mete out both justice and mercy. Now he looked back on that idiotic naivete and hated himself for it, for it had brought him here, to this.

Nothing about life at Sobibor, he thought, was remotely bearable, never mind as pleasant as Niemann had said it could be. He did not want to drink and play cards with the other officers; he did not want to take what would be seen as his fair share of the spoils. Almost all the officers dipped into the sorting sheds and took whatever they liked—a fur coat, a bottle of champagne, a diamond ring. Some of the prisoners even put things aside for an officer that they thought might be liked, as a way to curry favor.

Hans suspected he was already disliked for not taking part in such things; the other officers most likely considered him priggish and stupid. Even so, he could not make himself so much as go through the motions. He, who had stridden into this camp determined to make his mark and prove his worth, now only wanted to escape, unseen and forgotten. He wondered how long it would be before he was given different orders, and how changed he would be when that finally happened. How much of his humanity would he have lost?

.   .   .

In the third week after Hans had arrived in Sobibor, Gustav Wagner threw open the door to his little office where he'd been waiting for the money—the crumpled notes and handfuls of coins, some still warm from other people's hands—holding the arm of a man who looked both shocked and terrified. A Jew.

"Some company for you, Brenner," Wagner said with a laugh that sounded more like a snarl, and he threw the man toward Hans' desk, so he stumbled and fell, catching himself hard on the corner.

Hans half-rose from where he'd been sitting, one hand flung out to help the man, before he dropped it to his side. He thought of Wagner's warning from that second, awful transport. *You can't let them treat you like that.* He wanted to give Wagner no reason to pull out his gun and shoot the man in the head. Or him, for that matter. He was under no illusion that Wagner would treat him all that differently; many of the SS came to blows over petty disagreements, and Hans already knew the man disliked him.

He forced himself to sound cool, unimpressed even, as he turned to Wagner. "What am I meant to do with him?"

"He *says* he's a goldsmith. After Bolender's damned dog savaged the last one, I still want my gold ring." He let out an ugly sort of laugh. "Did you hear that, Jew? The last man who fashioned me a ring ended up as dog meat. You couldn't even make out his face after that mongrel had finished with him." He took a step closer to the man, who was huddled by the end of Hans' desk, his head lowered, so he could meet no one's gaze. "Don't lie to me," Wagner warned in a low growl.

The man shook his head, his gaze still on the floor, one hand fumbling to his side. It was only then that Hans saw the child cowering behind him—a boy, no more than ten or eleven, pressed close to his father.

Wagner glanced at them both, and Hans could have sworn he saw the man's fingers twitch toward his pistol. It felt as if everyone in the room were holding their breath. Then, with something like a grunt, Wagner turned and stalked away. As the door slammed behind him, Hans exhaled slowly and sat down.

The silence in the room was absolute, like concrete being poured over them, setting to stone. Hans had no idea what to say. What to think. What on earth was he to do with a Jew? *Two* Jews?

Then he saw that the boy was bleeding, an open wound by his eye, caused, he suspected, by a clout with the butt of a pistol.

"Your boy's hurt," he said quietly, and the man threw him a frightened, suspicious look and said nothing. "He needs stitches." Still nothing from either of them. "Let me fetch my sister," Hans said. "She's good with a needle."

He saw the man's hand flex on the boy's shoulder, fingers digging in, anchoring him in place. *As if you can keep him safe in a place like this*, Hans thought with a savage sort of sorrow. As if anything this man might do would help or postpone his fate. Both he and the boy were doomed, no matter how many rings they made. Anni had told him, having learned it from the maid, that the prisoners who served the first and second camps were changed on a regular basis, killed outright or sent to work in camp three, where no one, Hans knew, came back from. There were always fresh prisoners off the ramp to take their place.

"I'll fetch her," he said, and rose from the desk. The man and the boy still didn't speak. Hans paused by the door. "Don't leave this room," he ordered, and after a second's pause, the man nodded. His hand was still resting on his son's shoulder.

Back in their cottage, Anni was sitting at the table, tapping her pencil against her teeth as she worked out one of her math problems. She looked up, instantly alert as Hans burst through the door.

"What is it?" she asked in a tone of voice that suggested she'd been expecting the worst since they'd arrived. Perhaps she had; Hans had already noticed how her nails were bitten to the quick, her fingers redder and more raw than usual, and she never seemed to be able to keep still.

"I need your help," he said, and she rose from the table without question.

"Where?" she asked simply.

Quickly, he explained. Anni retrieved her sewing basket—she was a mediocre seamstress at best, despite what Hans had said about her skills—and followed him out of the cottage.

"They won't like you coming to the administration building," he told her in a low voice as they walked through the officers' quarters. "Niemann warned me not to let you wander about the camp."

"I've seen more of this camp than you have," Anni replied, and Hans shot her an uncertain look. He didn't know what she could mean—surely she hadn't gone *exploring*—but he left the matter as they walked through the courtyard where the men undressed—they were gone now, down the *Schlauch* as if they'd never even been—to his office.

The man was in the exact same place where Hans had left him, and the boy as well. He doubted whether they'd so much as twitched in his absence.

"It's the boy's eye," he said, and Anni walked up to the child with a confidence Hans didn't remotely feel.

"Let's have a look," she said, and guided him to a chair.

Hans stayed by the door, one hand pressed to the knob, in case anyone should come in. The building housed the offices of several other SS, as well as some of their accommodation and workshops run by Jews. He was usually left to himself, but who knew?

The boy remained still and silent under Anni's confident but somewhat clumsy ministrations. The man watched, gaunt-faced, hollow-eyed, a hungry, desperate look about him. His clothes were ragged and hung off thin shoulders, and he stank of piss and sweat, although Hans could hardly blame him for that, considering he'd spent hours, if not days, crammed into a cattle car with hundreds of other passengers.

"You're a goldsmith," he stated, and slowly the man turned and looked at him. He nodded. "Are you, really?" Hans asked quietly, because already he knew that many lied about their skills in a desperate attempt to stay alive. "Because Wagner…" He stopped, for he did not know what he could say about Wagner, and in any case, he did not want anything repeated.

"I am a goldsmith," the man said in careful German, and he nodded toward the boy. "And so is my son."

"Your son?" Hans couldn't help but sound skeptical. "He's only a child." There were a few children at the camp, wily boys who slipped from workshop to workshop, running messages, light-fingered and sly. The officers tolerated them with a grudging sort of amusement; Hans suspected their survival rate was better than that of their elders, although he already knew firsthand that a child could be killed as easily as a man.

"He's ten years old, and he's skilled," the man said firmly. "He has been learning at my side these last two years, and his fingers are nimble. We can make a ring. We can make a hundred rings."

And after that, Hans thought, *what happens to you?*

"Do you have tools?" he asked instead, and the man shook his head.

"They were taken—before. But the guard—the other one—said he would bring them back to us."

The other one. It took Hans a moment to realize that this man was equating him with someone like Gustav Wagner. They were both, in his eyes, guards, more or less the same—

they'd both shown mercy, of a kind, and yet they existed in this hellish system. They perpetuated it. Why should this prisoner trust one man over the other?

In any case, Hans wasn't sure he wanted him to. It was dangerous for them both. Yet the thought that someone could mistake him for someone like Gustav Wagner filled him with both horror and shame.

"There," Anni said, and stepped back from the boy. The cut above his eye had been lumpily stitched.

Hans turned to the man. "What is your name?" he asked, and the man drew himself up, reached one hand out for his son, to draw him back against his side.

"My name," he said, "is Daniel Weiss."

CHAPTER 16

LIBBY

I drive back home and walk into the house and a family who needs me, and I feel as if I don't know how to be needed. I don't know how to *be* anymore. Without my father, who am I? Without his love, my love for him, how do I define myself? They are questions that feel somewhat pathetic to be asking aged forty-eight, and yet I feel them right through to the core of my being. It's been my dad and me *forever*. A team, a partnership, an unbreakable bond.

"Lib?" Tim's voice is somewhere between concerned and exasperated as I walk past him. "What happened? Where did you go?"

"I needed to clear my head." Simply saying those words feels like too much.

I walk up the stairs, to our bedroom. After a few seconds, Tim follows me.

"*Libby*." He stands in the doorway while I curl up in my armchair, my head resting on my knees, as if I could somehow get small enough until I am not anything at all. "What's going on?"

I close my eyes.

"Did your dad say something to you? Have you learned something?" He takes a step into the room. "Talk to me, Libby. Don't leave me in the dark. Don't shut me out, please."

I force myself to open my eyes. "I'm not shutting you out." I am shutting everything *else* out, because I can't stand to think about any of it anymore. My brain feels too big for my head, my thoughts pressing on the edges of my skull. I feel as if I could explode, but instead I am collapsing inside myself.

"Why won't you tell me what's going on?" Tim asks.

"Please." I speak the words with numb lips as I let my eyes drift shut once more. "Please just let me be for a minute. I need to..." I trail off, because I am not sure what I need to do. My father is a Nazi. He's killed a man. He's as good as lied to me about my mother, made my whole life feel like a lie. My whole *self*. Even my name was a lie, I think numbly. I'm Libby Brenner. As for my dad, my hero, he was... I can't bear to think about what he was. What he did. "I just need a minute," I tell Tim, and after a few seconds he walks out of the room, shutting the door behind him.

I keep my eyes closed as I stay curled up in my chair, feeling utterly spent. My chest hurts from the futile screams that have torn out of me, and my eyes throb. I find myself thinking about my mother, obsessively combing through my memories, searching for every single scrap of remembrance.

A lullaby, in German. Soft, lilting, haunting—or am I imagining it? Maybe I've seen it in a movie. The same with my memory of a woman seated at a kitchen table, her dark hair falling down from a bun, her chin in her hand. Her gaze moving slowly over me, stopping on me as if she's not quite sure who I am. Or am I imagining that as well, a mixture of real life, the photograph I saw, and what I am feeling inside? Like my mother never knew me, just as I never knew her, and why? Because of my father. Because of what he did, who he was. How can I ever forgive him, never mind love him again? He took my mother from me, as good as if he'd shot her, just like he shot Daniel Weiss.

Did she think about taking me with her when she left? I wonder painfully. I picture her kissing me in my sleep, tiptoeing away in the night with tears in her eyes, but I know that is truly only a figment of my imagination. My father has always said, in a way that I thought was not meant to hurt, that my mother wasn't very maternal. He was the one who got up in the night when I was a baby, who changed my diapers, who taught me to walk. *Or so he said.* Am I to believe that now? Am I to believe anything?

Or, I wonder, was my mother glad to leave me, this child with Nazi blood running through its veins? Did she think that way, that I was somehow tainted? Did she look at me and think of my father, the life he'd lived, the man he'd killed, the horrors he'd seen and perpetrated?

I drop my head onto my knees, press my eyes into my kneecaps until lights blur and explode across my darkened vision. *I don't want to do this anymore.* I don't want to live this life. It's a weary, useless thought, one that goes nowhere. I *have* to do this—not for my sake, but for my children's. I don't have the luxury of basking in my own sadness, of mourning the easy and uncomplicated life I had just a few short weeks ago. It's gone, maybe forever. But for my children, I have to go on. I have to help them get through this.

Slowly, everything aching, I uncurl myself from the chair and walk out of the room. I find Lucas first, tapping on his door before, at his grunt, I poke my head in. He's at his desk, hands poised over the keyboard of his laptop, its screen angled away . from me. The look he gives me is guarded.

"What?"

"I just wondered how you were doing." I step into his bedroom, breathing in the teenaged boy smell of musty laundry and cheap deodorant, with only the merest hint of the sweet little boy he was a handful of years ago, when he smelled of sunshine and Band-Aids.

"Fine." The look he gives me is level, revealing nothing. Did he learn that from his grandfather?

I come in farther, picking my way through the piles of dirty clothes and damp towels on the floor, to perch on the end of his bed, the duvet rumpled and smelling none too clean. I need to tidy up in here, I think. I can't even remember the last time I vacuumed or dusted, changed the sheets, plumped the pillows.

"What are you working on?" I ask, with a nod toward his computer.

Lucas looks back at me, his eyes narrowed as if he's trying to figure out what my angle is, what I want. His hair, the same color as mine, is spiky and mussed, and his dark eyes have the most ridiculously luxuriant lashes, as if he wears mascara. He is always embarrassed by this, especially when old ladies comment on it. *What I wouldn't give for your lashes!* Now, with a jolt, I realize I see something of my father's sister in my son's eyes. *Anni.* The family I never knew I had.

"Nothing," Lucas says.

"Lucas." I manage a smile. We've been in monosyllabic territory for a good year now, but I still always try for more. "It must be something." I do my best to inject a note of playfulness into my voice but am pretty sure I fail. "You're not just staring at a blank screen."

"My chemistry thing." His teacher entered him and three others of the high school's best chem students into a state-wide science Olympiad; I don't know all the details, but they have to work on a research project together and present their findings in September. Tim has stated, with a beam of pride, that Lucas is taking after him.

"How is it going?" I ask, and he shrugs. "Are the other guys pulling their weight? Guys and girls, I mean." There's one young woman on the team, I recall.

Another shrug. "I guess."

"I'm sure you'll be great. You've always found chemistry easy, just like Dad." I give him an encouraging smile, but he's not looking at me. I know there's no point persisting with this line of inquiry; our conversation is starting to feel more like an interrogation. "How are you feeling about things with Grandad?" I ask instead, gentling my voice, cocking my head. I feel like a parody of parental concern, but I mean it, utterly.

Lucas turns back to his laptop. "Fine."

Fine? "Lucas, really. I want to know."

His shoulders twitch as he taps on his keyboard, his back now to me. "He's guilty, and he should be prosecuted, so yeah, I'm fine."

"Yes..." I allow, "but he's your grandad."

"So?"

Is it really that simple for him? And so, perhaps, it should be for me. Part of me wants it to be. "All I'm saying is, your feelings are likely to be complicated—"

"They're not."

"Okay." I breathe out. "Have you talked to him about any of it?"

"He asked me to look up the extradition trial thing on the iPad."

So that was what he wanted Lucas for. And part of me had hoped they were looking up chess masters or trivia, or something simple, easy. A sigh slips out of me like a whisper. "What did he want to know?"

"Whether he could avoid the trial, if he didn't contest anything."

Which is exactly what he did—but why? Because it was the right thing to do, or because, like Simon Baum suggested, he's hiding something? Something even more than what he has already, what I've learned.

"How do you feel about that?" I ask Lucas. I really should know better.

He lets out an annoyed hiss of breath. "Mom, please don't act like my therapist, okay?"

I give a grimace of apology. "Sorry, I just want to make sure you're okay—"

"I am. I am okay."

How? I think helplessly. How can anyone in this situation be okay?

"Are you angry with Grandad?" I ask and Lucas blows out another breath.

"He's guilty," he says, as if this is an answer. Maybe it is.

"Lucas..." My voice trails away as I realize I have no idea what else to say. I can't reach my father; I can't reach my son. But I know better than to push for some sort of emotional and heartwarming conversation we're clearly not going to have right now. "You can talk to me," I finally say, an admission of defeat. "If you want to. Whenever. About anything."

"Yeah." He nods, his gaze still trained on the screen of his laptop. "Sure."

I can't tell if he's being sarcastic or not. I rise from the bed and walk out of his room without saying anything more.

Next is Em, and I dread this conversation far more than the stilted conversation I had with Lucas, because I know how angry she is with me. It hurts, to have my daughter, my golden girl, act like she hates me. *Me*, when my father was the one who did something wrong, who worked in a concentration camp, who blew our family apart. Why am *I* the bad guy? Grace would say this kind of anger and angst was coming for me anyway, as soon as Em hit her teens, but I'd lulled myself into believing we could avoid all that teenaged trouble with her, because underneath her anxiousness, she's always been so sweet.

"Em?" Again I tap, poke my head in. She is on her bed, her

back hunched over something, and she doesn't even look at me as I step in her room, decorated in pink and purple and sparkles, when she was about eight. "What are you doing, sweetheart?"

"Nothing."

Children can be so predictable sometimes. "Seriously." I take another step in, and then I draw my breath in when I see what she's bent over. "Em, you're not allowed the iPad in your bedroom. You know that."

"Why not?" she flings at me. "Lucas is allowed his laptop."

"That's for school, and besides, he's fifteen." Tim and I quietly decided to take a harder line with Em than we did with Lucas when it came to tech and screens; Grace told me how social media can be so destructive for teenaged girls, and the last thing we wanted was for Em's anxiety to get any worse. "What have you been doing on the iPad, up here?" I try to keep my voice light, but a needling concern pokes through. What is she being so secretive about? What is she hiding?

Em lifts her head, pushing her hair away from her face to glare at me. "Nothing."

"Em." I don't really want to argue about the iPad right now, but I feel as if I have no choice, not when she's being so hostile. I can't let these things slide, not even now, when I am so tempted, when I know there are other battles to pick. "Let me have a look at it."

Wordlessly, her eyes practically burning into mine, she hands it to me.

I tap on the internet browser, only to discover the search history has been completely cleared. I didn't even know Em knew how to do that. I look back at her.

"Why did you clear the search history?"

She shrugs, folds her arms. "Why do you need to know every single thing I'm doing? It's, like, weird, you know. No one else's mom does that kind of thing. Ever."

Then they're foolish, I think, but don't say. I tuck the iPad under my arm. "I'll keep this for now."

"Of course you will." She snorts in derision, still glaring at me. She's so different from how she usually is, it almost feels like she's acting. *This isn't you*, I want to say, laughing, inviting her to share the absurdity of it, but, of course, that would be the worst thing to do.

I take a deep breath and sit on the edge of her bed. She scoots over, not to make room, but to get away from me. Her whole body is bristling. "Em, I know this is hard. I know you're sad about Grandad."

"You don't know anything."

"It's true there's a lot I don't know," I agree. "I certainly don't know the best way to act in this kind of situation. I don't know what's best for you or Lucas, or Dad or me, or Grandad. I'm just trying to muddle my way through the best I can."

"The best thing for Grandad," Em replies, her voice shaking, "is for him to stay here."

"You know that's not possible."

"Yeah, because you turned him in."

I stifle a groan. How did she figure that one out? Perhaps she overheard me talking to my dad tonight, or maybe one of Tim's and my conversations. We have tried to be discreet, but sometimes we haven't been. Sometimes circumstances—or emotions—have overtaken us.

"It's true I gave the Department of Justice some evidence they asked for," I reply levelly, doing my best not to sound defensive or on edge. "What was I supposed to do, Em?"

"Oh, I don't know? Not give it in?" she practically snarls. "Protect your own father, who never did anything to hurt you or anyone?"

"Em—"

"You know all he did was count money?" she tells me. "That's it."

Does she not know about Daniel Weiss, the real one? The man my father might have killed?

"We weren't there, Em," I say as gently as I can, even though her hostility is scraping me raw. "We don't know exactly—"

"I know," she bursts out. "I know my grandad. He didn't do anything *wrong*."

I hesitate, wishing Tim were here, not knowing how to answer these questions, not even knowing how I feel about them myself. I am angry at my father, yes, but I realize, humblingly, that it is as much for lying to me as for what he did seventy years ago. What, I wonder hollowly, does that say about me?

"According to the law, he did," I finally tell her carefully. "We all have choices, Em, about what we do or say, what we think or believe. What we're willing to allow to happen." *The only thing necessary for evil to triumph is for good men to do nothing.* The quote by Edmund Burke floats into my mind like a bubble, and then pops.

Em's face twists into a sneer. "Oh, and you think Grandad could have stopped the whole war by himself?" she demands. "What was he supposed to do? He couldn't have changed anything. He couldn't have even said no. Do you know what they did to officers and people who refused their orders?"

I was given a job and I did it. "Has Grandad been talking to you about this?" I ask, my voice turning sharp. Is my dad trying to get Em on his side? Is that what we've come to? A war with my children as the weapons?

"No, he won't. I've asked him and he always refuses to say anything." She tilts her chin up a notch, eyes flashing. "But I can think for myself, you know. And I've looked stuff up."

Clearly. "Em, I understand why you're upset and angry," I begin gently. "Truly, I do. This is all very confusing and upsetting.

For me, too." If I'm trying to get a small sympathy vote, it fails. She huffs, as if she is incredulous that this could be remotely as hard for me as it is for her. I feel like gritting my teeth; I feel like screaming. How are we supposed to give our children what they need when we are running on fumes ourselves? I have nothing to give right now, and yet somehow I have to dredge something up—something my daughter will reject, but still, I must make the offer, and so I persevere. "I want us to stick together," I tell her. "I want us to work together, as a family, because we love each other. That's the only way we'll get through this. By supporting one another."

Em eyes me coolly, unimpressed by my little heartfelt speech. "Maybe you should have thought of that before you turned Grandad in," she tells me, and then rolls over, so her back is to me.

Zero for two, I think dully as I leave her room. Neither of my children is willing to open up to me, and even though I don't remotely have the energy, I know I have to keep trying.

Downstairs, Tim is at the kitchen table, going through the legal paperwork I have not yet been able to do more than flick through. I don't suppose it matters anymore, anyway; the trial is no longer a trial, but a hearing. A formality. And then what happens? The next steps feel both inevitable and oblique.

I open the fridge and stare blindly into its depths. I need to go food shopping. "I spoke to Em and Lucas," I tell Tim.

"How are they?"

"Pretty uncommunicative. Em blames me. Lucas acts like he doesn't care about any of it."

"That's about what I'd expect." There is a lilt of weary humor in his voice and I close the fridge and turn around, a flare of anger burning through me, although I'm not sure what its source is.

"Really?" I ask. "That's what you'd expect?"

"Em can't bear to be angry with her grandfather, so she's

chosen you, because you're safe. Because she knows you'll never abandon her or get angry in return."

My lips twist, almost of their own accord, my bitterness and frustration spilling out to the person who deserves it least. A little bit like Em, then. "That's a neat bit of psychology," I manage, not quite able to lighten my tone as I meant to.

"And Lucas, like you, doesn't like showing emotion." A small, crooked smile quirks Tim's mouth. "So he pretends he's not feeling it."

"Wow, you picked the wrong career," I tell him, my voice coming out just a bit too sharp to be funny. "You should have been a psychoanalyst."

"I thought about it," Tim replies lightly, choosing to ignore my bitterness. He's a good man, maybe too good for me, especially when I feel like this—both jumbled up and empty. How is that even possible? And yet it is.

"I'm sorry." I take a deep breath. "I didn't mean to snap."

"You're going through a lot." Tim pauses, then adds quietly, "I wish you'd talk to me about it."

Which is exactly what I don't want to do, because everything feels so raw. Still, for his sake, I try. "Earlier... my dad told me my mom left because of this. He told her he'd worked in a camp and she left. Left him. Left me." Tears sting my eyes and rapidly I blink them back. Through their blur, I see that Tim is unsurprised. "You knew?" I guessed.

"I wondered."

"Since when?"

He shrugs. "I don't know, since this all started. She left so abruptly, no explanation... I'm sorry. Maybe I should have told you my suspicions."

"No. I think I needed to hear it from my dad." Not that he told me much. "I don't know why it hurt so much, to hear him say that," I admit slowly. I start wiping the counters, just to have something to do. "I don't know that it makes much difference, not really. She still left, after all." Left and never even tried to get in touch—unless my father has lied about that, too? Would he even tell me if I asked?

Tim is silent for a long moment. "Maybe this can be the beginning of something," he says finally, and I look up from swiping the already pristine granite.

"The beginning of something?" I repeat in disbelief. Everything feels like an ending. "Of what?"

"Of your father being honest with you, about everything."

"He doesn't want to speak about any of it." I draw a quick, steadying breath. "And I'm not sure I want to, either. I don't actually think anything he could say or do at this point will change how I feel. It won't change the facts."

"But you don't know what the facts are, Lib, not completely—"

"I know my father was a Nazi," I return sharply. "I know he worked in a concentration camp—a death camp. He saw horrible things, he *did* horrible things. I know he most likely killed a man. Shot him in cold blood. Maybe more than one."

"But you also know he loves you," Tim points out gently.

"Does he?" I echo bitterly. "You're so sure about that?" It's easy for Tim to say, with his uncomplicated parents up in Connecticut. His family goes back to the *Mayflower*. His dad worked a desk job in insurance, his mother was a part-time librarian, baked cookies, did the soccer mom thing. His upbringing was entirely different from mine.

"You know he does," Tim replies. The words sound like a reproof, and I can't keep all the emotion in any longer.

"I don't know any such thing," I snap, hurling the dish towel I was holding toward the sink. It misses and falls on the floor with a wet splat. "And I also don't know how you can keep so calm about this, like you're my therapist or something." I am echoing Lucas, which is humiliating. "It's like you don't even care," I add. I know it's an unfair accusation, but Tim has never even raised his voice this entire time. He's barely blinked, and here I am, feeling as if my soul has been split open. That dark hole right in the middle of me that I keep swerving to avoid? I've fallen into it, and I'm not sure I can climb out again.

I miss my mom. For the first time in thirty years, I miss my mom, and it's because of what my dad said. It's knowing that maybe she missed me too, after all, if not enough to stay or come back.

"I do care," Tim says quietly. Calmly, *still.* "You know I do."

I just shake my head, too angry to fight with him, because I know he won't fight back. He'll just get calmer and calmer, while I'll want to rage, but be afraid to. It's a dynamic that I appreciated, once upon a time, because his sureness steadied me, but right now it just feels like one more person who is giving me a flat stare of silence.

"I don't want to talk about this anymore."

"Okay." As unruffled as ever. For heaven's *sake.* I blow out a breath as I turn toward the fridge, take out the bottle of wine and pour myself a large glass. "We'll get through this, Lib," Tim says. "We will. I promise."

I nod, mostly because I don't know what else to do. Yes, we'll get through this. He's said it before, and I actually do believe it, even though right now I feel both lost and broken. But *how* will we get through it? How will we be, on the other side? My father will be gone. Our name will be dragged through the news, if today's reporters are anything to go by. Our children will be scarred, damaged. And what about us, our marriage? Maybe that will suffer too. Maybe it already has.

As if he can sense the nature of my thoughts, and I know he probably can, Tim continues, "I'm not saying everything will go back to the way it was, or that we'll all be the same. But we'll be together, Lib. And we'll get through it. We'll move on, one way or another."

One way or another. What does that even mean?

My phone buzzes in my pocket, and I slowly withdraw it, half-afraid of what I might see. It's a text, from Grace. *I'm so sorry. Is there anything I can do?*

My stomach drops, hollows out. She knows, then; it must be in the news already, the reporters crowding across the streets having filed their stories. Opening the door early this morning already feels like a lifetime ago, so it's almost surprising that it took this long. My thumb hovers over the Facebook icon as I consider checking what people are saying, but then another text pings on my phone, and another. And then the notifications start—my news app, all the social media, texts and WhatsApp messages. Ping. Ping. Ping.

"A news story must have dropped," Tim says, sounding pragmatic, like this won't bother him either.

I nod, feeling frozen inside. How can I possibly handle this, on top of everything else?

Gently, Tim pries the phone from my hand. "You don't need to look at any of that now," he tells me. "Or ever."

Except I won't be able to avoid it, not the way I once thought I would, when it felt distant, unreal. Ping. Ping. Ping. It's here, in my town, among my friends, in my own home, on my phone. Yet another fallout from my father's lies.

CHAPTER 17

Ninety-six-year-old Nazi to be tried for extradition to Germany, complicit in the murder of over one hundred thousand Jews.

Local Man Discovered to be in the SS, might be deported to Germany.

Nazi in Charlottesville!

The headlines, actually, aren't so bad. They state facts, more or less, sometimes in a sensationalist way, sometimes more plainly, but they generally do keep to the facts. I have found that I can handle the headlines. I can even, when I steel myself, handle the articles I've forced myself to skim through.

My father's case has made just about every national news-paper, as well as all the local ones, and it has been featured on all the main news channels. He's been the subject of interviews with Holocaust survivors, podcasts with history experts, discussions with various immigration lawyers—anyone who has an opinion about his situation, basically, and just about everyone does.

I've only watched short clips, and I've been able to handle those, too, for the most part, although an interview with a woman whose father was killed at Sobibor made my chest go tight as I fought to breathe—I was having a panic attack, I realized, the way I used to as a kid—and I had to turn the TV off.

But, no, amazingly, it's none of that that threatens to break me, because there's a certain theoretical and dispassionate cast to all the articles and interviews that makes them easier to read or hear, because it almost feels like they're talking about a stranger, someone I don't know. Someone I don't love.

No, it's the comments that really hurt me. I read them all, even though I absolutely know I shouldn't. I don't know if I'm punishing myself, or just macabrely curious, or maybe I want to feel prepared for whatever is next. I want to know what people really think, although I'm not sure the anonymous comments of a national news website are an accurate reflection of that. If they are, what people think is vile.

He should burn in hell forever. Or better yet, be slowly tortured to death—very slowly! Evil man. Evil family. They knew. Of course they knew. Are you kidding me???

And that's one of the more polite ones.

I've been sitting in front of my laptop for an hour, imbibing this poison. If Tim knew, he'd be furious, or maybe just disappointed. Concerned, certainly, because this isn't doing me any good, and he seems to find it so much easier to disengage, turn off his phone or the TV, while I can't stop. I need to know.

It has been a week since the first news story landed, and the messages started to come in. The concerned ones from friends, as well as the faux-friendly ones from people I hadn't heard from in months or years, wanting to get the gossip. Worse than those, though, was the radio silence from people I thought were my friends, who have suddenly decided to disappear.

The mom of one of Lucas's friends avoided me in the produce aisle of Wegmans, dodging behind a tottering display of pineapples rather than have to look me in the eye, even though we'd always been fairly chatty before. Tim said to expect it, not because people suspect or dislike me, but because they don't know what to say. He made it sound so understandable, and while it was, it hurt. It all hurts.

Even Grace has seemed a little distant, although maybe that's just me being sensitive, paranoid. I feel so raw, like my skin has been peeled back. Every single thing stings, inside and out. My eczema, the plague of my childhood, has come back, so my hands have become red and scaly, along with my eyelids—a rash I can't help but itch compulsively even though I know it only makes it worse.

I've been working from home, avoiding people as much as I can, even my father. Especially him, but then I'm pretty sure he is avoiding me. We've barely spoken since this all started, and when he does deign to speak to me, it's with a chilly politeness that both infuriates me and breaks my heart. *You're not the one who should be feeling aggrieved*, I think but never say. His refusal even to consider how I might feel, to offer an explanation, never mind an apology, only adds to my anger. But I swallow it down, for better or worse, for the sake of my family.

Not that this noble response is even noticed. Em is still furious with me, barely on speaking terms, slamming doors and stalking out of rooms as if she's auditioning for the role of moody teenager. Lucas, on the other hand, is morosely silent, more monosyllabic than ever, which I hardly thought possible. And Tim? His unflappable patience is wearing a little thin—there is an edge to his voice, a droop to his shoulders—and that is both frightening and gratifying. I almost want him to lose his temper, for that calm exterior to finally crack. I want him to prove to me that all this is hitting him hard, the way it is me, and yet at the same time, I know I don't want that at all.

The truth is, I know, that we are all feeling attacked, under siege, and not just from the newspapers, the social media sites. Even locally, among neighbors and friends, there is a decided sense of suspicion, their sympathy tempered with cautious questions—*You had no idea? Really?* A woman I barely recognized—she ran the PTA at Em's school—cornered me when I was taking a walk around the block at twilight, just to get out of the house.

"You must be devastated," she said in a tone that was somewhere between hushed and condemning. "To learn the truth about your father." I would have thought she was being sympathetic, save for the relish I saw on her face. Nothing like enjoying someone else's ill fortune.

"Yes," I told her flatly. "I am."

"You really had no idea?" she asked in a tone of such skepticism that I struggled not to flinch.

"No," I replied, wondering why I was bothering to answer this near-stranger. "I had no idea at all."

She cocked her head as she made a sound halfway to a tut. "You *must* have wondered."

"No."

"I've *been* to Auschwitz, you know. I've seen it, what they did there. Rooms full of shoes..."

I had a sudden, wild urge to laugh, except, of course, that would have been the worst thing to do right then, and nothing about this was remotely funny. But she'd *been* to Auschwitz? Snapped a few photos, maybe? And somehow that made her an expert, a judge. I opened my mouth, closed it. I was not going to argue the point, or any other.

She huffed a little, as if I was offending her with my silence. "It's awful, what they did," she finally said. "Absolutely awful."

"Yes." That I could agree with one hundred percent.

She shook her head, as if she couldn't believe my temerity in agreeing with her, and then she strode off, adjusting her smart watch as she resumed her power walk. I waited until she'd rounded the corner before I walked on.

Having such suspicion cast on me, on my family, was yet

another thing to learn to bear—and another thing to blame my father for. *He did this to us.* It felt petty, to think like that, and yet I couldn't help it. I was so angry, and beneath that, pulsing darkly, was an ocean of grief I could barely acknowledge, even to myself.

If he'd said sorry, if he'd tried to reach me, I thought I would have felt differently. If he'd done anything to help me understand, to acknowledge what this was doing to us... but he didn't.

He stood in the kitchen, grim-faced and silent, when I handed him a letter from the National Society of Accountants, informing him that, due to "the nature of circumstances" they'd terminated his membership. He ripped it in two and threw it into the trash without a word, a haughty look on his face, as if they were the ones who had done something wrong.

I swallowed down the bitterness that threatened to choke me. *Are you worried about Em, who isn't sleeping at night, but still won't talk to me? Or Lucas, who has become so sullen and silent? Are you concerned about me, Dad, and what this is doing to me? Do you see the eczema on my face, do you hear the break in my voice? And what about Tim, who has been like a son to you? Do you care about any of us?*

I didn't ask any of those questions clamoring to get out. "Do you want lunch?" I asked instead, flatly, and he gave me the same haughty look.

"If it's not too much trouble." In a tone that suggested it shouldn't be.

I didn't bother to reply, just got out a can of Campbell's.

"Libby?"

Quickly I close down the browser on my laptop, but not before Tim sees.

"Why are you looking at that stuff?"

"It's good to be informed," I mumble.

"Libby." Tim shakes his head, annoyed although trying to hide it. "You know nothing good will come of reading the comments on CNN, right?"

"I know." I'm not stupid. "I just want to know what people are thinking."

"The people who comment on those sites are not thinking. At all." He rests a hand on my shoulder. "I thought we could all go out to dinner."

I stare up at him as if he has just spoken a foreign language. Go out? My one trip to Wegmans and a walk around the block were perilous enough. Go out to a *restaurant*? With my father? With his stony silences, Lucas's sulks, Em's fury? I don't even want to go outside to face my neighbors, still fuming about the loss of their parking spaces and privacy. "I don't think so."

"Lib." He squeezes my shoulder. "Your father could be in Germany in a couple of weeks. If he's not contesting the extradition, there's no reason for them to delay. It could happen quickly. Really quickly." I just shake my head and he continues quietly, "These could be the last weeks any of us have with him, that are anything close to normal. It would be good for all of us, to get out of the house, our own heads."

"But it won't be normal." The words come out thickly. "People will recognize him. They'll stare, point, or worse." And, I know, even if they don't, it won't be normal with *me*. I don't know how to talk to him, or even if I want to. I still feel so angry; perhaps I always will. "Besides," I say, although this isn't really my reason, "it will upset him, Tim."

"I think it will upset you more than him," Tim replies. "I think your dad has been pretty stoical, pretty accepting of all the press."

And why shouldn't he be, I think, *when this is all his fault?* The thought, bursting into my mind like a firework, shames me again, because Tim has managed to rise above it and yet I can't. I can't keep myself from blaming him, not just for what he did seventy years ago or for not telling me about my mom after she left, but for what he has brought upon us now. It's *his* fault Em is so angry, Lucas so sullen. It's his fault my friends are blanking me and newspapers want my story. Yet blaming him, even now, feels wrong. Petty and mean.

"Let's go somewhere anonymous," Tim says, his manner comfortingly cajoling. "Mission BBQ or somewhere," he adds, naming a chain restaurant on the outskirts of town, with dim lighting and deep booths, that does burgers and ribs.

I hesitate, a tiny bit tempted, because as much as I am resisting, I crave for things to feel normal, or as close to normal as they can, even if just for an hour or two. And Tim is right. We all need a break. I need to at least try for normality, for my children's sake, if not my father's.

"Lib?"

"Okay," I say, wondering if I'll regret it, if something terrible will happen. Reporters will accost us in the street; the waiter will recognize my father and refuse to serve him. Em will have a meltdown, Lucas will become even surlier. My father will refuse to speak. Ever since Simon Baum showed up on my doorstep, I've been bracing myself for the next bombshell. The next devastating explosion.

But in the end, nothing terrible happens. No one recognizes us. The music is loud, the lights dim, the booth deep enough to hide us all. As the pounding music washes over us and we settle into the booth, I feel a wave of shaky relief. Normally, I would have turned my nose up at a place like this, preferred a trendy little bistro in Charlottesville's historic district. But now I am happy simply to be out, to feel free. Sort of.

We order burgers and ribs, baked beans and coleslaw, fresh-cut fries and green beans with bacon. The table is practically groaning under the weight of all the food, more than we can possibly eat. We let the kids get refills on their soda. Tim creates a mood of conviviality, challenging Lucas to some football game with a paper square batted back and forth across the table, and Em watches and cheers on, while my father smiles faintly, never meeting my eye. Everyone is laughing and smiling, but there is an edge of desperation to it all, a wild recklessness, as if we know how precious this is, how fleeting, and also how fake. And yet I savor every moment, because what else do I have?

In a few days, my father will be in court. Shortly after that, he will be stripped of his citizenship, deported, tried, and then, in all likelihood, sent to prison in a country he hasn't visited in seventy years, where he will remain for the rest of his life. And none of us say one word about any of it, not tonight, because we can still pretend. Almost.

When we return home, twilight is settling softly over our neighborhood, and thankfully the reporters camped across the street have gone home. It really does feel like a normal day, or almost.

My father thanks Tim and me for the night out, formally, as if he's a guest, little more than an acquaintance. It makes me ache, but I don't know how to respond and so I nod jerkily and he retreats to his room.

When we are in the family room, Em in the shower and Lucas downstairs, Tim asks quietly, "Have you thought about when he goes to Germany?"

I let out a shuddering breath. "No." Life after that feels like a blank screen, an empty space.

"You could go with him, you know."

"What?" I turn around, gaping at Tim. I have not envisioned anything beyond my father leaving my life. "I don't... Is that even an option?"

"Kate said he won't be considered a flight risk, since he isn't contesting the extradition. He can stay somewhere in Stuttgart, where the trial will be held. An apartment or house or a nursing home. Whatever is most suitable. But it will have to be arranged." He pauses. "And, you know, he might want the company."

Want the company? "Tim, he has barely spoken to me since this all happened." And I've barely spoken to him. I shake my head, sure now. "I think me going with him is the last thing he wants." And it's the last thing I want, even if I dread to think of saying goodbye. "From the beginning, he's been determined to handle this on his own. He won't want me hearing whatever comes out in the trial—"

"It'll be in all the newspapers anyway."

"Still, to see me there, know I'm hearing it." I shake my head again, resolute now. "Besides, I don't know that I want to hear it. That I... I can." I almost say something about how angry I feel, but I can't quite let myself. Tim obviously isn't struggling with the same kind of fury, and his reasonableness keeps making me feel petty, even though I know he doesn't mean it to. "And what about Em and Lucas?" I point out instead. I can't leave them when they're clearly struggling, even if they're showing it in very different ways. "School will be starting in another week, and things at Fresh Start will be getting going again..." I trail off at Tim's slightly disapproving look.

"Libby, this is your dad."

My hackles rise instantly. My dad who betrayed me, all of us, utterly. "I *know* that."

He sighs. "I just don't want you to regret your choices."

"The person who should be regretting their choices is my dad," I retort, and then feel guilty, like once again I'm being mean. Maybe I am. I rub my face, my shoulders slumping. I want to stop being so angry; it rears up its ugly head at the most inopportune moments. I certainly don't want to be angry with

Tim. "I'm sorry, it's just that I don't know if I have it in me. Especially if my dad doesn't want me to be there."

"You don't know whether he does or not."

"He certainly hasn't given the impression that—"

"You could ask him, Lib." Tim says this like it is easy. Obvious.

I take a deep breath, let it out slowly. I know he's right, that I should at least ask my dad what he wants. I should at least be willing to consider going with him, even if it's hard, even if it hurts. Even if I learn things I don't want to know, and understand more about my father's past than I ever wished to. Even if it means I face more judgment, animosity, hatred. For my father's sake, and maybe for mine, I should.

"I can't stay in Germany with him for months," I tell Tim, like a warning.

"I know, but maybe a little while, to get him settled?"

I knuckle my forehead. "Maybe," I relent. It's as far as I'm willing to go. I don't want to leave my job, my family. Not now, when everything feels so fragile and precarious. Besides, Tim's job is demanding, and while he does his best to help around the house, I still do the heavy lifting. And our children need my emotional support, now more than ever, no matter how they are pushing me away. I think of Em's anxiety, Lucas's sullen silence. They still need me; I can't just *leave*.

"We'll manage, Lib," Tim tells me gently. "If you go. I'll hire an au pair or something. We'll be okay."

Hire an *au pair*? A stranger in my home, taking care of my family? Suddenly I feel frightened. He is making it sound so *possible*.

"What about my job?" I ask, caught between belligerence and bewilderment.

Tim shrugs. "I think asking for compassionate leave isn't out of the question, in a situation like this."

No, it probably isn't. The CEO and founder of Fresh Start,

Karen Bain, has already called me, "to check in." Her gushing sympathy made me cringe. It felt false, and in any case, I didn't feel like I deserved it. Plus the "and you really had no idea?" she tacked onto the end of the phone call pretty much ruined the whole conversation for me. But go to Germany? Sit in on the trial? Face my father's stony silence, day after day, along with the media coverage, the scrutiny? I resist the idea instinctively, utterly. I'm afraid of what I'll learn there. I'm scared I'm not strong enough to face it.

"I don't know," I say slowly. "I need to think about it."

"Okay."

I glance up at Tim, who is looking as relaxed as usual, as competent and calm as he is always, and something spiky inside me rears its ugly head. "How can you just keep taking this all on the chin?" I ask.

Tim hesitates. "I love your father, but he's your dad, not mine," he finally says quietly.

Tim's parents live in Massachusetts. They're warm and lovely—keen golfers, avid gardeners, obsessive crossword enthusiasts, sucking the marrow out of their retirement. Right now, I envy him their utter uncomplicatedness.

"Still," I say after a moment, "has it been hard for you at work? Has anyone said anything?"

He shrugs, which is no answer at all, and I wonder what he has chosen not to tell me over the last few weeks, when I've been walking around in a haze of disbelief, a fog of fear and fury.

"Tim? Have they?"

"A few comments here and there, but nothing I can't handle. Don't worry about me, Lib. You've got enough on your plate."

I stare at him, wanting to believe him, feeling as if I am somehow letting him down. You certainly don't imagine this kind of scenario when you talk about *for better or for worse*. Is

Tim regretting being married to me and having to lug all my baggage? It's a question born of insecurity, because if I'm painfully, brutally honest, I've always felt I got the better part of the deal.

Tim and I met in New York, when I was working as a librarian at Columbia and he was a chemistry PhD student. He came to the library six times to check out books before he finally asked me out; I was shyly pleased, unable to hide my surprise, because at twenty-four, I'd only had a couple of casual boyfriends, relationships that had never gone anywhere, in part, I was able to understand later, because I didn't let them. Having your mother walk out when you were four can leave you with all sorts of relationship issues—some more obvious than others, some I'm still not willing to examine too closely.

But I've never had that fear with Tim. He's always been so steady, a true rock, when I'm the one that is foundering, even if I do my best to hide it. I can't hide it now, as much as I want to, as much as I want to get back onto an even keel, solid ground. But maybe the only way to do that is to go forward… to face whatever it is my father's still hiding. To know the truth, and learn to deal with it.

To go to Germany.

CHAPTER 18

OCTOBER, 1942

Sobibor, Poland

Almost as soon as Hans had sent Anni back to their quarters, Gustav Wagner strode into his office and dumped a pile of what looked like dishes and silverware on the table in front of Daniel Weiss.

"There, Jew. Make me a ring."

Daniel stared at him wordlessly, one hand still on his son's shoulder.

Hans held his breath, having no idea what Wagner was capable of—although he realized, he *did* know, and that frightened him all the more. There was a wild glitter in the officer's eye, and he was breathing heavily, one hand resting on the butt of his Walther pistol.

"Oh, wait," he said, with a laugh that sounded more like a growl. "You'll need some gold."

He withdrew a handful of what looked like gold pellets from the pocket of his jacket and showered them down on the goldsmithing equipment he'd tossed on the table. Hans watched as they tumbled and bounced, and Daniel's face drained of all color.

Then he realized what those little golden pellets were —*teeth*. They were gold teeth, some with bits of blood or bone still attached to them, taken, perhaps, from today's transport. His stomach heaved and it took all his strength not to clap his hand over his mouth to keep from vomiting. He took a deep breath instead, let it out slowly as his stomach continued to churn.

The very air in the room was taut as Wagner stared at Daniel Weiss, clearly enjoying this moment. He was mad, Hans thought wildly. He had to be quite, quite mad. They all did here, to do this. To *enjoy* it.

"I'll need some water," Daniel finally said, and his voice was amazingly steady. "To wash them."

Wagner laughed and clapped him hard enough on the shoulder to make him stagger. "So you will. So you will. All right, Jew. I'll get you some water. I'll fetch and carry for you." Although he was smiling, there was something ominous about his tone, as if he was warning Daniel Weiss that he would humor him only so far.

Daniel did not respond, and after another few seconds, Wagner strode out of the room, banging the door behind him.

Hans watched as Daniel sank into his chair, dropping his face into his hands for a moment. A shudder went through his body and then he lifted his head and drew his son to him, hugging him tightly in his arms. Hans found he had to look away, a lump in his throat, a stone in his stomach.

A few minutes later, Wagner burst through the door again, slamming a pitcher of water down on the table so that much of it splashed out.

"There. Satisfied?" he growled, and Daniel nodded minutely.

Wagner turned to glare at Hans.

"Why are you so silent? Cat got your tongue?"

Somehow, Hans found his voice. "I'm waiting for the money."

"Hasn't one of the Blackies brought it to you? Damned thieves. They're almost as bad as the Jews." Wagner glanced at Daniel then, almost as if he expected him to share in the joke, but the man's head was bowed, his son drawn against him, both of them completely silent and still.

Swearing under his breath, Wagner strode once more out of the room.

The ensuing silence felt like the aftermath of the storm, or perhaps only the eye. Who knew when Wagner would be back, what he would say. Do.

Hans opened his mouth to say something—what? To assure this man that he was safe here? But, of course, he wasn't. Hans was practically as powerless as he was, if not in remotely the same kind of danger.

So he remained silent, reaching for his ledger and opening it to a fresh page, even though the money hadn't come yet.

After a few moments, Daniel lifted his head, and he slowly started cleaning the gold teeth of their bits of blood and bone, taking each one and rinsing it in the basin of water, before drying it carefully. His son watched him silently for a few moments before he started helping, handing his father the teeth, one by one. Hans had to look away.

They'd been working in silence for nearly an hour—the guard had arrived with the money, and left again, without a word—when Daniel Weiss finally spoke.

"Please," he said, his German halting and careful. "Please, can you tell me what happens to all the others?"

Hans stared at him, unwilling to put it into words. He felt a flicker of something almost like annoyance, and it shamed him. But couldn't the man guess, based on what he'd been doing?

"Please," he said again. "I... I need to know." He swallowed hard. "My wife. My daughter..."

Hans looked back down at his ledger. They were, he knew, almost certainly dead.

"Can't you tell me?"

He swallowed and kept staring down at the neat columns of figures printed in black ink, Gothic script. "I think you know."

"Is there any way...?"

Hans let out an impatient breath. He felt, entirely unreasonably, he knew, angry at this man, and that made him feel wretched with guilt. Couldn't he let it go, for his son's sake?

"There must be some way," Daniel insisted quietly. "To be sure."

Hans closed his eyes. "Very well," he said, his tone terse to hide his discomfort, his fear. "I will look into the matter for you. What were their names?"

Daniel Weiss' voice wavered as he replied, "*Are.* Their names are Rachel and Hannah. Rachel and Hannah Weiss. Hannah is only four years old..."

Hans shook his head. "Do not expect good news. They are..." He paused, and glanced at the man's son, who had not said a single word. "They are almost certainly dead."

Daniel bowed his head. "Thank you," he whispered, "for looking."

Hans rose from his desk. "And stay here," he ordered. "If Wagner comes in again..." He shook his head. "Just make the damned ring and keep your mouth shut."

Daniel Weiss nodded, but Hans was already striding out the door.

He did not want to find out what had happened to Rachel and Hannah Weiss. He did not want to know, and he certainly did not want to go searching through the camp for answers. He might have only been here for a few weeks, but already he knew that the best—the only—way to survive was to keep his head down and do the work. Nothing else. Certainly not this.

Squaring his shoulders, he headed for "The Tube"—the narrow passageway shrouded in greenery and barbed wire, that all the Jews went down, and from which none ever came back. He didn't actually know exactly what was at the other end. He didn't want to know. He didn't even want to guess. And yet, for Daniel Weiss' sake, and yes, maybe his own, he kept walking.

It was at least a quarter-mile from the administration building to the end of the Tube, and it took him nearly five minutes of walking slowly but resolutely to get to the end, a strangely silent and surreal few minutes, where the only sound was the thump of his heart, the rush of blood in his ears.

Then he came to a courtyard of concrete, several squat buildings of brick behind them. As Hans reached the courtyard, he saw prisoners dragging bodies from the doorway of one of the buildings; it looked like a gaping mouth, a black hole, and the bodies—shaved, naked, pitiable—were stacked inside—no, not stacked, but jumbled and jostled, heaped any old way, lying on top of each other. And there were so many. Hundreds. Thousands...

Do the math.

He could almost hear Anni's voice, hard and unrelenting. At least two thousand Jews had come on trains today. Of course there were thousands.

"Hey, what are you doing here?" One of the Ukrainian guards approached him, a surly look on his face. Hans' SS uniform clearly was not enough to impress even a guard. He didn't reply, couldn't; it was all he could do to stare at the prisoners dragging out the dead bodies by the armpits. Their faces resembled those of the corpses they carried: haggard, blank, beyond shock.

"I'm looking for someone," Hans told the guard finally, his voice coming out in a commanding tone he was far from feeling.

"Just looking..." And yet he could look no more. He turned away, knowing there was no more to find. To know. Dead, they were all dead. How? Gassed, he supposed, gassed and then their bodies burned, and then he wondered how he knew that. Somehow he knew, had known all along, even as he'd insisted he didn't. Couldn't.

He walked back down the Tube, putting one foot in front of another, barely aware of where he was going. Where was there to go? Nowhere away from this hell on earth, this waking night-mare. Nowhere but the Front, but even then it would go on and on...

How many Jews are there in the world?

Anni had asked the question. Anni had seen and under-stood, instantly, while he'd blundered on, determined to be blind. He thought of aleph null, and he made a sound, some-thing between a laugh and a sob. Would all the Jews in the Greater Reich, in all of Europe, the whole world—would they end up here? And then what? After the Jews, who would be next?

Because even after just a few weeks in the camp, Hans understood that once men got a taste for savagery, they would never rest without it. Sobibor would never end. The war would never be over, even after the guns stopped, and the skies were blue and empty. Life itself, he knew, would never be the same again. Not him, not for Anni, not for anyone. There would be no going back to Stuttgart and picking up where they left off, not ever; once innocence was gone, it was gone forever. He could never be naïve again. And he wanted to be. Oh, how he wanted to be. To do his sums in his office, Anni making supper in the flat above. An evening of reading or listening to the radio. Right then, it seemed like the sweetest thing in the world, and utterly distant.

The administration building came into view as he emerged from the dreaded Tube. Steeling himself, Hans opened the door to his office, having no idea what he would find. Perhaps Daniel Weiss would have disappeared, or be lying dead on the floor, shot in the head, blood pooling around his blank face. Hans had no expectations of what could happen, of how bad it could get. Not after what he'd just seen. Not after what he now knew.

But, for better or worse, Daniel was in the same place as before, perched on a stool in front of a rickety wooden table, his goldsmithing equipment laid out neatly in front of him. He'd finished cleaning the gold teeth and was now melting the gold in a little brazier over a glowing piece of charcoal, a pair of metal tongs in his hand, his son standing by his shoulder, watchful and at the ready. He looked up as Hans came into the room, a question in his eyes.

Hans simply shook his head.

Later, while Daniel and his son went to the prisoner barracks, the ring having been molded and set, Hans returned to his cottage and Anni. She was sitting in a chair, staring out the window, making Hans wonder what on earth she did all day. There was nothing to do in this place, he thought bitterly, but kill. Kill and maim and *count*.

"Hans?" Anni asked quietly, and he realized he was glowering. "What's wrong?"

A sudden tidal wave of rage crashed over him, left him shaking with the futile force of it. He strode into the cottage and kicked the table, hard enough to send it spinning across the room. Then, with a growl, he threw a chair onto its side, splintering one of its rickety legs.

Anni simply watched him.

Hans let out another growl, this one of frustration, as he hurled his cap onto the floor and then raked his hands through his hair, turning away from his sister and her quiet, knowing stare.

"Hans," she said, and it was the tone of a parent to a child.

Hans stared blindly out the window at the blank wall, the railroad beyond. He didn't think he had ever felt so hopeless in his life.

"Has something happened?" Anni asked quietly. "Or is it just this place?"

Hans didn't reply. He simply stared out the window as understanding trickled slowly through him. He would lose his soul here, he realized. He would lose his soul, or, on the Front, he would most likely lose his life. He was under no illusion about that; Niemann or Reichleitner or whoever it was who sent him into battle would make sure he had the worst position, the most dangerous duty. He would be dead within days, maybe weeks. That, he knew instinctively and absolutely, was the price of walking away from Sobibor.

"Hans?"

Slowly, defeated, he turned around. "What?"

"What about the man? Daniel Weiss? And his son?"

"What about them?"

She looked impatient, her lips pressed together. "Are they all right?"

"Are they all right?" Hans let out a hollow laugh. "For now, I suppose." But tomorrow? Or the next day? The next hour, even? They were doomed, utterly doomed; it was only a matter of time. They were *all* doomed, he thought wretchedly. Every single one of them, in one way or another. All on the road to death, to hell, as sure as if they were walking down that dreaded *Schlauch*.

"And you must make sure they stay so," Anni stated, and he stared at her blankly.

"*I* must? How?"

"Whatever it takes—"

"I'm going to the Front," he burst out. "We have to leave this place, Anni. They offered me that—either Sobibor or Stalingrad. I didn't tell you before, but... I choose Stalingrad." The words came with a rush of sweetness. He could leave this place. He *could*.

If he expected to see relief in his sister's face, or perhaps respect, he was disappointed. She looked, if anything, annoyed. "You can't leave now, Hans," she said, as if it were obvious.

"I can," he insisted. "If I fight—"

"What about your weak chest?"

"I doubt they care about a thing like that anymore." The Wehrmacht were dying in droves on the Eastern Front. They were desperate for recruits. The requirements for the SS had been lowered; Hans was sure those for a common enlisted soldier had been, as well. They'd take anyone. They'd take him.

"Even so, Hans." Now Anni sounded severe. "You can't."

He let out an incredulous laugh, a sound more of despair than any possible humor. "Oh? And why can't I?"

"Because you have a purpose here now. You have someone to take care of."

It took him a few seconds to realize who she was talking about. "You mean the Jew?"

"Daniel Weiss," she returned sharply. "And his son Leo. They have *names*, Hans."

"I know they have names." He rubbed his hand over his face. "I *know*." And Hannah and Rachel Weiss, too, he thought wearily. They *all* had names.

"They are your responsibility, now."

He shook his head wearily. "Anni, there is nothing I can do for them. Wagner is as likely to shoot them in the head for looking at him the wrong way as he is to... to wear the damned ring they're making for him. I have no power here—"

"You are an officer in the SS," Anni reminded him with asperity. "And you are learned, compared to many of these louts. Make them respect you, and they might leave the Weisses alone."

"Make them respect me?" Once, a very short while ago, he would have liked such men to respect him. He would have hoped and tried for it. Now the idea filled him with revulsion.

"Yes, you have to play their game, Hans—"

He could not keep from shuddering. "I will never play their game."

"Not like that," she said quickly. "Of course not like that. But pretend you admire them. Act like having a Jew in your office is amusing, nothing more. Never let them see that you care—"

"I don't care," Hans burst out. "Not about him or his boy. I care about *you*, Anni—"

"Then do this for me," she replied steadily. "Because if we can save two people here, or even only one, then it will have been worth it, for us ever to have had to come to this godforsaken place."

CHAPTER 19

LIBBY

The reporters are out in full force the day of my dad's hearing. I glimpse them from the upstairs hall window, a mob across the street under a dank and heavy August sky. All my neighbors probably hate me for the intrusion, even though at least some of them are still pretending to be understanding. I'm so tired even my teeth ache, and I have no idea what happens after today.

The last week has been as difficult as all the ones before. I've done my best to maintain some semblance of normality, but after that night at Mission BBQ, the one brief, bright spot in an otherwise bleak parade of days, it feels laughable even to try. Em still won't talk to me, and Lucas is little better. My father continues to avoid me, and I'm avoiding him. I feel like we are all moving around each other in the house, silent and wary. Tim is the only thing holding any of us together, but even he is feeling the strain, I know—the reporters, the news stories, my father's stoical silence, our children's anxiety and anger, everyone in Charlottesville's rubbernecking... and my emotional outbursts. I feel as if I am a jumble of rusted parts, a handful of broken glass. Tim has been so very patient with me, considering. I am grateful for his kindness, as I try to manage all the disparate parts of my scattered life.

A couple of days ago, I finally agreed to meet Grace for a drink, even though I was weirdly reluctant. She was my best friend, and yet as I sat across from her on a high stool in the back of a dimly lit bar near the Grounds of UVA, she didn't *feel* like my best friend. Or maybe I didn't feel like hers. The truth is, since this grenade was hurled into my life, I haven't felt like myself. I haven't felt like I even know who that person is, or how to find her, never mind anybody else.

And when Grace asked me how I was, really, I didn't know how to answer. I didn't trust her with the truth, but I wasn't ready to lie, so I just shrugged and sipped my wine, and I saw the flash of exasperation cross her face.

"Libby. This is me. You can tell me what's really going on."

I felt a prickle of defensiveness, even fear. Did she just want the lowdown, the gossip? Was I wrong to think that way about my best friend?

"If you've read the newspapers, you know what's going on," I told her, and hurt flashed in her eyes, along with irritation.

"I want to hear it from you." I didn't reply and she continued, gently, "Is it really hard?"

"Yes." I reached for my wine.

"Was he really in a camp?" she asked hesitantly, and I tensed. "I mean, a death camp?"

"Yes."

"It's so hard to believe. I mean, your *dad*..." She shook her head slowly, seemingly unaware that every word she spoke scraped me raw, left me bleeding. "I guess it was different, then," she finished with a shake of her head, and my gaze narrowed.

"Different? What do you mean?"

"Well, you know..." She shrugged. "Nazi Germany... it must have been pretty hard growing up in that environment. Hard not to toe the line..." She sounded like Tim, but even more forgiving. Was it easier, I wondered, to forgive someone you didn't care too much about? Shouldn't it be the other way round?

"I'm sure there were ways if you really wanted to resist," I couldn't help but say. "If you knew it was wrong." Like I'm sure my father did.

"But it would have been dangerous," Grace protested.

"So?" I knew I sounded hard, but I couldn't help it. This was my *father* we were talking about, not some nameless, face-less boy in the Hitler Youth. My father should have known better. He should have been braver. The man I thought I knew, the man I loved, would have been. "Anyway," I told Grace, "no matter how he was back then, he should have *told* me. That's what I can't get over. He lied to me, Grace. Over and over again, about so many things." The pain vibrated in my voice, but instead of going all soft with sympathy, Grace looked uncertain, like she wanted to say something but was afraid to. "What?" I asked.

"It's just... how could he have told you the truth? Considering?"

"I would have understood," I said, although I wasn't sure I meant it. I didn't understand now, certainly. I didn't even want to.

"It would have put him at such risk. Look what's happening now, with all the press—"

"People like him weren't even able to be prosecuted until a couple of years ago," I told her. I sounded like such an expert, but I wasn't, not remotely. "Besides, this was me, his only child, not the police or the court." I shook my head, resolute again, even though it caused a deep, tearing grief. "It's more than that, though. These places... the death camps." I swallowed. "They were beyond horrible, Grace, unbelievably evil. And that's just what I've seen in documentaries. And my dad was there, for a *year*. How can I possibly look at him the same way again? Knowing he lived there? Endured it, was part of it, maybe even contributed to it? He won't answer any of my questions about it, which makes it worse."

Grace was silent, and once more I reached for my wine.

"What?" I said again, this time a bit belligerently, when she didn't seem like she was going to reply.

"I don't know..."

"Just tell me."

"I just think you have to walk a mile in someone's shoes," she said slowly. "To understand how it really was back then. Who knows what you or I would have done if we'd been living in Nazi Germany? How we would have responded, or caved to pressure, or reacted out of fear?"

"I certainly wouldn't have worked in a death camp," I replied, although I knew I couldn't be entirely sure. I hoped I wouldn't have. I know I wouldn't have shot a man. I wouldn't have pretended I had all these principles, I wouldn't have lied to my only child, I wouldn't have maintained a stony silence, acting angry when I should have been asking—*begging*—for forgiveness.

Would I?

Grace's face had fallen into weary lines and something in me prickled. "What is it this time?" I demanded.

Grace took a long time replying. "I don't know, Libby. Sometimes you seem a little... hard, on other people. Like you expect people never to make mistakes, never to have confused motives, never to mess up... like that stupid stained shirt."

I stared at her blankly. Why was she mentioning a *shirt*?

"You assumed the woman who donated it didn't care. That she was selfish, thoughtless, whatever. But... maybe she just didn't realize."

"Are we really talking about a shirt?" I asked in disbelief.

"Not just the shirt. Just... everything. You're so sure all the time, about what's right, what's wrong. *Who's* right, who's wrong. And sometimes life is a little more... complicated... than that. A little less black and white, and a little more gray."

"The Holocaust is not complicated." My voice was flat. "It's not a gray area, Grace."

"No, of course not," she replied quickly. "I'm not saying that. I'm just saying... Oh, I don't even know." She sighed and shook her head. "Just that we all make mistakes, we all mess up, we're all doing the best we can."

"Are we?" I sounded almost contemptuous, but I couldn't help it. I hadn't seen a lot of my father's best recently, and I felt both hurt and aggrieved that my best friend was making it seem as if I was being the unreasonable one, just as my dad had acted, as Em had accused. "I'm sorry." I shook my head as I slid off my stool, knowing I couldn't take any more. "I don't have the energy to argue with you about this, not with the hearing in a few days. I really am sorry."

"You're mad at me, aren't you?" she asked, making it sound like something else was my fault.

"No," I said. "I'm not." I was spinning, wondering if there was more than a grain of truth in what she'd said, wishing she'd just listened and been on my side. "I'm really not," I assured her, but she didn't look convinced. "I just... can't do this right now. Emotionally, I mean. I feel... tapped out. Used up. I'm sorry."

Grace looked conflicted, as if she wanted to both scold and hug me, and the truth was, I didn't think I could handle either. So with one more halfhearted, apologetic smile, I walked out of the bar, into the muggy night, wondering if I'd lost another person in my life.

Yet her criticisms—for that's what they were, if kindly meant—continued to needle me. Was I unreasonable? Unforgiving? Did I demand a perfection from other people when I knew I was such a mess myself? If I came across that way, I didn't mean to, I was sure of it. Maybe hiding all my own imperfections had made me seem as if I expected perfection in other people, including my dad. And yet it was my dad who had instilled that desire in me—to pursue justice, to love mercy, to do what was right. Had he been lying? Or just atoning for his own sins, without telling me so? Maybe Tim was right, and I'd idolized him a bit too much. Maybe that was what made his fall from grace harder now.

But could forgiveness ever be that easy?

As my father's hearing drew closer, I knew I didn't have any answers.

"Libby?"

Tim knocks on the door, looking tense. "It's time to go."

I nod mechanically. I feel weirdly distant from myself, as if I'm a spectator rather than a participant in my own life. Maybe it's the only way I can protect myself, to pretend I don't care. Last night, I read an editorial in *The New York Times* that picked apart the public statement Tim and I gave, with all its careful wording dictated by Kate. It was meant to be sincere, apologetic, heartfelt. The article tore it to shreds, claiming the statement showed we were just covering our backs, that we weren't really sorry, and of course we must have known all along. The piece didn't go so far as to accuse us outright, but it cast enough doubt to make any reader wonder whether we were complicit in my father's crimes, whether we shared his abhorrent sympathies.

I'd put the newspaper aside with a sigh, too weary or perhaps numb to summon any emotion about the most popular newspaper in the entire country more or less calling me a Nazi. I thought of what Grace had said, and I wondered how she could accuse me of judging my father, when it felt like everyone was judging me.

"Libby," Tim says again, and I nod.

"I'm coming."

Em and Lucas are staying at home during the hearing. Em wanted to go, got into near hysterics about it, but I knew at eleven years old she couldn't handle this kind of scrutiny and pressure. Lucas said he didn't want to go. Normally, I would have asked Grace to come over and keep them company, but unfortunately we're not really speaking now after our tense drink, and so Tim will drop my dad and I off and then come back to be with the kids. I could have used his support, even if I was reluctant to admit it, but I know it has to be this way.

My father is waiting by the front door, stiff and dignified in his best suit, his hair combed over his bald spot, a bright blue silk handkerchief in his blazer pocket. I know he's trying to look smart, but I fear the splash of color by his lapel will look too dapper, flashy. The newspapers will accuse him of treating this as nothing more than a show, a circus. I am wearing a navy-blue dress, somber enough for a funeral, but I'm sure they'll pick that apart too. *Brenner's daughter was trying to dress for the occasion, to look suitably sober.* I've come to realize no matter what we do, we can't win. We're not *meant* to win, because that would be wrong. I understand that, I sympathize with the sentiment, but if you're not meant to win, what are you supposed to do? How do you act?

There are two policemen to keep the reporters at bay as we run the gauntlet from the house to the car. Tim takes my father's arm, and we all duck our heads as the cameras click and the reporters shriek their questions.

"How are you feeling about your trial?"

"What defense will you be offering?"

"Did you kill Daniel Weiss?"

We make it to the car.

None of us speak as we are driven by police escort to the courthouse in downtown Charlottesville. My father is staring straight ahead, his expression both remote and grim; Tim glances at me in concern and I look away. The only way to get through this is to stay numb.

Stay numb, and do my best not to think about the toll this is taking on my family, my marriage, my friends. My life and my home. Everything, absolutely everything, has been damaged, and I can't even assess how much yet.

There are even more reporters in front of the courthouse, a cluster of avid journalists and their endlessly clicking cameras. My father squares his shoulders. He has not looked at me once, but then I haven't really looked at him. I think about him teaching me to dance, kissing me goodnight, wiping away my childish tears, and then I push all the memories away, because I know I can't handle them right now.

The reporters outside the courthouse are even more aggressive, thrusting microphones near our faces, standing in our way despite the police escorting us, trying to keep them back and not, I think, doing a very good job of it. I can't help but feel that even the police think we deserve this—a little scrutiny, a dose of judgment, maybe even the odd shout or shove. And maybe we do.

Once we're in the courthouse, Tim kisses me goodbye and slips out the back to head home. He wanted us to present a united front for the media, but he really needs to be with Em and Lucas.

I glance at my father, who is staring straight ahead.

"Are you ready?" I ask, and he lifts his chin a notch.

"Yes."

I swallow past the tightness in my throat, wishing there was something I could say in this moment. I wish I could tell him I love him, but the words won't come, and I can't think of any other ones.

The doors open, and a bailiff ushers us in. Compared to all the media drama outside, the hearing is a bit of a letdown, as well as a much-needed relief. We enter a space that looks like a corporate conference room rather than a courtroom, with a few rows of folding chairs and a couple of tables. The judge is an African-American woman in her fifties with graying hair and a brisk, no-nonsense manner. When Kate tells her my father is not contesting the extradition, she simply nods and then reviews the evidence—stating what I already know in a couple of sentences before going on to summarize all the legalities, using jargon that washes over me in an incomprehensible tide, but the result is that, in less than an hour, it has been decided my father will be stripped of his citizenship before being extradited to Germany, at a time to be determined by the Department of Justice in conjunction with the German government.

My father hasn't said a word. Neither have I. My head aches and my jaw's so tight, it is throbbing. When I glance at him out of the corner of my eye, he looks like a stranger and yet I want to put my arms around him and weep.

We walk out in silence, only to be mobbed once again by the reporters, the sound and fury of them like walking into a wall. They're like a pack of dogs, practically snapping and biting at us, a dangerous glitter in their eyes as they push their microphones toward us, shrieking for answers to their questions. Instinctively, I reach for my father's hand, and thankfully he takes it; it feels small and frail in mine, slender bones beneath papery skin. When was the last time I touched him?

I hold onto him as I do my best to push my way through the melee, a couple of policemen trying to keep the crowds back, although not with much effort or effect. Then I feel my arm being yanked and my father's hand slips out of mine. I turn back to see a woman reporter getting in my father's face, pushing a microphone toward him as she shouts a question while he simply blinks at her. There is a glob of her spittle on his cheek. He looks so small, so vulnerable, so *old*, and no matter what he did in the past, the urge to protect him overwhelms me. This is my *dad*, and I love him. I know I do, even if it's hard. Even if I'm not sure I should anymore.

I whirl around, grabbing the woman's shoulder to get her off my father.

"Get away from him," I say in a low voice.

"I'm just asking a question," she shrills, and something in me finally boils up to overflowing, all the emotions I've suppressed, all the times I've tried to be fine. I can't, now. I won't. I need to protect my dad.

"Why can't you just get *off*," I snarl, the words escaping me in a rush of something like satisfaction before I can bite them back, my hand still hard on her shoulder. I swear there is a look of glee on her face before she takes a step backwards and then, quite deliberately, falls to the ground, as if I've pushed her.

I stare at her in numb disbelief as the cameras click and people shout and then someone grabs my arm. I turn to see it's a policeman, and I think he's trying to hustle me out of there to safety, until I see the handcuffs coming out and I realize what's happening. He's arresting me.

The last thing I see is my father staring at me in wordless shock, one hand pressed to his spit-smeared cheek.

CHAPTER 20

LIBBY

I am, unbelievably, in a jail cell in downtown Charlottesville, handcuffed and taken here like a criminal, to the obvious delight of all the reporters. What a story. I'll be on the front page of every newspaper in the country, I think numbly. A video clip of the moment the reporter fell on all the news channels, everyone watching, shaking their heads, assuming I'm some kind of Nazi too. *She's as bad as he is.*

Still, I know I only have myself to blame, at least this time. I can't believe I was so stupid, so foolishly uncontrolled, as to shout at and shove a reporter—even though I'm certain she fell down on purpose. I'm sure the video clips and photographs will make it look like I really pushed her. And I thought things couldn't get any worse.

The police were polite but firm. I would be kept here until bail was decided. *Bail.* I've never been in trouble with the law in my life. I've never even jaywalked. I can't believe this case will be taken seriously; the woman was manhandling my father, after all, and I didn't actually *push* her. I was just trying to get her off my dad. No matter how the media plays it, I have to believe I will be treated fairly by the courts, and this case will be dismissed. I absolutely do not have the mental or emotional space to consider anything else, and I cling to the idea that justice must triumph. Isn't that what this has all been about?

But then Kate comes to the police headquarters, and when I sit across from her in a small room with a table and a couple of folding chairs, she looks at me gravely.

"This is serious, Libby." Her voice is grim.

I pry the lid off of the coffee she brought, my stomach roiling too much to attempt even a sip. "I know I shouldn't have touched her, but she was manhandling my dad."

"She didn't actually touch him."

"She did," I protest, but then, with a jolt, I realize I'm not actually sure; she might have just got all up in his face. I remember the spit on his cheek, though. "She fell down on purpose," I tell Kate.

"That's not what she's saying."

I let out a groan of frustration. "Of course it's not, but there were plenty of people there to see—"

"No one is saying that, Libby," she states quietly. "They're all saying you pushed her, and she seems pretty determined to press charges."

I groan again, pressing the heels of my hands into my eyes hard enough to hurt. "I can't believe this."

Kate sighs. "It is very unfortunate," she says, with something close to sympathy, but I suspect she blames me, and the truth is, I blame myself. I never should have lost my temper.

"Is my dad okay?" I look up, blinking Kate back into focus. "The police were practically useless. Did he get back home safely?" I realize how much it still matters to me.

"Yes, he's back at your house." She clearly doesn't want to talk about my dad. Her expression is as sober as if she's a doctor about to give me a terminal diagnosis. "Libby, I need to tell you, the penalty in the state of Virginia for assault and battery of a person based on their religion or ethnicity is a six-month prison sentence, *minimum*."

"What?" For a few stunned seconds the words simply do not compute. Assault and battery? *Prison?* "I didn't... What does her religion or ethnicity have to do with anything?"

"She's Jewish."

I close my eyes. "I didn't know that."

"It doesn't matter."

"Surely it should matter, because I can hardly assault someone based on their religion if I didn't know what it was!" My voice both rises and shakes; I am furious, but more than that, I am terrified. I can't go to *jail*. "Kate, I'm not a Nazi."

"I know." Her expression softens briefly. "But it's the optics of it all, Libby. They matter the most, and, in all honesty, they look really bad right now." She shrugs, more in acceptance than apology. "The truth is just a casualty."

Spoken like a true lawyer.

I stare into space, too tired even to think, to react, to feel. My terror is replaced by a familiar numbness, a cloak that covers me. I cannot believe this is happening, and yet some part of me is unsurprised, just waiting for things to get even worse.

"So what should I do?" I finally ask.

"Apologize publicly, for a start. And hope the reporter decides to be forgiving."

I can't believe I have been put in this position, and yet it is my own fault. I can't blame my dad for this; maybe I shouldn't be blaming him at all. "Okay," I say wearily, because I know I have no choice. "Can I get out of here?"

"You need to wait to see if you can be posted bail."

Good *grief*. My shoulders slump, and my head lolls forward. I simply cannot take anymore, I think. Not one thing more. I will snap. I will break. Then I wonder if I already have.

"That shouldn't be a problem, considering your history," Kate tells me bracingly. "If your father's not seen as a flight risk, then surely you won't be, either." She sighs. "The truth is, Libby, this is all something of a circus. It's all about what makes good news."

"Tell me about it." I shake my head. What I've learned is that no one even cares about the truth; they just want to be vindicated, scandalized, or better yet, both. But, I realize, I don't actually know what the truth *is*. If only my father would talk to me. If only I could be strong enough to hear whatever it is he has to say. If only I could let go of this anger and hurt and just... *be*. Be honest, like I want him to be. But I don't even know what that would look like anymore.

"I'll be in touch as soon as I can," Kate says, and she's gone before I can ask her if I'm likely to be in here for an hour or a day or worse.

I trudge back to my cell, still too tired to do anything but curl up on the thin mattress and close my eyes.

Maybe I sleep; maybe I just drift in a haze of despair, but time passes—minutes, hours—and then I receive another visitor. To my surprise, it's Simon Baum.

He looks as rumpled as always, his curly hair a bit disheveled, as I am unlocked from my cell. I feel a flicker of humiliation, but no more, because I am simply too weary to care.

"You're free to go," he tells me. "The reporter dropped the charges."

"What?" I blink at him, stunned. "She did? But... why?"

"Let's get a coffee," he says, and ushers me out of the police headquarters. I nod wearily, too exhausted to ask any more questions.

We end up at The Nook, an old-fashioned diner with deep, mahogany booths around the corner from the police station. Simon orders us both coffee and then glances at me.

"Have you eaten today?"

Wordlessly, I shake my head. He asks the waitress to bring

two "all the way" breakfasts—eggs, bacon, toast, grits, even though it's past lunchtime. I protest a little, saying I'm not hungry, and he shakes his head.

"You need to eat, and so do I." He hands the menus to the waitress with a smile, and then we are alone, facing each other.

"Thank you," I say belatedly. "I don't know what you did or why, but I'm very grateful not to be going to jail for a minimum of six months."

He shakes his head. "That never would have happened."

"My lawyer seemed to think it could."

"Your lawyer loves the drama as much as anyone else," he replies dryly. "That's the thing with these cases—it becomes less about what actually happened and more about how people feel about it, how they want to feel about it."

The waitress returns with two cups of black coffee and a pitcher of creamer. I wrap my hands around my cup as I watch Simon put no less than three packets of sweetener into his.

I still feel dazed. "So why did the reporter drop the charges?"

"Because I asked her to."

"You did?" I stare at him in surprise, wondering if I have misjudged him. This is just about the last thing I would have expected.

"I know how hairy it can get outside a courtroom. And I knew the reporter in question. And," he adds, taking a sip of his coffee, "I know you, at least a little."

I feel myself flushing, although I'm not sure why. I'm touched by his kindness, but also embarrassed by my own obvious failing. "I didn't know she was Jewish."

He shrugs. "It clearly wasn't a religiously motivated assault." A pause. "Although that's how the media will play it. And the reporter in question will get to look magnanimous, for dropping the charges."

"Of course." I let out a sigh that comes from the depths of

my being. "I'm so tired of it all," I tell him. "Tired of the media attention, tired of everyone in my family being tense or angry or sullen or silent. Tired of not knowing how I'm supposed to feel." I'm not sure why I'm telling Simon Baum this, but weirdly it feels right.

He nods in understanding. "What has happened is completely emotionally draining for you. I get it."

"You must see this a lot in your line of work." I think of the other people he's prosecuted, the families he's known. Did they fall apart like mine seems to be doing? "Do you ever feel sorry, for the... the pain you cause, to the families, the friends? Indirectly, I mean? I know it's not your fault or anything." *But it would have been better if you'd just let this all lie.* I don't say the words, of course, I don't even think them, not really, and yet, even so, they seem to hover between us.

"No," Simon replies flatly. "I don't ever feel sorry, not in that way. But I do feel sympathetic. Especially if the family had no idea. Although often they do."

So does that mean I'm different? My dad is? I realize I don't want to pursue that line of conversation just now. "Well, thank you, anyway," I tell him. "For getting me out of jail. Literally."

He nods, and the waitress returns with two enormous breakfasts, more food than I could possibly eat. I toy with my fork while Simon digs into his grits. After a few minutes of eating in silence, he lays down his fork and looks at me.

"Look, I don't usually get involved with the families of those I'm trying to bring to justice, but the truth is you seem different. Most people wouldn't have handed that evidence in, for starters." I grimace, and he nods as if I have spoken and he is agreeing with me. "It was hard, I know that. And I respect you, for doing it. It was brave, but a lot of people won't see it as courage."

I stare down at my barely touched breakfast. "My daughter doesn't."

"She's angry with you?"

"That would be an understatement."

He lets out a small sigh. "I'm sorry."

"Thanks."

"You shouldn't blame yourself for what your father did, you know, or beat yourself up for not knowing."

"I don't blame myself," I tell him. "At least, I don't think I do." I swallow hard and then admit painfully, "But maybe I blame myself for loving him. How could I have loved someone and not known what they were capable of? Am I that bad a judge of character?"

"I think," Simon answers, "that it's not as much about having loved him before, but how you feel now. How you choose to feel. What you have to decide—and I can tell it's eating you up—is whether you can still love him now. And I'm not going to make any judgments about whether you should or not, because I don't know. But after the media attention dies down, after your father goes to Germany, or jail, or wherever he ends up, that question will remain. And it's one only you can answer."

I stare at him as he resumes eating his eggs, and I realize he's right. I've been tying myself in knots, filled with a despairing uncertainty, because I feel like I can't love my father anymore and yet I *want* to. Even though I'm angry, even though the hurt I feel still cripples me, I want to love him and be loved back. It's a desire that is at the absolute core of my being, shot through my heart and soul, and yet it feels almost impossible now, as well as wrong. Too much has happened, too much has become known. And yet I still long for it, utterly.

"He won't even talk to me about it," I tell Simon. "How can I decide whether I can still love him if I can't even get any answers?"

He takes a sip of coffee, putting his cup down as he meets my eye. "You are never going to get the answers you want," he tells me matter-of-factly. "Because they're not there. They don't exist. That I know." I swallow hard. I know he's right, but I don't want him to be. "Your father isn't the man you thought he was," he states clearly. "He never will be again. What you need to decide is if you can still love the man you now know him to be."

After paying for my meal on his own insistence, Simon drives me home. As I walk into my house, I feel as if the tectonic plates of my world have shifted—again. Earthquake after earthquake. When will I find my balance?

"*Libby*." Tim is in the kitchen, his phone in his hand. "Where have you been? Kate told me you'd been released hours ago. I've been calling and calling—"

"I'm sorry." I'd switched off my phone in the courtroom and, with all the events of the morning, had forgotten to switch it on again when the police gave it back to me. I walk to the fridge as a matter of habit, although after eating some of that enormous breakfast, I'm not actually hungry. "It's been quite a day."

"We were worried." There is an uncharacteristic edge to Tim's voice and I stiffen.

"I'm sorry," I say again.

"Where were you?"

"Talking with Simon Baum."

"Simon *Baum*?" Tim sounds understandably disbelieving.

"Yes. He was surprisingly sympathetic. He's the one who managed to get the reporter to drop the charges."

Simon is silent, and I turn from the fridge to look at him. His expression is almost angry, his jaw tight. I feel a flicker of fear. "What?" I ask.

He puts his phone down on the counter, carefully, as if it might break. "You didn't call me," he states, and I stare at him uneasily.

"I switched my phone off when we went into court."

He nods slowly, his gaze now on the floor. "Yes, but after. When you were arrested. When you were taken to the police. When you were released, when you went out with Simon Baum for who knows how long. You didn't call me *once*."

"They took my phone when I was... incarcerated." I try for a smile, but Tim's expression is uncharacteristically stony. I abandon my attempt at lightness for a genuine apology. "I'm sorry, Tim. It was all kind of overwhelming, and I... I didn't think. But it's finished now. The reporter's dropped the charges." Of course I know it isn't really finished; it's barely begun. It will be on tonight's news, and even after that, it will always be online, dissected on blogs and posts and editorials. Besides, beyond my arrest, we've still got my father's extradition to face, his criminal trial in Germany, whatever happens afterwards. But it doesn't seem Tim is even thinking of any of those things.

"Libby..." He looks down at the floor for a few seconds and then back up at me, shaking his head slowly. "Did you not even think of calling me?"

"I..." What can I say? "I knew you had Em and Lucas. I didn't want you to worry." I didn't want to admit what I'd done, or fall apart on the phone.

"Didn't want me to *worry*?" His voice rises, a throb of anger in it. "You must have known I'd see it on the news? That Kate would call me? That your dad would come home and tell me what had happened? Of course I'd damn well *worry*."

I feel a shrinking inside, as well as a hollowing out, as if I am becoming smaller, emptier. "Tim..." What can I say? "I'm sorry. I really didn't think."

"I think you did think," he returns flatly. "I think you chose not to tell me, because you want to handle things on your own. You don't ever want to *need* me, Libby."

I bite my lip, caught between guilt and a weary exasperation. There's a lot of truth in that, I know there is, but in this case, it was really that I just didn't think. Although, I realize uncomfortably, was that simply because it was second nature not to bother Tim with my troubles? Not to show him my weakness? "I really am sorry," I say humbly.

"I know." He blows out a breath as he rakes his hand through his hair. "It's not that I'm angry," he tells me, and then amends, "All right, yes, I am a little angry, but I guess more than that, I'm hurt. Why won't you let me help? Why won't you tell me this stuff? You unloaded to Simon Baum of all people, but you can't even send me a text when you've been *arrested*? Did they give you a chance to phone someone?"

"I... I don't remember. I am sorry," I say yet again, because I don't have any other words.

"It's not even about that, Lib." Tim looks at me full in the face, and there is so much pain in his eyes that I have to look away. "Today is just a... symptom. It's like you're keeping part of yourself from me. Like you always have. This isn't... this isn't an issue that's suddenly come up and surprised us both. It's always been there. This has... revealed it, maybe." He lowers his head, his voice quiet and sad. "Stress doesn't create the fault lines, it just shows us where they are."

I'm still not looking at him. I know he's right and what he's saying is important, but I also know, absolutely, that right now I cannot handle any more strain in my life, my marriage, without breaking down completely. "I hear you," I say, and Tim's mouth tightens as he senses my prevarication. "I really do," I insist. "But... can we please not do this now? With everything else going on?"

"But there will never be a good time, will there?" Tim retorts, his voice full of frustration even as his shoulders slump in defeat. "Because when it is a good time, when the media palaver has finally died down, when your dad is... when that's resolved, we'll just go back to the way we were. And we'll pretend that it's fine, it's good enough, because that feels easier. Well, I'm telling you now, for me, it isn't. I don't want only the shiny parts of you that you're willing to present to the world. That's not a marriage."

I finally look at him, and I see an implacability in his face that shocks me to the core, even as it somehow fails to surprise me. Was I expecting this, on some level? I think of all the disaster scenarios I envisioned as a child, lying in my bed, peering into dark corners for spiders, monsters under the bed. Well, here they are, just as I knew they would be, and yet I never predicted how it would happen. In my what-if scenarios, I took control. I stayed strong in the whirlwind, I defeated the monster, I averted the disaster, all by myself. Now it seems that was my weakness all along.

"So what are you saying?" I ask after a moment, my tone flat. "That you want a... a divorce?" The word feels foreign.

"A divorce?" The incredulity in Tim's voice would be heartening if I didn't feel so wretched. "No. No, of course not. Libby..." He takes a step toward me, and for a second, I feel a flicker of hope, a tremor of happiness, like a pulse enlivening me. Whatever is going on here, we can get through it. We can move past this. Together, if we try. If I do.

Then Em comes running into the kitchen, her face pale, her eyes wide. "Mom, there's a police car outside."

The police, again?

I glance at Tim, who sighs and gives a little shrug. "I guess there might be some follow-up," he says quietly.

I stare at him, stricken, for a second before I head for the front door. What if the reporter has changed her mind? Is she going to press charges, after all? Can she do that? My stomach is churning as I open the door to two burly blue-uniformed officers, just like I imagined, back when Em first called me. When this all began, a lifetime ago.

"Mrs. Trent?"

I have to swallow hard before I speak. "Yes?"

The police look somber, like they've just been to a funeral. I am already bracing myself, but even so, I am flattened by what they say next.

"We're here to talk to you about your daughter, Emily Trent."

CHAPTER 21

JANUARY 1943

Sobibor, Poland

There was a foot of snow on the ground, a hard, grimy, icy crust throughout the camp, and soft, pristine pillows of it in the forest, weighing down the boughs of the trees, decorating them like mounds of icing on a cake. All around, there was beauty, and yet after three months at Sobibor, Hans knew he had become far too accustomed to ugliness. It felt impossible for him not to; it stole into his very bones and rotted his heart right out.

All autumn, the transports had come in fits and starts; sometimes two a day, sometimes none for a week. It was horrific when they came, but in some ways, it was worse when they didn't. Hans had seen how the officers became restless and bored, if they didn't have enough to do; he'd soon realized that was when they were at their most dangerous. He saw how their speculative gaze moved around the camp, looking for an easy target. He had watched, trying to hide his horror, while they'd made up their evil, intolerable games, forcing prisoners to jump up and down or walk like ducks while they shot at them at random, almost lazily, not interested enough even to watch them fall.

Once, when a particularly unpleasant officer, Gomerski, was forcing a Jew to eat an entire salami whole, while he choked and gagged, his face red, his eyes bulging and desperate, Hans had intervened.

"What's the point?" he had asked the other officer, trying to keep his voice light, bored, as if he found it all as trivial as Gomerski did. "You're wasting a perfectly good salami."

Gomerski, with his craggy face and weary expression, had given Hans a quick, searching look. "What are you, a Jew-lover?" he had sneered.

"Hardly," Hans had replied, doing his best to scoff. He forced himself not to look at the choking prisoner. "But I don't like to see good food go to waste."

"Too true," Gomerski had replied, and then, with an ugly, gloating sort of smile, he had taken out his pistol and shot the man in the head, the same way Wagner had done that first day.

Hans had stiffened, doing his utmost to keep his expression neutral as the man fell, dead, at his feet. That was the second death he was responsible for, he thought, whether he'd meant it or not. He had stared down at the ground, watching the blood soak into the dirt, before he forced himself to look up and meet Gomerski's narrowed, knowing gaze.

"You've still wasted a salami," he had forced out, managing to keep his tone curt, and then he had made himself stroll away as if the whole matter had been negligible, tedious.

That had been back in November, when everything had felt new and raw and shocking; by January, Hans realized he was as inured to the violence and sadism as if he'd been born to it himself. He barely blinked when one of the officers got his gun out, when a prisoner fell down dead, dragged away by his ankles, leaving nothing but a rusty streak of blood on the sandy yard. It had become commonplace, practically dull; death was everywhere.

The sweetish, rotting smell of the place—the smell of burning bodies and rotting corpses, when they piled up in front of the crematorium—was on his clothes, his hair, even in his skin. It was part of himself, and he thought it would be forever; fifty years from now, if he lived that long, and he doubted very much that he would, he knew he would still smell it on himself. He would never be free of the stench.

He realized he now barely heard the screams and cries from the courtyard as he worked through a column of figures in his little office, focusing on the numbers, just like Anni did—or used to, she seemed less inclined to wrestle with a complex math problem these days. Still, the numbers were solid, unchanging, trustworthy. They were his friends now.

And yet he could not stay staring at a column of figures forever, as much as he longed to. There was Daniel Weiss, toiling next to him every day, his son Leo so silent and watchful, knowing which tool to hand his father, or how to fan the charcoal to a glowing ember. Hans had done his best to be civil but curt, not trusting himself to be anything more, but with Anni that proved impossible.

Anni, Hans realized, was still somewhat protected from the utter grimness of their surroundings, and that felt like the one small mercy in this godforsaken place. He could not save himself, he saw that plainly now, but he could still save Anni. He could make sure she was protected from the worst of it, at least; he could keep her a little innocent. Of course, Anni didn't consider herself innocent; she acted as if she were as knowledgeable as Hans, as if she'd seen the horrors of the ramp alongside him, but he knew she hadn't, not really.

She hadn't witnessed the weeping crowds whipped down the dreaded *Schlauch*, mothers clutching children, husbands stoically holding the hands of their sons; she hadn't watched the prisoners scrub the yard of its bloodstains after they'd gone, their heads bent low to avoid catching anyone's eye.

She knew about camp three with its gas chambers and crematoria, but only in theory; she had not seen them drag the bodies out; she had not heard the agonized screams when the doors were sealed, fists hammering against steel. She had never watched Wagner or Bolender or any of the others gaze on dispassionately while that monstrous dog ripped a person to pieces. She knew about it all, or at least suspected some of it, but she hadn't *seen*. Not like he had. It was the difference, Hans knew, between hearing the echo of a gunshot and having the still-warm blood fleck your face.

Anni kept to their cottage in the officers' quarters, but, after Daniel Weiss' arrival, she began to appear in his office. Hans had tried to keep her from returning, but it was like holding back the tide. She was determined to be kind to Daniel and his son and, reluctantly, Hans allowed it—not that he could have stopped his sister anyway—because it brought her joy and it assuaged his guilt, if only an infinitesimal amount.

The friendship that had sprung up between the pair of them had happened surprisingly, yet by design. Anni's design. A week after Daniel Weiss had set up his little goldsmithing table in Hans' office, she had come into his office with a basket over one arm and a stubborn look on her face that he knew well.

"I've brought lunch," she had announced, setting the basket on the table. "Bread and cheese and some tinned ham. It's a pity for food to go to waste."

"Anni," Hans had said, a warning, but she'd thrust her chin out and glared at him, and he had fallen silent. Who was he to begrudge a starving man the pleasure of a round of cheese, a loaf of bread? Or, he realized, the chance to chat, listen, even laugh.

Of course, that hadn't happened right away. The first time Anni had brought lunch, Daniel and his son had eaten it with their heads lowered, not meeting her gaze, mumbling their thanks before stuffing the food into their mouths. Anni had watched them, head cocked, lips pursed thoughtfully.

The second day she had come, she had brought her notebook with all its numbers. "I thought I might teach Leo," she had told Daniel, who had stared at her in wordless shock. "It has to be dull to be standing there all day, watching you work. Does he like numbers?"

"He only speaks a little German," Daniel had said after a moment.

"Then I will teach him that too," Anni had replied immediately, unfazed. "Although I prefer numbers." She had smiled playfully at Leo. "Perhaps you could teach me to count in Polish."

"This isn't a good idea," Hans had told her later, when they were back at their cottage. "Teaching a Jew, being friends with one. Anni, you'll only bring disaster on them as well as you. The other officers, the guards—they don't like it." Hans had heard the gossip, how an officer had been transferred after an affair with a Jewess, the ultimate transgression, it seemed.

"That is, if anyone finds out," Anni had scoffed. "And why should they?"

"If they come into the office—"

"But no one ever does, unless it's to deliver the money, and I wait until they've gone." She had shaken her head, smiling, but also scornful. "Do you think I'm stupid?"

No, Hans had thought, *but reckless, yes*. Reckless and naïve in her own way, although she didn't realize it. She hadn't been there when Bolender had burst into the office a few days before, furious that Weiss was making Wagner a ring and not him, after he'd demanded one for himself and the goldsmith had told him he would make it after he'd finished Wagner's.

Bolender had punched him full in the face, knocking out a tooth, while Hans had simply stood and watched. Then

Bolender had taken out his pistol and pressed it to Weiss' temple, the look in his eyes reminding Hans of a maddened dog.

"Really, you shouldn't cost Wagner *two* goldsmiths," Hans had said, disguising the shaking of his voice with a cough. "It's hardly worth it. Besides, I heard the commandant saying he wanted rings made for all the officers, with the SS insignia on each. He has been quite impressed by the Jew's skills."

The pistol had wavered. "Did he?" Bolender had asked, with a cautious lilt of interest.

Hans had shrugged indifferently. "So he said." Actually, Reichleitner *hadn't* said; he had not even seen Weiss. Hans had thought of the notion on the spot, but he would find a way to plant the idea in the commandant's head, somehow.

After another tense few seconds and one more careless punch, Bolender had lowered the pistol and left.

Weiss had let out a shaky breath, clasping his silent son to him. He'd looked over at Hans, not as a prisoner to his captor, but a man to a man. "Thank you," he'd said quietly, wiping the blood from his chin. Hans had jerked his head in the semblance of a nod, and they'd both gone back to work.

Anni hadn't seen any of that. She didn't understand.

"Do you know what will happen, if you are discovered?" Hans had asked her in a low voice. "Can you imagine it?"

"I don't need to."

"Anni... these men... they will shoot a Jew in the head as soon as look at him. And worse things—"

"I *know*."

But she didn't, Hans thought, not really. She couldn't.

And so he had let her come, because trying to stop her seemed even more dangerous, and he had watched out of the corner of his eye as she taught Leo both German and numbers, and he taught her some Polish in return, heard Anni's laughter and caught Leo's shy smiles.

One day in mid-November, he had seen Daniel eyeing both

Anni and Leo, their heads bent together, with something like dread, and he wondered if he felt the same fear Hans did, that nothing good could come of this, that they were all courting danger.

"My sister means well," he had told him one afternoon, after Anni had gone. "She is trying to help."

Daniel had nodded once, his gaze on his little brazier with its smoking charcoal. "Yes."

"I know it is not easy."

Daniel had let out a huff of hopeless laughter, staring at the small, smoking brazier in front of him. "You could say that, yes," he had said, and something about his tone, the weariness of it, the driest of humor, made Hans pause.

Even now, months later, he realized he'd separated Daniel Weiss and his son in his head; he'd still assumed they were somehow different to him. The idea that they were not, not at all, was too horrifying to contemplate for very long. It was part of the reason why he hadn't asked the man any questions, why he barely talked to him, even as Anni seemed determined to be his friend, along with the boy's.

"Were you always a goldsmith?" he had asked suddenly, and Daniel had given him a wary, measured look.

"Yes," he had said after a moment, "as my father before me. But I did not always want to be one, although it was expected."

"No?" Hans had recalled his own reluctance to train as an accountant, as his father had, when he was eighteen. He'd had vague dreams of going into the Wehrmacht, or even the Luftwaffe. Of course it had come to nothing; he supposed he should be glad of that now.

"No, I wanted to be a musician." Daniel had smiled faintly, the creases around his eyes deepening. Although he was only about thirty, he looked far more haggard than Hans, the years etched on his face. "I played the violin, once upon a time."

Leo had said something in Polish, and Hans had looked at him in curiosity. "What did he say?" he had asked Daniel.

"He said I was good, when I used to play."

"Why don't you play anymore?" Hans had asked, realizing after he'd spoken how stupid a question it was. "I mean, not here, but..." He had trailed off.

"The Gestapo destroyed my violin when they burst into my apartment in 1939," Daniel had replied, almost conversationally. "They suspected I was a member of the Secret Polish Army, an underground resistance movement." He had shrugged. "I wasn't, but in any case, we were all deported to Warsaw in 1940. We weren't allowed to take anything with us."

Hans had been silent. He'd had no idea what to say. He'd known the Jews had been forced into ghettoes, of course; he'd seen it in Stuttgart. But he hadn't heard it from a man's own lips, he hadn't been able to imagine a family, a family like *his*, being herded along the street, into a train, with nothing but the clothes on their backs—and why? *Why?* Because they happened to be Jewish.

He had let out a shaky breath. He did not like having these thoughts. It had been easier, he realized, when he hadn't known. When he hadn't let himself think, when he'd been able to believe that Jews were different, contentedly complacent in that attitude. After a few seconds, he had reached for his column of figures. They didn't speak again.

Hans did manage, however, to speak to Reichleitner about the SS rings, during a night of cards; he'd made himself go, at Anni's bidding, even though he found the evenings interminable. Reichleitner, thankfully, was quite taken with the idea. Weiss would have enough work to keep him alive for months, or so Hans had hoped.

And, meanwhile, Anni came to his office almost every day, as merry as a cricket, often bringing lunch in a cloth-covered basket, teasing Leo till he smiled, asking Daniel questions about his life back in Poznan while Hans listened silently. He learned that the Weisses came from a long line of goldsmiths, and Daniel's grandfather had made medals for the Prussian military; that his wife had worked as a seamstress in a tailor's shop and he'd bought a suit he didn't need just so he could see her. After a few weeks, he even talked about his daughter Hannah, only four years old when she'd been gassed to death. With a tremor in his voice, Daniel told Anni how they'd nicknamed her *Mala Mis*, or little bear, because she'd loved honey so much.

All these details scraped and chafed him; they made Daniel as real a man as he was, not just flesh and blood, but heart and soul. And yet, each evening Hans walked out of that office and into the horror that was Sobibor and found himself getting hardened to it all, to all the flesh-and-blood men like Daniel whose lives held unimaginable suffering until they were condemned to die, because it was impossible not to do so and live.

In January, he was given two weeks off, to be spent at one of the SS rest huts. There was no question of returning to Stuttgart. Hans thought if he could have gone back home, he would have found some way never to come back.

"I don't want to go," Anni stated flatly when he told her about the holiday. "Two weeks is far too long to be away."

Hans let out a huff of sound, something caught between despair and a weary, defeated humor. "You'll miss this place?"

"I am counting the days until we are able to leave here," Anni replied tartly, "whenever that blessed time comes. But we cannot leave Daniel and Leo alone and vulnerable. You know that, Hans. Your presence protects them."

Hans shook his head. "I don't think my presence matters one whit, Anni." It hurt to say. Even now, he clung to some small, stubborn shred of pride that he was important.

"Nonsense. You arranged for him to make the rings—"

"And he's still making the rings. He's safe until then, at least, so we could go."

Anni shook her head and, to his shame, Hans found himself bursting out, "Please. Please, Anni. I... I must get away from here. Just for a few days, if not the whole two weeks." He covered his eyes with his hand, embarrassed by his own weakness. "Please," he whispered.

"Oh, Hans." Anni rose from her chair and came over to put her arms around him. "I'm sorry. I didn't think."

"Just a few days." His voice was no more than a whisper. He pressed his cheek against Anni's hair, breathing in the sweet, clean smell of her. She was everything good in his life—the only good, amidst all the wreckage and horror.

"A few days, then," she agreed. "I suppose it will be all right."

Those few days passed in a blink of an eye; Hans could have stayed at the holiday camp for a month or more. The place was in the mountains, a simple wooden chalet tucked high among the pines, the air cold and clear, the only sound the hoot of an owl or the whisper of wind in the trees.

Most of the SS officers played cards or went hunting; the few women—SS auxiliaries from another camp, Auschwitz—went on walks or sat about chatting and flirting with the officers, none of them seeming to have a care in the world. Hans and Anni kept to themselves; neither of them had any desire to socialize. Hans went on long walks through the snowy forest, trudging through the heavy, wet snow that came up nearly to his knees, breathing in the cold, pure air as if could cleanse him. He walked for hours, enjoying the pull on his muscles, the way his breath came in tearing gasps and his chest burned. He walked as if the mere act of it could somehow both strengthen and absolve him, as if he could actually get somewhere.

The day before they were to return to Sobibor, Anni brightened, as if she was about to go on holiday rather than leave the only respite they'd had. While Hans had walked in the forest, she'd written new lessons for Leo, pages and pages of arithmetic problems and German phrases. She had them all in a neat pile, ready for their return. Hans saw her smile to herself and he wondered how she had managed to hold onto hope, even as he was glad that she had. And he would make sure she held onto it, he told himself. He would go back—and God knew he dreaded the thought with a terrible, numbing dread that crept over him in a horrified paralysis—but he would keep Anni innocent—or as innocent as one could be, in a place like Sobibor.

That night, Hans climbed into his bed, pulling the scratchy blanket up over him as he pressed his face into his pillow, and could not keep the hot tears from seeping out from under his lids.

CHAPTER 22

LIBBY

The policemen are apologetic but firm as I numbly usher them into our kitchen. Tim has sent Em upstairs, with a sterner word than he normally would have, and we are seated at the kitchen table, our hands neatly folded, waiting for them to speak. I have absolutely no idea what they could possibly have to say about my eleven-year-old daughter.

"We're here informally," the first one says, a kindly-looking man in his forties with hazel eyes and close-cropped sandy hair, "but I'm afraid we have received reports that your daughter's online activity constitutes hate speech."

Tim and I both goggle. *Hate speech?* From *Em?*

I open my mouth, scramble for thoughts, words. I had no idea what to expect, and yet it still wasn't this. "I... What online activity?"

"Some tweets—"

"Em's not even on Twitter, or any social media." I speak quickly, firmly. "She has no social media access at all." Except I am remembering how she brought the iPad to her room, the cleared search history, her angry defiance. It would be easy enough for her to create a Twitter account, an email address, whatever she wanted. We have some parental controls on the device, but they're for things like porn and violence. We didn't think we needed to restrict apps I wasn't even sure she knew about.

"I'm afraid she is on Twitter," the second police officer tells us. He's older, with a belly hanging over his belt, a tired, jaded air about him. "The account is in her name, and the tweets were made from the IP address of this location. We received a report—"

"From who?" I demand, and the officers exchange glances.

"That's confidential, but it was someone who knows your daughter and is concerned for her."

Which makes me feel both angry and ashamed, like I'm the one who has done something wrong. Who went to the police rather than to me directly? What kind of *concern* is that?

"You're here informally," Tim says after a moment. "What does that mean, exactly?"

"Given... the current situation," the older officer says, "we felt we needed to follow up on this. But we're not going to arrest her," he adds, and I can't tell if he's joking or not. Is arresting an eleven-year-old actually a possibility? "We're here really to give her a warning. Could we talk to her?"

"No," I reply swiftly. "Absolutely not. We're her parents, we'll talk to her about this." Em would be terrified to be *warned* by two big, burly police officers. And yet... hate speech. *What*?

The older officer shifts in his chair. "While this isn't a punishable offense, it can have serious consequences. If it comes to the attention of her school, for example, she could be looking at a suspension or even expulsion." He gives me a significant look, and I wonder if he knows I was arrested this morning.

"Thank you, noted," Tim says. He rises from his chair. "We'll certainly take this matter in hand. Hate speech is, of course, a serious issue. A very serious issue."

He ushers the officers out of the house while I simply sit

there, staring into space. My brain feels as if it has stalled out, and I cannot get it back into gear.

"We need to talk to Em about this," Tim says when he comes back into the kitchen.

"Yes." I shake my head slowly, still disbelieving. "What could she have possibly posted?" That was bad enough to warrant a visit from the police?

"I don't know." He rubs his cheek. "But she's been pretty angry lately, and kids can be stupid. Really stupid."

My stomach cramps. What if she is suspended for whatever thoughtless thing she wrote? Expelled, even? The repercussions from Simon Baum's visit, from my dad's past, just keep going on and on, in ways I never could have imagined. Never would have wanted to imagine.

"Let's go upstairs—" I rise from my chair, only to have Tim put a hand out to stop me.

"Maybe I should talk to her, Lib."

"What?" I blink at him, too surprised to be hurt. "What do you mean?"

"By myself. I know it's not fair, but she's been angry with you. And considering you were arrested only this morning..." He trails off, shrugging, not quite in apology.

"I don't have a leg to stand on, you mean?" I finish. I can see he has a point, but I've always been the one to talk to Em about the serious stuff. I've walked her through her anxieties; we've done the whole puberty-and-periods conversation, awkward questions included. I've listened to her worry about whether she'll have someone to sit with at lunch, or if her PE uniform makes her look too gangly. I want to be the one who walks with her through this. Besides, if I slink away like I've done something wrong—and all right, maybe I *have*—what kind of message is that sending to my daughter? "Let's talk to her together," I tell Tim. "I don't want to just absent myself entirely."

He looks like he wants to protest, and I'm reminded of the

argument we were having before the police arrived—more than an argument, more like the tectonic plates of our marriage shifting. Cracking.

"All right," he relents, and I am filled with relief. We'll talk about our marriage another time. Right now, we need to focus on our daughter.

Upstairs, Em is huddled on her bed, bony arms wrapped around her knees, face tear-stained yet defiant.

"What?" she throws at us before we've barely stepped through the door. I can see the guilt and fear written on her face plainly, and my heart aches.

"Em..." I begin, keeping my voice gentle, "the police were here because of something you posted online."

Her gaze darts away she hunches her shoulders. Tim sits next to her on the bed, and there's no room for me, so I end up standing, when what I really want to do is sit down and put my arms around my daughter.

"Can you tell us what it was, Em?" Tim asks. "What you posted?"

"Just... stuff."

"Stuff they said constituted hate speech," I fill in, my voice sharpening just a little, and Tim gives me a quelling glance. Maybe I am too close to it all. Too raw, as if I've been split wide open. But first my father, now Em? *My whole family.* I realize this might be yet another conversation I can't handle.

I wait for Em to speak.

"Everything is hate speech these days," she declares with a shrug. "But of course you believe them rather than me." As if this is some sort of habit we've fallen into, to doubt our daughter, to think the worst.

I bite my lip to keep from saying something else sharp.

"Why don't you just show us what you posted," Tim suggests. "And then we can talk about it."

Her arms tighten around her knees and she doesn't reply.

"Em." Once again I sound too stern, mainly to hide my fear. "Show us the iPad."

"It's downstairs," she retorts, and I take an even breath, let it out.

"I'll go get it."

I walk downstairs slowly, using the few moments it takes to get the iPad to calm myself. As I head back out of the kitchen, Lucas pokes his head through the basement doorway.

"What's going on?" he asks, frowning, and I shake my head.

"Nothing you need to worry about." I walk quickly out of the room before he can ask any more questions.

Upstairs, Tim has his arm around Em and she is leaning into him, which should make me feel encouraged, but I struggle not to feel excluded, as if this is somehow a rejection of me.

Wordlessly, I hand the iPad to Em and she takes it reluctantly, holding it on her lap like she's not going to do anything with it.

"Em," I say after a moment, and she glares at me. "Please show us what it was you wrote."

She sighs heavily, gives me another glare for good measure, and then swipes to turn on the device. I wait, with held breath, as she taps and swipes the screen until her Twitter account loads. Then she hands the iPad to Tim before flinging herself back on the bed, arms folded as she stares up at the ceiling.

Tim scans the tweets on the page, his forehead furrowed, and my fingers twitch with the urge to snatch the device from him, to see what is on that screen. After a few endless minutes, he hands it to me, looking troubled.

I gaze down at the screen and for a second I can't believe what I'm reading. This cannot be my daughter's account. And yet it obviously is—EmTrentVA is her username, no hiding it at all.

And yet... the words. The awful absurdity as well as the utter vitriol. *Did u know the Holocaust was actually a HOAX?*

So many of the photos were FAKED. With a link to a Holocaust denial site I know I don't want to see.

And other tweets too, all with offensive claims—that the Allies faked the pictures to incriminate Germans; that the Allies committed more atrocities than the Nazis ever did; that the Jews that died in the camps were already diseased, the Nazis didn't actually kill them. There are even a few slurs against Jews themselves, which chills me right through. Most of it looks copy and pasted, with lots of links and hashtags, but how could she have endorsed this stuff? God help us if she actually believes it.

My stomach churns as I force myself to read through them all—about twenty in total, over the course of the last few weeks.

I look up at my daughter, who turns from her study of the ceiling to give me a coolly appraising look, as if she stands behind every awful word she wrote.

"Em," I say, and my voice is hoarse, choked. "What on earth were you thinking?"

Instantly, she turns mutinous. "What do you know about it?"

"More than you do," I fire back before I can think better of it. Out of the corner of my eye, I see Tim give me a recriminating look, but I keep going. I have to. "Em. *Em*. You must know the Holocaust isn't a... a hoax. There's so much evidence. Photographs, eyewitnesses, survivors... your grandmother's family all *died* in a camp!" She looks uncertain for a second, and realization slams through me. "Did you not know that?" Had I never told her, because I've never talked about my mother? I should have, I realize. Of course I should have. "In Theresienstadt," I tell her, my voice shaking. "She survived because she was considered only half-Jewish, and so she wasn't put in the camp, but everyone else died. They were killed, Em, in gas chambers." *My family*. Strange, how I've never really thought about it like that before. My mother's family was as ghostlike as she was.

Em thrusts her lower lip out and I continue more stridently, "Sweetheart, if you talked to Grandad about it, he would tell you the same. He was at a camp, too. He knows it really happened. That's why..." *He's being prosecuted.* I stop, try again as I gesture to the iPad. "I can understand, a little bit, why you would think..." I stop once more, because it's abhorrent, what she posted, and I can't let myself justify it. *But she's only eleven,* I think, *and she's hurting so much.* "Em, you have to delete these tweets immediately. This instant. They're wrong. They're... evil."

"Libby," Tim says quietly, and I swing around to face him.

"You know they are! I appreciate Em is hurting, but this is... this is inexcusable. Vile."

"*Libby.*"

I draw a shuddering breath. I try to rein back the words, the emotions, for Em's sake, but part of me wants to take her by the shoulders and shake her. *Do you realize what could happen now?* I want to shriek. If the school gets wind of these tweets... Em will be disciplined, maybe even expelled, the story will find its way to the press, on top of my arrest this morning, and our family will be utterly vilified. Forever.

I thrust the iPad toward her and her face twists as she takes it, looking at me with what only can be described as hatred. Em, my Em, looking at me like that. Is it my fault? Am I expecting too much, like Grace said? Being judgmental? And yet... those tweets. What parent would turn a blind eye to something like that?

"That's all you care about, isn't it," she tosses at me as she swipes and taps. "How things look."

Where on earth did she get *that* idea from? "I'm just trying to protect you."

"And what about Grandad?" she flares. "You weren't trying to protect him, were you, when you turned him in!"

"I didn't turn him in," I snap, goaded into a sharp retort. "I provided evidence—"

"They wouldn't have arrested him if you hadn't!" Her face is blotchy with both fury and grief as she screams at me, the torrent let loose. "You made it possible for them to arrest him! To take him away! Your own father! How could you *do* that!" And then she's sobbing, my poor little girl, as if her heart could break. She tosses the iPad aside and it lands on the floor with an alarming crack while she flings herself face down on her bed, her whole body shaking with the force of her feeling.

"Em." I take a step toward her, but she jerks away from me. My fists clench even as my heart aches. *How did we end up in this place?* "I did the right thing," I tell her, my voice trembling, though I try to keep it steady. "Sometimes that feels very hard, and it may have consequences that you don't like or want, but that doesn't make it *wrong*."

"Libby." Tim puts a hand on Em's shoulder as he gives me a quiet, restraining look. "I think... I think maybe just leave her alone right now."

It takes me a second to realize he means with him. I'm only making things worse, trying to justify my own actions. Actions that still make me feel guilty, even though I honestly don't think I could have done anything other than what I did.

I take a deep breath, make myself nod, and then walk out of the room to my own bedroom.

I pace back and forth, rubbing my arms, feeling a deep coldness inside that I fear I'll never shake. When the children were little, I could go down rabbit holes of potential disasters, spending nights awake worried they might choke on a Cheerio, or fall off a slide and hit their head, or develop meningitis or sepsis and I'd realize too late. I'd imagined so many ways things could go wrong, but I'd never once envisioned something like this. That my child would as good as hate me. That I'd wonder if I deserved it.

After a few minutes, there is a tap at my door. "Yes?" I call as I stop pacing.

Half of me is futilely hoping it might be Em, but it is Lucas who pushes open the door, leaning his shoulder against the frame. "What's going on with Em?"

"She's upset about Grandad." He gives me a well-duh look and I sigh wearily. "And she... she has acted out in ways that aren't helpful."

"She shouldn't blame you, Mom," Lucas tells me, and I blink, surprised, gratified.

"Thank you for saying that."

He shrugs. "Speaking out can be really hard."

I have a strange sense that he's not talking about me or my father, but then he shrugs again, pushing off the doorframe, and disappears. That was a more heartfelt conversation than we've had in a long time, and I am encouraged, even though I still feel spent, despairing.

Then my phone rings. When I fish it out of my pocket, I see, with a sinking sensation, that it is Karen Bain, the CEO of Fresh Start, and I'm pretty sure this can't be good. Yet something else to go wrong in my life, I think, and I almost want to laugh. What else can happen? What fresh disaster?

"Libby?" Her voice is taut, with no pretense of caring concern or friendly interest.

"Hi, Karen."

"Look," she says without preamble, "I've just been on the phone with our board of trustees, and we are all in agreement that considering the recent media coverage and today's unfortunate events, it's best if you take a step back from your position."

"A step back?" I realize I should have been expecting this.

"We appreciate your service, but obviously having one of our area managers act violently toward a woman is not the kind of representation we want for Fresh Start, and what it stands for. Understandably, you've been under some stress, and we've taken that into account. We think a three-month suspension at this point is both appropriate and necessary, and we'll re-evaluate at the end of October."

"I didn't push her," I say, uselessly, and Karen just sighs.

"Like I said, you're under stress. This isn't meant to be a punishment, Libby. With everything that's going on, I'm sure you could use some time off."

Except it is a punishment, obviously.

"Yes," I agree after a pause, because I know there's nothing else I can say. "Thank you."

She offers a few more brisk pleasantries and then she ends the call.

I sink onto the bed, my phone in my hand. In the course of a single day, I have been arrested, imprisoned, made national news for all the wrong reasons, and potentially lost my job. But amidst all that, it's Em's rejection of me that hurts the most. Makes me feel as if I've failed her. *What kind of mother...*

I don't know how long I've been sitting there, staring into space, when Tim comes into our room. "Em's taking a shower," he tells me. "The account is deleted and I've written an email to Twitter's complaints department, explaining the situation. The fact that she's only eleven will go some way to mitigating the situation, I think."

"The media won't care about that."

"Maybe the media will miss this one," he replies. "Think about all the vitriol that's spewed on Twitter on a daily basis. In any case, there's nothing more we can do."

I shake my head slowly. "Why would she write those things? I know she's angry and she wants to—I don't know, excuse my dad, I suppose—but the Holocaust a *hoax*...?"

"She didn't mean it. She barely knows what the Holocaust

is. It was just a way for her to make sense of it all, Lib." He sits down next to me on the bed. "Don't take it to heart."

I take a deep breath. This is where I tell Tim that I won't, and I get up briskly and move to the next thing. Where I convince him, along with myself, that I'm fine... except I'm not. I'm not remotely fine.

"I'm sorry," I say stiltedly. "I feel like I keep making everything worse."

He puts his hand over mine. "This is a really hard situation."

"Simon Baum said I needed to decide if I could still love my dad," I tell Tim slowly. "Instead of finding a way to excuse or make sense of things. I need to decide if I can live with the truth."

Tim squeezes my hand. "That sounds wise."

"I don't know if I can. I'm not even sure I want to... it's not just what happened at that camp, although God knows that's beyond horrible. It's also the lying to me, about my mom. It's refusing to talk about her to cover his own guilt."

"He made a lot of mistakes."

"But he's not even acknowledging them!" My voice rises, more in frustration than anger. "He won't talk to me."

"And you're not really talking to him. I understand why you aren't, but maybe you can be the one to take the first step."

I turn to face Tim, his seemingly inexhaustible sympathy. I've always been secretly worried that it will run out, if I burden him too much, show too much weakness, but maybe it won't. Maybe it would run out if I *didn't*. Or maybe it wouldn't run out at all.

"I'm sorry I didn't call you earlier today," I blurt. "I should have. I know that." He nods slowly, and I force myself to continue, even though it hurts. "And I know, like you said, it's not just that. I haven't... I haven't wanted to lean on you, or really, to seem like I'm leaning on you, even though I have been all along, no matter whether you knew it or not. I have, I promise."

"Libby—"

"Let me say this." Because I never have before, and I should have. "I've been thinking about my mom a lot lately, after years and years of trying not to, at all. But she was always there, you know. On the edges."

Tim squeezes my hand again, gently. "Of course she was."

"And I know that in some ways I've been just like my father. Not talking or even thinking about her leaving, pretending it didn't affect me, when all along it did. All along it made me be so careful, thinking that if I could just keep myself together, or at least seem like I did, then I would be fine. We would be fine. I'd never give you an excuse to... to walk away."

Tim's breath comes out in a soft rush. "Libby, I never would walk away."

"I'm more of a mess than you think," I tell him in a shaky voice. It feels huge, to say that, even though I think he's probably not all that surprised.

"We're all a mess, Lib. Every single one of us. That's the human condition."

"Maybe," I say, not completely convinced, even now.

Tim gazes down at our clasped hands. "All I've ever wanted," he says quietly, "is to share life with you. All of it—the good, the bad, the boring, the hard. And have you share it with me too."

I feel a tear pool, start to slip, and for once I don't blink it back. It trickles down my cheek, and Tim brushes it away with his thumb. "I'm sorry," I whisper.

"You don't need to be sorry. I just want you to be honest."

I nod jerkily. "I'm trying to be."

"We will get through this," he tells me, not for the first time. "Maybe not back exactly to where we were, but stronger, all the same. We are already. Look at us here, having this conversation." He smiles faintly, and my heart aches and aches.

"Yes," I whisper. I want to believe him so badly.

We sit there for a few moments, let the silence soak into us. It's not a strained silence, or a bad one. It's weary and accepting, maybe the beginning of something good. And in that moment of quiet I realize what I need to do.

I turn to Tim, a new resolve firing through me. "I need to go to Germany," I tell him. "And see this through."

Tim nods, unsurprised, maybe even a little proud. "Yes," he says, leaning over to kiss me. "I think you do."

CHAPTER 23

LIBBY

There are no reporters or cameramen outside the Andrews Air Force Base, thankfully. There's been a shooting somewhere in Minnesota and the focus of the news has turned to that. I am not the kind of person who would ever rejoice in someone else's ill fortune, but I am at least relieved that my father's case isn't making today's headlines. The story of his extradition was all the way back on page six of *The New York Times*, which felt like a blessing.

It's the first week of September, three weeks after my dad's hearing, and the day of his extradition to Germany. I will be accompanying him to Stuttgart.

The last three weeks have been hard, but in a good way, a healing way, at least I hope so. Tim and I feel stronger than ever, even though it's still challenging. After the police came to tell us about Em, I woke up in the middle of the night and went to check on her, out of instinct. She was curled up on her side, but she stirred when I came in, blinking blearily, and then, to my immense gratitude, she suddenly flung her arms around me, burrowing her head against my shoulder.

I clasped her in my arms, thankful to have my girl back, if

just for these few minutes. We sat there in the dark, our arms around each other, neither of us speaking, neither of us needing to, and it felt like a watershed moment. We were going to be okay. I was sure of it then, even if the next morning Em was still tense, a bit irritable. I still felt the fundamental shift in our relationship, the turn back to shore, and I was glad.

Last night, as I was packing for Germany, she came into my bedroom—something she would have done easily, thoughtlessly, before this—before my father—but hadn't in recent weeks. She hovered in the doorway, looking so much like she used to, her hair in a soft, strawberry-blond cloud about her face, one leg twisted round the other. She'd grown taller over the summer; her T-shirt looked too small. We hadn't done our usual pre-school shopping trip, for both jeans and pencils, a brand new backpack, that September sense of expectation and hope.

"How long will you be away for?" she asked.

"I don't know, really. Not too long, I hope. A couple of weeks?" I smiled at her, willing her to unbend a little more, to spin this moment out into something even better. "I'll miss you."

She was silent, absorbing my words, at least, and not rejecting them. "Will we be able to visit Grandad, in Germany?" she finally asked, in a small voice that made my heart ache.

"I hope so, Em." We'd arranged for my father to move into an assisted-living facility in Stuttgart during the trial, but as for afterwards? I had no idea what might happen. He might be in jail then, but I don't have the heart to tell that to my daughter. I barely have the strength to acknowledge it myself. "I really hope so," I told her, and she nodded, stoic now, her shoulders squared.

When we left early this morning, she wrapped her arms around me and hugged me tightly, silently. She hugged my father too, trying not to cry, burrowing her head against his frail shoulder, and I felt a pressure in my chest, that this was happening at all, and yet knowing it had to. Knowing, even, that it was right.

A few reporters had camped outside our house for the occasion of our departure, but my father didn't answer their barrage of questions—the same ones, as always, *are you a Nazi, did you kill Daniel Weiss, do you regret your actions, do you have anything to say*—as he walked out, accompanied by two immigration agents, to the military-issued four-by-four that would transfer us to the air base. We rode in a silence that felt surreal. At the base, a Gulfstream jet was waiting to take us directly to Stuttgart, and from there the German police would escort us to my father's living facility. I felt as if I were living in the pages of some spy thriller, or on the screen of a movie I would have put on while making the popcorn.

It all felt like a huge operation, simply to get my father to Germany, and yet it had happened so *quickly*. John Demjanjuk's case had taken over ten years; my father's only two months. But then he hasn't fought against any of it, and I doubt he will when we get to Germany, although we haven't talked about that yet. He *is* different, I wanted to tell Simon Baum, but Simon wasn't anywhere to be seen now. His job was done, and my father's fate rested in the hands of the German government.

In the three weeks since the hearing, my father and I have not had a single serious conversation. He's kept to his room, sleeping more and more, as if he can just shut the whole world out. When I told him I would accompany him to Stuttgart, he got a stubborn look on his face.

"You don't need to do that."

"I want to, Dad," I said, and he swung his head around to give me a sharp, suspicious look, as if he didn't trust what I'd said, but I'd actually meant it. I was trying to find a way forward, and sometimes it felt like hacking through a jungle, other times like staggering across a desert, but I was trying. I hoped he would, too.

It's hardly appropriate to have any meaningful conversation on the plane, in the hearing of blank-faced immigration agents, however, and so the journey feels interminable, endless. My father sleeps most of the way and I stare into space, wondering what the future holds, if I'll ever learn the truth. Or maybe I've already learned it, all there is to know, and I just have to learn to live with it, like Simon Baum said. I have to decide if I can make peace with it all; if I can love my father.

It's raining when we arrive at the US Army airfield in Stuttgart, a dreary, relentless drizzle that blankets the city in gray mist. The agents who meet us as we deplane are courteous but brusque, a bit officious, or maybe that's just how the German language always sounds. I don't understand a word; my father never wanted to teach me, but I watch his spine stiffen, his expression become that now-familiar mix of disdain and indifference. Is it all an act, I wonder, or does he really not care? I wish I knew; I wish I felt like I could know, because I knew my father.

I see the agents' lips twist, how they shoot glances at one another as if to say, *See? Just another Nazi.*

And maybe he is.

We are driven to his residence, a facility called Parkheim Berg in the center of the city, near the grounds of a park called Villa Berg. It's all very gracious and green, and it's strange to think my father knows this city, grew up here. He doesn't say a word as we drive from the airfield to the nursing home; he doesn't even look out the window.

At the home, the administrator meets us at the door, her face determinedly impassive. My father has a room separate from the others, on its own corridor. He is, she tells me in precise English, encouraged not to take part in the home's activities while the trial is going on, as it could be upsetting to other residents. I can hardly see my father wanting to join the choir or break out the Scrabble, and so I simply murmur my agreement, even though part of me resents the request. He hasn't been convicted yet, I think, but I am already realizing that everyone just assumes it is a matter of time, even me.

By the time my father is settled in his room, and the agents and administrator have left, I am wilting with exhaustion, both emotional and physical, as well as jet lag. I can't believe we are here, that this is happening. I start to unpack his clothes, and the sight of his neatly folded trousers and shirts, the same ones I washed and ironed and put in his dresser back home, brings tears to my eyes.

I blink them back and start putting his clothes in the drawers. "This is quite a nice room," I tell him, trying to sound chatty even though it feels both false and forced. "And the park outside looks very pretty." I glance at the window, streaked with rain. "Did you live near this neighborhood, Dad?"

For a second, I think he's not going to answer even that innocuous question, and then he gives a little shrug. "I lived in Stuttgart-Mitte, about two kilometers to the southwest, closer to the center. An apartment over my office."

I straighten, turning to look at him; he is staring out the window, but his gaze seems unseeing, his mind far away. "Is it strange to be back?" I ask quietly.

Another shrug, this one more like a jerk. He doesn't speak, and I am about to turn wearily back to the shirts when I realize tears are trickling silently down his wrinkled, withered cheeks, and I go completely still, utterly shocked. I have never seen him cry like this before, not ever.

"Dad." I take a step toward him, one hand outstretched. "Dad."

"I'm sorry," he whispers brokenly, his gaze still on the window, the tears still streaking down his face, catching in the wrinkles. "So sorry for everything."

I remain still, hardly able to believe he is finally apologizing. Finally he's opening the door to the conversation we've never been able to have. Then I walk slowly toward him and sit down on the end of the bed, opposite his chair. "What are you sorry for?" I ask quietly. "Won't you tell me, Dad?"

He shakes his head slowly. "How can I tell it? How can anyone understand? I couldn't understand it myself." He lapses into silence and I wait, sensing there is more. "You do not realize the capacity for evil in a person," he finally says quietly. "You can't, until... until it is there, right before you, and even then, you think, *well*, there must be a reason. These things— they happen for a reason, don't they? Until you realize they don't. Not one reason at all." He sighs and leans his head back against his chair, closing his eyes.

A moment passes, then another, as I hold my breath, waiting.

"And then," he says quietly, so quietly I can barely hear him, "you realize the capacity for evil in yourself."

I know what's coming next, even though I don't want to.

He opens his eyes. "I am responsible for Daniel Weiss' death," he tells me. "I killed him. You knew it, I think, but you didn't want to believe it. You hoped there was a mistake, or maybe a reason. Your old father, capable of causing a man's death. Of killing him." He shakes his head. "I didn't believe it myself."

"What happened?" I ask in a whisper. I ache for my father in a way I never have before.

My father closes his eyes again. "He betrayed me. We were friends, Daniel and I, of a sort. As much as we could be, considering the circumstances. He was a goldsmith, he worked in my office. I protected him as best as I could, which wasn't very well, as it happened. I was a coward—you should know that." He opens his eyes to look at me directly. "I was naïve at first, naïve and stupidly arrogant, and then later I was a coward. Anni..."

His voice chokes. "Anni was always the courageous one." I can tell from his tone how much he loved her. There is a world of memories in his words, of sorrow and regret and, most of all, love. It makes me wish I'd known her, or at least known of her. All I have now is a single photograph, and my father's fading memories.

"And what about Leo?" I ask after a moment, my voice gentle.

My father stares at me, seeming confused. "Leo?"

"Leo, his son. He saw you—with Daniel Weiss at the camp gates." I can't bring myself to say *shoot* or *kill*, not when my father is still struggling to contain his emotion.

"Leo..." He shakes his head slowly. "I did my best by Leo. I know that wasn't very much, in the end, but I tried. I was so sorry when I found out he'd died."

"Died?" Now I am the one feeling confused. "Dad, Leo's not dead. He's the one who instigated this trial." Is it possible my dad doesn't know this? I think of how it was explained to him—the Department of Justice, the German government. Due to privacy constraints, Leo's name was never mentioned, and because my father has refused to talk about it, I never brought him up. Now I do. "Leo Weiss saw a photo of you from one of my fundraisers and identified you," I tell him, trying to keep my tone gentle, in case it is too much of a shock.

"Leo did?" My father goggles at me, one hand pressed to his chest. "*Leo?*"

"Yes, Leo." I frown. "He... he started all this. Why did you think he'd died?"

"Because... because when I went to find Anni, right after the war... He'd been with her, you see. They left the camp together, after the revolt, went to Dresden, to stay with some distant friends. But their building had been bombed, there was nothing left, the authorities said. They couldn't even identify the bodies. Anni... Anni and Leo. I assumed they were both gone."

My mind whirls as I attempt to process this new information. "Why would Leo Weiss have left with your sister? How could that even happen, since he was Jewish?"

My dad doesn't seem to hear me. He shakes his head slowly, tears glistening in his eyes. "All this time," he says softly. "All this time."

He keeps shaking his head, almost in wonder. He looks both moved and hopeful, as if Leo Weiss being alive and well after all these years is good news. And maybe it is, because I am realizing that there still is much I don't know. There are secrets my father has kept, and maybe they will make a difference, after all.

But then I think of what he has already said, and a realization unfurls inside me. My father killed a man... and I still love him.

CHAPTER 24

FEBRUARY 1943

Sobibor, Poland

When Hans returned to Sobibor after their time away, he felt as if he were entering the camp almost as a prisoner, the gates shutting behind him, the guards in their black uniforms, rifles at the ready, standing sentry, staring him down. As he and Anni headed toward the cottage, a bitter February wind funneling in from the forest, he glanced toward the dreaded *Schlauch*, the Road to Heaven, as the others laughingly called it, and he had a sudden, mad impulse to run down it himself, to finally find release.

Death, he realized, would be preferable to more of this life, and yet, despite feeling and believing such a thing in his very bones, he still chose to live. For Anni's sake, if not his own. Although perhaps, he acknowledged, he was not as selfless as that; even though he longed for release, his instinct to survive remained, stubborn, persistent, like a weed pushing up through the soil.

And so he kept his head down as he went to the administration building to report for duty the next morning; there had apparently been no transports all week and the officers were restless, at their most dangerous, fingering their pistols, their expressions both lazy and murderous.

Wagner sat with his feet on his desk, a bottle of schnapps held carelessly in his hand as he looked at Hans with bored malice. He was wearing a new leather trench coat, purloined from the prisoners' effects, Hans supposed. It had a fur collar and the leather strained across his broad shoulders.

"Your little goldsmith got into trouble while you were away," he drawled, and it took everything Hans had in him to simply lift an eyebrow.

"Oh?"

"Gomerski got bored." Wagner shrugged. "It happens."

Hans stared at him, doing his best to keep his hands from clenching into fists. "What?" he asked as if it didn't really matter—and he realized wearily, maybe it *didn't*. "Is he dead?"

"No, not quite, and you can thank me for that. I want another ring." He let out a laugh. "And a badge, as well. I've commissioned it, so he'd better heal up soon."

"Where is he?" Hans asked, and realized at once he sounded too interested, too concerned.

Wagner's lip curled. "Gomerski said you were a Jew-lover."

"Hardly," Hans scoffed. "But he's a decent goldsmith and the only one in this place, as you know. I was hoping he'd make a ring for my sister."

Wagner continued to give him a hard stare, and Hans kept his gaze steady with effort. He felt the sweat trickle down the back of his neck, between his shoulder blades. He wasn't entirely sure he wanted to force a confrontation by defending Daniel Weiss, and yet for Anni's sake, and the sake of his own soul, he would. He had been given the opportunity to protect the man in this hellish place, for better or for worse. He wanted to have enough honor and courage to do it.

"They took him to the hospital," Wagner said finally, and

Hans worked to keep his expression neutral. The "hospital" was no more than a tin-roofed shed with a guard and a pistol. Anyone sick or suffering who was sent there got a bullet in the head before their body was hauled to camp three for burning. "But don't worry," Wagner continued with a sneer. "I saved him. He's resting up in your office. And, like I said, he'd better heal quickly."

Hans considered asking about Leo, but then decided not to draw attention to the boy, if he was still alive. "When is the next transport?" he asked instead.

Wagner lifted his heavy shoulders in a weary shrug. "Who knows?" He let out a hard guffaw of laughter. "They're running out of Jews."

Could that actually be possible? Hans wondered. They had managed, in the space of a year, to kill all the Jews in Europe? He thought of Anni's penetrating question—*how many Jews in the world?* Aleph null had an ending, he thought bleakly, and it was here.

"And what happens when there aren't any more Jews?" he asked Wagner.

"Then we close the camp. They're going to close Belzec soon. Besides..." Wagner grimaced. "We're a little too close to the Reds, aren't we?"

Hans acknowledged the grimly knowing glint in the other man's eye and he did not reply. Stalingrad had been retaken by the Soviets only last month, and February had seen further losses of the Axis army in Russia. Sobibor was less than ten kilometers from the Ukrainian border. How long before the Soviets marched on the camp? Before Germany lost the war?

With a nod—no one did the *Hitlergrüss* here, Hans had learned long ago—he left the deputy commandant's office. His mind was still spinning with unwelcome new thoughts as he headed toward his own small office.

As he opened the door, he saw Daniel lying on a makeshift

bed, no more than a heap of sacks and raggedy blankets, with Leo sitting next to him. His breath came out in a rush as he surveyed the other man. His face was a mess of bruises and cuts, one eye swollen shut, his hair matted with blood. He was cradling his arm close to his body and Hans feared it was broken. He could only imagine what the rest of his body must look like, underneath his ragged clothes—as bloody and bruised as his face, no doubt. He hoped there weren't any internal injuries.

"When did this happen?" he asked, and Leo answered, in careful English.

"Three days ago."

"Three days!" Hans shook his head, caught, as ever, between a deep, abiding fury and a pervasive, creeping fear. "I'll get you some proper bandages," he told Daniel. "Your arm will need to be set, I think."

Daniel nodded, his face taut with pain. "Yes, it is broken, I think."

Hans shook his head, a burning in his chest that made him feel as if he could choke. "I'm sorry this happened to you," he said after a moment, and Daniel, his face too swollen and bruised to speak, merely nodded again.

Hans turned on his heel and left the room. He strode through the camp, collecting what he needed from the various storage sheds, sure that if someone asked him what he was doing, he would tell them exactly—*I am helping a Jew*—even as he realized he wouldn't. He wouldn't dare. He collected bandages and clean blankets, antiseptic ointment and soothing lotions before he steeled himself to see Anni, knowing she would be furious.

"What is it?" she asked immediately, before he'd so much as said a word. She eyed the basket of provisions he'd gathered. "Is it Daniel?" she asked sharply, and Hans nodded.

"He's been beaten. His arm is broken—"

"I'll set it, then." She sounded so sure, but Hans had his doubts.

"You've never done such a thing before, Anni—"

"It's another kind of mathematics," she dismissed. "It's all about the angle."

And Hans supposed it was.

Hans stood apart while Anni crouched in front of Daniel, bathing his face gently, dabbing at the cuts and bruises, while he tried not to wince. There was something strangely intimate about the scene that made him feel a little uncomfortable, uneasy, but Anni seemed oblivious to it. She'd turned eighteen last month, without any fuss or celebration. At a drinks party at the commandant's house, Wagner had given her a purloined box of chocolates which she'd accepted with stiff politeness, before passing them on to Leo.

As Hans watched her now, her eyes narrowed with concentration, her hair half falling down from its twist, he was conscious that his sister was a lovely young woman and Daniel not all that much older, only thirty or so, and a handsome man, even beaten to a pulp as he had been. The thought alarmed him, and then he dismissed it as absurd, outrageous.

"They must stay with us," Anni announced after she'd set Daniel's arm, his face white with pain as she'd worked with crisp efficiency. It really had been about the angle.

"With us?" Hans stared at her blankly.

"It's too unprotected in here, as well as cold. They can have the back room. We will share the front."

Hans stared at her in disbelief. "Anni, that is utterly impossible, you *know* that. There are no Jews in the officers' quarters —they'd be shot on sight if there were."

Anni's face was settling into mutinous lines that he well recognized. "Then we'll sneak them in, at night."

"No." Hans shook his head, firm now. Clearly he'd indulged his sister far too much, for her even to consider such a thing. "They must stay here. Anything else is a risk to them as well as to us. You do not want their deaths on your conscience, do you?"

"He is right," Daniel said quietly, speaking painfully through swollen lips. "We will stay here."

"Then I will stay here—"

"*Anni*—"

"As much as I can," she amended swiftly. "For their sakes."

Hans knew he would not be able to dissuade her. He gave Daniel a long, fulminating glance, hoping the man would understand his disapproval of such a situation.

"Wagner is waiting for his ring," he told him. "And I don't know how patient he will be." He glanced at Daniel's splinted arm. "Will you be able to make it?

Daniel shook his head. "Not like this. But Leo can do it."

Hans glanced skeptically at the boy. He was only eleven years old. "Leo?"

"He is an accomplished goldsmith, and his fingers are nimble. Wagner will know no different."

"You'd better hope so," Hans told him, the hopelessness of the situation overwhelming him, and he turned away before any of them could see the desolate expression on his face.

It took Daniel three weeks to fully recover from his injuries; thankfully, Wagner was fobbed off with the ring Leo had made, which was, to Hans' surprise, an exquisite piece of work. Anni spent every spare moment she had in Hans' office, forcing Hans to do likewise, although he was called out twice to the ramp for transports. He stood there wearily as they whipped and herded the Jews, these from Greece, toward the *Schlauch* and their deaths, and he found he couldn't even care very much. He supposed the human soul had only so much capacity for horror; perhaps it was why the officers and guards were able to be so unmoved. They even struggled to work themselves into the enraged frenzy they once had, Hans noticed; it had all, appallingly, become ordinary, mundane. Dull.

As winter thawed into a damp and muddy spring, fewer and fewer transports arrived at the camp, leaving the staff bored and dangerous. The news coming from Russia didn't help, either; the Soviets were coming ever closer. Hans heard the mutters about how they'd captured Vyazma and were marching toward Smolensk.

There had also been, over the course of a few months, two unsuccessful assassination attempts on Hitler, and while these were hailed as victories for their God-given leader, the fact that there had been any attempts at all had made Hans feel an unsettling mixture of unease and hope. They were, he suspected, losing the war... and everyone was starting to realize it. What that meant for any of them in the future, no one wanted to consider.

"Of course we are losing the war," Anni had replied with a dismissive shrug when he'd mentioned it to her. "We lost it first when we invaded Russia, and again when America joined with the British. It is only a matter of time, Hans, and that depends entirely on how mule-headed Hitler is." She sighed. "Very mule-headed, I fear."

"Aren't you worried about what will happen if we lose?" Hans asked, mystified by her brisk, pragmatic manner.

"I would be more worried about what happened if we didn't," Anni replied. "Now let us talk about more important matters. I want to have a birthday party."

"Your birthday was months ago, Anni—"

"Not mine, you silly!" She laughed, shaking her head. "Leo's. He will be twelve in May, and we are going to have a party."

Hans shook his head slowly. "Anni, you are crazy."

She laughed again, a pure, clear sound. "Maybe, but we are still going to have it, Hans, and you are going to help me."

In retrospect, he was not quite sure how he came to agree, but somehow he helped her to arrange a party for the boy. He went to Chelm for supplies, as Anni refused on principle to use stolen goods taken from the storage sheds. She made a cake from a little flour and sugar and precious eggs on their wood stove, and decorated it with flowers foraged in the forest. She'd taken to walking, in the mornings, skirting around the land-mines to meander through the forest that surrounded the camp, not quite as forbidding now that the countryside had softened into spring—skies of blue porcelain with cotton-wool clouds, sunshine like an offering, air like a balm. She even fashioned presents for the boy—one of her precious mathematics books, and a shirt she'd made, with clumsy diligence, from an old ripped-up dress. Never mind that Hans could have taken from several dozen shirts in the clothing shed; this wasn't tainted, and he knew that was important to Anni, and most likely to Daniel and Leo, as well.

They held the party on a quiet afternoon in the middle of May, when many of the camp staff were on leave, and others were lazing about in the sunshine, drinking or playing cards or dice. There hadn't been a transport in weeks, and the mood in the camp was both soporific and dangerous, like a sleepy-eyed snake about to strike. There were rumors that Treblinka would be closing soon, just as Belzec had, and if Treblinka, then Sobibor. Hans had overheard some of the officers joking about the running totals of deaths for the three camps—Sobibor, the small-est, was, Reichleitner had said with a laugh, losing the competi-tion. Hans had looked away quickly, not trusting the expression on his face.

If Sobibor closed, he knew—and it seemed likely that it would, and soon—then the six hundred Jews who served the camp, including Leo and Daniel, would be killed—sent to the gas chambers of camp three, just as all the others had been. They had to know it, too, surely. Although he did not interact with any prisoners save Daniel and his son, he saw how they listened, watched, waited, knew. There was nothing in this camp, he suspected, that the prisoners were not aware of, and in any case, it did not take any great logic to envision how things would have to end.

He realized he'd become fond of both Daniel and Leo, in a cautious sort of way; he appreciated the goldsmith's dry sense of humor, and Leo's shy smile, when Anni had explained something to him, lightened his heart. If the world were different, Hans had thought more than once, they would have called the Weisses friends. Perhaps they would have even had them over to dinner, for evening conversations over a glass of schnapps, a game of chess. As it was, the Weisses were almost certainly doomed, and in a matter of months, if not weeks, and Hans knew there was nothing he could do to save them.

Such thoughts were occupying his mind as he sat at his desk for Leo's little party, and Daniel covered his son's eyes while Anni brought in the cake.

"*Wszystkiego najlepszego!*" she exclaimed and at Hans' blank look, Daniel explained.

"It is 'happy birthday' in Polish. Leo has been teaching Anni a little."

"Has he?" Hans had not realized that Anni had learned any Polish. She'd spent hours with her head bent close to the boy's, sharing whispers, looks, giggles. Hans supposed it was natural the boy might teach her some of his language, and yet...

He let out a sigh, a sound of frustration, impatience, despair. Was Anni so stupid as to think Leo could have a normal birthday, a ridiculous party, when his death warrant was as good as signed, along with his father's?

"And now your presents!" Anni cried, reaching for the paper-wrapped parcels she'd tucked out of the way. Leo's smile burst onto his face like sunlight, and Hans let out another discontented sigh as he looked away.

"What troubles you?" Daniel asked quietly as he moved to stand next to Hans.

Hans glanced at him narrowly, wondering how much to say. What would be the point? And yet he felt compelled to honesty. "You have heard the rumors that Treblinka is closing?"

"Yes." Daniel's expression was impassive, unmoved.

"And Belzec is already closed."

He nodded, something almost like humor lightening his eyes. "It seems you will be out of a job soon, *Herr Buchhalter*." How could Daniel speak so calmly?

Hans could not manage an answering smile. Yes, he would no longer be the camp accountant, for there would be no camp. Perhaps he would be sent back to Stuttgart, at last. And yet the thought brought little relief. It was too late, Hans thought. He had seen too much; he was too changed. And as for the prisoners...

"You know what that means?" he asked Daniel, his voice so low the other man had to stoop a little to hear it. He could hardly believe he was having this conversation. If any of the other officers heard, they would be appalled, disgusted. He would be disciplined—who knew, maybe even shot.

"Yes," Daniel replied, and his voice was sure.

"Papa, look!" Leo held up the shirt Anni had made, grinning, and his father's face softened with love.

"What a handsome boy you will be in that, *zabko*," Daniel told him, smiling.

After a few seconds, he turned back to Hans.

"I know what is going to happen." His voice was strong, sure, and Hans looked at him in surprise.

"Daniel—" It was, he realized, the first time he'd called the goldsmith by his first name. He'd never called him anything before now, had tried not to think about him too deeply as anything more than a prisoner and a Jew. Before he said anything more, however, he stopped at the look on the other man's face—a knowing, watchful look. Realization slammed into him, left him breathless. "You are planning something." As he said the words, the fragments of a dozen disparate memories slotted into place. The shifty looks across the yard, the hushed whispers on the ramp, the ways the prisoners would melt away whenever an officer or guard came by—as they always did, and yet there had been an intention about it, these last few weeks. A knowingness. "The Jews, I mean," he said, his voice dropping even more. "You must be."

Daniel did not reply, but Hans saw the bright flare of panic in his eyes before his expression turned impassive once more.

"A revolt," he whispered, knowing it, feeling the truth of it like a thudding through his bones. "How many of you? What will you do? How will you manage it? You have no weapons..." His mind raced as he tried to think of what they might be planning. "Are the Blackies in on it? No, they couldn't be. You can't trust them, you know. Most of them would sell their mothers for a wristwatch." He shook his head, his narrowed gazed moving over Daniel. "But something. Something else..."

Daniel's face was pale, beads of sweat pearling on his forehead as he stared steadily back. "I will not speak of it," he stated with quiet, firm decision. "You can do what you like, kill me even, but I will not tell you one thing."

"I'm not going to kill you," Hans exclaimed, then lowering his voice, he found himself saying, "I want to help you." The look of blatant surprise on Daniel's face hurt him, perhaps absurdly, more than a little. He'd meant what he said, but it was clear Daniel would never trust him. "Do you not believe me?"

"I do not know what to believe, *Herr Buchhalter*." Mr. Accountant, as he'd called him before. It almost sounded like a nickname, but Daniel's voice was deathly grim.

"You will not succeed without help. You have no weapons, for a start."

"You would be risking your life," Daniel replied quietly. "As well as your sister's. Even if you were willing, I could not ask such a thing of you. Or of Anni."

Anni. Hans did not miss the familiar way Daniel spoke her name, as if he knew her, liked her.

As Hans continued to stare at him, he realized how foolish he was being. What on earth had he been thinking, suggesting such a thing? He couldn't help the Jews *escape*. Their attempt would assuredly fail, and he would, as Daniel had said, most certainly be shot on sight, and Anni, as well. And that was the *best*-case scenario. The worst was prison, ruthless beatings, unbearable torture, and then, inevitably, death, for both him and Anni. What kind of idiot was he? For a second, he'd let himself get caught up in imagining leading some righteous charge, an atonement of sorts, but now, like Daniel, he saw the utter absurdity of it. He couldn't do anything. He *wouldn't* do anything, as always... for Anni's sake, and yes, for his own.

"Hans, Daniel, come see Leo's presents," Anni called, her tone playful. "And stop with the serious talk! We are going to play *Würstchenschnappen*." She had, Hans saw, hung up a sausage on a string for the typical birthday game; Leo would have to stand on his tiptoes as he tried to bite it.

"Don't tell me of it," Hans told Daniel flatly as the other man started forward to join the game. "Don't speak one word of it to me."

After a second's pause, Daniel nodded.

Hans stood by his desk and watched as he put his arm around his son, laughing as he encouraged him to jump at the sausage. He thought of the officers, forcing that wretched prisoner to eat an entire salami; this, at least, was innocent, even joyful, and yet it made him ache inside, for he wondered if he would ever be able to enjoy innocence again. To believe in it.

"And you must have a try as well, Daniel!" Anni exclaimed, pulling him by the hand. "I've put one up even higher for you!"

Hans' gaze narrowed as he watched Anni lead Daniel by the hand to the other sausage; she laughed and clapped her hands as he gamely played along, going on his tiptoes, his hands clasped behind his back. When he'd managed to jump up and bite the sausage, he threw his arms up in victory and, laughing in delight, Anni gave him a hug, Daniel returning it for an instant, his hand spanning the dip of her waist, before he stepped quickly away.

It all lasted no more than a few seconds, if that, and yet shock had Hans standing rigidly in place. How had he missed the friendship that had sprung between his sister and the goldsmith? Of course, he'd seen how friendly and even affectionate Anni was toward both Daniel and his son, but he had quickly dismissed anything more as ridiculous. Now, as he recalled Daniel's hand on Anni's waist, he wondered.

"I think we have had enough party games," he said.

"Oh, Hans..." Anni sounded as disappointed as a child. She glanced toward Daniel, who looked away.

"We have been reckless enough." Hans started taking down the string. "What if Wagner came in right now? Can you imagine what might happen?"

"I don't care," Anni insisted.

"He's right, Anni." Daniel's voice was gentle, and, Hans thought, far too familiar. As if he *knew* her, knew her even better than Hans did.

Something in him prickled, an unsettling mixture of jealousy and suspicion. Daniel was smiling at his sister as if he had the right to, as if he understood her.

"Get back to your work, goldsmith," Hans commanded shortly before he could think better of it, and Daniel's eyes blazed for a brief second before he lowered his gaze and nodded.

"As you wish, *Herr Buchhalter*."

It no longer sounded like a nickname.

CHAPTER 25

LIBBY

Stuttgart, Germany

It takes a week for my father to recover from jet lag and the strain of the journey. A week of me sitting by his bed, watching him sleep or stir, wondering if he looks even older, frailer. Less than, somehow. He certainly seems smaller, in this unfamiliar bed, this unfamiliar room. One of the staff of Parkheim Berg checks in on him occasionally; I can't tell from her expression what she thinks about having a bona fide Nazi under the nursing home's roof. She twitches about the room, puts the back of her hand against his forehead, pours a glass of water from the pitcher, and then leaves again.

I find I am glad I don't understand German. I can't understand the news on the TV that blares from the home's living room, or the stark headlines I glimpse displayed in newspaper kiosks when I stroll around the park. My father's trial is on the front page of the *Stuttgarter Zeitung*, but only a small article near the bottom. Perhaps there will be more coverage, when the trial begins, set for next week.

The rain has continued, a steady drumming, so I have not

ventured far or long, and only when my father is deeply asleep. I wander through the park, everything drenched and green, my mind as misty as the rain-dampened air, and then I hurry back to my father, to sit once more by his bedside and wait.

Tim has called every night, and we text throughout the day, although there is not much to say. Now that my father is off American soil, he is no longer of interest to the media outlets there. Em and Lucas are busy with school, although Tim tells me that Lucas still seems quiet. Em, thankfully, had no repercussions from her time on Twitter; she has become obsessed with our photo albums, leafing through pages of her as a baby, in my father's arms, or as a toddler, taking his hand, wanting to know the details of each one, asking Tim to tell the story behind every picture.

"It's a way to grieve," he tells me, as if it needs explaining.

"I know." This, in a way, is my own kind of grieving: sitting quietly, watching my father sleep, letting the memories drift through my mind like flotsam on a lazy current. I am remembering the Grimm's fairy tales he read to me as a child, editing out the gruesome bits and making them silly instead, so I'd lose myself in giggles, his arm snugly around my shoulders. I think of watching the Sunday Disney movie together on our old, battered sofa, the smell of burnt popcorn in the air, the big ceramic bowl on our laps. How he came to all my field hockey matches, even though I was only an alternate on the C team. The twinkle in his eye when I told him about Tim for the first time. "Ah," he said, "this one sounds special."

My dad was always looking out for me, loving me through practical, selfless acts of service. When did it change? I wonder. When did I start feeling that I needed to look out for him? I remember he had a brief scare about fifteen years ago; a funny turn we worried might be a stroke or a heart attack, but the scans came up with nothing. The first time I realized he was getting forgetful, and I could see he knew it, too. When I started helping him on the stairs, my hand cupping his elbow as he navigated down the front steps of our house.

Although, I realize, I was looking out for him even before then. Before he got truly old. I remember creeping out of bed one night when I was about nine or ten, and seeing him sitting at the kitchen table, his shoulders slumped, his gaze distant. There was something so weary and defeated about his pose, his stare, that I felt a rush of love, a ripple of fear. Even then, as a child, I felt a need to protect him.

It was the reason I stayed close for college, why my dad became the deal-breaker for the few boyfriends I had. He was always going to be part of the package. It's why, at least in part, this has all been so difficult—because that ingrained need to protect him has had to war with what I know—what he taught me—is right. In my black-and-white way, I thought it had to be one or the other, but now I am starting to realize that life and love are more complicated, more gray, than that, and I wonder if maybe I can do both. Maybe he can, too.

He has a meeting with a court-appointed lawyer on Monday, eight days after we arrived in Germany. I don't know what will happen at that meeting; my dad has told me he'll meet with the lawyer alone, and I respect his wishes. I already know that, under German law, defendants don't have the option to enter a plea, and so there must be a trial of some kind. The truth will come out.

The day before his meeting with the lawyer, the sky finally clears. It's a fragile blue, fleeced with cottony clouds. An hour after I arrived at Parkheim Berg from the rented studio flat I've been staying in, my father finally rises from his bed, hobbling to the chair by the window to look out at the park.

"Why don't we go out today, Dad?" I suggest and he gives me an uncertain look.

"Eh?"

"Why don't we go out?" I say, stronger this time, because I really mean it. "This is your hometown. I'd love for you to show me some of the sights."

"The sights," he huffs, shaking his head.

"Stuttgart is meant to be a beautiful city."

"Its sights were bombed during the war."

"But there's some very interesting modern architecture replacing the old buildings." Or so I read on the internet. "Anyway, I don't care so much about that. I want to see *your* Stuttgart —where you lived. You and Anni." I hesitate, feeling almost as if I shouldn't have said her name, yet still glad I said it. "I want to know more about her. About you." Before the opportunity is gone forever.

My father doesn't reply; he is staring out the window, his gaze distant, his shoulders stooped. I wait, hoping, uncertain, as his body sags a little, the deep wrinkles of his face collapsing, and then he slowly, grudgingly nods.

"All right," he says, and I'm not sure whether it's a victory or a defeat, a rallying or a giving up. Still, I keep my voice upbeat as I reply.

"Great. I'll arrange a car."

An hour later, we are in a hired car with a driver, moving smoothly through the city's steep, green valleys, golden-stoned, red-roofed buildings clustered below like something on a postcard. Stuttgart is leafy and green, with an old-world feel that is suddenly and jarringly interrupted by various sleek modern buildings of glass and chrome—museums for both Mercedes-Benz and Porsche, the Weissenhof Colony, the *Rathaus*.

We bypass the tourist shops on Königstrasse and the imposing Palace Square for the quiet Oberer Schlossgarten, with its manmade pond stretching placidly in front of us. I help my father out of the car as we walk slowly toward the water.

"Anni used to feed the ducks here," he tells me. "She kept a bag of stale bread in the kitchen for them. I always told her they were overfed. Fat, even during the war." He shakes his head, smiling, but there are tears in his eyes, and I am grateful he is giving me these memories, offering them up like gifts.

"What was she like?" I ask hesitantly, afraid he might stop talking if I press too much, and yet I want to form a picture of this woman I never knew, whom my father loved, his only sibling, his last living relative.

"She was..." He pauses, casting his gaze to the sky as he tries to think of a way to describe her. "Stubborn," he says at last. "And full of life and humor. She exasperated me to no end, but I loved her so much." He glances down at the water; a duck is paddling hopefully near us. "After... after Sobibor closed, she went to Dresden, to live with friends of our family. When I came to find her, after the war... I couldn't believe she had gone."

"You said it was an Allied bombing?"

He nods. "Yes, in February 1945, one of the worst of the war. There was nothing left of the apartment building where she'd been living... nothing there but a crater. Emptiness." He shakes his head slowly, his expression both stricken and distant. "I'd been hoping we could rebuild our lives somehow. She was only twenty, after all, there was so much ahead of her, and the worst had surely passed. It took me years to accept her death... I simply couldn't imagine life without her."

And yet I'd never known about this woman who meant so much to him. He'd never even spoken of her. "Is that why you decided to go to America?" I ask gently.

"I thought there was nothing left for me in Germany." I want to ask about Leo, but then his expression hardens a little and he turns away from the pond. The conversation is clearly over, and I let it go, at least for now. "Let's get going," my father says.

When we get back in the car, my dad gives the driver an address and then sits back, a determined look on his face. I'm surprised, unsure where we are going as we leave the Schloss-garten for a narrow, unremarkable street in Stuttgart-Mitte, but I realize I can guess. My dad tells the driver to stop halfway down the block.

"Here," he says, and nods toward one of the terraced houses, four floors of faded brick with long, narrow windows. "My father's business was on the ground floor, and we lived in the flat above. Frau Werling, our neighbor, lived above us. She looked after things for us while..." He glances at the driver. "While we were away."

I gaze at the nondescript house, gracious and identical to many others on the street. I am trying to imagine my father there, my aunt. I picture that dark-haired young woman striding down the street, a bag of stale bread in her hand, a ready smile on her lips. What was she like, Anni Brenner? Am I at all like her?

"And after your father died, you worked in the office?" I ask.

"Yes."

"And Anni?"

My father's lips twitch in a smile. "Anni kept house, but quite badly. She wasn't interested in domestic pursuits. She was a terrible cook, and even worse at housekeeping. She used to tell me if I didn't like sneezing, I could dust the rooms myself." His smile widens, and I find myself smiling too. I like the sound of Anni Brenner, I decide.

"What did she like to do?"

My father lets out a soft sigh. "Anni loved numbers. Loved them the way someone might love their friends, or even their children. She was obsessed with mathematics—not just arith-metic or algebra, but the philosophy behind it. The beauty and purity." He sighs. "I wasn't smart enough to understand her, but I tried."

She sounds even more interesting, and I feel a rush of something like loss. "I wish I'd known her."

My dad nods slowly. "So do I." He turns to me, finding a smile. "You look a bit like her, you know. That always felt like a gift to me, to see Anni in you."

"I thought she looked familiar in the photo, and Tim pointed out the resemblance." I give a small laugh, shaking my head. "I didn't even realize."

To my surprise, my dad reaches for my hand, and when he speaks, his voice is choked. "I thank God for both of you," he says, squeezing my hand. "And your mother, too. I should have spoken of her more to you. I know that."

My throat thickens as I grasp his hand. "I understand why you didn't," I tell him, and for the first time I mean it.

"She loved you, in her own way. I should have made that clearer to you, especially when you were a child. I should have told you, again and again, so you knew you were loved. But I just wanted to forget. And I think I wanted you to forget too, at least a little, because you were all I had left. You were my everything." His smile trembles at its corners. "You still are."

"Dad..." I have no words as I blink back tears.

"I failed you all," my father continues, "you, your mother, Anni, in different ways, because of my cowardice. I will always be sorry for that, Libby. I hope you know that." He draws a shuddering breath and continues, before I can make a reply. "You are going to hear things at this trial, and they will mostly be true. Not completely, because they do not know all the facts—"

"Then you tell them the facts, Dad," I burst out before I can help it. "If there were any mitigating circumstances, then—"

"No." His voice is flat. "There weren't. Not in the way you think. Not enough, certainly. I know that full well."

I fall silent, recognizing the stubborn look on his face. A bit, perhaps, the way Anni might once have looked.

"Whatever you hear," he continues, "whatever you believe, I want you to know that I have always loved you. And I have always been ashamed of what I did—but, moreover, what I *didn't* do. Always."

"I wish you'd told me this before," I whisper. I think of those weeks back at home, the way he'd looked so disdainful, so scornful, and how I hadn't pushed back. I hadn't demanded he tell me, because I had thought I hadn't wanted to hear. I wish we both could have done things differently.

"I was too ashamed," he tells me. "And too proud. It has always been my failing. Even when I knew I should die, I fought to live. It's hard to let go of that, eh?" He smiles sadly, shaking his head. "For seventy years, I have done my best to act as if I never had been at Sobibor, never seen..." He presses his lips together for a moment before continuing. "But it was there all the time. Here..." He taps his head, "and here." He presses a shaking hand against his heart. "I've never been able to leave it behind. I knew I wouldn't, a long time ago, but I still tried."

"And now?" I ask, hardly daring to ask the question, not sure I want to know the answer, yet knowing I need to ask. To know.

My father squeezes my hand once more as his expression irons out into implacability. "And now," he says, "it finally ends."

CHAPTER 26

There is a small cadre of cameramen and newspaper reporters outside the courtroom, but since they're speaking in German, I don't know what they're saying, although I imagine it's the same kind of thing as back in America. *Are you a Nazi? Do you regret your actions?* The click of the camera shutters sound like some invasive insect, making me tense as I escort my father inside, past a group of demonstrators. I can't read the German of the banner they are holding, but my father tells me, quietly, that they are the relatives of concentration camp survivors.

We have been in Stuttgart for two weeks, and I am aching to get home, even as I dread leaving my father. After our tour through Stuttgart, things mellowed between us, and the moments became all the more precious. With each passing day, I am realizing that this whole ordeal has taken something from my father, most likely forever. It has sapped his strength, but more than that, it has taken his will. He has slept most of each day, while I have sat by his bedside. When I asked him about his talk with the lawyer, he merely shook his head, smiled.

"It's finished," he said, in a tone of something almost like satisfaction, and I wondered exactly what he meant.

Last night, Tim called me with news that once would have filled me with both guilt and grief; Lucas had been disqualified from the chemistry Olympiad after his teammates were found to be cheating.

"He knew about it," Tim said heavily, "but he was afraid to say anything. They've all been disqualified from this year's competition, and they won't be able to compete in future years, either. That's it for him, I'm afraid, when it comes to these competitions."

"Oh, Tim." I ached for my husband, who sounded so disappointed, as well as for my son. I recalled what he had said, about speaking up being hard, and I understood his sentiment so much more now. I wish he'd been able to tell us what had been going on, but I also understood why he didn't.

"I'm worried I pressured him," Tim told me, his voice laced with regret. "All my jokes about how he was following in my footsteps, a chip off the old block. That couldn't have been helpful."

"You were proud," I reassured him. "That was understandable, and nothing to feel guilty about."

"But if he felt he couldn't speak up, that I'd be disappointed somehow—"

"He told me it's hard to speak up," I replied. "And so it is. Maybe this will be a good lesson for him, in the end." Because, I was realizing, we don't grow or learn through accomplishment or success, through getting it right first time, or at least pretending to, but rather through failure—depressing, shaming, unavoidable failure. I'd been so frightened of showing my own failures, exposing my weakness, my *wrongness*, but that's exactly what I've had to do in order to get past this. To grow and to heal. And maybe Lucas does, as well. Maybe we all do. "How is Em?" I asked, and Tim sighed.

"She's okay. A little clingy. Missing you."

"Is she?" I was heartened, because things had still been

tense between us when I'd left, despite our silent hugs. "I miss her."

"She misses your dad too, of course. She sits in his room, sometimes, by herself."

Tears stung my eyes. I imagined my daughter curled up on the sofa, my dad's chair empty, *Storage Wars* on the TV.

"I want to go home," I told Tim.

"I want you home. But you're needed there. Your dad needs you."

"Yes." I couldn't deny that coming to Stuttgart had been important, necessary—even, in its own way, good. "He's so tired, Tim. He sleeps all the time."

"This whole thing has to have taken it out of him."

"Yes..." But I feared it was more than that. I thought of my father saying *it finally ends* and I didn't think he meant the court case, which in any case hadn't even begun. I think he meant something bigger, deeper. I was afraid he had given up on life; that he was ready to die.

The memory of that conversation is fresh in my mind as we make our way into the courtroom, the doors closing behind us on the barrage of questions. This room is as unpretentious as the one back in Charlottesville, with a couple of conference tables equipped with microphones on either side, and then the witness stand and judge's bench on a small dais. There are only a few dozen people in attendance—mainly court officials, a few relatives of camp survivors, the prosecuting lawyer, and, of course, Leo Weiss.

I glance over at him curiously, wondering about this man who has affected my life so much, yet whom I've never met, never even seen. He is sitting by his lawyer on the opposite side of the room, an elderly man with stooped shoulders and white hair, which jolts me, because, for some reason, I had been picturing someone young and vigorous, in their thirties or forties, maybe, which I realize is, of course, ridiculous. He couldn't be young, not if he was at Sobibor, and yet in my head I'd made him so, perhaps because I'd known he was a child at the time, and so had always thought of him as young. Now I am struck that he looks almost as old as my own father—they are two feeble, white-haired men, both bent over their tables, squinting into the distance, stooped and frail. It saddens me, that it has come to this, for them, for us.

I've already learned that there are only a handful of Sobibor survivors—three or four at most—who are still alive, and none of them were either able or willing to travel to Stuttgart for the trial, although two have helped to bring the case to court as Leo Weiss's co-plaintiffs. I wonder who they are, whether they actually knew my father. Did they speak to him? Did they see him on the ramp? Perhaps I'll find out today.

As we take our seats, Leo Weiss looks over at us and his expression hardens, his eyes turning flinty, his mouth thinning. I can sense the force of his feelings from across the room, and it both chills and humbles me. Even after all this time, he is angry, and of course he has a right to be. I still haven't heard the whole story from my father, about how he came to shoot Daniel Weiss. Perhaps I'll hear it today.

My father, fumbling for his seat, doesn't notice Leo Weiss' dark look. He has seemed even more tired today, as well as a bit disoriented; a couple of times this morning, he forgot what he was doing, and I ended up having to help him do his tie, lace up his shoes. Now I put my hand on his arm to steady him as the judge enters the court and we all rise. The trial, finally and yet already, has begun.

Of course, I don't understand a word. It's all in German, and even though I can pick a few words out—Sobibor, *buchhalter*—I can't make sense of any of it. The opening statement by the prosecuting attorney is lengthy and florid, with many sweeping hand gestures and ringing proclamations as the man, somber and in his fifties, moves about the room. Seated behind his table, Leo Weiss looks stony; my father is looking down at his lap. I wish I knew what was being said, but I realize I am also glad that I don't. It's hard enough not knowing, but hearing the tone, the condemnation, the judgment, knowing they are warranted and yet aching all the same.

Finally, the lawyer finishes, sitting down with a flourish, and I expect him to call Leo to the stand, his only witness as far as I know, although my dad's lawyer told us the other Sobibor survivors have issued statements as co-plaintiffs that will be read out in due course. But then, to my surprise, I hear another name called.

"Hans Brenner."

My father rises from his seat, a resolute look on his face, his bearing frail yet dignified. The whole room seems to be holding its breath as my dad makes his laborious way to the stand, one step after another, his expression remaining determined. He is going to testify, I realize, and in a flash of understanding, it all suddenly makes sense. *It finally ends.* He is, I know with a flare of soul-deep certainty, going to testify against himself.

The lawyer asks his name, and he responds with quiet dignity, first in German, then in English. "For the sake my daughter, so she may understand what I am about to say," he tells the lawyer. "I would like to answer in both languages, if it is acceptable to the court. My German is also not as good as it once was."

The lawyer glances at the judge, who nods.

I sit, transfixed, my heart starting to thud. I have no idea what my father is going to say, but I know with every fiber of my being that he needs to say it—and I need to hear it, even if I don't want to.

"You may make your statement, Herr Brenner," the judge says. "You may speak in English first, and then German."

My father murmurs his thanks and then takes a piece of paper out of the inside pocket of his jacket before slowly, painstakingly, unfolding it, and I realize this must have been arranged beforehand. This was what my father spoke about with his lawyer.

Slowly, haltingly, looking down at the paper, my father begins in English. "I came to Sobibor as a young man of twenty-three. I had already attempted to join the SS, out of pride and ambition more than any ideology I held, when I was summoned to the regional headquarters here in Stuttgart and told they had a particular job for me. There was no question of refusing it, not without serious repercussions, but in any case, I did not want to refuse. I was, I admit, excited by the idea that I had been chosen for a special task, as well as a bit apprehensive about the unknown. Still, it seemed particularly fortuitous that the regional officer had arranged for my sister, Anni, to accompany me. Our parents were dead and she was only seventeen. I felt responsible for her, and I was very glad for her company, at the start."

He pauses to clear his throat, and I glance around at the courtroom, the faces of those listening—some look rapt, others skeptical, a few even angry. Do they not want my father to be a human being like anyone else, with all the accompanying foibles and vagaries? Perhaps it's easier, I think, to be as black and white as I once was—to think everyone is either a monster or a saint. The truth, I am realizing more and more, is far more complicated.

My father continues. "When we arrived at the camp, I was pleased with its appearance. It looked like a mountain village, a holiday destination, everything very pleasant. There were many white cottages with painted green trim, baskets of hanging flowers. I was pleased," he states, his voice becoming more strident, "because I wanted to be pleased. I wanted to see what I saw, and so I did.

"My sister, however, was far more perceptive than I was. She realized almost immediately, based on the size of the camp, that the Jewish prisoners had to have been killed upon arrival. It took me several days to come to that conclusion—it happened during the second transport I witnessed, when Polish Jews were beaten as they were herded toward the Tube that led to the gas chambers." His voice wavers and he bows his head. "I saw an officer shoot a man in the head right in front of me. I saw the same officer swing a baby against the side of a train car to kill it. I could not believe what I was seeing, and yet there it was. I walked away from that ramp a changed man."

He takes a deep breath. I realize my eyes are full of tears. "I requested a transfer the next day and was refused. I was told that if I wished to leave Sobibor, I could go to the Eastern Front, as a soldier. I refused, although in retrospect I wished I had not. It would have been far better to lose my life than my soul."

A ripple of emotion moves through the crowd, but I'm not sure what it is. Respect? Empathy? Or maybe just a determination for my father to pay for his crimes, no matter what heartfelt sentiments he offers now. They come too late; they can never be enough.

"I met Daniel Weiss about a month after I had arrived. He was a goldsmith, and another officer, Gustav Wagner, wished for him to make him a ring. Daniel and his son, Leo, worked in my office. My sister developed an attachment to them both, and it was her wish that I did what I could to protect them."

Another ripple—this one more shocked, definitely angry. *Protect* Daniel Weiss? And yet he'd killed him.

My father looks up from his notes. "I failed in that regard," he states, and then he searches the crowd for Leo Weiss. "I failed utterly." His gaze fastens on Leo, who is looking back at him stonily. "Your father was my friend," he continues, his voice breaking now. "As much of a friend as he could be, considering the circumstances. I know I am responsible for his death. I accept that fully, and whatever penalty or punishment it requires. It was a moment of madness, of rage, of hurt, and I have always, *always* been sorry for it."

He takes a deep breath and then looks over the whole court. Looks at me.

"Moreover, I am complicit in all the atrocities of Sobibor, for I did not walk away from that camp, as much as I wanted to. I did not question my superiors or their actions; I did not resist them in any real way. I acted out of cowardice, rather than courage, and for that I will be forever ashamed and guilty. Even more than that, I am ashamed of how I let the camp change me. I watched the transports arrive; I heard the screams and cries and gunshots and I let myself become inured to it all, because I knew I could not survive otherwise, and I wanted to survive. No matter what I told myself, that I had no choice, that I had to protect my sister, I wanted to survive, and I let that guide me both then and for the last seventy years." He puts down the paper, lifts his chin. "I was, and am, guilty of assisting in the crimes that were committed at the Sobibor death camp. I am complicit in the deaths of the more than one hundred thousand Jewish people who died while I worked there. Let the court decide as it pleases, as is right."

He repeats his entire statement in German and then his words fall away into a silence, a stillness, that is hushed and absolute. I feel the tears streaking down my face, tears of sorrow and grief, but also love and pride. *I know who my father is.* He glances at the judge and then, with dignified precision, he rises from his seat at the witness stand. There are only two steps down from the dais to the floor, and he takes them carefully. I want to run to him, to take him in my arms, but I can't, and so I wait, my breath held, my face still damp with tears.

As my father takes the second step, his leg shakes, his face goes pale, and then, as if happening in slow motion, he collapses to the floor while a collective gasp is heard around the court as I rise from where I am sitting, a silent cry caught in my throat.

. . .

"There's nothing visibly wrong with him, besides that he is an old man. A very old man."

The doctor, who thankfully speaks English, smiles at me in sympathy. I wonder if she knows who the frail man asleep in the bed behind her is—a Nazi, about to be convicted of war crimes.

I take a deep breath and let it out slowly. It's been six hours since my father collapsed in court. An ambulance was called as people gathered round, and he was taken here, to Klinikum Stuttgart, one of the best hospitals in the region, that accepts patients from all over the world.

"Are there tests you can do? To see if anything is wrong?"

"Yes, there are tests." She pauses, and then rests a hand on my arm. "But he is ninety-six. Sometimes the body has had enough. It just gives out."

And sometimes the heart does, as well. The soul. Why would my father want to live anymore, now? All he has to look forward to is prison. He has admitted his guilt, and I hope, made his peace. But I'm still not ready to let him go.

I thank the doctor as she leaves and then sink into the chair next to my dad. His eyes are closed, his breathing slow and deep, his skin papery. He hasn't regained consciousness since his collapse. I wonder if someone can simply will themselves to die, and I pray my father won't. Not yet, anyway. I still have things I need to say, things I didn't fully understand or accept until I saw him there on the witness stand.

He is guilty and I love him.

It felt so impossible months, or even weeks, ago, to have both those things be true, and now it seems simple, or at least right. I think of Simon Baum telling me that only I can figure out if I can still love my father, and now I know the answer to that question. I can.

"Libby?"

I turn to my father, my heart rising like a balloon in my chest as I see his eyes flicker open. "Dad." I reach for his hand resting on the sheet; it feels like a bundle of twigs under my own fingers.

"I'm... sorry."

"I know you are, Dad." Gently, so gently, I squeeze his hands. "It's okay."

He blinks back tears as he looks up at me. "For your mother, I mean."

My throat goes so tight I have to force the words past the lump that is forming there. "I know."

"She loved you, in her own way. It was hard for her, but she did."

I just nod, because now I find I can't speak at all.

"I should have told you the truth... about everything."

"I know it was hard—"

"I have been a coward to the last." He closes his eyes and, for a second, I think he has fallen asleep, but then he speaks, his voice barely a thread of sound. "I hoped that if I... did enough, I could make it right. If I taught you what was good, if I showed you how wrong they all were..."

I think of him at the Holocaust Museum, with tears in his eyes. "I know, Dad."

He opens his eyes. "But there is no making it right, without honesty. Without truth. I am guilty. I deserve to pay for my crimes. I accept that, at last. And I am glad of it, in the end."

I can only nod. A sob is rising in my chest, breaking against my lips, but I hold it back.

Then my father lifts his head from the pillow, the look in his eyes one of burning intensity. "Libby... I must ask you to do one last thing for me."

I don't want to think about last things, but I nod. "What is it, Dad? What do you want me to do?"

"There is someone I need to see. To talk to. I want you to ask him to visit me, here."

I am full of both wonder and dread as I shake my head slightly. "Who, Dad?" I ask, although I think I know whom he means. Who else could he mean? And then he says it.

"Leo Weiss."

CHAPTER 27

Sobibor, Poland

All summer, the air in the camp crackled with expectation, with tension, with dread. The transports of Polish Jews had stopped months ago; in June, the last of the Dutch Jews had come through. There simply weren't anymore, Gomerski had told Hans with a laugh. Hans had thought of aleph null and said nothing. The transports had tapered off to one every few weeks or less; by August, there weren't any at all.

The only activity happening at Sobibor was the clearing of trees and the building of barracks in what was known as North Camp, for the possibility of storing weapons there in future, but Hans didn't know much about it and he thought it hardly seemed likely. Sobibor was a place, he felt, teetering on the edge of destruction. Belzec had already closed and Treblinka would not be far behind; it was common sense that Sobibor would be next. And what then, would happen to the last remaining Jews? To him and Anni?

He had not spoken again to Daniel of the planned revolt. He did not want to know, and yet he remained watchful as he moved about the camp, noticing how the prisoners could sidle silently from one place to the next, how easily they melted into the shadows, and most of all, how many of them there were. Six hundred to a handful of officers and guards, many of whom were away on leave on any given day, or drunk and idle.

Admittedly, the prisoners were haggard and weak, and moreover, weaponless. Yet how hard would it be for them to get their hands on some guns? There was an arsenal that could be broken into; a guard or officer killed in a moment, his gun snatched. But at the same time, such a plan seemed impossible, hopeless. Even if they grabbed some guns, stormed the gates, they would be shot down by the guards high up in their towers. Even if they made it out of the camp, Wagner and his ilk would hunt them through the forest, the same way a man might hunt rabbits. And yet, Hans thought bleakly, what did any of them have to lose?

His relations with both Daniel and Leo had cooled a little, since the birthday party. Hans felt guilty for the way he'd put the man in his place, and he had tried to apologize, without ever putting it into words. He smiled at Leo and gave him some paper and pencils he'd bought in Chelm; he asked Daniel about his goldsmithing. He missed the small sense of camaraderie they'd shared, such as it had been, but it felt impossible to get it back now. And perhaps that was for the best, considering. There was no future here, for either of them.

In July, Hans had been given leave to return to the rest hut they'd gone to in February, and, to his dismay, Anni had refused to go.

"You may go," she had told Hans flatly, "but I am staying here."

"Anni, you cannot stay here on your own!" Hans had told her in exasperation. "You know that."

"I'm not going," she had replied mulishly. "Look what

happened last time, Hans. You must know as well as I do how dangerous it is, especially now."

"Dangerous for Daniel Weiss," he had finished bitterly. "I wonder if you care more for him than you do me." He'd thrown the words at her like a careless challenge, not really meaning them, and yet, at the still, watchful look on her face, he'd fallen silent, appalled. "Anni..." he had begun, helplessly, and she cut him off quickly.

"I simply want to protect him and Leo," she had said. "If I can. If *we* can. Hans, if we can save lives..."

"Anni, they are all doomed," Hans had told her in a low voice. "You must know that. They will be shot or gassed when this camp closes. It's only a matter of time—"

She had said nothing, and a creeping new suspicion took hold.

"Is there something you're not telling me?" he had asked sharply. "Something you know?" Surely she wasn't in on this wretched revolt, whatever it was? Surely she wouldn't risk both their lives that way? He felt guilty enough for staying silent, when he knew he should warn the other officers. His ill-thought out offer to help Daniel he refused to think of again, and he'd hoped Anni would have enough sense not to, either. Yet when had Anni ever had sense?

"What could I possibly know?" Anni had replied, which Hans knew very well was no answer at all.

They did not go to the rest hut in the cool pine-covered hills, but suffered the humid, mosquito-laden heat at the camp, the simmering tensions that would suddenly explode in an act of violent sadism—a guard would make the prisoners crawl on all fours, or run in circles or do circus tricks, before shooting them lazily or demanding their fellow prisoners beat them, often to death. As much as he dreaded the end, Hans felt the closure of the camp couldn't come fast enough. He had to get out of this place before he lost his mind along with his soul.

"You won't go back to Dresden, you know," Niemann had told him one afternoon when they were having drinks outside the commandant's house, with something like amusement when Hans had dared to venture that he was looking forward to going home.

"Stuttgart," he had corrected levelly. "Why not?"

Niemann had let out a bored sigh as he looked away. One of the officers was setting up a camera, as if anyone wanted to record this moment for posterity, Hans thought with a spurt of bitterness. Anni had come reluctantly, not wanting to arouse any suspicion, but she'd kept herself apart, not bothering to disguise her disgust, her boredom.

"Because it doesn't work that way, Brenner," Niemann had told him. "Haven't you realized that yet? Rumor has it, we'll all be transferred to northern Italy after the camp closes, to deal with the Jews there."

There really were an infinite number of Jews, Hans thought numbly, and they would all be killed. First in Poland, then in France and Holland, and next Italy. And he would be part of it all. He did not think he could bear it, and yet all the same he knew he would.

"*Jetzt bitte lääächeln!*" the man had called, hefting the camera, and Hans had looked away. He did not want to be remembered as ever having been at this place.

In mid-September, when the heat had finally broken, the mood in the camp changed, for both the prisoners and officers. The news from the Front was dismal; the assault in North Africa had collapsed, Italy had surrendered to the Allies in Sicily, and Hitler had had to call off the Kursk Offensive, even though the Soviets continued fighting. They were losing the war everywhere they looked, and the simmering tensions in the camp turned into something taut and dangerous, like a rope about to snap.

Reichleitner ordered all the Jews to be kept in their barracks as a transport came in—the first one in over a month. Hans went to the ramp with a dread-filled curiosity; what was different about this transport compared to the others? Why did the Jews have to be kept away?

He found out when they slid open the cattle cars; this time there were no shouts of "*Raus!*" or "*Schnell*"; the officers simply raised their pistols and shot the Jews where they stood, huddled together in the cramped cars, blinking in the sudden spill of sunlight.

Hans watched, appalled, wondering how he could still possibly be surprised by anything that happened there.

"Why are you shooting them?" he asked Wagner, who gave a careless little shrug.

"They're the inmates from Belzec, the last crew. It's closed now." He gave Hans a humorous look. "Don't worry, book-keeper, they won't have any money for you to count." He let out a laugh that turned Hans' stomach.

Hans swallowed down any reply he might have made, and then turned on his heel and walked quickly away. So they wanted to keep the Jews from knowing how they were dealt with. Did the officers think they were stupid? That they hadn't already guessed? There had been a scattering of escape attempts over the summer—a few Jews had bribed some guards in North Camp to look the other way when they went to fetch water; a Polish Jew had tried to tunnel under the fence. None of it had ever come to anything, and the Jews remaining had been punished severely for the attempts. Perhaps, Hans reflected, the officers simply trusted that the prisoners would do whatever they could to preserve their miserable lives, as long as they believed it wasn't futile. Wasn't he the same?

And yet it *was* futile, utterly futile, for all of them. He knew that absolutely.

A week passed, and then another, time seeming to crawl by, every day utterly fraught. Would today be the day they closed the camp? Hans could picture it so clearly—they'd bring the prisoners out into the main square, where they had roll call. Perhaps they'd promise them something—extra rations, or some sort of news. And then they would shoot them, like fish in a barrel, like birds in the sky, one by one by one, without emotion, without care, without even interest.

If he knew it, they must know it too. Yet what could they do? How would they rebel, if they managed to find the strength, the strategy, the courage?

At the end of September, a transport came of Russian Jews who had been captured at Minsk, many of them having served in the Soviet army. All were killed, save for a few who had been selected to unload bricks for the barracks they were still building at North Camp. Hans watched from his empty office as the guards whipped those last prisoners into a near-frenzy; if they stumbled or fell, they were shot. They would work them to death, he thought. Perhaps it was simpler than gassing.

He glanced at Daniel, who was quietly working on a badge for Beckmann—one of the more reasonable officers. In charge of the stables and sorting barracks, he was, Hans thought, a man who did not seek out opportunities for sadistic punishment but was willing enough to mete it out if necessary.

Hans hesitated and then said quietly, "There's not much time."

Daniel gave him a swift, searching look but said nothing.

Hans took a deep breath. "I know I said I did not want to hear of it, and I don't, but you should know. There's not much time."

Daniel gazed down at his smoking little brazier, the gold a shimmering, boiling liquid. "Do you know what they found in the pockets of the prisoners from Belzec?" he asked, his voice so low Hans strained to hear him. He glanced at Leo, who looked quickly away.

"I didn't realize you knew about them."

"We hear and see everything, *Herr Buchhalter*."

Just as he'd thought, then. "What was in their pockets?"

"Notes, on scraps of paper. Almost all of them had written one. The guards didn't bother to look."

Hans registered the scorn in Daniel's voice, the fury blazing in his eyes. "And what did the notes say?" he asked, with a sickening wave of dread.

"'If they kill us, avenge us.'" He took a mold and began to pour the gold carefully into the lead-lined tray, his gaze lowered to his task. "And we will," he said, so quietly Hans could almost convince himself he'd imagined the words.

By the beginning of October, when the leaves had started to turn and Hans realized he and Anni had been at the camp for an entire year, his sister became both animated and restless, pacing the confines of their cottage, often slipping out to go heaven knew where.

"You should not roam the camp, Anni," Hans told her, his tone both severe and hopeless, because he knew she would not listen to him. "It's dangerous."

"I know what I am doing, Hans," she replied with confident asperity, and once more he had the feeling that she knew more than she would ever tell him, that she was involved somehow in whatever the prisoners were planning. It was bad enough, he thought, that he had not spoken of his suspicions to the commandant. But what if Anni actually *helped* them? If it became known, which it almost certainly would? Anni would not hide the fact, he knew. She would be proud of it.

He was afraid to ask her directly, and he despised his own cowardice.

The fourteenth of October dawned like any other day—crisp, clear and sunny, yet with a familiar heaviness in the air, in himself, that Hans couldn't shake. He wondered if he ever would, or if he would still feel this way, thirty, forty, fifty years from now, if he lived so long.

As he walked through the camp toward the administration building—he spent his days in his office, although there was little to do besides tally the amounts that had been used to buy bricks—he stopped.

The yard was empty, still, swept clean. Back in July, they had poured chlorine over it all to disinfect it after a hundred Jews from the Majdanek camp had lain dying on the sand, too weak to be taken down the Tube. Now there was nothing, and yet the back of Hans' neck prickled. He turned quickly, and saw a prisoner slink into the shoe shop across the yard.

He took a deep breath, let it out slowly. Then he walked into the administration building. It wasn't until he was seated behind his desk that he realized what had been odd about the prisoner he'd seen—although the day was warm enough, with just a hint of autumn in the air, the man had been wearing a heavy coat and winter boots.

When Daniel and Leo came in to work a short while later, Hans sensed their edginess. Daniel spoke sharply to Leo in Polish, and then took a deep breath, as if to calm himself. As he set to his work, Hans watched him, his stomach hollowing out.

Something was happening. Certainly today, maybe even right now.

The hours crept past. He worked on the same column of figures, unable to turn his mind to anything. Daniel worked steadily, his head lowered.

Hans ate lunch, a hunk of bread and cheese, at his desk, wanting to keep his eye on Daniel. Leo stood silently by his side, his head lowered. Nothing was amiss, and yet...

The sound of someone calling from outside had Hans moving to the door. As he gazed outside, he saw that a couple of prisoners were inviting an officer, Wolf, a man Hans thought was particularly stupid and slow, into the storage shed to try on a leather jacket. It was nothing out of the ordinary; prisoners were often trying to curry favor, by keeping back items for certain officers.

Hans turned back into the building, just as the prisoner called out to another officer, Beckmann, to also try on a coat. He paused. Wolf hadn't come out yet, and it was strange for the prisoners to invite two officers at the same time; they would argue over the clothes, and the Jews would suffer. They always did.

Halfway across the yard, Beckmann hesitated, and then he went into the shop. The silence felt absolute, the air languid and heavy. Slowly, Hans returned to his office.

When he came in, he saw Daniel was not at his desk, and he stopped where he stood, trying to make sense of it. Then he felt a hard blow to the back of his neck, and he stumbled and fell to his knees, stars dancing before his eyes, his ears ringing.

When he looked up, blinking the room back into focus, Daniel was in front of him, his arm still raised, a grim look on his face.

"I was told to kill you," he said, "but I can't, because I think that deep down you are a good man. But I cannot have you interfering with what we do today. I am sorry, Hans." And then he raised his hand and clouted Hans hard on the side of the head, so the whole world went black.

. . .

Hans did not know how much later it was when he awoke, groggy, his head aching abominably. The office was empty, Daniel and Leo both gone. With a groan, Hans put his hand to the side of his head; it came away sticky with blood. He clambered onto his hands and knees, his stomach heaving. He threw up right there on the floor, before he staggered to his feet.

Anni. He had to get to Anni.

Outside, to his surprise, the camp still seemed calm; some of the Jews were lining up in the yard for roll call, as they would on any normal day. What was happening? Hans wondered, his mind fuzzy, his head throbbing with pain. Had he imagined it all? But, no, Daniel had hit him. And there had been something strange about the officers going into the shed... but what? He struggled to think, to make sense of it all.

He looked around for other officers, but there was no one in sight; the roll call was being conducted by *kapos*. Had the officers all been killed, as he was meant to have been? Where were the guards?

He forced himself onward, staggering past the yard to the officers' quarters, and to Anni.

When he came into the cottage, he found her sitting at the table, her hands laced around her middle, as if she were waiting for something. She jumped up as soon as she saw him.

"Hans! Your head! What happened to you?"

"Daniel Weiss tried to kill me."

"What!" She sounded shocked, but not in the way Hans expected. She'd known, he realized numbly. She'd known what was going to happen, and she'd been willing to sacrifice him for it.

"You knew," he said, slumping into a chair. Blood trickled down his cheek. "You knew he would try, and you allowed it." The realization left him hurt and heartbroken in a way he hadn't thought possible. *Anni...* Anni, the only good thing in his life, the whole reason for it, had been willing for him to die?

"He wasn't going to kill you, and he didn't," she stated calmly. "You must not interfere, Hans."

"Interfere!" he repeated in disbelief. "Is that how you see it? Anni... how many officers have they killed?"

She hesitated, a familiarly stubborn look coming over her face. "I don't know."

He let out a groan, covering his eyes with one hand. "You know it's hopeless, don't you?"

As he dropped his hand, he saw her spine stiffen, eyes flash. "I don't know any such thing."

He shook his head slowly, even though it made it ache all the more. "Most of the Jews won't see any difference between you or I and someone like Wagner. They'd kill us in a heartbeat, do you realize?"

"I'm willing to take that risk."

"Why? Just to save Daniel Weiss?"

"Yes." She sounded so firm, so sure. Hans stared at her in helpless disbelief as she stated with quiet, ringing certainty, "I love him, Hans."

He gazed at her, caught between dismay, grief, and a complete lack of surprise. Hadn't he suspected some affection between them? And yet he had, in his stubborn naivete, not believed it could be true. Not *love*.

"You could be shot for saying such a thing," he told her flatly.

"Then so be it."

"And if he escapes? What then?"

She shrugged. "Then nothing. He doesn't love me, not like that. I've always known that. He is still grieving his wife."

"I am glad to hear it," Hans retorted bitterly. "It is bad enough, that you harbor some stupid, schoolgirl crush—"

"It is not a crush." Her hand went to her throat, and Hans' gaze narrowed as he saw her clasping a necklace he hadn't noticed before. He leaned across the table to peer at it; it was a ring on a chain, a ring of twisted gold; he recognized it as Daniel's work and he felt a sudden blaze of fury. He reached out and yanked the chain from her neck in one short, sharp jerk. She let out a gasp.

"He gave you this, I suppose?" he demanded, hurling the ring to the ground. It bounced and rolled into a corner of the room.

"He did," Anni replied. Spots of color had appeared on her cheeks and her chin was tilted at a defiant angle. "He made it for me."

Right in his office, under his nose! "He could have been killed," Hans told her, "for using the gold for his own purposes, never mind making a ring for an Aryan woman."

"He could have been killed for looking at Wagner, or Gomerski, or Bauer the wrong way," Anni snapped. "You *know* that. How can you defend them?"

"I'm not defending anyone." Hans shook his head, his teeth gritted against the pain. "So he gave you a ring. He returned your affection in some way, then?" He could barely stomach such a thought, and he knew it had nothing to do with Daniel being Jewish. It was the subterfuge, the treachery, the betrayal. Had they both been laughing at him?

Anni was silent, but then Hans saw her hand creep to her middle, press lightly there, and a terrible, new suspicion, too awful even to be put into words, dawned on him, took him over.

"Anni," he said in a low voice, half-rising from the table, his heart beginning to thud. "Anni, don't tell me... you *can't*..."

"Yes, I am," she flung at him. "I'm carrying his child, and I'm glad. *Glad*, Hans—"

"*No.*" With a guttural shout, he hurled the table onto its side. "No, my God, I'll kill him—"

"*Hans—*"

"And he's leaving you here, knowing you are carrying his child?" he demanded. "Leaving you to your fate?"

"What else can he do?" Anni returned, her eyes glittering with both rage and pride. "He has no choice. He will be killed if he stays here, Hans, and Leo too—"

"The bastard. The *bastard*." He raked a hand through his hair, smearing blood across his palm.

"I told you, I love him. I am not ashamed."

"Do you know what they would do to you," Hans demanded, "if they discover you are carrying a Jewish bastard?"

"Do you think they can tell, just from looking at a baby?" Anni returned scornfully. "Do you suppose they can determine it, by measuring the space between its ears? You're as bad as the rest of them, Hans, and you don't even realize."

"Oh, I realize," he answered in a growl of both bitterness and anguish. "I've known all along. I've fought hard against it, God knows, I've tried to hold onto my soul in this godforsaken place, for your sake, Anni, as much as mine, but *this*..."

Anni's furious expression softened and she held her hands out to him. "It's a baby, Hans, that's all. An innocent child."

He opened his mouth to reply, only to stiffen at the sound of gunshots—not one or two, but a sudden barrage. He stared at Anni, saw the flash of something like triumph in her eyes. Then he heard a guard scream: "*Ein Deutsch kaput! Ein Deutsch kaput!*"

This was it, Hans realized numbly. The Jews were escaping.

He whirled away from Anni and ran outside.

The main yard was a maelstrom of activity. Prisoners were running everywhere, screaming and shooting into the air, clubs raised as they rushed the gates, others the fences, a storm of humanity unleashed at the bitter last. Hans pressed back against the porch as he heard the mines begin to explode outside the walls, and clouds of acrid smoke billowed up in the air. One of the guards started shooting at the prisoners who were running toward the officers' quarters, and Hans watched, horrified, as a woman fell to the ground right in front of him, dead.

Several hundred prisoners were now at the main gate as the guards fired on them. The fences were bending under the weight of their bodies, as others scrambled upward in a desperate bid for freedom. Others, Hans saw, had cut the fence right behind Reichleitner's house, the Merry Flea, and were scrambling across the unmined meadow beyond, to the safety of the forest.

It was happening, he realized in amazement, hardly able to believe what was right in front of his eyes. They were actually escaping. Some of them, he thought with incredulous wonder, might even make it.

"Brenner!"

He jerked his head round to see another officer, Frenzl, toss him a pistol. He caught it as a matter of instinct, the metal hot and unfamiliar in his hand. In all his time at Sobibor, he'd never been given a gun.

"Get the bastards," Frenzl said, and started running.

Hans stared around him, paralyzed, horrified. He did not think he could shoot anyone. Then, in the distance, he saw Daniel, running toward the main gate.

"*Weiss!*" he shouted, and started sprinting toward him, heedless of the melee, the dead bodies littering the ground and strung across the fences like scarecrows. He thought of Anni, pregnant and alone, and his blood surged through his veins, roared in his ears. "*Weiss!*" he roared again.

Daniel turned, and something hardened in his face as he caught sight of Hans. Hans hadn't realized he'd raised the pistol and was pointing it at Daniel until he felt his fingers tremble on the trigger.

"How could you," he said in a low voice. "How *could* you."

"I didn't kill you—" Daniel protested, his voice caught between anguish and anger.

"It's not me I care about!" Hans roared. "It's Anni. *Anni*. You used her—"

A flicker of shame crossed Daniel's face like a shadow. "It was a moment of weakness," he told him raggedly. "I'm sorry, but Hans, please. *Please*. This is my only chance, mine and Leo's." He glanced to his side, and Hans realized Leo was there, hovering a few feet away. Both of them looked toward the forest, no doubt wondering if they could outrun Hans' shot, lose themselves in the streaming crowds.

"She's pregnant," Hans told him, his voice shaking. "Did you know that?"

The look on Daniel's face was all the confirmation Hans needed. He'd known, and he'd still intended to leave her. Forget her.

He levelled the pistol, his mind a haze of rage.

"Hans, please..."

The prisoners were still streaming through the gate. It would be easy, all too easy, to kill Daniel where he stood, one fallen among many. He'd never shot a man before, but in that moment he was sure he could do it. He'd seen it done enough times, and now he realized just how easy it was. It was his duty as an officer, after all, and yet... his finger started to press the trigger while a look of terrible resignation came over Daniel's face. He didn't move, simply waited.

Was this what he'd become, Hans thought with a sickening thud of realization, his finger still on the trigger. One more death meant nothing, less than nothing? The death of a man he'd come to know, even to care about? It seemed he could kill as well as watch the killing, speak as well as stay silent, in the midst of all this madness and cruelty? Was this the bitter endpoint of all he'd endured, all he'd seen?

Regret swirled like acid in Hans' stomach. He'd failed many times before, he knew that full well, but he would not be that man. He started to lower the gun.

"Brenner!"

The short, sharp bark had him stilling. It was Wagner, striding across the yard, having just returned from leave, his pistol aimed right at Hans.

"What the hell do you think you're doing?" he demanded. "Shoot the bastards, you idiot," he said, and then he turned, and without so much as a flicker, shot Daniel Weiss right in the chest.

Stunned, Hans watched Daniel fall, and from somewhere behind him, he heard Anni's scream. The whole camp fell away as he stood there, amidst the carnage and ruin, and in shock watched as Leo, having seen it all, ran forward and fell to his knees and cradled his father's limp body in his arms.

CHAPTER 28

LIBBY

Stuttgart, Germany

"Leo Weiss has refused. He does not wish to see or speak to Hans Brenner ever again."

"That's understandable," I murmur, trying not to feel stung. It is what I expected, and yet I know my father will be distraught. Ever since he made the request of me last night, he has been waiting for Leo to appear, like some ghost of times past, forgiving, healing. He wants to make amends, and yet how can he, if Leo Weiss won't let him? Forgiveness, I am realizing, is just as complicated as being wrong is. It doesn't happen naturally or easily; now that the trial has been suspended, I have seen how disappointed people are, how angry. They want their pound of flesh from my father, and maybe they deserve it, but they aren't going to get it. Not in the way that they wanted, anyway.

"My father is dying," I tell Leo's lawyer quietly. Stating it aloud, even though it's what the doctors intimated last night, still shocks me. "The doctors don't think he has long. For Herr

Weiss' sake, as much as my father's, could they not speak and make peace?"

The lawyer sighs on the phone. "I will ask again," he says, sounding doubtful.

I murmur my thanks before ending the call. Last night, I phoned Tim and told him, with tears thick in my throat, all the news. My father's statement and subsequent collapse. His apology to me, the doctors' dismal prognosis.

"There's nothing actually wrong with him," I said, my voice clogged. "He's just... giving up."

"Maybe it's better this way," Tim replied quietly, and I gulped and nodded.

"Yes... yes." Better than going to prison, perhaps, but it still felt so hard. Wrong, even if it was, at its essence, right. *It finally ends.*

I walk back into my father's room; he is lying still, his eyes closed, his breathing shallow, barely lifting his chest. It feels as if the life is draining steadily from him, minute by minute, hour by hour. How long will there be left? Not long, I fear. Not long at all.

I sit down next to him and carefully take his hand in my own. It's so thin, so fragile, the skin almost translucent. "I love you, Dad," I say, even though he is asleep, because they feel like the only words I have, and I don't know how much longer I'll have to say them. "I love you."

The minutes tick on and my father doesn't stir. Will he just silently slip away, I wonder, between one breath and the next? It would be more peaceful that way, and yet I dread it. I can't believe it's going to happen, even though I know I should have been more prepared for this moment.

I don't know how long I sit there, holding my dad's hand in mine, willing him to wake up so I can see him smile, hear him tell me he's here, he loves me as I love him. Hours, maybe, because the light fades from the sky; the hospital begins to quiet, no more than muffled murmurs and footsteps from the hallway.

And then—

"Frau Trent?"

I turn, and even in the dimness of the room, I know immediately who it is. Leo Weiss. He stands in the doorway as if he's still thinking of turning and leaving, an old man, stooped and sorrowful.

"Herr Weiss." It feels strange to call him that, what for so long I believed was my father's name. Gently, I lay my father's hand on the sheet as I stand to greet him. "Thank you so much for coming."

"I did not want to, but my wife..." He shrugs, offering a small smile. "She said enough time has passed. Forgiveness is for the wronged as much as it is for anyone else. It will go better this way, for both of us."

"Thank you," I say, the words heartfelt. I glance at my dad. "He's been sleeping a lot. I don't know..."

"I'll sit and wait." He takes a few shuffling steps toward the chair I'd been sitting in. "If you don't mind?"

"No, of course not." I take the other chair, at the end of the bed.

Leo Weiss sits down slowly, with a creak of joints, a groan of satisfaction. "That's better. It has been a long few days."

"I can imagine."

He glances at me, his expression both knowing and shrewd. "For you, as well?"

"Yes."

We are silent for a few moments as my father sleeps.

"You really didn't know?" he finally asks, and I shake my head.

"Not until we were told, by the US Department of Justice, a few months ago."

Leo nods slowly. "I have been looking for him all my life."

The words sadden more than chill me. "And now that you've found him?"

"I don't know," he admits, passing a hand across his face. "I don't know."

"My father thought you were dead," I venture hesitantly, after a few more moments of silence. "He thought you'd been killed with his sister, Anni, in an Allied raid."

Leo's face darkens in memory. "I escaped Dresden, with Aliza. Anni did not. She'd been working. She came back too late, and was caught in the raid."

I nod in understanding, even though I am confused. I still don't understand why Leo was with Anni in the first place. "Aliza?" I repeat uncertainly, and he looks at me in wary surprise.

"Do you not know—?"

I shake my head. "No, I don't know who she is." And I'm pretty sure my dad doesn't, either.

"Anni's daughter. She was born in March 1944."

"Her daughter..." I can barely believe it. "My father never said. I... I don't think he knew."

"He knew," Leo replied, and for the first time I hear bitterness edge his voice. "He confronted him about it before he shot my father."

It takes a moment for me to put the pieces together. "You mean... Daniel Weiss and Anni..."

"Yes." He presses his lips together and looks away. "She told me, after, when we had made it to safety."

I shake my head slowly, my mind reeling with questions. "How did you escape Sobibor?" I picture him as a child, standing by the gates, watching his father fall. How did he get from that moment to living with my father's sister in Dresden?

Leo hesitates and then says, "I went with Anni. In the confusion of the camp after the revolt, Hans was able to find us a safe place to stay nearby, until I was able to get forged papers.

He told the commandant that he was taking his sister to safety, and that I'd been killed. He stayed to close the camp while we made our way to Dresden, with a friend of their family's. I was passed off as a cousin on the other side of the family." He gives a grimace of acknowledgment although I have not said anything. "He saved me, I know, for Anni's sake, I think, because he couldn't stand for her to be angry with him. For that I am grateful, but he still killed my father, right when he was about to finally have his freedom. For that I cannot forgive."

"I believed him, when he said he regretted it," I tell Leo quietly. "He wants your forgiveness, Herr Weiss. Truly."

Leo nods slowly. "I don't know if I can give it, but as we are both old men and I have heard how much he regrets, I will try."

"Where did my father go, when you and Anni were in Dresden? After the camp closed?" That is something else my father has never told me, how he spent the rest of the war.

"He fought on the Eastern Front."

I sit back, my mind whirling. My father *fought*, and never said? I've heard the horror stories of the Eastern Front; how much more did he endure? "And you and... and Aliza?" I ask. "After the bombing?"

"We were rehoused with a family. Aliza was only a toddler. We were accepted thanks to our false papers. We stayed there until the end of the war, and then we went back to Poznan, but there was nothing left. Not one member of my family, besides Aliza and me, survived the war. We made it back to Germany... it was not easy, with the Soviets and Allies carving the country up like a cooked goose." He gives a small, sad smile. "We've lived in Dresden our whole lives."

"I'm so sorry," I whisper. It takes me a few seconds to realize that Aliza is my relative as well as Leo's. My *cousin*. My family. "Is Aliza still alive?" I ask uncertainly.

Leo looks bemused. "She's with my wife. They're paying for

the parking," he tells me, and I can't help but give a little laugh at the mundanity of this moment, amidst all the emotion.

"I'd love to meet her," I offer hesitantly. "And my father would, too—"

"Yes." My father's voice, no more than a hoarse whisper, surprises us both. We turn to look at him, lying in bed, his eyes open, a faint smile curving his mouth. How long has he been listening? "I would like to meet my niece, Leo, if you will allow it."

Leo's eyes brighten for a moment as he stares hard at my father. Is he reconciling this dying old man with the monster he made in his head? "I never thought I'd see you again," he says finally.

"Nor I, you," my father replies. "I thought you had died, in the bombing."

"You wanted me dead, perhaps."

I stiffen, but my father accepts this as his due. "No." He shakes his head against the pillow. "No, never. I always regretted causing your father's death—"

"Causing it?" Leo repeats in a tone of disbelieving scorn. "You mean shooting him right in the chest in cold blood."

My father stares at him for a moment, his brow furrowed, his mouth agape. "Leo, I didn't shoot him," he says finally, and my mouth drops open along with Leo's. *What?*

"You did." Leo's voice is shaking. "I saw you—"

"I was going to, yes. I thought about it, God knows, because I was so angry, in that moment. Everything was chaos, I couldn't think clearly... but I didn't. I lowered my arm, I was turning away... and Gustav Wagner shot him instead. He told me I was being an idiot for standing there." He struggles to sit up, and I help him to lean back against the pillows, his body feeling like a bundle of dried twigs beneath the thin hospital gown. "I thought you always knew," he exclaims hoarsely. "I understood why you blamed me—if I hadn't called out to him, confronted him the way I had, he would have made it to the forest. You both would have been safe. I know that I caused his death as good as if I pulled that trigger, but I didn't. I *didn't*." He reaches out for Leo's hand, but he doesn't move, simply sits there, looking stricken. "I couldn't let myself be that man," my father whispers. "I couldn't, Leo. I couldn't be that man."

My throat closes up and I blink back tears. I realize I've known my father all along.

Slowly, looking stunned, Leo shakes his head. "I didn't see..." he whispers. "I was only looking at you, the gun in your hand, and then I saw how my father fell." He swallows hard. "All this time," he whispers. "All this time."

"I looked for you, after the war," my father tells him. "When I came back from the Front. They said everyone in the building had been killed. Anni, you, the baby. That's what I thought. That's what I believed. I would have never gone to America if I'd known—"

Leo is still shaking his head. "I've hated you for more than seventy years," he says quietly.

"And I understand why," my father exclaims, his voice close to a gasp. "I have been ashamed of myself, for so long, for so much. So much cowardice, so much complicity—I am guilty, Leo. I know I am. But I beg you to forgive me."

Leo is silent for a long time. I sense his struggle—to reconcile this truth with what he has believed for so long, the hatred that has fired his soul, even given meaning to his life. Is my father still guilty? Yes, I realize, he is. He served at Sobibor; he was complicit, just as he said. But guilty people, I realize, can be forgiven.

"I forgive you," he says at last, the words heavy, heartfelt. He bows his head.

"Thank you," my father whispers. "*Thank you.*"

There is a light tap on the door, and then a woman with white hair and dark eyes, and an intelligent, laughing expression on her face pops her head into the room. She looks, I realize, how Anni might have looked, had she lived that long. She looks like someone I want to get to know.

"*Guten Tag*," she says, stepping into the room and closing the door behind her. "I am Aliza."

My father, I see, is weeping. I watch, overcome, as Aliza's expression softens and then she comes forward and clasps his hands, as if she has always known him. Then, as my father blinks up at her gratefully, she kisses his cheek. Leo looks on with tears in his eyes, and he gives me a small, sad smile, silently acknowledging both the beauty and the pain of this moment.

It is a family reunion, unlike any I could have imagined, unlike any of us could have wanted, and yet I am so thankful we are all here. I wipe my own eyes as my father clasps his niece in his arms for a moment before, smiling, she steps away.

"You're here," my father says wonderingly, looking around at all of us, blinking back his tears. "You're all here."

If things had been different, would Anni and Daniel Weiss have married, I wonder. Would we live in Germany, would my father have raised Leo as his own? Would this be my family, not a handful of strangers I've come to know at the very last? It's painfully bittersweet, thinking that way, but I am still glad we have made it to this moment. It's through the suffering we grow, I remind myself. It's through pain that we become stronger.

Aliza and Leo leave after about an hour, when my father is clearly tired out, and is slipping toward sleep.

"Will I see you again?" I ask, and it is Aliza who answers.

"Yes," she promises, "because we are family."

Family. I nod, amazed at the connection I already feel to this woman I didn't even know existed a short while ago. I glance questioningly at Leo, and he nods and squeezes my hand. He still looks shaken, and I know it will take some time for him to come to terms with what he has learned, but he has changed, just as I have. "Yes," he tells me, his voice hoarse, "we will."

As I return to my father's side, his eyes flicker open and he smiles faintly—that old smile of his, whimsical and wry, a hint of Anni in it, even if he never saw it. He had some of her courage, in the end. "Danke, *liebe*," he tells me softly, and I reach for his hand as his eyes slowly close and his breathing evens out.

They are the last words he speaks. I'm not sure when his soul slips from his body; sometime in the night, when I am trying not to doze, savoring every moment with him, his hand in mine, and darkness covers the room like a cloak. I do know when he is gone; I feel it, an absence, an emptiness inside myself. Lying in my own, my father's hand is cool and still.

I remain there in the dark, holding my father's hand, letting a surprising sense of peace creep slowly over me, along with the dawn. In the morning, I will tell the doctors, the lawyers, the reporters.

I will arrange the funeral and read the newspaper stories of how Hans Brenner, former SS officer, slipped away quietly in his sleep. He faced justice yet did not suffer the consequences. And yet, I know, my father suffered the consequences for the length of his whole life, and perhaps that was impossible to avoid. Perhaps it was right.

Still, I am glad he is at peace now. I am glad he is gone, even though I miss him with every fiber of my being. I wanted one more chance to tell him I loved him. One more chance to assure him I finally understood. But maybe what I had was enough. I'm pretty sure he knew.

Gently I lean forward and kiss his forehead, my lips grazing his skin. I close my eyes, anchoring myself in this moment, this final farewell, as a thousand memories tumble through me— riding my bike with him behind me, the gentle clasp of his arms, the rasp of his laugh. Dancing with my feet on top of his. The way he'd kiss my forehead goodnight, just as I am kissing him now. *Goodnight, Dad. Sleep well.*

Then I rise from the room and head for the door, to tell the doctor what has happened.

My father has gone home, and I am ready to, as well.

Finally, it is finished.

EPILOGUE

New York, 1947

The immigration hall at Ellis Island is awash with Germans. Political refugees, battered and shellshocked, gaunt and hollow-eyed. They come from a war-wrecked Germany, starving, grieving, hopeless and alone. Hans Brenner clutches his single suitcase, eyeing them all uncertainly, unsure if he really belongs here. He lost everything in the war, the same as every other person in this room, and yet still he wonders if he deserves this second chance. A chance to make it right, if he ever can. If that is even possible.

He'll be different now, he has told himself, again and again. It is a promise he means utterly. He won't be a coward. He won't stay quiet. He will show mercy, practice justice. He will fight for the weak. He will champion the helpless. He will no longer be Hans Brenner, former SS officer, overcome by guilt, dogged by shame.

This is his second chance, even if he doesn't deserve it. And he doesn't, Hans realizes afresh. He knows that full well. He was given a chance that thousands, millions, more worthy were not. He cannot change that, but he will do his best, his utmost, to make his life count. To give back. To atone... if he can. A new man, with the name of the man who should have been here, who deserved this opportunity so much more than he does.

He slips his hand in his pocket and feels for Anni's ring, curls his fingers around the tarnished gold. He found it, after the revolt had been put down and Anni and Leo had gone, in a crevice in the floor, beautiful and forgotten. It is his greatest treasure now, along with the photograph he has of his sister, taken outside the commandant's house, a lifetime ago, a life of bitterness and regret. But things will be different now, he thinks. He will make sure of it. He will try so hard... for Anni's sake, and for Daniel and Leo's.

"Next," the immigration officer calls, and Hans steps forward, grasping his suitcase, his heart in his mouth. "Name?" the officer asks in a bored voice, and he lifts his chin, throws back his shoulders.

"My name," he states clearly, "is Daniel Weiss."

A LETTER FROM KATE

Dear reader,

I want to say a huge thank you for choosing to read *When We Were Innocent*. If you found it thought-provoking and powerful, and would like to keep up to date with all my latest releases, just sign up at the following link. Your email address will never be shared and you can unsubscribe at any time.

www.bookouture.com/kate-hewitt

Writing this book was so challenging, as it stirred up many questions of moral guilt and responsibility, ones that are important, I think, for everyone to consider. Researching the details of Sobibor was also incredibly heart-wrenching, and many of those scenes are rooted in fact. All of the officers, except for Hans Brenner, were real people, and the atrocities they committed happened as described, related by survivors of the camp. Daniel Weiss and his son Leo are inspired by Stanislaw Szmajzner, a fifteen-year-old goldsmith who managed to save his brother, cousin, and nephew by insisting he needed their help with his craft.

I hope you loved *When We Were Innocent* and if you did, I would be very grateful if you could write a review. I'd love to hear what you think, and it makes such a difference helping new readers to discover one of my books for the first time.

I love hearing from my readers—you can get in touch on my Facebook page, through Twitter, Goodreads or my website.

Thanks again for reading!

Kate

www.kate-hewitt.com

 facebook.com/KateHewittAuthor
twitter.com/author_kate

ACKNOWLEDGEMENTS

As always, I must thank everyone on the incredible Bookouture team for helping bring this book to life. First and foremost, my wonderful editor Isobel, whose input and guidance I value hugely. I'd also like to thank Jade, my copy editor; Tom, my proofreader; Sarah and Kim in marketing; Richard and Peta in foreign rights; and Saidah, Rhianna, Alba, Sarah, Iulia, and Laura in editorial and audio. They work tirelessly on behalf of their authors and I am so grateful!

Thanks to writing friends who have supported me as I've grappled with the issues in this book, in particular Emma and Jenna, and also to all my readers. Thank you for reading my books, and thank you so much for letting me know how much you enjoy them.

Lastly, thanks to my family, as ever, for bearing with me when I'm deep in a book. Thanks in particular to Teddy and Anna, and the interesting dinner-table discussions we had on this topic! Love you all.